SLOW AND EASY

Cara Lynn buried her face in his chest as they slowed down to a two-step. Jordan smelled of soap and a spicy aftershave. His body was like chiseled granite. She could feel the muscles in his back playing against her fingertips.

"You smell good," Jordan said in her ear. His lips gently caressed her temple.

Cara Lynn was suddenly shy. No one had touched her like this since she broke up with Bill—and it never felt this good.

"I thought you said you didn't dance well," she said, trying to take her mind off its present riotous track.

"That only applies to square dancing. I could get used to this," Jordan said, rubbing her back. "Are you cold? You're trembling."

"No, no, I'm fine," she answered, smiling up at him.

"I'm holding you too close," Jordan said. He loosened his hold, leaving more space between them. "It's easy to forget we just met. I feel like I know you already, or maybe I'm too eager to get to know you better."

"My instincts are telling me to go full speed ahead, but my common sense is saying slow down because my emotions have always gotten me in trouble."

"Well, slow is good," Jordan concurred with a smile.

Affair of the Heart

JANICE SIMS

PINNACLE BOOKS
KENSINGTON PUBLISHING CORP.

PINNACLE BOOKS are published by

Kensington Publishing Corp.
850 Third Avenue
New York, NY 10022

Pinnacle, the P logo, and Arabesque are Reg. U.S. Pat. & TM
Off.

First Pinnacle Books Printing: July, 1996
10 9 8 7 6 5 4 3 2

Printed in the United States of America

This book is dedicated to the memory of my two fathers, James Jones and Isaac Hammond, because they were instrumental in shaping the person I am today.

I would like to acknowledge the following people for their invaluable help in bringing this work to fruition. Leticia Peoples for her kind encouragement. My editor, Monica Harris, for her diligence. And last, but not least, my husband, Curtis, for his unerring faith in me.

Once there was an ebony princess
who was fair of form and face.
   All in the kingdom loved her for
she ruled with gentleness and grace.

   There was but one flaw Her
Highness did suffer.
   A broken heart had caused her to
erect a buffer.

   Keeping away all suitors who
dare to love her too well.
   A handsome prince vows to win her
Look closely now, for the story will tell . . .
                    —From *The Book of Counted Joys*
                         by Janice Sims

One

Cara Lynn Garrett felt that familiar sentimental tug at her heart when she saw the roadside sign along the stretch of Kentucky highway: SHELBYVILLE, TEN MILES. On this early May morning, the dew was still on the grass, the air fresh and bracing. She had seen many motorists heading in the opposite direction toward Louisville, where she'd come from, but few going into Shelbyville, which was an hour's drive from the city.

Her father, Frank, often told her to take a more traveled route when she visited him. If she ran into trouble, she wouldn't be so isolated. Cara Lynn, however, enjoyed the scenery, miles of open country generously endowed with nature's greenery, along this winding back road. Frank would be the first to concede that his daughter, though he loved her dearly, was obstinate and always insisted on doing things her way.

Besides, Cara Lynn thought as she accelerated, she could speed on this road and not have to worry about Smokey clocking her. She already had the Jeep Cherokee up to sixty-five, and the numbers on the speedometer were steadily climbing.

A sound like a wounded animal pierced the silence of the peaceful morning. Cara Lynn immediately reduced her speed, glancing into the rearview mirror at the flashing lights atop the state trooper's cruiser.

The car pulled alongside her Jeep, and she saw the grim-faced trooper point to the side of the road. She pulled onto the shoulder and waited in her car. Caught red-handed. She wouldn't be able to talk her way out of this one.

"Miss, would you mind stepping out of your car?" the officer asked as he walked up to her car door.

Cara Lynn got out and looked up into the clean-shaven face of the young man.

I know him, she thought.

"Do you realize you were going seventy-eight miles per hour? The speed limit on this road is fifty-five, not sixty-five as it is on some interstate roads."

He turned his attention to his ticket book, writing down her license plate number.

"May I see your driver's license, please?"

Cara Lynn handed it to him.

"Cara Lynn Garrett, DVM" he read, then looked up at her and smiled. "I'll be damned, it *is* you. You don't remember me, do you?"

Cara Lynn searched his face. An attractive man with a tan, close-cropped blond hair and brown eyes. He must have been around her age, twenty-eight. She knew she'd seen him before but not in a long time.

Suddenly it came to her. "We went to high school together," she exclaimed. "You were on the football team, right?"

"Tight end, three years in a row," he said proudly. "You were valedictorian of our class. I'll never forget that. It was the first time a . . . pretty girl was chosen."

Cara Lynn ignored his slip of the tongue. There was no use antagonizing a man who was about to ticket you for speeding. So what if he was about to say it was one of the few times a black student had been chosen valedictorian of the senior class?

That explained why she couldn't think of his name. He'd remembered her because she'd made an impression on him.

They had probably rarely spoken to each other during their high school years a decade ago.

"So you became a veterinarian," he said. "Nice going, Cara Lynn. I'm sure your folks are proud of you."

"Thank you," Cara Lynn replied, smiling at him. "But my father won't be happy with me once he finds out I was speeding. You know how parents worry. He won't sleep for days wondering if I'll go out and do the same foolish thing again."

"Forget it," the trooper said, closing his ticket book. "I'm letting you off with just a warning. Slow it down, huh?" He grinned at her. "Wait till I tell Laura I saw you. You know we had our tenth reunion last June. Why didn't you come? Lots of people were asking about you, wondering whatever became of you. Laura, that's my wife, graduated with us, too. Her maiden name's Fisher. She was the editor of the yearbook."

"I remember Laura," Cara Lynn said truthfully. "She's tall with dark brown hair and blue eyes. We were in the Beta Club together."

The trooper nodded happily. "That's Laura. We were married a year after graduating. Our firstborn, Christopher, was on the way," he laughed. "We have three others now, two boys and a girl. Laura's expecting number five soon. Are you married? Got any kids?"

"No. I guess I never met the right person."

"You brainy types always have trouble in the love department," the trooper said jokingly. "Take my advice, Cara Lynn, don't act so smart and show a little more leg."

Ticket or no ticket, that did it.

"Look, my love life is none of your business," Cara Lynn rounded on him, dark brown eyes flashing. "And I'm not going to behave like a twit in order to attract some lowlife. Now, if you're going to give me a ticket, get on with it so I can be on my way."

The trooper went pale underneath his tan. However, he didn't react in the manner Cara Lynn assumed he would.

"I did get too personal there. I'm sorry, Ca—Dr. Garrett," he said apologetically. He replaced his hat and sunglasses, then turned to walk away. Cara Lynn felt terrible. Okay, maybe the guy got too chummy too quickly but that was no reason to snap his head off. He'd been nice to her, offering to forget about the ticket, and he appeared genuinely glad to see her after so many years.

"Wait a minute," she called after him.

He turned.

"What's your name?" Cara Lynn asked, walking toward him. "Besides the MacAllister on your name tag?"

"Lucas, Luke," he replied, the smile back on his face.

Cara Lynn took his hand and shook it. "It's good to see you again, Luke. Tell Laura I said hello."

Moments later she was back behind the wheel of the Jeep, dutifully watching her speed. Her week-long vacation away from sick animals had gotten off to a shaky start, but the day was still salvageable.

Due to the speeding fiasco, she was a good twenty minutes behind schedule. Because she was rarely late for anything, Frank was probably getting concerned about her.

She often wished her father had remarried after her mother's death ten years ago. The Garretts were horse trainers by trade. Frank learned the skill from his father, and there had been a tradition of horse handling in the family dating all the way back to before the Civil War.

When Frank married Lillianne, he taught her everything he knew about horses and soon found she had a better feel for it than he had. Lillianne used a gentle touch in training the thoroughbreds. They'd become well known over the twenty years they were partners.

Given the degree of implicit danger in horse handling, it was ironic that Lillianne had met her end in a train derailment that occurred during a trip to visit her mother in up-state New York.

At the time, Cara Lynn was a senior in high school. She and her father held each other together throughout the sad ordeal. The only details she could recall from the year involved either school or working on the ranch. If she stayed busy, she didn't have time to think about her mother. The rare moments she found herself idle, she'd invariably broken into tears. Her beautiful mother was gone forever.

The ranch house sat in the middle of two hundred acres of verdant horse country. The crunch of tires on gravel must have alerted old Sam to Cara Lynn's arrival because the golden retriever mix came running toward her the minute she stepped from the car.

Cara Lynn knelt to hug the pooch. "Hello, boy. How are you? Where's Dad?"

Sam licked her face, wagging his tail excitedly.

"Hey, don't I take precedence over a dog?" Frank Garrett said as he rounded the corner of the house.

Cara Lynn went into her father's outstretched arms. Frank lifted her up off the ground in his customary bear hug.

"You're lighter than you were last time—haven't you been eating right?"

"What are you, a human scale? Put me down," Cara Lynn said, laughing.

At six feet, three inches and in superb physical shape from hard work, Frank was a big man with a personality to match. After putting his daughter back on solid ground, he took a good look at her.

His wife's lovely almond-shaped eyes were glaring at him in mock anger. He couldn't get over how his little girl looked more like her mother with each passing year.

Cara Lynn had the same jet-black hair that was so thick, long, and unruly that, out of frustration, she usually wore it in a simple braid. And unfortunately she'd inherited her father's height. Frank didn't think a woman should stand practically six feet tall in bare feet. Cara Lynn was five feet, ten inches—and he could still recall her bemoaning the fact when she was in ninth grade and towering over most of the boys.

Everything else about her, the flawless golden brown skin, short, well-shaped nose, and wide, full mouth all reminded him of Lillianne.

"Dad, I've told you over and over again: stop picking me up like that," Cara Lynn said, shaking her index finger under his nose. "One of these days you're going to put your back out."

Frank ignored her warning, as usual. Grinning down at her, he hugged her again. "Shut up and give your old man another hug."

Cara Lynn knew when to give up. She kissed his sunburned cheek, and they went into the house, followed by a tail-wagging Sam.

"So Mavis Edwards is courting you with homemade pies. I told you she was serious about you," Cara Lynn said as she sliced tomatoes for a salad. "Is she any good?"

Frank was at the stove removing fresh trout from a cast iron skillet. "I wouldn't know. I haven't stayed the night yet."

"I meant her pies," Cara Lynn replied, grimacing. "You've been a widower far too long."

They sat down at the kitchen table. Cara Lynn filled two bowls with salad, and Frank placed the trout on plates.

He poured a generous amount of hot sauce on his fish and bit into it with relish.

"Eat all of that salad," Cara Lynn admonished.

"Rabbit food," Frank complained, picking up a roll and slathering it with butter

"Ye gods, the way you eat, Frank Garrett. It's a wonder your heart's still beating."

"Sixty-four and I'm still as strong as a horse," her father said, biting into the roll.

"Horses have been known to have coronaries, you know."

"You worry about me too much, Cara. What you need is someone else to mother. Why haven't you mentioned Gil?"

Cara Lynn ate a mouthful of the trout. It was delicious, seasoned with just the right combination of spices. Her father had a way with food. Roles were reversed in their household when Lillianne was with them. Lillianne worked the ranch as much as Frank, but Frank did most of the cooking. His talents stemmed from the fact that he was in his midthirties before settling down. He knew as much about running a household as any woman.

"His name is Bill, Daddy, Bill Dunlevy. You don't have to try to remember his name anymore because we recently broke up. There was no pleasing that man. He kept pestering me to work shorter hours so that I would be at his beck and call. I never bothered him about his hours. There were many times we'd be in the middle of dinner, his beeper would go off and he'd disappear."

"The man *is* a surgeon, Cara Lynn."

"I understood completely, but did I get the same consideration? No. He wanted me to work around his schedule," Cara Lynn said, her voice rising with emotion. "My practice is important to me, too. I have an obligation to my patients just as he does to his, even if mine aren't human."

"Well, I hope you got him told," Frank said. "You were not put on this earth to cater to his whims. If he couldn't understand how hard you've worked to be where you are today, you're better off without him." He paused. "Are you sure it's over?"

Cara Lynn reached across the table and squeezed her father's hand affectionately, "I'm sure, Daddy. You're so sweet when you're not being hardheaded."

"You mean when I'm agreeing with you, young lady."

Cara Lynn feigned a hurt expression. "You make me sound so controlling."

"You're bossy, frequently overbearing, and you think you know best how I should live my life. But I wouldn't say you're controlling," Frank returned, getting into the rhythm of their usual banter.

"You're the one who taught me to be aggressive," Cara Lynn said, hardly able to maintain a straight face.

"Now I'm to blame? Little did I know what a pain in the butt you'd become. Eat right, Daddy," he mimicked. "Get out and meet others, Dad. Hire someone to help you with the horses, Daddy."

"They were all good suggestions. I just want you to be here long enough to see your grandkids. Is that too much to ask for?" Cara Lynn countered.

"I'm going to be here, Cara. I'm going to be here long enough to be as much a burden on you as you are on me. Believe that."

"You promise?"

"I promise," her father said emphatically.

"Okay. Now eat your salad."

"I've got to find you someone else to pester."

"I'd always find time for you, Father dear," Cara Lynn said, a mischievous gleam in her eyes.

"That's what I'm afraid of," Frank replied, obediently eating a mouthful of lettuce.

"Hiya, Cara Lynn. Mr. Frank said you were coming home. How long you stayin'?" Junior Barnes, Frank's apprentice, greeted her later that day as she joined him at the corral.

They were both watching as Frank gave instructions to Jake Mahoney, the ranch's exercise jockey. Jake was astride a Kentucky-bred stallion whose owner was hoping would be a contender in next year's Derby.

The sun was bright, and Cara Lynn squinted as she turned to look at Junior. "Just a week. I was lucky to get away for that long. How've you been, Junior? Dad treating you all right?"

"Doin' good," Junior said, grinning. He was about five inches shorter than Cara Lynn but was powerfully built. He reminded her of a bull: dark, low to the ground, and physically imposing. At twenty, he'd been working with her father since he was a boy of seventeen. "And Mr. Frank's the best, the best!"

"I heard you and Lynette are expecting a baby," Cara Lynn said, returning his smile.

"She's four months along. Lynn's excited, I'm petrified. What do I know about babies?"

"Oh, you'll be fine," Cara Lynn assured him. "No parent knows everything about a child in the beginning. You'll learn."

The thoroughbred in the corral whinnied ominously. It was not taking the prodding from Jake as good-natured coaxing.

Cara Lynn glanced at her father, wondering why he hadn't yet gotten out of the corral. He'd let go of the horse's bit while he spoke to Jake. Now he was standing a few yards from horse and rider, observing as the horse became increasingly irritated with its rider.

Cara Lynn saw him motion to Jake to let up on the reins. Some horses resented being aggressively restrained. Jake, however, obstinately refused to let up. It was now a war of wills between beast and man.

Frank ran toward her and Junior, climbing across the fence to stand next to her. "That damned fool. I have half a mind to fire him for this. I told him to gradually work up to control for this horse—he's part Arabian, and they're temperamental by nature."

The stallion was now protesting vigorously and had begun cantering in circles.

"He's going to throw him," Cara Lynn predicted.

Almost the second she finished the sentence, the thoroughbred tossed Jake over its mighty head and ran off in the direction of the adjacent paddock.

Cara Lynn, Frank, and Junior ran into the corral to assess the damage.

Jake was already on his feet brushing sand off his jeans when they reached him.

"I guess you were right about that one, Frank," he said. "I needed to see how he'd react to firm handling though."

"You okay?" Frank asked.

"Yeah, I'm fine," the tough, diminutive Irishman said, grinning sheepishly. "I'm just sorry I didn't take your advice. No hard feelings?" He held out his hand in apology.

"None. Go on and leave for the day if you like. Junior will give him a good rubdown, and we'll start fresh tomorrow," Frank said.

They shook on it, and Jake turned to leave, but not without his usual playful wink at Cara Lynn. She winked back. It was a little game they'd been playing since she was eleven or twelve when Jake had first started working with her father.

Cara Lynn knew her father wasn't serious when he threatened to dismiss Jake. They'd worked companionably together for nearly twenty years, and she'd witnessed only a handful of arguments between them. They respected each other too much to let anything spoil their friendship.

"Let him run off some steam," Frank instructed Junior about the stallion. "Then give him a good rubdown, that should relax him."

"Yes, sir," Junior said amiably. "I'll finish cleaning the tack room until he settles down."

"Thanks," Frank said.

He and Cara Lynn began the three-hundred-yard walk back to the ranch house.

"Jake sure hasn't changed," Cara Lynn observed. "Still bullheaded."

"Yeah, but he knows his stuff," Frank said, defending his old friend. "What are you going to do while you're home?"

"Oh, I thought I'd aggravate you, ride a little, take Sam for long walks, and spy on you and Mavis." Cara Lynn lowered the brim of her Stetson against the sun's glare and grinned. "So you and Mavis are actually getting serious. I remember her telling the kids to turn the music down when we'd drop by the diner after school let out. Her husband was alive then. As I recall, he used to flirt outrageously with the girls."

"He flirted with anyone in a skirt. He never treated Mavis well, Cara. Mavis deserved better, she's a sweet lady."

"She must be," Cara Lynn said, hugging his arm affectionately. "My dad's sweet on her."

Sam came running up to them. He jumped up on Cara Lynn, his sad-looking eyes pleading with her to play with him.

"Oh, okay," Cara Lynn relented. "I never could resist a pair of big brown eyes. It's a walk you want?"

"See you later," Frank said, still walking toward the house.

"We won't be long," Cara Lynn said, placing Sam back on the ground and brushing his paw marks from her yellow blouse.

Sam began running south, toward the woods.

"I'm not about to spend the rest of the afternoon picking ticks off of you," Cara Lynn called after him. "Stay out of the woods."

Sam ignored her as he happily ran ahead, no doubt imagining he was on a hunt. He'd stop occasionally and prick up his ears, thinking he heard a rabbit or some other prey. But no such luck. It was only grasshoppers in the tall grass, and although he liked chasing the jumping insects, they were no challenge to the hunter in him.

After about an hour of following an unrepentant Sam through the brush, Cara Lynn decided to let him have his way. He'd come home when he got hungry.

She was near the old Collins plantation and wondered if she could relive her childhood, if only for a moment, by visiting her castle. Actually, it was a rundown mansion perhaps a mile from her father's ranch. It had once belonged to Josiah Collins, the biggest slaveholder in Jefferson county. Twenty-five years ago, Josiah Collins the fourth fell on hard times and had to sell the property.

The buyer, Eric Bader, a notorious gambler, kept the place less than a year before the bank foreclosed on him. Since then the property was deemed unlucky by the locals. Some said it was haunted by the spirits of the slaves who had built it, then given their lives maintaining it.

Whatever the reason, it had remained vacant since the foreclosure.

As she was approaching the ramshackle antebellum mansion, she couldn't believe what she was seeing: the grounds were neatly manicured and the house had a fresh coat of paint.

She paused at the edge of the property. There was a black Range Rover parked in front of the house. The bank had apparently found a buyer after two decades. What kind of person would invest his time and money in this rundown place?

Curious, she moved closer for a better look. She had been certain the house was beyond repair. The last time she was in it, the stairs were crumbling, all the windows had been broken out, even the floors were collapsing. Who could afford to replace virtually everything in that white elephant?

She heard the front door creaking open and watched with interest as a tall, dark-skinned man walked out of the house carrying a red toolbox. He opened the hatch on the Range Rover and placed the toolbox inside.

Cara Lynn was standing near a clump of trees, perhaps

thirty feet away from him. She supposed the polite thing to do would be to introduce herself.

However, when she looked down at her blouse and saw how soiled Sam's paws had left it and realized how her hair must look after traipsing around in the woods for over an hour, she decided against it. Besides, from the feel of the breeze on her skin, she was perspiring, and there was no telling when the effectiveness had expired on her twenty-four-hour deodorant. Even from this distance it was quite clear the stranger was a looker. She'd at least like to have a clean face when they met.

The guy probably had a wife and family, anyway. What did a single man need with all that space?

Halfway back home, Sam caught up with her. She looked down at him. "Where have you been?" she asked accusingly. "Chasing defenseless baby rabbits?"

Sam looked up at her as if to say, Can we discuss this after a meal and a dish of water? I'm bushed.

"You ought to be tired," Cara Lynn said. "You ran wild. I'll bet you're covered with ticks."

He was. Cara Lynn spent the better part of the afternoon picking the blood-sucking bugs off of him and giving him a bath.

After supper she and her father sat on the front porch, gazing at the star-filled sky.

"I don't suppose you want to talk about it," Frank said.

"Talk about what?" Cara Lynn inquired, turning to look at him.

"What happened between you and Will."

"Bill."

"Cut it out, Cara," her father said sharply. "Are you going to tell me why you broke up with the surgeon or not? The *real* reason this time."

Cara Lynn sighed. "He asked me to marry him, Daddy."

"Well, put the man on death row," Frank quipped. He got up from his rocker and sat down on the edge of the porch beside Cara Lynn. Placing an arm about her shoulders, he gave her a warm hug.

"When did you come to the conclusion you weren't going to fall in love with him?"

"I tried to love him, Daddy," Cara Lynn replied, laying her head on his shoulder. "That's when I knew something was wrong. I mean—shouldn't loving someone come as naturally as breathing? I kept envisioning myself as Mrs. Dr. Dunlevy, doing all the 'proper' things, socializing with only the 'right' people. Having two point five children, a Mercedes, no, a Volvo station wagon, and a purebred dog. Do you know how neurotic those critters are? Give me a mutt like Sam any day."

"Stay on the subject, sweetie," her father reminded her.

"Oh, Daddy, Bill was so anal retentive I couldn't breathe around him, and he was slowly trying to convert me. I was beginning to feel like a Stepford wife. I truly believe he wanted to recreate me in his image."

Her father nodded sympathetically. "Didn't I tell you a man who has achieved what he has didn't get there without having to exact control in every aspect of his life? It's probably second nature to him to want to mold the woman in his life into someone he feels is a perfect complement to him. What you need is a man who will love you just the way you are with all your faults, all your little quirks that tend to drive the average male nuts," he finished, lightening the mood.

"Such as?" Cara Lynn said, looking up at her father.

"That annoying streak of temper," Frank said as an example.

"Temper? I don't have a temper," Cara Lynn denied, her voice rising.

"Sure you do. There it is now."

"Okay, I have a temper," Cara Lynn admitted, laughing. "What else?"

"You're too independent. Not that being independent is

a bad thing, but sometimes you carry it a bit too far. I know most of the fault rests with your mother and me. We raised you to think for yourself. But a man has to feel like he's needed, at least a little, to feel like a man. I think it has something to do with his testosterone or something. Anyway, you've got to make them feel like they're necessary, not simply wanted."

"I must be desperate," Cara Lynn said. "Here I am taking advice from a man who just had his first date in ten years."

She leaned over and kissed his cheek. "How did you get so wise?"

"I watch reruns of the *Cosby* show," Frank said with a straight face.

He got to his feet. "I'm beat. I think I'll turn in. Good night, tadpole."

"Good night, Daddy."

She sat on the porch a while longer, enjoying the gentle breeze, the sound of the crickets. She lay back on the porch, staring up at the stars, and wondered if she would ever know real love, the kind her parents shared. Some part of her longed for it, and still another held out no hope of finding true love and resisted the notion of its very existence. Something was missing in her. She wished she knew what it was.

Two

No one sleeps in on the Garrett ranch. Cara Lynn was up at dawn to help her father put the horses through their paces. Frank trained racehorses, teaching them to take direction from the jockey. After years of experience, he was able to judge whether or not a horse would be a good candidate for the racetrack.

Jake Mahoney did the actual track work, riding the horses around the mile-long track, coaxing as much speed from them as possible. Cara Lynn, untrained in that type of riding, simply went over the various signals the jockey communicated to the horse while riding: right turns, left turns, more speed, less speed. They were signals any well-trained racehorse should be able to recognize and respond to.

She also enjoyed letting them run free in the paddock. There was nothing as exhilarating as riding an animal that was bred for speed.

It was after noon by the time the last thoroughbred had had its daily workout. Cara Lynn went to the house to wash up and get lunch started while Frank and Junior stayed behind to rub down the horses.

She was splashing water on her face at the downstairs bathroom sink when the phone rang.

Grabbing a towel, she went into the kitchen to answer it. "Hello, Garrett residence," she said a little breathlessly.

"Hello. May I speak with Frank, please?"

She didn't recognize the deep male voice on the other end of the line.

"Dad's with the horses right now. I'd be glad to take a message so that he can get back to you."

"You must be his daughter, Cara Lynn. I'm Jordan Davidson. I bought the old Collins place not far from your dad's ranch."

So this was how the walking dream she'd seen yesterday sounded. Nice.

"I always liked the Collins house. I used to play in it when I was a kid, but you don't want to hear about that."

"Sure I do, what did you play?" Laughter filled his voice.

"It's too embarrassing," Cara Lynn insisted, responding to his warm voice. "Look, welcome to Shelbyville, Mr. Davidson—"

"Jordan."

"Jordan," Cara Lynn repeated. "I hope you and your family will be happy here."

"Thank you. But it's just me. No wife or children, but it seems I've got a dog now. That's why I'm calling. I wanted to ask for the name of a good veterinarian."

"You recently adopted a pet?"

"It's more like he adopted me," Jordan said, laughing shortly. "I went jogging this morning, and he followed me home. I think he was hungry. Anyway, he looks like a German shepherd but he's probably a mixed breed. He doesn't have any tags, and he looks pretty exhausted—like he's been on his own for some time. I thought I'd better have him checked out by a professional, just in case."

"That's a good idea," Cara Lynn said. "I can come over in about an hour."

"I'd love to meet you," Jordan Davidson told her. "Would you know the name of a qualified vet?"

"Jordan, I'm a veterinarian. Since you knew my name, I assumed Dad had also told you what I do for a living. Dr. Harry Bailey is the local vet. He doesn't have weekend hours unless there is an emergency, but I'd be glad to take a look at your stray as a favor to a neighbor."

"Frank told me how good you are with horses and a few other things we're going to have to compare notes on," Jordan said with a chuckle. "I'd really appreciate it if you'd examine him, Cara Lynn."

Cara Lynn quickly glanced up at the wall clock. It was twelve thirty. "Is two o'clock okay?"

"Perfect. I just gave him a bath, he should be reasonably dry by then."

"What's our new neighbor like?" Cara Lynn asked her father as he walked into the kitchen about forty minutes later.

"Give me a minute to get some of this grime off, hon. Would you pour me a tall glass of water while I wash up?" he replied, going straight back to the bathroom.

When he returned, Cara Lynn handed him his water. He drank deeply then looked at Cara Lynn. "What was it you wanted to know?"

"I was asking about Jordan Davidson. He phoned a few minutes ago. He wanted you to recommend a vet. I'm going over there after lunch to examine a stray that followed him home."

"You are?" her father said.

Cara Lynn was bemused by her father's reaction to her announcement. Frank Garrett was a man who believed in being a good neighbor.

"It's the neighborly thing to do, isn't it?"

"I guess so," he allowed noncommittally.

Cara Lynn dropped the subject for the time being. She'd wheedle the truth out of him after he got his stomach full.

She had baked a frozen pizza and made a tossed salad. Her culinary skills weren't as honed as her father's. She got the pizza from the oven and placed it on a wooden cutting board in the center of the kitchen table.

They sat down across from one another. Frank said the blessing and they began eating. When the pizza was gone, Cara Lynn said, "What's wrong with Jordan Davidson?"

"Nothing that I know of," Frank began.

He took a sip of cola before continuing. His reluctance to talk about their handsome neighbor only made Cara Lynn more curious.

"I don't know him well, that's all. He comes up here every Friday. Leaves Sunday. He says he's in the construction business. He must be making good money to be able to afford two hundred and fifty acres. I know the bank hadn't had a nibble in a while, but they weren't giving it away."

"Maybe his parents left him a big inheritance," Cara Lynn suggested.

"Really big," her father said obviously unconvinced.

"Dad, you're too suspicious. What is it you suspect him of, drug dealing?" Cara Lynn asked incredulously.

"You never know. He appears nice enough, but I'll wait and see. I think you should do the same."

"I can't see how going over there to examine a stray will get me in any trouble," Cara Lynn said lightly.

"Don't misunderstand me, Cara. I don't have anything against Jordan. He's just a stranger who's spreading a lot of money around, and I'm not sure of how he's earning it. You know that if there's one thing I can't stand, it's the drug business. Too many of our boys have been lost to it," Frank said vehemently.

Cara Lynn sighed. "Aside from the wealth Jordan Davidson has access to, what makes you think he's involved with drugs?"

"Like I said, there's nothing sinister about the man. We've spoken on a few occasions. He told me about his work, his family up in Maine, and the renovations he's making on the

house. I told him about you and my work. He's new to the
area, and that's reason enough to be wary," Frank reiterated.

"Fine. I can see your point," Cara Lynn conceded. "I'll
just examine the dog and beat a hasty retreat."

"Hello?" Cara Lynn found the front door of Jordan Davidson's two-story Southern-style mansion standing open.

She stood in the foyer with her black bag in her right
hand and her car keys in the left. Dressed in a pair of khaki
walking shorts, a bright royal blue T-shirt, and a pair of
brown leather sandals. She had taken the time to shower,
braid her hair, and apply a little lipstick before coming over.
She'd still made it by two o'clock, so where was he?

He certainly couldn't have gone far since he'd left the
door wide open.

She was a bit apprehensive about meeting him face-to-
face, especially after her conversation with her father. Se-
cretly she was hoping her father's suspicions would be
unfounded. The sound of Jordan's voice and his physique
aroused her interest. What would the rest of him be like?

She took the opportunity to look around while she
awaited his arrival. The great room straight ahead was under
construction. The far wall was being torn down, and there
was a stack of lumber piled across two sawhorses. A red
toolbox sat underneath one of the sawhorses.

There were other signs of newness about the room. The
Collins's ancestor, Josiah Collins, had built the house well
over one hundred years ago, yet the stairs were brand new.
The staircase hadn't been painted, so it looked out of place
next to the white walls and the black-and-white checker-
board floor, which also looked like a new addition.

She remembered gliding down the old stairs as a little
girl, imagining herself as a princess entering a ball with
everyone attending gazing raptly up at her as she slowly
descended. Her parents would have been furious with her

if they had known the old house had been her secret hide-away. It hadn't been structurally sound even then, and she could have been injured running up and down the rickety stairs. An eight-year-old is blissfully unaware of danger.

"Cara Lynn?" a voice said from behind her.

Cara Lynn turned to look up into the most beautiful pair of light brown eyes she'd ever beheld.

Jordan Davidson smiled broadly, revealing even, white teeth in a square-chinned, dark copper-colored face.

He extended a hand in greeting. "Hello, Cara Lynn, Frank didn't tell me how pretty you are."

Cara Lynn's hand was engulfed by his much larger one.

He left out quite a few adjectives about you, too, she thought as she smiled up at him.

Leave it to her father. Not only did he think Jordan might be a drug dealer, he had probably pegged him as a womanizer as well. Maybe that was why he had been less than enthusiastic about her meeting their new neighbor.

Jordan was wearing blue denim overalls with a sleeveless white T-shirt underneath. He was at least four inches over six feet minus the work boots he was wearing, Cara Lynn judged, and had the body of a seasoned athlete.

He ran a hand over his black, natural, neatly shorn hair as he continued to smile at her.

Cara Lynn had fixated on his mouth. And what a mouth. It was wide and full, with a sensuous curve that made her imagine how it must feel on a woman's skin.

"Huh?" she managed. Get it together, girl, she chided herself. He's gorgeous, get over it. You're not a teenager any longer, for God's sake.

"I called out for you when I came in, but I guess you didn't hear me."

"I was in the backyard. You're tall like Frank but other than that, nothing," he said, openly admiring her.

"Everyone says I look more like my mother. Dad didn't tell me much about you, either." She looked around quickly.

"I can see you've done extensive work on the house. It looks wonderful. You couldn't have done it all by yourself."

Jordan covered her hand with his other one. "That's right, you told me you used to play here as a child. Your parents didn't know that, did they? I can't imagine their allowing you to come here alone. And no, I had a crew do the walls and floors, and I'm doing the detail work in my spare time. It's a chore, but I enjoy restoring old houses."

He finally released her hand. "Let me show you around."

Cara Lynn followed him into the living room, a huge high-ceilinged room with a floor-to-ceiling fireplace as its most remarkable feature.

"I had a hell of a time restoring this," Jordan said. "I almost gave up on it until a friend who's a stonemason gave me a few pointers. Now I'm glad I didn't brick it up."

"It is distinctive," Cara Lynn said with approval. "They really built them big back then, didn't they?"

She ran a hand over the cool bricks along the surface, liking the feel of the rough texture.

"You have to remember that back when the house was built, this was their sole source of heat in winter," Jordan explained.

He led her to the kitchen. "Everything in here had to be redone."

Cara Lynn liked the kitchen immediately. The cabinets were a rich oak which lent a certain warmth to the room. The appliances were white as was the floor. But the countertops were red tile, giving the room a splash of contrasting color.

"Very cozy," Cara Lynn said admiringly.

"It's my favorite room," Jordan told her.

Cara Lynn leaned against the counter, her face framed in the stream of sunlight coming through the window.

The breath caught in Jordan's throat. The sunlight cast reddish lights throughout her dark hair and gave her eyes a golden hue.

Catching his eyes on her, Cara Lynn blushed.

Jordan smiled. "I'm sorry. I was staring, wasn't I? Forgive me, but I'm a painter, oils mostly. I appreciate good lines when I see them."

Cara Lynn felt as though she'd abruptly awakened from a deep sleep. That was the best come-on line she'd heard in years.

She pushed away from the counter and looked into his eyes.

"Gee, thanks. Where's the dog?" she said sharply.

"Did I say something to offend you?" Jordan asked, puzzled by her behavior.

"You appreciate good lines when you see them? Well, I can recognize them when I hear them."

Jordan reached out and firmly grasped her by the arm. "Come with me."

Cara Lynn allowed him to lead her toward the back stairwell.

"Is the dog upstairs?" she asked suspiciously. She was beginning to think her father's estimation of his character was on the mark. "I'm not going upstairs with you."

"Do I look like a rapist or a murderer to you, doc?"

Cara Lynn humphed. "What does a rapist or a murderer look like?"

They stood at the bottom of the stairs, sending challenges with their eyes.

"I just want to prove that I wasn't coming on to you. I'm no fool. Do you suppose I'd attack you in my own home, knowing full well that your father is aware of your presence here?" To her ears his "here" sounded like "he-yah." "Get real, lady."

Cara Lynn assented and followed Jordan upstairs. He stopped at the second door on the right.

He pushed it open and stepped aside. Cara Lynn walked into a large airy room that was flooded with sunlight. Two floor-to-ceiling windows dominated the room. Otherwise the room was empty except for several easels and drop cloths on the polished hardwood floor.

On the walls, however, were various paintings of different sizes and subjects. Cara Lynn stepped closer in order to inspect them further.

The first painting she came to was of a child. An angelic, brown-skinned girl of four or five, sitting in a field of poppies playing with a brown and white floppy-eared puppy.

"My niece, Bianca," Jordan told her. "She was five at the time. She's eight now."

"She looks sweet," Cara Lynn said and moved on to the next one.

This painting was of the desert at dusk. Jordan had visualized the colors in various shades of gold and red. Cara Lynn felt emotion welling up within her. A lump formed in her throat. It was the sort of full feeling one gets when an exceptional voice is raised in song. He was good, really good.

One of them struck a responsive chord in her. It was of a young, unsmiling black woman. She sat stiffly on an ornate settee, dressed elaborately in a white lace wedding gown.

"She looks so sad," Cara Lynn commented, hoping Jordan would tell her something of the portrait's subject.

"I suppose she was when the photograph I copied the painting from was taken. That's my mother. My father had to force her to take that picture on their wedding day."

"Why was she so camera shy?"

"Her father was a minister in a very strict religion. He didn't believe in graven images. My mother doesn't follow his religion today, but back then she was just leaving his house and after years of indoctrination, I suppose she really believed being photographed was a sin."

Intrigued, Cara Lynn faced him. "Did she allow her children to be photographed?"

"My father insisted on it. After a while, she stopped protesting."

"Did you know your grandfather?"

"I'm afraid he died before I was born, and because of his beliefs, I don't even know what he looked like."

Cara Lynn moved to the next painting. Jordan reached up to straighten it on the wall. "That's an old farmhouse in Bangor. It was the first house I remodeled when I started my business."

"Is that where you're from, Bangor, Maine?"

"Yeah," Jordan said. "I was born there."

Once again, Cara Lynn thought his "yeah" sounded like "a-yah" and his "there" like "they-uh."

"That would account for your accent," Cara Lynn said, smiling at him. "It's different, but nice."

"It took me a while to get used to the way you all speak here in Kentucky, too," Jordan said.

"Tell me about Bangor," Cara Lynn asked him, looking into his unusual eyes.

"It's a small town in southern Maine. It's the seat of Penobscot county. The main industry is lumber, but we do have other businesses such as a shoe factory and several electronic equipment manufacturers. Then there's the tourist industry. We're near the Penobscot and the Kenduskeag rivers, so we get a lot of campers and hikers."

"I hear there aren't that many black folks in Maine," Cara Lynn said. "Is that true?"

"Yeah, my family was one of the few black families in town. I learned fast what it meant to be black. My dad was a captain in the army before he and Mom married and settled in Bangor. When he tried to start a construction business, he was boycotted." He paused, and there was a warm light in his eyes as he continued. "But there was an elderly lady, Mrs. Lowell, who hired him to build an extra room for her. When her neighbors saw he did better work than the other company in town, he started getting plenty of business. Dad still puts fresh flowers on Mrs. Lowell's grave to this day."

"What a great story," Cara Lynn said, smiling wistfully.

She went on to view the remaining paintings while Jordan watched her every nuance.

He wondered if she felt it—the strong magnetism that grabbed his attention the moment he looked into her eyes. His heart was pounding so hard, he could barely breathe and he hoped he didn't look as excited as he felt.

What was wrong with him? No other woman had ever evoked this kind of reaction from him. Certainly he was physically drawn to her. She was beautiful, from her big, soft brown eyes, to her pert nose and full, exquisitely formed mouth. But it wasn't simply her visual beauty that appealed to him, there was something else, some indefinable quality about her that was acutely compelling. He wasn't a believer in love at first sight. He was too jaded for that. He'd known too many women, lived too many years. And yet, there it was, making him feel like a hot-blooded teenager with the first blush of love causing his hormones to run wild.

"You're good," Cara Lynn said at last, turning to give him a wan smile. "I owe you an apology. Forgive me?"

Jordan moved closer to her. "You couldn't have known I was on the level. I *am* attracted to you. However, I'd think of something more creative to say to you than that corny line."

"Oh, really? What sort of line would you use?" Cara Lynn asked, her eyes tinted with humor.

Jordan moved even closer. Cara Lynn backed up a few steps and found she'd been maneuvered against the wall. Jordan imprisoned her between his two muscular arms, his body leaning in toward her.

She could feel his cool minty breath on her face. Butterflies clamored for space in the pit of her stomach. She held her breath.

Jordan smiled at her. "You don't look like the sort of woman a man uses a line on, Cara."

Cara Lynn exhaled slowly. Their eyes met and held. Then his gaze lowered to rest upon her full red mouth. Cara Lynn moistened her lips. She wanted him to kiss her. Willed it.

But he didn't. He inhaled her heady essence, imagined what that luscious mouth would taste like. He envisioned her jet-black hair unbound, untamed, trailing across his naked chest after they'd made slow, sweet love. Still he didn't touch her.

"I think you've made your point," Cara Lynn said, her voice a hoarse whisper.

Jordan pushed away from the wall and took her hand. "Okay, doc. Ready to see your patient?"

"That *is* what I came here for," Cara Lynn said, laughter bubbling up. "I hope you don't subject all your guests to this kind of treatment."

Jordan looked back at her as they descended the stairs. "Only the lady veterinarians with doe-eyes."

"That ought to narrow the field a bit," Cara Lynn said.

The dog, whom Jordan had dubbed Peabo, was in good shape aside from a little malnutrition. Cara Lynn prescribed a healthful brand of dog food, vitamins, and plenty of fresh air and exercise.

"He's young, maybe a year old, I imagine," she told Jordan as she inspected Peabo's teeth and gums. "Someone probably abandoned him because they could no longer afford to care for him. He's friendly enough, isn't he?" Peabo was repeatedly licking her hand. "He'll make a good pet. Are you thinking of keeping him?"

"Well, my apartment building does allow pets, and we have gotten acquainted—huh, boy?" Jordan said, scratching Peabo behind the ear.

Cara Lynn stood, finished with the examination. "He's fine, Jordan. No sign of anything health threatening. But you should get his shots done, especially his rabies shot.

He looks like a runner to me—you won't be able to keep him from the woods. Ask Harry about some heartworm medication."

"Oh?" Jordan said, concerned. "What's a heartworm?"

"It's a nasty little parasitic nematode worm that attacks the heart and arteries of dogs, especially young ones like Peabo. If left untreated, it can cause death. But you don't have any need to worry. Harry will take excellent care of Peabo."

"You sound like you know him well," Jordan said, wondering if Harry Bailey was some young, robust country vet Cara Lynn might be interested in romantically. He hoped not.

"Harry's my mentor, and he's a friend of the family."

They went back into the house through the kitchen, leaving Peabo in the backyard.

"I'd like to wash up," Cara Lynn said as she removed her rubber gloves.

Jordan directed her to the downstairs bathroom, which was located beneath the stairwell.

She joined him in the kitchen afterward, and he handed her a tall glass of ice-cold lemonade.

"You looked thirsty."

Cara Lynn gratefully accepted the glass, and they sat down at the breakfast nook.

"Now that that's over with, we can talk," Jordan said. "Tell me you're not involved with anyone. I don't want to hear anything else."

"I'm not involved with anyone."

"Truly?"

Cara Lynn took a sip of the tart lemonade. "Three months ago I stopped seeing a man I'd been with for two years."

"Oh, I'm sorry. Would you mind if I asked you what happened?" Jordan said, giving her his undivided attention.

"Who knows?" Cara Lynn began, feeling very comfortable in his presence. "He wanted something I didn't? We didn't have enough in common? Or we didn't love one another enough to overlook what should have been small things?"

"*Was* it love?" Jordan asked, encouraging her to open up.

"I respected him a lot. The major thing we couldn't agree on was our careers. He wanted me to treat mine like a hobby and put his on the front burner. Neither of us was willing to compromise on that."

"What does he do?"

"He's a heart specialist, a surgeon."

"I see. I take it he wanted to marry you?"

"We talked about it."

"And he wanted you to be the perfect wife. Organize his social life, give him a male heir. The whole nine yards."

"Do you know him?" Cara Lynn said, smiling. "That sounds exactly like Bill."

"I know the type. He has separate drawers for his brown socks and his black socks. His maid irons his shorts, and he wouldn't dream of going a whole week without a haircut. Am I close?" Jordan joked.

"I was lucky to get away unscathed, huh?"

"Extremely."

"It isn't that I don't want to get married someday," Cara Lynn explained. "I want children, too—but I want them with a man who's going to be around to be a good father to them. I have a great dad, so I want the same thing for my children."

"My old man is pretty great, too. He was always easy to talk to, and he taught me practically everything I know about construction."

Cara Lynn drank more of the lemonade, then, setting her glass down, she regarded him with questioning eyes.

"Why did you leave Maine?"

"There were two reasons, actually. The woman I was engaged to eloped with my best friend."

"Oh, no!"

"Yeah. They left town together the week before our wedding was to take place. I didn't even get a letter of explanation or any kind of warning. Her mother phoned to tell me what had happened. She kept apologizing for her daughter's behavior, as if it was her fault." He could smile about it now. "A month after they eloped, they were back in town acting like newlyweds. I couldn't take it. Every time I saw them together, I wanted to shoot them. So instead of committing murder, I moved away."

"Well, that was preferable," Cara Lynn said, laughing.

Jordan laughed along with her. "That was six years ago. Every time I go home for a visit, I hear about a new addition to their family. Life goes on."

"And the other reason?"

"I got a job offer I couldn't pass up. A conglomerate in Louisville accepted my bid to build a high-rise in downtown Louisville. I was twenty-nine and had a successful business in Augusta, that's in southwest Maine, not far from Bangor, but I saw the chance to grow, to learn more, so I took it. I've been in Louisville ever since."

"How did you end up in this house?" Cara Lynn wanted to know. A house I always wanted to own, she thought.

"I was out for a long drive one Sunday afternoon and wound up in Shelbyville, which I thought was a quaint little town, so I decided to investigate the countryside. I passed this house and had to stop. I thought to myself, What would this monstrosity look like restored to its former glory? I had to find out, so I bought it."

"It's beautiful," Cara Lynn said, admiring the kitchen again.

"It's not the only thing around here that's beautiful," Jordan said, his eyes on her face.

"You asked me if I'm involved with anyone. Are you?" Cara Lynn asked, adeptly changing the subject.

"I was up until about a year ago. She was a realtor. Her

father developed Alzheimer's disease, and Sharon moved back to Florida to be closer to her family."

"That's an awful disease. I know several families affected by it," Cara Lynn said sympathetically.

"Yes, but a couple of positive things came out of her move home. She says she's much happier being near her parents, and an old beau she knew from college came back into her life."

"How do you feel about that?"

"I'm happy for her," Jordan said lightly. "She deserves all the happiness life has to offer."

Cara Lynn smiled at him. "That's sweet of you."

"I'm a sweet guy," Jordan said with a charismatic grin.

Cara Lynn finished her lemonade, then stood. "I should be going. Dad's expecting me back."

Jordan got to his feet as well. "This has definitely been a banner day for me," he said, looking down into her up-turned face. "I got to meet you."

Blushing, Cara Lynn didn't exactly know how to take his declaration. "You may be eating those words soon. To quote my father, I'm bossy, bullheaded, and frequently overbearing. I'm not an easy person to be around."

Jordan reached out and gently caressed her cheek. "Let me be the judge of that. Name the time, place. I'm there."

"Okay," Cara Lynn said. Her brown eyes held a mischievous glint. "Tomorrow, downtown in the park. It's Founder's Day. There's going to be a big barbecue and a square dance afterward."

"Square?" Jordan said, a quizzical look on his handsome face.

"Wear your cowboy boots." Cara Lynn grinned at him and ducked out of his reach.

She picked up her black bag from the counter, then walked swiftly through the house to the foyer where she'd left her car keys. Jordan caught up with her at the front door.

"As in the Virginia reel?" he said, referring to her square dance comment.

"I'll teach you," Cara Lynn promised. "It'll be fun."

"I'll probably flatten your pretty toes."

"I'm beginning to think you're trying to get out of this. You said anytime, anyplace."

"I was hoping you'd suggest dinner for two at a secluded restaurant with dancing at a rather dimly lit club afterward. Not eating ribs with the entire town, followed by a foot-stomping hoedown."

Cara Lynn laughed at his description of square dancing. "Some people would be offended by the colorful way you refer to a great American tradition. You're lucky I'm not one of them. The barbecue starts at seven. Pick me up at Dad's around then."

She was running down the front porch steps to the Cherokee before he had the chance to say anything else. She waved as she sped out of his driveway.

Jordan sighed. "Her father's right, but she's got great legs."

Frank was in his favorite rocker on the wraparound porch when Cara Lynn returned. She sat down on the swing, bending to pat Sam, who was lying underneath, on his furry head.

"How'd it go?" her father inquired.

"It went fine. The dog is pretty healthy, just needs to be in a loving home."

Frank responded by propping his elbow on the arm of the chair he was sitting in, placing his chin in the palm of his hand, and staring at her.

"Oh, okay," Cara Lynn said, knowing her father could read her better than anyone else on earth. "We're going to the Founder's Day celebration together."

"I knew you'd like him," Frank said smugly.

"What's that supposed to mean?"

"Didn't the way I was acting pique your curiosity just a wee bit?"

"You mean you wanted me to meet him?"

"I liked him the moment I met him. He's one fellow who has his head on straight," her father told her, a satisfied grin on his still handsome face.

"Then all that talk about drugs . . . ?"

"A ruse. His phoning, well—that was providence. But, yes, I would have thought of some way to have you two meet before you had to return to Louisville."

"Why didn't you just tell me you wanted me to meet this nice guy you knew?" Cara Lynn asked.

"You know daughters don't like their fathers choosing their male friends. And speaking of male friends, Keith Freeman phoned while you were out."

Shocked, Cara Lynn stared at her father. "What did *he* want?"

"I didn't ask. He wants you to call him back. Listen, Cara, I know it's none of my business—but what happened between you and Keith is best left in the past. He was no good for you then, and now that he's divorced from Diana—"

"Divorced?" Cara Lynn cried. "You never mentioned that before."

"I didn't think you cared. Did you or did you not tell me you detested Keith Freeman? Weren't you the one who was ranting and raving about how he broke your heart and took advantage of your inexperience? You can thank your lucky stars I didn't insist you explain that statement," Frank said evenly.

"Apparently you never forgot it," Cara Lynn noted with some irritation. "The truth is, I don't care about him, Dad, but that doesn't mean I'm not curious about what goes on in his life."

"Especially when it's something bad, right?" her father surmised.

"I know it's petty. But I was in love with the creep, and he said he loved me. Yet he chose money over me. Why shouldn't I want a little secondhand revenge?" Cara Lynn reasoned.

Her father shook his head and sighed. "Baby, revenge is never as sweet as it's cracked up to be. You only end up getting hurt. Chalk it up to first love. No matter what the romantics would like to think, your first love is rarely your true love. You recognized too late that Keith was an opportunist. You're mature now. Forget about him."

Cara Lynn knew her father was right. But even the mention of Keith's name brought back bitter memories of four summers ago.

She was twenty-four and fresh out of veterinary college. Dr. Harry Bailey had hired her for the summer, allowing her to assist him on his rounds in an effort to hone her clinical skills before embarking on her own private practice.

She accompanied Harry on a house call to the Freeman farm. John Freeman, Keith's father, was a cattle rancher. One of his prize Herefords was having a difficult labor, and Harry had to turn the calf while it was still in its mother's womb.

It wasn't an easy process. Normally the calf moves down into the birth canal when the time's right, but this time the calf wasn't budging, so Harry manually pushed the calf through the birth canal. Luckily the mother was spent from hard labor and didn't require anesthesia. Harry was afraid that due to her exhausted state she might not have survived the effects of the drug.

So there Harry was with his arm up to his elbow inside the cow, trying to facilitate the birth of the calf, and Cara Lynn at the opposite end attempting to keep the mother calm.

Several intense minutes later the mother delivered a healthy male to Mr. Freeman's delight.

Keith had been in the barn with them throughout the birth, occasionally looking away when the sight of the birthing left him a bit green. He had been brought up on the ranch, but he had never gotten used to such spectacles.

Cara Lynn sympathized with him. Seeing Harry with his arm up a cow did things to her stomach, too, and she was a qualified veterinarian.

A couple of times during the labor, Cara Lynn had looked up to find Keith watching her. She was thrilled. She'd had a crush on him ever since she was a freshman in high school and he a senior.

Back then practically every female at Shelbyville High School had a crush on Keith. He was captain of the football team. He was the quarterback his junior and senior years, a big deal in their small town because black quarterbacks were a rarity.

Not only was he strikingly handsome and a lettered athlete, he was also intelligent. He could have been a classic example of the young black athlete who peaks too soon and goes on to a life of anonymity. But he worked hard and earned a four-year athletic scholarship to the University of Kentucky in Lexington, and in his second year he was drafted by the Miami Dolphins. He played three years before a knee injury forced him into permanent retirement. Then he went back to college and got a degree in business administration.

He had opened a sports shop specializing in athletic apparel in Lexington when his mother fell ill, and he came home to Shelbyville to visit her.

That was when he first saw Cara Lynn. Really saw her. He had known her in school, and he remembered seeing her photograph in the *Courier Journal* on a number of occasions. She was a junior rodeo champion, winning several trophies in calf roping. Besides, at her height, she was hard to miss.

That day in the barn, however, he'd seen a very desirable woman who was competent and a bit cocky. He liked that in a woman.

So as Dr. Bailey packed up his equipment, Keith had pulled Cara Lynn aside.

"Your dad and mine have been friends for years. Why is it I never see you around?"

"It could be because you live in Lexington," Cara Lynn said jokingly.

"Well, I'm going to be home for a while. Mind if I give you a call?" he asked, flashing a brilliant smile.

"It's a free country," Cara Lynn replied, trying to appear cool. Inside she was smoldering.

That summer was magical. They were together every chance they got, and it soon became evident to Cara Lynn that Keith was the man she'd been waiting for all her life. She fell in love so hard she totally dispensed with her usual cool reserve. Still a virgin at twenty-four, she willingly and exultingly gave herself to him. He was the man she thought she'd spend the rest of her life with.

Then along came Diana Childs, only daughter of Lexington real estate magnate, Carter Childs. Diana didn't possess Cara Lynn's natural beauty or quick mind. She was spoiled and petulant, the model poor little rich kid. When she wanted something, she whined to her father until he acquired it for her.

Keith Freeman became the object of her avarice, and she went about buying him just as she would any other possession. As it turned out, Keith was easier to own than Cara Lynn ever imagined. He was ambitious and saw the opportunity to expand his business more rapidly than he'd initially anticipated. They were made for each other. The only casualty was Cara Lynn, who took their breakup badly.

She hadn't seen or spoken to Keith since then.

"As long as I don't see him, I can forget about revenge," she said now. "But if I see him, I really can't be held accountable for my actions."

"He still has a hold on your heart, Cara. Maybe that's why you haven't allowed yourself to fall in love with anyone else."

"What I feel for Keith could never be construed as love, Daddy," Cara Lynn said with emotion.

"If you can't let go of your anger, then you surely feel something for him. Stop fooling yourself, girl. You're not over him yet, and I suggest you see him face-to-face and do whatever it takes to get over him."

"Oh, now you want me to see him? A minute ago you said I should let it stay in the past."

"That was before I saw your reaction, Cara. I've noticed how you've behaved since your breakup with Keith. You date someone, begin getting close, and the next thing I know, it's over. If your unresolved feelings for Keith are causing you to mistrust every man who comes into your life, you need to talk to him."

Cara Lynn stood and stretched her legs. Sam got up from his comfortable bed beneath the swing, thinking she was preparing to take him for a walk. Cara Lynn sat down on the edge of the porch and hugged him.

"I despise Keith Freeman," she said, but her voice lacked conviction.

"You hate what he did to you, but do you hate *him?*" her father asked.

Looking out at the picturesque rolling hills of the ranch, Cara Lynn honestly didn't know.

Three

Later that afternoon Cara Lynn thought a ride might help to clear her mind, so she saddled up a spirited mare her father was boarding for a friend and took off across the field west of the ranch.

She loved the feel of the animal's muscles moving beneath her as it galloped. It was still a joy to ride, even though she'd been doing it all her life.

She firmly held on to the reins with her gloved right hand, sensing the pent-up need for speed in the mare. She felt that desire herself at the moment and urged the mare on with a quick tap to its rump with her hand. She deplored the use of riding crops.

Dad could be right, she thought as the horse raced across the meadow. Maybe I do need to see Keith and cuss him out so that I can get on with my life.

If Keith hadn't betrayed her four years ago, maybe she would have been capable of loving Bill. No, she couldn't subscribe to that. The chemistry between her and Bill had been lukewarm at best. When it came down to it, the only thing about him that excited her was his intellect—and you couldn't make love to a man's brain.

She couldn't place the blame on Keith for her failed relationship with Bill. She did see the need for closure where Keith was concerned though.

He'd left her for another woman, giving her no explanation. He had simply broken their regular Saturday night date. When she tried to contact him, he refused to return her calls. A trip to his store in Lexington left her feeling foolish and desperate. The saleswoman told her he was out, but as she was leaving, she recognized his distinctive white Chevy Blazer in its usual parking space at the back of the store. Like an idiot she sat in her car across the street, waiting for any sign of him. Two hours later he emerged, got into his Blazer, and drove away.

Still a glutton for punishment, she followed him. For a half hour she wove through Lexington traffic, staying two or three cars behind him, hoping to avoid detection. Then he pulled into a fenced estate.

She parked a block away, watching as he spoke into an intercom. The electric gates slid open, and the Blazer disappeared behind them.

So she never got the opportunity to vent her anger. She'd kept it bottled up inside, and the hurt had been debilitating because against her better judgment, she'd fallen in love with Keith Freeman. And to make matters worse, he was her first love, lover, and the provider of her first broken heart. She learned to distrust her instincts about men. She learned to trust men even less.

Now she had only two uses for a man, and she truly hated to face this truth about herself: a man could stimulate her intellectually with nothing more intimate between them, or a man could serve as a conduit for sexual release. That wasn't to say she was promiscuous because, to date, she'd had only two lovers. She just recognized the tendency in herself, and she wasn't the type of person to ignore lessons when life was trying to teach her one.

She could see Jordan's place up ahead. She looked for his car and saw it parked behind the house.

The mare slowed to a trot, and Cara Lynn guided her toward the mansion. She dismounted and tied the horse's reins to a low-hanging branch of the huge oak tree in the front yard.

She removed her gloves and riding helmet as she walked onto the porch.

The door was open. "Jordan?" she called. "Are you here?"

"Come on in, I'm upstairs. I'll be right down," came his deep baritone.

A couple of minutes later he was running down the stairs barefoot and wearing nothing except a pair of stonewashed jeans. He was carrying a white T-shirt, however, and put it on.

Don't bother on my account, Cara Lynn thought rather disappointedly. She'd never seen pecs so well defined, and his abdominal muscles were like a washboard.

His smile was sensual as he regarded her. "What a pleasant surprise. Did you come to give me dancing lessons? Afraid I'll embarrass you tomorrow night?"

"No, actually I came to check up on my patient. Where is he?" Cara Lynn replied, returning his smile.

"He's outside destroying one of my best work boots."

Cara Lynn placed her helmet and gloves on the bottom step of the staircase and turned to go outside.

Jordan followed her. "I'm a little hurt that it wasn't me you came to see."

"Oh? I was here a few hours ago and I'm back again. Doesn't that make you wary? Aggressive women don't turn you off?"

"It depends on who the aggressor is," Jordan said as he opened the back door for her.

Their eyes met. "Well, it's beside the point," Cara Lynn maintained. "Because I really did come to see Peabo."

She whistled for him. "Here, boy!"

Peabo dropped the leather boot he was gnawing on and came running, happily wagging his tail.

Cara Lynn squatted so that she'd be on eye level with

Peabo. Even after only a few hours he looked much better than he had on her previous examination. His eyes were clearer, and it was apparent he'd been well fed. "Hello, pretty boy, feeling better? Yes, I can see you are."

Peabo licked her hand in appreciation of her kindness. Something in the way he was looking at her told her he wasn't used to being treated humanely. She was glad Jordan had decided to take him in. She let him get back to his boot.

"Your care agrees with him," she told Jordan as they walked back inside. "Did I take you away from something?"

"I was retiling one of the upstairs bathrooms," Jordan said.

"Can I help?" Cara Lynn offered.

"Sure you don't have anywhere to be in the next few minutes?"

"Nowhere. I just need to get back before dark—my transportation doesn't have headlights."

"Are they broken?"

"No, horses don't come with headlights," Cara Lynn said, tongue in cheek.

Laughing, Jordan took her hand. "Come on, Doc, I'll teach you how to lay tile."

In the upstairs bathroom Cara Lynn sat on the edge of the tub. "Mind if I take my boots off? I don't think they'd be too comfortable while I'm laying tile."

"Take off anything you like," Jordan said, giving her an exaggerated leer.

"Just the boots," Cara Lynn said quickly and began nudging the heel of the right boot with her left foot.

"How do you get those things on in the first place?" Jordan asked. He bent down to help her off with the tight riding boots. Holding firmly to the heel, he pulled while Cara Lynn tried to slip her foot out.

"They're easy to get on, hell to get off," Cara Lynn said, grunting.

They finally got the right boot off, but the left one wouldn't budge. Jordan pulled and Cara Lynn pushed—to no avail. Then Jordan turned around so that he could get a better grip and advised Cara Lynn to push against his bottom with her bootless foot.

After a few seconds of this, Jordan said, "Put a little power into it, doc."

Cara Lynn took a deep breath and did exactly as he said. Suddenly the boot slipped off her foot, Jordan went headlong into the bathroom wall, and she fell backward into the bathtub.

Scrambling to her feet, Cara Lynn gingerly touched her backside. Fortunately she was adequately padded back there, so she didn't think she was injured. She got out of the tub to see how Jordan had fared.

He sat on the floor nursing a bruised shoulder. Cara Lynn knelt beside him, automatically placing her hand on the injured shoulder. She carefully checked him for broken bones. There were none.

"How do you feel?" she asked, still examining him.

Jordan's heart was hammering in his chest, and his brow was wet with perspiration—but not due to any pain from his fall. He was reacting to Cara Lynn's close proximity.

"You seem to be okay," she said softly, peering into his eyes.

Pulling himself together, Jordan said, "I'll be sore in the morning, but I'll live."

Relieved Cara Lynn helped him to his feet. "I'm sorry, Jordan. I pushed too hard."

"I told you to push hard," Jordan reminded her.

"Still, I know my own strength. I'm not a petite person. I could have hurt you."

"You *are* petite next to me," Jordan said. "You don't have the 'tall girl' complex, do you?"

Cara Lynn avoided eye contact.

"You do," Jordan said quietly.

He gently touched her cheek, and Cara Lynn turned to meet his gaze.

"If you mean do I think I've always been too big, the answer is yes. You don't know how it feels, from a female point of view, to be the tallest person in your class, including the male teachers. By the time I was thirteen, I was already my full height. I felt like an ostrich, and if I could have, I would have hidden my head in a hole."

Jordan stepped into the tub and began spreading adhesive onto a six-inch-square block of beige glazed tile.

Cara Lynn sat beside him on the tub, watching.

"I guess you didn't date much in high school, knowing how insecure the average male is about his size," Jordan said, looking at her sideways.

He carefully placed the tile on the wall and smoothed the excess adhesive with a notch-edged trowel.

"Not much," Cara Lynn said as though the memory was still painful. "What guy in his right mind would want a girlfriend who looked like the horses she was so wild about?"

Jordan laughed at her comment. "Cara, you look about as much like a horse as Halle Berry does."

"I know that now, but that's how I felt when I was a shy, skinny teenager." She changed the subject. "Can I try that, it looks pretty foolproof."

Jordan handed her the trowel. He watched as she spread on the adhesive.

"Put it on evenly," he instructed her. "That's good. Now make sure it's level with the last tile that was placed."

She did it almost as well as he had.

"You're a fast learner," he complimented her.

"You're a good teacher."

"Tell me, when did the dense fellows around here start giving you a run for your money?"

Cara Lynn laughed softly. "I was out of college before anyone showed any real interest."

She concentrated on her tile laying, trying not to come across as nervous under his scrutiny.

"And?" he prompted her.

"He broke my heart," she said simply.

"Is that the beginning, the middle, and the end of the story?" Jordan said. "He broke your heart. Does that mean you were in love with him?"

Cara Lynn looked him in the eyes. "It seems I was half in love with him since I was in ninth grade. I had a crush on him through high school and college. Then the summer I graduated from veterinary school, we met again—and I fell in love with him. By fall, he was married to someone else."

Frowning, Jordan stayed her hand as she tried to pick up another tile. "How did that happen?"

"I suppose I just didn't mean anything to him. I was hoodwinked. Used. Dad says it was probably the money. Keith never told me why he dumped me." She sighed. "All I know is, why should I waste my time worrying about what went wrong when he couldn't care less about my feelings?"

"Because each relationship affects how you'll react to the next person who comes into your life. Take me for example. After Gail eloped with my best pal, I didn't trust women for a long time afterward. I saw them as predatory and greedy, and I just knew I'd eventually get stepped on by them. So I couldn't get close to anyone," Jordan said, his voice emotion filled.

"What happened to bring you out of it?" Cara Lynn asked with interest.

"I realized I was my own worst enemy. Oftentimes you get what you expect in life because subconsciously you're directing your own fate. You know what I mean?"

Cara Lynn nodded.

She liked this man. The trouble was, she couldn't lump him in either of her categories for men because he was both intellectually *and* sensually stimulating. She was in a quandary, albeit a very pleasant one.

"You seem to have it all together," Cara Lynn said, her eyes on his mouth. She quickly raised them to his eyes, hoping he had not sensed what she had been thinking.

"Don't be fooled," Jordan advised her, lowering his eyes to her mouth. "I've got my problems. But you don't live over thirty-five years without acquiring a certain amount of wisdom."

"Name your biggest problem," Cara Lynn dared him, her voice seductive.

"Right now it's restraining myself from kissing you," Jordan said, moving closer to her.

"Some problem," Cara Lynn said a bit breathlessly.

"What should I do about it?" he asked, his cool, clean breath caressing her cheek.

"Cold showers are known to help the condition," Cara Lynn suggested sweetly.

She placed the last tile, smoothed it with the trowel, then stood.

Jordan helped her out of the tub.

"Now whenever I shower in here, I'll think of you," he said.

"I'm glad to have been of service," Cara Lynn said, standing directly in front of him. "But back to your problem—"

"Yes?" Jordan said, leaning in.

Before she could lose her nerve, Cara Lynn stood on tiptoe and kissed him squarely on the mouth. She knew she had made a mistake the moment their mouths touched because her core seemed to melt. There was no other way to describe it. Her arms went around his neck and his pulled her fully into his embrace. He tasted sweet, and the scent of him was woodsy and male. Her senses were aflame, and although she could have willfully been consumed by them, a cautionary voice in the back of her mind was screaming *"run!"*

When they came up for air, they stood there staring at one another for a few moments, a look of wonder on both their faces.

Cara Lynn wiggled out of his arms. "I should be going," she said, swallowing hard. "It's getting dark."

Jordan nodded dazedly. "Of course. Thanks for helping me solve my problem."

"Anytime."

"Tomorrow night?"

"Wear your dancin' shoes," Cara Lynn said as she reached down for her boots. Sitting on the edge of the tub, she quickly pulled them on.

Finished, she ran downstairs, Jordan behind her. He was becoming quite fond of the view from his vantage point.

She turned to smile at him as she put on her gloves and riding helmet. "Do you ride?"

"A little, as long as there are no surprises like jumping barrels or something."

"You *are* a greenhorn," Cara Lynn said. "What are you doing tomorrow, say at around eleven?"

"I'm at your disposal."

"Good. Would you go riding with me? I'll show you the countryside."

"I'd like that very much."

Cara Lynn gave him another rather shy smile, then she bounded down the front steps and mounted the mare.

Jordan would have watched her until she was out of sight, but his phone began ringing.

It was his construction foreman, Vince Walker.

"Bad news, boss. Somebody came onto the site last night and lifted some materials, mostly lumber. We're going to come up short on Monday if something isn't done."

"Where was the security staff last night, sleeping on the job?" Jordan asked.

"They all claimed they didn't see anything," Vince replied, sounding skeptical.

"You wouldn't be phoning me if it wasn't major. What's the damage?"

"We're looking at a five or six grand loss at the minimum."

Angry, Jordan sighed heavily. "Get me a new security crew, Vince. We can't eat those kinds of losses—besides, I suspect the thieves are on the payroll."

"I'll get on it right away," Vince assured him.

"Thanks, Vince. I'll inspect the site and see if I can call in a few favors. We've got to bring this project in on time."

"Be careful, boss," Vince advised. "Charlie and his crew aren't going to take being fired kindly. There could be trouble.

By the time Jordan arrived at the construction site of the new children's hospital in Louisville, it was pitch dark. He drove the Range Rover around to the mobile home that was serving as the office.

Climbing the wooden steps two at a time, unlocking the door, he went inside to get the powerful halogen lamp he kept in the bottom drawer of the file cabinet.

On the way back out, he was surprised by a bright light being shone in his eyes. He stumbled back but not before someone swung part of a two-by-four at his head.

Reflexes sharp, he blocked the blow with his right hand, grabbing hold of the board and pulling his assailant toward him. His attacker dropped his flashlight, and Jordan could make out his form well enough to throw a punch at his head.

The man went down hard. Jordan switched on the overhead lights.

Charlie Wilson, his former head security guard, lay facedown on the floor.

Jordan went to his desk, picked up the phone, and began dialing the police.

"Put the phone down," came a male voice from the doorway.

Jordan calmly replaced the receiver and looked up. He had seen the young black man before but didn't recall his name. He was also a member of the defunct security staff.

The man held a revolver in his shaking right hand. "Move over there," he told Jordan, motioning in the direction of the closet.

"What you guys have done so far is petty, but if you go through with this, you could go to prison for life," Jordan said, trying to reason with him. "Why don't you give me the gun and turn yourself in?"

"I'm not gonna kill you," the man said, clearly nervous. "I want enough time to get Charlie and get the hell away from here."

"Uhh . . ." Charlie moaned. He was coming to. The man turned to look down at Charlie, and the chaos which ensued after that, Jordan was not clear on.

A ferocious wolflike creature leapt through the doorway onto the man holding the gun. Terrified, the man screamed, dropped the gun, and fell into a fetal position to protect his throat.

At the same moment Jordan jumped across the desk and picked up the gun. That was when he recognized his rescuer as Peabo.

Peabo stood over the cowering man, growling like a mad dog.

Jordan quickly completed the call to the police, then sat down on the edge of the desk to wait, the gun trained on the two would-be thieves.

"Who would've thought it," he said to Peabo. "A guard dog. I reckon you've earned your dog chow for at least a year, boy."

Peabo let down his guard long enough to switch his tail

happily at the sound of praise in his master's voice, but when the man he was holding at bay moved, he growled menacingly at him to show he meant business.

Twenty minutes later the police were driving away with Charlie Wilson and his partner in custody. Jordan had agreed to follow them to the police station and press charges.

Before the night was over, Charlie and Stephen Wilson, Charlie's kid brother, had given the police the location of the stolen materials in exchange for a lesser charge.

Jordan got his lumber back, the Wilson brothers received time in jail, and Peabo was rewarded with a nice juicy steak.

The next morning Cara Lynn listened intently as Jordan related the goings-on of the previous night. When he'd finished, she smiled at him. "I told you he was a good dog."

They were sitting on the grass beneath a spreading oak after dismounting and tethering the horses to a low-hanging branch.

There wasn't a cloud in the sky, and there was a gentle breeze with the fragrance of honeysuckle in it.

She closed her eyes.

"What are you thinking?" Jordan asked, his voice sensual.

Cara Lynn looked into his eyes. "I'm thinking: why do I feel so comfortable with you? We've just met."

"Do you believe in fate?" Jordan said, a slow smile bringing out his laugh lines.

This morning his eyes were more golden than brown.

"I believe in God, I believe in angels—so I suppose I do believe our lives are directed by some unseen power."

"For months I've been asking myself what drew me to this town, the house I couldn't resist buying," Jordan told her. He reached out to grasp her hand. "Then out of the blue, I phone your father's house, you answer and tell me how you used to play in that very house. A chill came over me. We feel comfortable with one another because we were meant to meet," he said with confidence.

"For what purpose?" Cara Lynn inquired, going along with his theory for the moment.

"That, my dear, is left to be seen."

They leaned back, holding hands, quietly enjoying the breeze and the sunlight on their faces.

Four

"Your date's here!" Cara Lynn called to her father, who was upstairs getting dressed for the Founder's Day celebration.

She peeped through the living room drapes at Mavis Edwards as the older woman walked spiritedly onto the front porch.

Mavis owned and operated the Home Cookin' diner in town. She was in her late forties and a widow of five years. Petite with smooth, medium brown skin, she had one of those faces that defied aging.

Cara Lynn opened the door and stepped aside as Mavis entered the room. "My, aren't you pretty tonight," she complimented her.

Mavis kissed Cara Lynn's cheek, then swatted her on the behind.

"Why haven't you been around to see me? If I hadn't phoned your father yesterday, I wouldn't have known you were in town," she said in her high-pitched, almost squeaky voice.

"I haven't made the rounds yet. I've been sticking close to home," Cara Lynn told her, laughing. "You're stronger than you look."

Knowing her way around, Mavis made herself at home, going over and sitting on the couch. "Frank told you we're officially an item? The whole town's wondering when we're going to set the date. You wouldn't mind having me for a stepmother, would you?"

Cara Lynn joined her on the couch. "I think you'd make anyone a great mother."

Mavis flashed her pearly whites. "Seriously, Cara Lynn, I've been alone so long, I wouldn't know how to begin to share a house with another man. And Frank? He's so set in his ways, a woman would have to be loco to consider becoming his wife."

Cara Lynn thought she detected a hint of sadness behind Mavis's bravado. Could the attractive widow be falling in love with her father?

"You qualify for that," Frank said from the bottom of the stairs.

Picking up his black Stetson from the hall tree, he winked at Mavis. "Come on, pretty lady. I don't want to miss the first dance with you."

Mavis leapt to her feet, beaming at Frank. "Isn't he the most charming man you've ever known?"

"Absolutely," Cara Lynn agreed and ushered them out the front door. "Have a good time, you two."

She watched them walk to the car hand in hand, then Mavis gave her car keys to Frank, and Gentleman Frank opened the car door for her.

"My dad dating. There's a concept that's going to take some getting used to," Cara Lynn said to herself before turning away.

A few minutes later Jordan arrived. She invited him in and then took a step back, admiring his new footwear, a pair of black snakeskin cowboy boots. They were so shiny, you could see your face reflected in them.

"Where'd you get those babies?" Cara Lynn asked, also appreciating the way his jeans and denim shirt fit him.

Jordan grinned. "I was told they were handcrafted by a Mr. Hart Sumter."

"That's Howard Sumter," Cara Lynn explained, laughing

softly. "You must have patronized the Sumters' shoe shop downtown. Mrs. Sumter probably waited on you. I know it sounds as if she's saying 'Hart,' but she's actually saying 'Howard.' You'll eventually get used to the accents around here."

Jordan stepped forward and took her hand, pulling her toward him. "Turn around for me, will you?"

She did and her skirt, which was designed for such movement, twirled, forming a perfect circle around her shapely legs.

She was also wearing a denim shirt, tucked into the skirt, which fell a couple of inches above her knees. Both a pale blue, the skirt was cinched at the waist by a thick black leather belt with a silver buckle in the shape of a butterfly. She wore her best black cowboy boots and had twisted her hair into a French braid. In her earlobes were silver butterfly stud earrings.

"You look beautiful," Jordan told her.

"I'm at my gaudy cowgirl best," she joked. "You look pretty great yourself, I'm going to have to beat the other ladies off with a stick."

"You flatter me," Jordan said, but he appeared pleased.

"Hello, Cara Lynn, how are you?" Dr. Harry Bailey said as he bent to bestow a fatherly kiss on her forehead. In his midsixties, Harry was a rugged-looking man with steel gray eyes and a full head of thick, wavy hair to match. Sara Bailey, his blond, green-eyed wife of thirty years, waited her turn to embrace Cara Lynn.

"Let go of her, Harry," Sara said impatiently.

Cara Lynn hugged Sara. "Being married forever seems to agree with you two."

Sara let go of her in order to get a good look at her. "How come you don't surprise us more often? I've missed you," she said, smiling. "And as for that one—" motioning to her husband "—I've taught him how to put his dirty clothes in the hamper, and he makes a darn good cup of coffee. I'm not about to give that up."

"There are other things you'd miss if I weren't around," Harry said with a wicked gleam in his eyes.

"Oh, yeah—he takes out the garbage without being asked first," Sara added, deadpan.

Harry grinned at his wife, his love for her shining in his eyes.

"How long are you going to be home?" he asked Cara Lynn.

"A week," Cara Lynn answered. "How are Amy and Harry Junior?"

"Amy's been burning up the phone lines ever since she learned she's expecting," Sara said. "You would think she's the only woman ever to have a baby. Harry Junior's fine. This is his last year of undergraduate school at Tulane. He's been accepted by the medical school there."

"That's fantastic news. The last time I spoke with H.J. he was worried that he might not make the grade. I've got to give him a call and congratulate him."

"Do that," Harry said. "You know how he looks up to you." Turning to Sara, he placed his arm about her slender waist. "They're playing 'Skylark,' sweetheart. Let's hit the dance floor."

"Wait a minute," Sara said, holding back. "I want to know who's that great-looking fellow Cara came with."

"Mind your own business," Harry said, pulling her along.

"We'll talk later," Sara promised Cara Lynn. "I want to hear all about him."

Cara Lynn nodded, grinning at their antics. They were still very much in love with each other, and it was gratifying to watch.

They waved good-bye to her as they hurried toward the dance floor.

Alone in the middle of the crowd, Cara Lynn looked

around her, wondering what had become of Jordan. He'd gone to get cold drinks for them more than ten minutes ago. It was difficult to spot anyone in this sea of people. It seemed as though everyone in town had shown up.

Shelbyville was a melting pot, its population consisting of about equal parts blacks and whites with Mexican Americans, some Native Americans, a few Korean families, and more recently, Middle Eastern immigrants.

Largely a farming community, many of its residents worked either on the area's farms or ranches. But industry hadn't overlooked Shelbyville. There was a potato chip factory and a new shopping mall the residents were rightfully proud of. Downtown was lined with antique shops, a quaint grouping of family businesses such as a pharmacy, a hardware store, various restaurants, a frozen yogurt shop, a video rental store, and two supermarkets: a mom-and-pop grocery that had been a mainstay and a new chain that offered lower prices but less personal service. Loyal customers kept the mom-and-pop store afloat.

Two small boys were chasing each other, not looking where they were going and ran into Cara Lynn. Her heel caught on a root coming up from the tree she was standing under, and she lost her balance.

A pair of strong arms wrapped protectively around her waist, bringing her back to her feet.

Thinking her rescuer was Jordan, Cara Lynn turned to smile at him. Keith Freeman grinned at her.

"What do you think you're doing?" she exclaimed, glaring at him.

Keith's grip tightened. "Keeping you from falling on that cute little behind."

"Well, my behind and I are fine now, thank you. You can let go."

"Can I, Cara? I don't think I want to let go of you."

"Either remove your hand, or I'll scream bloody murder," Cara Lynn warned him, teeth clenched.

Keith released her, and Cara Lynn walked away from him, eager to put some distance between them.

Keith was right behind her. "Why are you running away, Cara?"

Cara Lynn stopped in her tracks and faced him. "If you want to talk to me, Keith, we do it on my terms, not yours. I don't want to get into anything with you here. Besides, I'm with someone."

"You mean Davidson?" he said, one eyebrow rising the way it did when he was sure of himself.

Cara Lynn's dark eyes narrowed. "What are you up to, Keith?"

"My aunt's keeping him busy."

"Miss Lena?" Cara Lynn said, voice rising.

Keith closed the distance between them. "Right now, he's about ready to put on the spare tire. Who could refuse to help a sweet little old lady?"

Cara Lynn sighed. "Of all the duplicitous, rotten—"

"Save the adjectives, Cara. We need to talk."

"Hi, Cara Lynn!" It was Trudy Johnson, a former schoolmate.

"Hey, Trudy, how are you, girl?"

"Doing good, how about you?"

"Great. Say hello to your parents for me."

"I will. You take care now."

Trudy kept walking, moved along by an impatient six-year-old who wanted a ride on the merry-go-round.

"Can't we go someplace more private?" Keith implored. "I've missed you."

"I haven't missed you, you jerk," Cara Lynn said menacingly. "Now move or I'll go through you."

"You have a right to be angry with me. I treated you badly," Keith said. He ran a hand through his long, dark brown hair. Naturally wavy, he held it back with a rubber band. "Do you hate me so, Cara? There was a time you loved me, I know that. Is there anything I can do to make it up to you?" He even managed to look remorseful.

Cara Lynn simply stared at him. This was the face of the man she had fancied herself in love with? She wondered if Diana had suggested he wear that ponytail. It seemed like an affectation to her. And the mustache was new. Otherwise, he hadn't changed much since the last time they were face-to-face. He was still in great shape judging from the hard-muscled body showing beneath the snug-fitting jeans and polo shirt. Impeccably groomed, a woman would have to be comatose not to be aware of his sex appeal. He hadn't lost any of his attractiveness. The problem was, she was no longer ruled by her glands.

Her father had been correct. What she had interpreted as love four years ago had been sexual attraction. To be honest, she had not been with Keith long enough, just that one summer, to get to know him as a person. Lust was a dangerous thing—often mistaken for the real thing. She had to see him again in order to come to that conclusion.

"You don't want me to tell you what I'd like you to do with yourself, Keith."

"Please, Cara. It took me four years of being in an unhappy marriage to face the fact that I gave up the best thing that ever happened to me."

"I don't believe that. And if I did, do you actually think I care after what you put me through?" Cara Lynn cried. "Why couldn't you be a man and tell me how you felt, Keith? It would have only taken one phone call."

Keith's voice was low and deliberate. "Because I knew if I heard your voice, I'd never be able to marry Diana and—God help me—I needed her. My business was failing, Cara. I saw Diana as a lifeline. How could I come to you and admit that?"

He sounded sincere. And looking into his eyes, Cara Lynn was inclined to believe him. She could believe him, but she could never trust him again.

"Didn't it occur to you that I might be involved with someone else after all this time?" Cara Lynn asked. "Just yesterday Daddy was telling me I needed to see you and tell you off, but I don't feel the need any longer, Keith. For years I wondered why you left me. What was wrong with me that you would even think of treating me with such disrespect? A minute ago you gave me the answer: there was nothing wrong with me. You were just greedy." She laughed abruptly. "Thank you, Keith. Thank you for seeking me out tonight." She grasped his hand and firmly shook it.

With that, Cara Lynn turned on her heel and left Keith Freeman standing there catching flies with his mouth.

"But Cara—" he called after her.

"No, don't say another word. I want to remember you exactly as you are right now," Cara Lynn told him, her voice cheery.

Cara Lynn saw Jordan before he noticed her. He was standing beside Lena Freeman's old blue Chevy, wiping his hands on a paper towel. Lena looked up, saw Cara, and smiled weakly.

Cara Lynn smiled at the sweet-faced septuagenarian as she bent to kiss her cheek. "Keith and I had that talk. You're free to go now."

"You aren't angry with me, are you?"

"No, why should I be? I know how persuasive that nephew of yours can be."

"Are you two getting back together?" Miss Lena asked hopefully.

"No, Miss Lena. There was nothing to try to save."

"Too bad. That boy needs someone like you."

Cara Lynn put her arm around the elderly woman's shoulders. "Don't worry about Keith, he always lands on his feet."

Miss Lena sighed sadly.

She and Cara Lynn watched as Jordan placed the jack in the Chevy's trunk.

Jordan looked up, saw Cara Lynn, and grinned. "Miss Freeman needed help changing a tire. I couldn't let her get that pretty dress dirty."

Cara Lynn was amused to see Miss Lena's café-au-lait complexion color slightly.

"He's a sweet young man. Hang on to him. If I were forty years younger, you'd have some competition, Cara Lynn."

Miss Lena thanked Jordan for his help, gave him a quick peck on the cheek, and bid them farewell.

"What was all that about?" Jordan asked after Miss Lena had sped away in her Chevy.

Cara Lynn hooked her arm through his. "Miss Lena told me I'm lucky she isn't younger because if she was, she'd be all over you."

Jordan laughed. "I've got a feeling Miss Lena was quite popular in her day." He looked down at his hands. "Where can I wash up?"

Cara Lynn pointed out the facilities next to the concession stands. "Now don't get waylaid by another little old lady in distress. I'll wait for you by the merry-go-round."

On the dance floor Jordan pulled her into his arms as they began the merengue. The fast, spirited dance originated in the West Indies, and the syncopated beat of the drums brought out deep-seated sensuality in the dancers.

As Cara Lynn and Jordan got into the music, their bodies instinctively moved in sync. The point in the dance where the man pulls the woman close to him and then quickly pushes her away again left them both hot and bothered. Their eyes were locked, sending messages of mutual longing. For them, the dance had become a heated ritual of foreplay.

They were both relieved when the song ended and the band went into an old standard: Lorenz Hart's and Richard Rodgers's "Blue Moon."

Cara Lynn buried her face in his chest as they slowed down to a two-step. Jordan smelled of soap and a spicy aftershave. His body was like chiseled granite. She could feel the muscles in his back playing against her fingertips.

"You smell good," Jordan said in her ear. His lips gently caressed her temple.

Cara Lynn was suddenly shy. No one had touched her like this since she broke up with Bill—and it had never felt this good.

"I thought you said you didn't dance well," she said, trying to take her mind off its present riotous track.

"That applies only to square dancing. I could get used to this," Jordan said, rubbing her back. "Are you cold? You're trembling."

"No, no, I'm fine," she answered, smiling up at him.

"I'm holding you too close," Jordan said. He loosened his hold, leaving more space between them. "It's easy to forget we just met. I feel like I know you already, or maybe I'm too eager to get to know you better."

"I feel the same way, it's just that . . ." Cara Lynn tried to explain.

"I know. You recently ended a relationship, and you're not ready for anything more than friendship. I understand," Jordan finished for her.

"My instincts are telling me to go full speed ahead, but my common sense is saying slow down because my emotions have always gotten me in trouble."

"Slow is good," Jordan concurred. "But something tells me my water bill is going to be astronomical next month. I'm taking a lot of showers lately."

Cara Lynn laughed. "Do you ever let up?" she asked, her cheeks dimpling.

The set ended with a waltz, and Cara Lynn was pleasantly

surprised when her father tapped Jordan on the shoulder and asked if he could have this dance with her.

They changed partners, Jordan dancing with Mavis, who wanted to know everything about him, beginning with his conception.

"You seem to be enjoying yourself," Frank said, expertly twirling Cara Lynn around the dance floor.

"I know what you want to hear," Cara Lynn told her father, an amused expression on her face. "You want me to say you were right about him."

"From the way you two were clinging to each other, I already know I was right about him."

Throwing her head back, Cara Lynn laughed. "We'll tone it down. I wouldn't want to start the tongues to wagging."

"People are going to talk anyway. Have fun, tadpole. It's been a long time since I saw you really letting go. If Mavis and I were doing half the things they say we are, there'd be a stupid grin on my face all the time."

"You do have a stupid grin on your face most of the time," Cara Lynn joked. "Anyway, Dad, it's only a date. But I like Jordan a lot. I haven't felt this way since—"

"Keith, am I right?"

"Yes. But Jordan's not like Keith, and I'm not that naive girl who played with fire and got burned. Don't worry, Dad, I've learned my lesson."

"I'm not worried about you, Cara," Frank assured her. He hugged her briefly. "Better get back to Mavis before she talks Jordan's ears off. Don't wait up tonight, I may be late."

"You're a big boy. You know the way home. You *do* know the way home, don't you?" Cara Lynn said, giving him a playful shove away from her.

"Would you like to come in for coffee?" Cara Lynn asked Jordan after he'd seen her to her door.

"It's late. I don't think it would be a good idea."

"Afraid you'll ruin my reputation? I'll let you in on a secret, Jordan. I live a mile from our nearest neighbor, and that's you. No one's going to know if you come into my parlor for a cup of coffee."

"That's not it. To be honest, the sooner I start running up my water bill, the better," he joked.

"Whatever you think is best," Cara Lynn said with an exaggerated sigh.

Cara Lynn took his hand in hers. "Good night, Mr. Davidson. It was a real pleasure being in your company tonight. Perhaps you'll call again when I have a suitable chaperone."

Jordan brought her hand to his lips, turned it palm up, kissed it, then worked his way up to her wrist.

Heart racing, Cara Lynn touched his cheek with her free hand. "Why, Mr. Davidson, what are you doing?"

Jordan slowly pulled her into his embrace, his hand on the small of her back. He bent his head to nuzzle the gentle curve of her neck.

Cara Lynn moaned. What was it about this man? she wondered. He made her weak just being near him.

She was aroused and afraid all at once. What if he didn't feel the same way she did? Her track record where men were concerned wasn't very good. Two broken relationships in four years. Maybe she was doomed to make foolish choices. Oprah had recently done an entire show on the subject. Shut up and kiss him, she interrupted her thoughts, dispensing with the psychobabble.

Jordan wasn't prepared for the emotional onslaught of her mouth on his. He knew then that she had been holding back yesterday. It was his intention to be gentle, in control. But when their mouths met, the taste of her, the feel of her body in his arms all worked together to ignite his senses. He wanted to go on holding her forever, meld with her. His need for her was immediate and entirely too strong. It was sweet torture.

The kiss deepened and Cara Lynn found she had wrapped her arms around his neck, her body pressed into his. She moved her hands downward to his powerful back, past his waist, until they rested on his firm buttocks. Unbidden, erotic images of the two of them making love came to her feverish mind.

Jordan raised his head and looked into her eyes. "I'm leaving now," he said breathlessly.

He released her, and Cara Lynn, none too steady on her feet, backed into the porch swing. Jordan reached out and caught her by the waist to prevent her from falling, and they were kissing again.

He picked her up, and Cara Lynn wrapped her legs around his body.

"This is crazy," Jordan breathed. "You're much too perfect for me. We don't have a damn thing in common."

Cara Lynn kissed his earlobe, then took it between her lips, gently sucking on it. "Of course we do. We drive each other wild."

"You're educated. The only time I set foot on a college campus, I was there to build something."

Cara Lynn sighed. "I'm a vet, not a brain surgeon. Who cares about differences? You're a self-made man, Jordan. One hell of a man. Take me home with you tonight." She couldn't believe she'd uttered those words.

Jordan responded by kissing her with added passion. When he lifted his head this time, he smiled at her. "I've never had such an enticing offer, and I'm probably going to regret this before morning comes." He quickly kissed her forehead. "Good night, beautiful."

He ran down the front steps to his car, giving Cara Lynn little opportunity to protest.

Cara Lynn exhaled. He's right, she thought. I'm lonely— that's why my resistance is low.

She felt something warm and wet on her right leg. Sam stood next to her wagging his tail.

Reaching down to scratch him behind his ear, she laughed. "Hey, boy, did you see me make a fool of myself? You won't tell anyone, will you?"

Five

"The Horsemen's Ball is coming up," Frank said to Cara Lynn the following evening when they'd settled down on the front porch to enjoy the nightly breezes. "Since you're only a skip and a hop from home, are you going to try to go this year? The proceeds will go to the Boys' Home."

"I'll make a contribution," Cara Lynn replied, swatting a mosquito. "That citronella candle isn't doing a bit of good. No, Daddy, I loathe those dances. All those stuck-up blue bloods deigning to mingle with us common folk one day a year. It isn't for me."

"Oh, I love 'em," Frank said, his voice buoyant. "Their uppity attitudes don't bother me. Like I always say: When it's raining, a fellow with his nose in the air drowns much swifter—"

"Than a fellow who humbly bows his head," Cara Lynn finished with a laugh. "You've got a million of 'em. Which blue blood is hosting the shindig this year?"

"Evan Fitzgerald, remember him? I trained a couple of his thoroughbreds. One of them came in second in the Derby last year. Desert Wind."

"Sure, I remember Evan Fitzgerald. I must have been around eighteen the last time I saw him. Isn't he pretty young?"

"He's in his late thirties, I should think. Unmarried. Not

that the ladies give him any rest. With money like his, he has his pick of the females in this county."

"Isn't it unusual for a youngish bachelor to be hosting the ball? The past hosts have been practically in their dotage. I thought it was a prerequisite," Cara Lynn said, laughing.

"Well, it's time we broke with tradition. I think Evan will inject new life into the party. And more African Americans than anytime in the history of the ball are attending, no doubt because they feel comfortable with the notion of Evan being the host. He's always made generous contributions to the United Negro College Fund, and his company is known as a place where a black person has just as much chance for advancement as a white person does," her father said, trying to sell her on attending.

"That must please some of the old guard," Cara Lynn said of her father's assertion about more blacks attending the ball this year.

"I wouldn't miss it," he said. "You might even enjoy it. Bring Jordan."

"He doesn't seem the ballroom type," Cara Lynn said.

"He seems like a man who can handle any type of situation," Frank said diplomatically.

"Can't Jordan and I have a second date before I ask him to a serious social function like the Horsemen's Ball?" Cara Lynn asked, sighing heavily.

"There you go again, thinking negatively."

"I'm not thinking negatively," Cara Lynn defended herself. "I'm only being realistic."

"You don't want to fail again."

"I wasn't thinking of failing, Daddy," Cara Lynn denied, rising from her seat on the edge of the porch.

"Yes, you were. That's exactly what you were thinking. In fact, if I know you—and I do—your fear of failure is so strong, it's getting in the way of your feelings for Jordan.

You like him, but you'd rather not have real emotions creep in and catch you off guard. Am I right?"

Cara Lynn smiled at her father. She supposed that since he'd been a single parent for so many years, very little about her was bound to escape his scrutiny.

"Don't you have a date with Mavis or something?" she asked as she called to Sam by slapping her jeans-clad thigh. "Come on, Sam, let's take a walk and let the professor's brain cool off after that keen observation."

"I'm right," her father said to her retreating back.

He was smiling contentedly as he got to his feet. Actually he did have a date with Mavis tonight.

Cara Lynn and Sam walked along their favorite path, just meandering. She had no place in particular to go.

There was a rustling sound in the brush, probably a small animal hiding in it. Sam pricked up his ears, pausing to sniff the air. He disappeared into the thicket.

"I hope that isn't a raccoon you're so eager to tangle with," Cara Lynn said more to herself than anyone. "Don't come home all scratched up like you did last time."

She heard him barking happily as she walked on.

She missed work, which wasn't surprising. She had never wanted to be anything else besides a veterinarian. From an early age, animals, especially horses, were her focus.

Her mother used to complain that every stray in the county eventually found its way to their house.

By the time Cara Lynn was twelve, Lillianne had had enough, making a stipulation: Cara Lynn could nurse the strays back to health, but as soon as they were ambulatory, she had to give them away. The last stray she'd taken in was Sam, and she had been unable to give him away. Besides, Sam had a way of ingratiating his way right into your heart. Even Lillianne had loved the mutt.

At seventeen, Cara Lynn was graduated from Shelbyville

High with the promise of a full academic scholarship to the University of Kentucky. On breaks from school she worked with Harry, the family's veterinarian and the husband of her mother's dearest friend, Sara.

Harry took her under his wing, giving her insight into the profession she could not get anywhere else. At twenty-one, she was a full-time student at Tuskegee Institute's School of Veterinary Medicine and, thanks to Harry's tutelage, her hard work and dedication, at the top of her class.

Today, at twenty-eight, she was a doctor of veterinary medicine, owned a clinic in Louisville—well, she and the bank owned it. However, she was in the black, could afford to pay Carly and herself very decent salaries and give them two weeks' paid vacation yearly, plus major holidays. She had no complaints.

She stopped and looked around her. She'd done it again. All the years of coming to the Collins mansion and weaving her dreams around it was going to be a hard habit to break. And now, she willingly admitted, Jordan's presence would make it doubly hard to stop coming here.

The porch light was on, but she knew he had it on an automatic timer. It came on two or three times a night to discourage prowlers.

She sat down on the top step, remembering the initial thought she'd had about Jordan after she'd learned he'd purchased the Collins place. She'd been a little put out by him. After all, he'd destroyed her dream of one day buying the house herself.

She'd had plans for this house since she was eight years old. She saw herself living here, being married here, raising her children.

The property had a guest house that could be converted into a first-rate veterinary clinic. And there was a decent barn several hundred feet from the house where horses could be boarded.

Then along came a tall, handsome Yankee who spoke

with an unusual accent, had eyes the color of an autumn sunset and a voice so sexy you could listen to him read the phone book and beg for more.

True, he'd confounded her plans, but he'd also become the subject of her recent daydreams. Daydreams that were often downright embarrassing.

No use brooding, she thought as she started walking back to the ranch. She'd go into town and catch a movie or something.

Or something turned out to be a visit to the local video store, where she browsed through their considerable selection of movies.

The store was busy for a Monday night. Cara Lynn was standing in the romantic comedy section when someone tapped her on the shoulder.

"Hello, sweetie," a feminine voice said.

Cara Lynn turned to find Sara Bailey standing behind her.

"Sara! How are you?" They hugged.

"I thought I saw you come in here. Harry and I were across the street at the hardware store. He's finally going to repair that leaky faucet in the guest bathroom." She paused. "Oh, I'm okay. I could use some sleep though. I haven't been sleeping well lately."

"Is that why you have dark circles under your eyes? Nothing more serious?"

"Nah, I'm fine, Mother," Sara said, smiling. She always referred to Cara Lynn as "Mother" whenever Cara Lynn started obsessing about her.

After Lillianne's death, Sara, as Lillianne's best friend, took a special interest in Cara Lynn. She loved her like a daughter. However, just as Cara Lynn had a penchant for nursing sick animals back to health, she was that much more attentive to the people she loved—and she had a tendency to worry overmuch about them.

"Don't tell me you're going home tonight and watch a movie alone," Sara lamented.

"Okay, I won't tell you," Cara Lynn said jokingly.

"Where's that big, good-looking Jordan Davidson?"

"Back in Louisville. He has a business to run."

"When are you going to see him again?" Sara inquired.

"This weekend, I suppose. Why do you ask?" Cara Lynn said, playing with her. She already knew the answer. Both Sara's children were happily married, and she'd like nothing better than to see Cara Lynn likewise shackled.

"You two looked so good together last night, I just knew something like work couldn't keep you apart. Anyway, Harry and I want to have you to dinner so that we can get to know him."

"So that you can interrogate him at your leisure," Cara Lynn said, smiling knowingly.

"That, too," Sara said, unashamed, her green eyes sparkling, probably in anticipation of the actual event. "Last night he answered my questions rather politely."

"You mean under the pretext of a dance, you put the poor guy on the spot?"

"I just asked him if he realized how special you are, and he said, yes, he did. He knew you were exceptional the instant you two met."

"He was being a gentleman, Sara," Cara Lynn said.

Sara shook her head. "No, I could tell he was being honest. He has honest eyes. I know people. I wouldn't be my mother's daughter if I didn't. He's good people."

"I'm not going to argue with you about that," Cara Lynn said, picking up a Tom Hanks film.

"A romance?" Sara noted. "You miss him, huh?"

"I miss romance," Cara Lynn allowed, sounding wistful.

Sara quickly kissed Cara Lynn's cheek. "I've gotta run. Tell Jordan hello for me. See you."

"You go home and get some sleep," Cara Lynn admonished. "None of that staying up all night watching Cary Grant movies."

"Got to have my daily dose of Cary," Sara said lightly as she walked away.

In spite of Sara's claims to the contrary, Cara Lynn was worried Sara was ill. For one thing, Sara's normally tanned skin was pale. Sara had inherited her half Navajo mother's naturally dark complexion, her Nordic father's green eyes and blond hair. Another thing that disturbed her was how much weight Sara had lost. Sara was five feet, three inches and usually plump, but recently she'd become so slender, her clothes hung on her.

Cara Lynn tried to put it out of her mind. If Sara was seriously ill, wouldn't she confide in her? Not if she wanted to protect her from the knowledge . . . Maybe she'd drop by Harry's office tomorrow and have a chat with him about her suspicions.

Leaving the video store, she nearly collided with a couple who were going in.

She recognized them at once. Jerry Younger and Deborah Sanford. They were both in her graduating class in high school. Jerry was a successful disc jockey at a popular radio station out of Chicago. He was undoubtedly on vacation, too. It took a good deal of self-control for her to smile at Deborah Sanford, who had bullied her throughout their school years. She hoped Deborah had grown into a nicer woman.

Jerry was grinning at her. "Cara Lynn Garrett. How are you, girl? You're definitely looking good."

He was perhaps five-eleven, dark skinned, and wore a full beard which he kept smartly trimmed. Cara Lynn had always found Jerry friendly and easygoing.

"Hi, Jerry, Deborah. It's so good to see you. I'm doing fine. Visiting your folks?"

"Uh huh," Jerry said, nodding. "I try to make it back at least once a year. What are you up to these days? I haven't seen you since we graduated. I don't see a wedding ring on your finger."

Before she could reply, Deborah cut in, laughing. "A wedding ring? Cara Lynn is much too involved with her career for marriage."

Cara Lynn noticed that her ring finger was naked as well.

"I'm a veterinarian," she explained to Jerry. She moved aside as a customer entered the video store. "I have an office in Louisville. I'm visiting my dad for a few days."

"How is Mr. Frank?" Jerry inquired as he reached into his coat pocket and retrieved one of his business cards.

"He's doing great, as active as ever," Cara Lynn replied pleasantly. "And your folks?"

"They're all doing just fine." He reached for her hand and placed the card in her palm. "Call me sometime. You can usually reach me at one of those numbers."

Cara Lynn couldn't help noticing the angry expression on Deborah's face when Jerry gave her the card. She was unaware of any romantic involvement between them. Wasn't Deborah seeing Bobby Johnson?

"Sure," she said politely. Turning to Deborah, she added, "I hope your dress shop is doing well, Deborah."

"I've been very successful. You're not the only one who has made something of herself, Cara Lynn."

Taken aback, Cara Lynn continued to smile. "I'm sure lots of people we went to school with have been successful, Deborah," she said, hoping she was able to keep the edge off her voice.

It never failed. Whenever she and Deborah were in the same room, the shorter girl invariably tried to pick an argument.

"Well, I'm sure we're holding you up, Cara Lynn," Jerry intervened, sounding uncomfortable.

"Yes, I should be going," Cara Lynn agreed. "You take care, Jerry." She paused. "You, too, Deborah."

Cara Lynn walked away so she didn't hear Deborah tell

Jerry to go on into the store without her. She wanted to go across the street to buy a cup of frozen yogurt.

Cara Lynn was getting into her Jeep when Deborah caught up with her.

"Aren't you satisfied with one man?" she shouted at Cara Lynn through the closed window.

Cara Lynn rolled down the window. "What did you say?"

"I saw you last night with Jordan Davidson. And still you had to flirt with Jerry," Deborah said contemptuously. "A person would think you're hard up for male companionship."

"You were standing right there—you know I wasn't flirting with Jerry," Cara Lynn said, matching Deborah's tone. "What is your problem?"

Deborah's dark eyes narrowed. "You are my problem. You haven't changed a bit. Still playing the shy innocent. I didn't like you then, and I like you even less now. So, you're a big doctor, drive around in a nice car with your nose stuck in the air. Deep down you're still that skinny, awkward egghead."

Sighing, Cara Lynn pushed the car door open, making Deborah quickly move away or risk being hit.

She looked at Deborah, her expression cold, unrelenting.

"You are one sick human being, Deborah Sanford, if you think you can intimidate me. The last time you tried that, I was in mourning, having just lost my mother. I thought you were a heartless bully then, but I can see now that you're much worse." She shook her head sadly. "Girl, we've been out of high school for eleven years. How can you behave so childishly? You need to grow up and stop being an ass."

"You can't call me that," Deborah huffed.

"I call 'em as I see 'em," Cara Lynn said, standing her ground. "If you don't want to be knocked into next Tuesday, I suggest you get out of my face."

There were times when being five-ten had its advantages.

Deborah slunk away but not without one last weak comment. "Stay away from Jerry."

"He's all yours," Cara Lynn called after her. "Enjoy him until poor Bobby returns from Alaska."

She got back into the Jeep, started the engine and drove away. She finally knew why Deborah had always been belligerent toward her. Jealousy, plain and simple.

"Dr. Garrett, how are you? I didn't know you were coming by today," Angela Conner, Harry's secretary exclaimed upon seeing Cara Lynn.

Angela had been with Harry for ten years, she was African American, in her early thirties, around five-six, fair skinned, and wore her brown hair in braids that were shoulder length. She was married and the mother of two preschool boys.

"Hi, Angie," Cara Lynn said, smiling. "I didn't phone ahead because I was hoping to see Harry between appointments if you can work me in."

"No problem," Angela said. She smoothed a couple of braids behind her ear as she stood. "I'll go see how far along he is with his present patient. Mr. Ketchum brought Boomer in, says he's listless. It's probably his advanced age. You remember that irascible old hound dog?"

"Who doesn't know Boomer? He must have terrorized every kid in town at one time or another."

Angela humphed. "Yeah, well those days are long gone," she said as she left the room.

Cara Lynn sat down on a chair next to an elderly woman holding a very fat Siamese cat on her lap.

"Good morning," Cara Lynn greeted the cat lady.

"Good morning. Did I hear Angie refer to you as 'doctor'?"

"I'm a veterinarian."

The woman shifted the cat on her lap so that Cara Lynn

could see it better. The cat was pure white with lavender eyes. It would be quite a showpiece if the woman didn't spoil it by overfeeding.

"Maybe I ought to bring my Seymour to you," the woman said. "Dr. Bailey, bless his heart, doesn't seem to be able to do anything for him." She kissed Seymour on the top of his head. "Poor baby, he just lays in one place all day, doesn't even come to me to be petted anymore."

That's because you're overfeeding him, lady, Cara Lynn thought, amused.

She reached over and stroked Seymour's head. "What did Dr. Bailey tell you to do for him?"

"Oh, he told me to feed him less and encourage him to get some exercise by putting him out once a day."

"Excellent advice," Cara Lynn said. "Cats are instinctual creatures. He needs to be outside sometimes doing what comes naturally to his species. Do you have a fenced backyard?"

"I have a huge fenced backyard."

"Then let Seymour out to play. You'll have a healthier, happier cat in no time."

"That's exactly what Dr. Bailey suggested." She hesitated. "I'm afraid Seymour might run away."

Cara Lynn held her laughter. "Do you think Seymour is going to be climbing fences as heavy as he is?"

The woman looked down at the cat then back up at Cara Lynn. "No, I suppose not," she said. She smiled and grasped Cara Lynn's hand. "You're sweet. Thank you, doctor. But you know—" her voice dropped and her tone became conspiratorial "—you don't look old enough to be a doctor."

Angela returned at that moment and told Cara Lynn she could go on back to Harry's office.

"He's finishing up with Boomer now," she said. "He'll be right with you, Mrs. O'Brien."

Harry was effusive as always. He gave Cara Lynn a warm bear hug.

"To what do I owe this unexpected visit?" he said, pointing to the burgundy leather chair across from his desk in his oak paneled office.

Cara Lynn sat down and Harry went around his desk, sitting in the swivel chair behind it.

"I'll be brief, Harry. I know you're busy," Cara Lynn began. She took a deep breath, exhaled. "How do I say this without appearing to be sticking my nose where it doesn't belong?"

"Come out with it, Cara," Harry urged her. "We've never stood on ceremony."

Cara Lynn leaned forward in her chair. "Harry, I'm worried about Sara. She's lost a lot of weight, and she looks tired every time I see her."

"She told me you were concerned about how haggard she looked last night. Sara hasn't been sleeping well, Cara. She has insomnia—it's affecting her appetite, even her personality. She gets depressed and irritable."

"Who's she seeing about this?" she asked, voice rising.

"George Ackerman in Louisville. He's a good physician."

"George is a general practitioner. Maybe Sara needs to go to a specialist. I've never known Sara to be anything but robust."

"I know," Harry said, his gray eyes sad. "These have been difficult times for us, Cara. But by the grace of God, we'll get through them."

Cara Lynn had the strangest feeling that Harry was talking about something entirely different from what they were discussing. She didn't press the point.

She rose. "Let me know if I can do anything." She smiled at him. "I'll let you get back to work. I'm glad to know it's nothing life threatening, Harry. Sara means a great deal to me."

Harry saw her to the door. "Sara feels the same way

about you, we both do. Don't worry, Cara. We're taking care of it."

Cara Lynn left Harry's office feeling as though he'd sugar-coated Sara's condition. She had been told by the both of them that Sara was fine. A little sleeplessness, loss of appetite, but basically all right. She tried to set her mind at ease and stop obsessing as Sara had accused her of doing.

After leaving Harry's office, she drove downtown. She needed to pick up some conditioner for her hair since Jordan was taking her out Friday night, and she wanted to look her best.

She was greeted enthusiastically by Mrs. Greenwald, wife of the pharmacist in the small, family owned drugstore.

Transplants from Brooklyn, the Greenwalds still spoke with a Yiddish accent, even though they'd been in Shelbyville since 1948 when Benjamin was discharged from the army, and a pal of his, who was from Kentucky, convinced him of the lucrative opportunities down South.

"Hello, Miss Fancy Doctor," Tovah Greenwald said, without a trace of malice. "It's been a long time since we've seen you. How's big-city life treating you?"

Cara Lynn laughed at Tovah's description of Louisville as a big city. True, it was a large city by the South's standards, but it still had that small town rhythm to it.

"Hello, yourself!" Cara Lynn said, stopping at the front register where Tovah was stationed. "You're looking wonderful, as usual."

Tovah prided herself on her appearance. She'd been quite a beauty in her youth. A redhead with green eyes and a perfect figure.

She once told Cara Lynn how "the fellas," as she called them, used to woo her. Her parents, however, were strict Orthodox Jews and wouldn't allow her to see any young man who didn't meet their requirements. "Oh, the handsome fellas they turned away," she said, sighing. "But if they hadn't, I wouldn't have met dear, sweet Ben and he was the cream of the crop."

"Thanks for the compliment," Tovah said now. "But between you and me, I have to put in twice the time to look half as good." Her clear eyes twinkled. "You, on the other hand . . . if I had legs like yours, I'd never wear slacks. Show off your assets while you've still got them."

"Believe me," Cara Lynn said, leaning over the counter. "When the time is right, I've been known to display my assets."

"I'd like to see that," said a humor-laced male voice behind her.

Cara Lynn's face grew hot with embarrassment. She turned to find Evan Fitzgerald standing behind her.

At six feet, he was only a couple of inches taller than Cara Lynn, so they were on eye level. His eyes registered delight, hers held something akin to panic. The last time she'd seen Evan, he'd stopped by the ranch to discuss a horse he'd left in Frank's care. Cara Lynn had interrupted them in her father's study. She was excited because a woodpecker she'd found in the woods with a broken wing had improved so much it had flown away.

She'd burst into the room talking hurriedly. "Daddy, Woody flew away, he's completely recovered. I knew he would make it!"

That was when she saw Evan sitting in the wing chair across from her father's desk.

"Oh, I'm sorry," Cara Lynn had stammered, her hand going to her dirty face. Her clothes weren't in better condition. She'd been working on the ranch all day. Feeding the horses, cleaning out the barn, rubbing down the horses, all sweaty jobs.

Don't let him remember me, she prayed fervently.

"Evan, you rascal," Tovah said. "Our conversation was not for your ears. Now apologize to Cara Lynn."

Thanks so much, Mrs. Greenwald, Cara Lynn thought, chagrined.

Evan offered his hand in apology. He smiled, revealing straight white teeth in his deeply tanned face.

He bent his curly, dark brown, almost black, head courteously. He looked into her eyes, an amused expression in his topaz eyes. He reminded Cara Lynn of the actor, Antonio Banderas, only Evan had a thick mustache.

"My apologies, Miss Cara Lynn," he said, his voice low. Then it dawned on him. "You're not Frank Garrett's little girl, are you?"

"I haven't been a little girl in quite some time," Cara Lynn replied with a wry smile. "How've you been, Mr. Fitzgerald?"

Cara Lynn grasped his hand. He didn't shake, he just held it, continuing to look at her as though he were seeing her for the first time.

He released her hand after a moment and placed the basket with his purchases in them on the counter to give Tovah something to do. She was listening to their exchange with rapt interest.

"Call me Evan," he told her, his golden brown eyes on her face. "May I say you've become a very lovely woman. The last time I saw you, you must have been fresh out of high school."

"I was eighteen," Cara Lynn confirmed, pleased with the compliment but bewildered as to how she should take it. Hopefully Evan Fitzgerald was simply being polite. The Southern Gentleman. Complimentary but above impropriety.

"Yes, I remember," Evan said, smiling. "Your father and I were discussing business when you came into the room shouting about a bird that had flown away. I couldn't tell whether you were happy about it or upset—"

"Happy. It was a bird I'd nursed back to health, and he'd

flown away only moments before I interrupted you and Dad."

"Well," Evan said. "You were pretty back then but nothing that compares to what you've become. I hear you're a veterinarian now. Are you married?"

That blew her theory to kingdom come.

"No, but I am seeing someone."

"Seriously? Talk of an engagement, that sort of arrangement?"

"No, but—"

"Excellent, then you aren't committed to anyone."

Tovah finished ringing up his purchases, and she was practically leaning over the counter in her attempt to hear what they were saying. Evan paid his bill and, turning to Cara Lynn, said, "Would you do me the honor of having a cup of coffee with me?"

"I'm a little rushed. I need to pick up a few things and then I have to meet Dad by eleven thirty."

It was nearly eleven. Cara Lynn hoped he'd get discouraged by her excuses not to have coffee with him. A man of Evan's looks and social status was probably accustomed to women tripping over themselves to be with him.

Her reluctance didn't deter him though.

"I'll go across to the diner and order for us," he suggested. "That will save time. Go ahead and do your shopping."

He's just being friendly, she reasoned. "Okay, I'll meet you there in about five minutes."

Evan left the store. Tovah shook her head. "And in slacks yet! You'd better stick to hiding your legs. The stuff you've got would be too powerful in a dress."

"You should stop, Mrs. Greenwald," Cara Lynn said, laughing. "Give me a bottle of conditioner, and I'm blowing this joint."

"Evan's okay," Tovah said as she punched in the price of the conditioner on the cash register. "He's not half the ladies' man people claim he is. It's not easy being the wealthiest man in Jefferson county. If you don't live up to people's expectations, they start making up things about you."

"It's just coffee," Cara Lynn said, picking up her package. "So long, Mrs. Greenwald."

"Bye, and don't be a stranger."

A cup of coffee, a gentle let down, and I'm outta there, Cara Lynn thought of her date with Evan.

The Home Cookin' diner was busy, every table occupied. A restaurant whose atmosphere was just as its name implied, people came here to eat well and feel at home.

Mavis Edwards was a solicitous hostess, flitting from table to table, chatting up the customers. She was a tiny dynamo.

She was standing next to Evan's booth now, giggling at something he'd said.

Her eyes lit up when she saw Cara Lynn approaching. She playfully punched Evan's shoulder. "When you said you were expecting a lady friend, I didn't know you were talking about Cara Lynn." To Cara Lynn, she said, "Hello, sugar."

"Good morning," Cara Lynn said in a low voice, standing close to Mavis. "What were you and Dad up to so late last night?"

"None of your beeswax," Mavis said with a grin. "You sit down and have some grits, put some roses in those cheeks. Both pair," she added, then left them alone.

"She's a character," Evan said.

"That she is," Cara Lynn agreed.

Their eyes met across the table, and Evan smiled at her. "You only came because it would've been ill-mannered not to, didn't you?"

Cara Lynn arched her eyebrows and thought of hedging. "I think you're very nice, Evan, but I did try to tell you I'm seeing someone."

"He's a lucky man. Who is he?"

"I don't think you know him. He's new in town. Owns a construction company in Louisville."

"It's a small town, Cara Lynn. You sound like you're describing Jordan Davidson."

"You know him?"

"We've had some dealings. His company built my new office building in Lexington. Did a fine job. Came in under budget," Evan explained. "He's a good guy, never heard anything negative about him. I wish I had."

Amused, Cara Lynn said, "No, you don't."

"Okay, I don't," Evan conceded. His eyes caressed her beautiful bronzed face, taking in the little cleft in her chin, high cheekbones, and pink, heart-shaped mouth. It's funny, he thought. She's gorgeous, yet she doesn't behave as if she's even aware of it.

He was used to beautiful women having a certain haughty, even petulant, air about them. But Cara Lynn was so down to earth she intrigued him.

He reached across the table to playfully touch the tip of her nose. "I've been out maneuvered by Mr. Davidson. That doesn't mean we can't be friends, does it?"

"You can never have too many friends," Cara Lynn said lightly.

"Good, because I could use your help."

"How?"

"You've heard of the Horsemen's Ball?"

"Only every year since my birth."

"I've been roped into hosting the event this year, and I don't know a waltz from a polka. I'm afraid that part of my education was sorely lacking," Evan said, sighing. "My secretary has been on leave since her husband fell ill. The party planners I hired are turning my house upside down. What I need is someone who can tell me if they're doing an adequate job or if I should give them the boot."

His eyes pleaded with her.

"Are you serious?"

"Very. Are you game?"

"I'm as ignorant on the social graces as you are," Cara Lynn told him.

But it might be interesting to tour Baymoor. She'd often wondered what the palatial estate looked like on the inside.

"I figure two heads are better than one," Evan was saying. "The idea is to avoid utter embarrassment. I refuse to go to one of those old battle axes who've hosted in the past. They think I'm so much garbage because I haven't married one of their daughters yet."

Chloe, one of the waitresses, brought them steaming cups of coffee and slices of freshly made apple pie. "On the house," she said.

Cara Lynn thanked her and took a sip of the coffee, still pondering Evan's request. So, the other blue bloods were sitting back waiting for Evan to fall on his face.

"Why haven't you married one of them?" she asked, postponing her answer to his query.

"Because I'm attracted to women with substance and style. Women with big brown eyes and skin like silk," he said, touching the tender inside of her arm.

"Stop that," Cara Lynn said and meant it. "I'd be willing to come over and see what the planners are doing, but only on a friendly basis."

"Great. Is tomorrow good for you?"

"Wednesday or Thursday, I'm free both days."

"Then tomorrow it is. The planners will arrive at around nine in the morning."

"I'll be there about five minutes earlier. You can say I'm your cousin from out of town," Cara Lynn said jokingly.

Evan tried Mavis's pie. "Mmm . . . delicious."

For the next few minutes they consumed the pie and drank the coffee in silence. Finished, Cara Lynn glanced at her watch. "I've got to go," she announced, getting to her feet.

Evan stood, too, leaned over and kissed her on the cheek, close to her mouth.

"We can't leave without giving Mavis's customers something to gossip about."

I'm going to have to keep my eye on this one, Cara Lynn thought, surprised by his nerve.

The news spread fast. That night at the supper table, Frank told her someone had told him she'd been spotted brazenly kissing Evan on the street.

"It wasn't a kiss, it was more like a buss on the cheek, and we weren't on the street, we were in Mavis's diner."

"Well, how did this come about?" her father wanted to know.

"I'd just agreed to help him plan the Horsemen's Ball," Cara Lynn stated. Frank's bushy eyebrows shot up in surprise. "Don't look at me like that, Daddy. Evan and I met this morning, we took an instant liking to one another. I told him I'm dating Jordan. He said, 'Fine, but can't we be friends?' I didn't see any harm in it. I have plenty of male friends I don't date."

"No harm in it?" Frank said, his voice rising. "Evan is a white man, Cara Lynn. You're too young to remember, but I know the lack of respect they've shown our women in the past. On top of being white, he's richer than Rockefeller. Didn't it occur to you why he's interested in you?"

"My sparkling personality?" Cara Lynn said dryly.

"Be serious," Frank said, irritated. His expression most definitely was.

"All right, already," Cara Lynn returned, exasperated. She put down her fork and regarded her father. "I know Evan Fitzgerald is interested in me only because he's attracted to the package. I thought it would be a lark to get to know him, that's all. Yes, he is a wealthy, good-looking bachelor—but I'm not going to date him. I've already made that perfectly clear to him."

Frank put up his hand. "Enough said. I wanted you to

know my opinion on the situation. I have nothing personal against Evan, he's always treated me fairly—but I draw the line at watching him take advantage of my child. You keep your eyes open. Rich men are a different breed of men."

"Point taken," Cara Lynn said. "By the way, Mavis wouldn't tell me what you two were doing until the wee hours, maybe you will . . ."

"When you're older," Frank promised. "Much older."

Six

Cara Lynn arrived at Baymoor, a Colonial-style mansion surrounded by more than ten thousand acres of prime Kentucky property, promptly at five till nine.

The housekeeper, Mrs. Earlene Washington, a middle-aged woman she knew from St. Paul AME church, greeted her and showed her to the sunroom right off the kitchen.

Cara Lynn could tell by Mrs. Washington's sour demeanor that the woman thought her involvement with Evan was an unsavory one. She'd given the woman a cheery, "Hello, Mrs. Washington, so good to see you again." In return, she'd received a mumbled "morning," after which the housekeeper fixed her with a malicious stare.

Cara Lynn had to remind herself that it was still some people's opinion that races should not mix socially, and if a black woman was seeing a white man, then she was probably of low character.

Mrs. Washington grudgingly asked if she'd like a cup of coffee.

"No, thank you," Cara Lynn answered politely.

Mrs. Washington turned to leave.

"Oh, Mrs. Washington?"

"Yes, Miss Garrett?"

"See you in church Sunday."

Earlene Washington's face was expressionless. "I'll go see what's keeping Mr. Fitzgerald."

In about five minutes Evan joined Cara Lynn in the sun-room, looking well rested and relaxed in a pair of Levis, a crisp white long-sleeved shirt that set off the darkness of his skin, and a pair of tan Italian loafers.

He went right to Cara Lynn, grasping both her hands in his. "I'm sorry I wasn't down here to greet you, but I had an unexpected business call. Did Mrs. Washington make you feel welcome?"

"She was very nice," Cara Lynn said, getting to her feet.

"You look lovely," Evan told her. "The party planners will be a few minutes late. But I suppose we should get right down to business. The ballroom's this way."

The ballroom was approximately the size of a school gymnasium.

"This is beautiful," Cara Lynn said as she stepped onto the polished hardwood floor. She gazed up at the crystal chandelier hanging from the center of the ceiling. "Did your parents give many parties when you were growing up?"

"Mother loved giving parties," Evan said, enjoying her reaction to the room. "Twice a year, usually in the spring and New Year's, they would host a big bash. The New Year's dance was invariably a costume ball. It was great fun that I'd spy on since I wasn't allowed to attend them until I turned twenty-one." He grinned infectiously. "You see, there was always an abundance of spirits at these soirees. Some of the revelers got a little wild after a few rounds. One night a woman stripped and took a swan dive off the bal-cony into the pool."

"Was she injured?"

"Fortunately, no. Mother never invited her back though."

Cara Lynn looked at the room from all angles: the ele-gant, understated green and gold wallpaper, the bandstand, the French doors that opened onto the balcony, the grand piano next to the bandstand.

"I can imagine this room filled with people," she said, her voice low, dreamy.

"Tell me what you see," Evan encouraged her, spellbound by her impassioned response to the room.

"The room is romantically lit, not too dark, mind you—you want to be able to see your partner's face. The band is playing 'Embraceable You' or 'Someone to Watch Over Me,' one of the standards that never goes out of style."

She was captivating in her spring dress with her hair like an ebony halo framing her luminous face. Evan couldn't take his eyes off her.

"No waltzes?" he said, his voice barely audible.

"Oh, no. Who wants to waltz on a night like this? There is a chanteuse. She's standing in the spotlight, singing about a lost love."

Evan circled her. "More practically," he interjected. "Tell me what happens from the moment you arrive at the dance."

Cara Lynn closed her eyes. "You step from your car at the entrance, the valet takes your keys and parks your car for you. Then you check your coat. After that, you and your date go into the ballroom. The first thing you notice is the music and then the chandelier. When you walk into the room, it's as if you've been transported back in time. Straight ahead is the bandstand. To your left are the buffet tables and the bar. The French doors are left open, allowing the night breezes to circulate throughout the room and to give lovers an escape route to sneak a kiss on the balcony."

In his excitement, Evan went to her and grasped her hands in his, turning her around to face him. "Now you see what I meant when I asked for your help. You may not be used to balls, but you know what you like. What's more, you have superb taste. When the party planners arrive, I want you to tell them what you told me. I want a night exactly like the one you described."

He pulled her into his arms, and they danced around the ballroom, laughing like children.

Evan sang a lyric to "Someone to Watch Over Me." He had a pleasant, clear baritone. Cara Lynn was impressed.

"Although he may not be the man some girls think of as handsome. To my heart he carries the key. Won't you tell him please to put on some speed. Follow my lead, oh, how I need. Someone to watch over me." Cara Lynn picked up the song.

"You have a beautiful voice," Evan said.

"Choir practice," Cara Lynn laughed.

"Cara Lynn . . . To think that the girl of my dreams grew up right down the road from me, and I've been looking all over for her."

"Excuse me, Mr. Fitzgerald," Mrs. Washington interrupted from the doorway. "But Miss Danson and Miss Roberts are here."

Evan frowned and sighed. "Maybe we can finish our dance later. Would you show them in, Mrs. Washington?"

The morning passed quickly. The party planners were relieved that Evan had a concise idea of what he wanted them to do for him. Miss Danson, Estelle Danson, the owner of Partys Galore, was especially curious about Cara Lynn. Estelle was an attractive blond in her early thirties, and she was hoping to parlay this job into an entry to Evan's world.

She raised an expertly tweezed eyebrow when Evan introduced Cara Lynn as a dear friend. Estelle was careful not to show her disgust at the genuine admiration Evan appeared to have for the girl.

Judy Roberts, on the other hand, was instantly taken with Dr. Garrett. Judy hung on every word Cara Lynn said and instantly agreed with every suggestion she made, which irritated Estelle.

"I love the idea of a chanteuse," Judy said, nodding so hard her chestnut curls bounced. "It's so forties."

"Most of our clients appreciate a more refined choice in music," Estelle said, barely able to hide her annoyance. "Gershwin, even Vivaldi."

"I don't think so," Evan spoke up. "I'm more fond of

Duke Ellington, Sammy Cahn, Johnny Mercer. That's the kind of music we want."

"Well then, it's agreed," Estelle said, a bit too brightly. "We'll take care of everything: hire the caterer, the band, the sing—chanteuse, hire the waiters and drivers. Don't worry about a thing, Mr. Fitzgerald."

"I won't," Evan said.

He thanked them for coming and then asked Mrs. Washington to see them out.

"That's my cue to leave," Cara Lynn said, looking over the ballroom one last time.

Evan smiled at her. He enjoyed watching her move. She had such grace, such fluidity of motion.

"I can't wait to see you on the night of the ball," he said.

Cara Lynn faced him. "I hadn't planned on coming, Evan."

"You must come. Are you going to miss your dream night?"

Cara Lynn began walking toward him from across the ballroom. "My father and I have already had this conversation. I don't mix well with—"

"People like me?" Evan said.

"I was going to say I have a strong aversion to anyone looking down their noses at me."

"The Horsemen's Ball is supposed to be for everyone in the business, Cara. From the owners all the way down to the stable boy. Everyone's invited. That's why there is no minimum donation for the charity that's chosen each year."

He grinned. "Afraid you won't have a date?"

"No, I'm not," Cara Lynn said sharply.

"I'll tell you what," Evan ribbed her. "If you don't have a date a week before the dance, call me and *I'll* be your escort."

Not waiting for her answer to his proposition, he took her by the hand. "Before you run away, there's something I'd like to show you."

He led her through the house, out the back door to the stables.

"Wait until you see this," he said, as they walked through the double doors of the stable.

Two young men, one black, one white, were stacking hay.

"Hey, Joey, get the Sheik for me, will you? I'd like Dr. Garrett to have a look at him."

The black youth propped the pitchfork he'd been using against a nearby wall and hurried to open the stall of the Arabian stallion.

Joey gently placed the bit in the Sheik's mouth and led him out by his reins. The Arabian behaved well, allowing himself to be put on display. He even stood still as Cara Lynn patted his flanks and ran her hand along his powerful neck. He was the color of the desert sand and magnificent. He held his head as though he were cognizant of it.

"What's his lineage?" Cara Lynn asked.

"He comes from a long line of winners. Desert Wind is his father," Evan replied proudly.

Desert Wind had placed second in the Kentucky Derby last year.

"Whatever happened to Desert Wind?" Cara Lynn inquired.

"He's retired from the track, of course. But he's commanding quite a sum for stud fees."

Cara Lynn brushed the Sheik's mane. "Dad would probably love to get his hands on this one. He has great lines."

"Like father, like daughter?" Evan said of her ability to spot good physical attributes in a horse.

"I love horses," Cara Lynn replied, setting him straight. "But Dad's the expert. All I want to do is ride them. I don't care if they win races or not."

The Sheik had been patient long enough. He began prancing.

"Take him back to his stall, Joey," Evan said.

"Thank you, Joey," Cara Lynn said.

"You're welcome, Dr. Garrett," Joey said, giving her a shy smile.

"Nice young man," Evan said when Joey was out of ear-shot. "He came here about a year ago, right out of high school. Has a special touch with horses. If anyone else had gone in there after the Sheik, he would have put up a fuss."

Cara Lynn nodded, agreeing with Evan's opinion of his stable boy. "Well, Evan, you've been a gracious host. I should be going. You're a busy man."

"I'd gladly cancel all my plans if you'd spend the day with me," Evan said, moving closer to her.

Looking around them and realizing they were alone, Cara Lynn took a step backward. "Remember our agreement? I told you I'm dating Jordan. You're going to have to find another princess to share your kingdom with. Estelle Danson seemed interested. Give her a call."

Catching her in his arms, Evan looked down into her eyes. "But it's you I want. How long could you have known Davidson? Maybe you're mistaken about your feelings for him. And besides, there is no rule that says you can't date us both."

Laughing, Cara Lynn said, "Evan, you're interested in me only because I'm different from the other women you're accustomed to dating."

She calmly removed his arms from around her waist. "I'd like to believe we can be friends, but if you insist on trying to change my mind around to your way of thinking, I have to tell you now, I can't see you anymore. I don't want to lead you on."

"If that's the way it has to be," Evan said resignedly. "I won't make any more passes at you. But you must come to the ball. Bring your 'Maine' man."

Cara Lynn sighed. "All right, I'll come."

"I'll turn away all snobs at the door," Evan promised, pleased she'd relented.

"You'd better."

Evan placed his arm about her shoulders. "It's settled then. I'll walk you to your car."

"I can see why you're such a successful businessman," Cara Lynn told him as they left the stables. "You never take no for an answer."

"I just did," Evan reminded her.

Frank was breaking for his midday meal when Cara Lynn drove into the yard. He waved off Junior, who was going home to have lunch with Lynette, then walked over to the Jeep and opened Cara Lynn's door for her.

"How did it go?" he asked.

"He was the perfect gentleman, Daddy," Cara Lynn said as she got out of the car. "You had nothing to worry about."

"Earlene Washington still his housekeeper?"

"Uh huh."

"Then it'll be all over town by nightfall. I've got plenty to worry about. My daughter is the object of desire of the wealthiest man in the county. Powerful men don't give up easily. I'm wondering what his strategy is going to be."

They walked toward the house at a leisurely pace.

"Evan knows I'm serious about Jordan, Daddy."

"You admit it?" Frank said, surprised.

"I haven't been able to get him off my mind," Cara Lynn said quietly.

"What are you going to do about it?"

Sam ran up to Cara Lynn to be petted. She took the time to bend down and scratch him under the chin.

"What can I do about it? He had to go back to work, and I'm on vacation."

"Use your imagination, tadpole. He has to work, but you have plenty of free time. Call him up and invite him to lunch, only you will go to him. Pack a picnic lunch."

Cara Lynn smiled up at her father with newfound respect. "You romantic fool, you."

"Kept your mother happy for years."

"I'll phone him tonight."

"Before he phones you? He's been phoning every night since he left. I'm beginning to feel like you're back in high school. Did you and Carly ever tie up the phone lines!"

"Yeah, but now the caller's a male. Be grateful for small favors," Cara Lynn laughed.

They entered the house through the back door and Cara Lynn immediately opened the refrigerator to get out the tuna casserole and warm it in the microwave while her father went to wash up.

"The question is—" Cara Lynn said when Frank returned "—what can I prepare for the man that won't kill him? You know my cooking."

Her father sighed. "You could cook if you took your time."

"You've been telling me that for years, and I haven't improved yet."

"That's because you never had a reason to," her father said, getting himself a glass of water. "You don't cook for yourself very much because with only one mouth to feed, why bother? You didn't cook for Bill—hey, I got his name right," he laughed, "because he preferred expensive restaurants. Jordan is more down to earth. As a bachelor, he probably cooks. Maybe he'll teach you."

The timer sounded on the microwave, and they sat down to lunch. Frank told her about his morning and she told him about hers, making sure to mention the Sheik.

When they'd eaten their fill, Cara Lynn did the dishes while her father excused himself, saying he should be getting back to work.

Cara Lynn went upstairs to change her clothes after she was done with the dishes. As she passed the door that led to the attic, she hesitated. She'd promised herself she wouldn't do it on this visit home. It only made her melancholy and start toying with the notion of what might have been.

Her hand was on the doorknob, and before she knew it, she was climbing the stairs to the room her mother had used as a sewing room. The door to the room creaked as she pushed it open, and the musty smell of dust and stale air hit her in the face.

She guessed this wasn't her father's favorite place. It held too many memories of his beloved Lillianne.

She went over and drew the curtains, then opened the windows. Bright sunlight spilled in, illuminating the dark corners of the small room. Cara Lynn felt the hair on the back of her neck stand on end when she saw the dressmaker's dummy in the corner. For one split second she thought someone was in the room with her.

She knelt before her mother's hope chest. It was an intricately carved, five-foot-long pine box that had been handmade by her father, Justin DuBois. It had been his wedding gift to her.

She raised the lid and removed the patchwork quilt that lay on top. The quilt had been in the family for over a hundred years. Lillianne's great-grandmother, Edna, made it the year the family settled in Buffalo.

Lillianne had sealed the multicolored treasure in plastic more than ten years ago, and that's how Cara Lynn had left it.

She gently placed it on top of the open lid, then she pulled out a leather-bound photo album.

The first photograph was a black-and-white snapshot of her mother and father on their wedding day.

The two of them were cutting their wedding cake. Lillianne must have been all of twenty at the time, Frank was already over thirty. They're so young, Cara Lynn thought, sadly. The way they're looking at each other, it's as if they believe they'll always be together.

She turned the page, and there they were on their honeymoon right here at the ranch. They were poor but happy in those days, the both of them would tell her later.

There were photographs of the house and the adjoining property as it was then, woodland but beautiful. They had cleared the land and made improvements to the house as they could afford them.

After a year of marriage Lillianne found she was expecting. The young couple was ecstatic. Unfortunately something went wrong and she miscarried. The crisis drew them closer together. It was two years before Lillianne conceived Cara Lynn. By that time they had met and become friends with Harry and Sara Bailey, the local veterinarian and his teacher wife, newcomers from Phoenix.

When Cara Lynn arrived, on one of the hottest days in August, Harry and Sara were keeping Frank sane while they sweated it out in the hospital waiting room.

The remainder of the photographs showed all three of the Garretts at various stages in their lives: Cara Lynn at one, a chubby beauty with a quizzical expression on her face as she stared up at her mother. Cara Lynn at three on her Shetland pony, Baby. She couldn't recall why she'd called him Baby. Maybe because, even at that tender age, one of her fondest wishes was for a brother or sister. Her parents were never to be blessed with another child though.

She turned the page. Her mother's pretty face smiled at her. It was rare to find Lillianne in a photograph alone. She did not like posing for pictures. This one was even more poignant because it was the last photograph ever taken of her.

Remembering that day at the railway station, the first tear rolled down Cara Lynn's face. She had begged her mother to let her go with her. It was the beginning of December, and Cara Lynn had midterms coming up the following week. Lillianne refused to allow her to go out of town when she should be studying for tests.

The next day Frank received the phone call from the rail-

way company saying his wife had been among the six fa-
talities in a massive derailment.

Until then Cara Lynn had never seen her father cry. She
could still envision his face as he hung up the phone and
turned to her. His eyes were panicked, and they were rapidly
filling with tears. He seemed to be having trouble breathing.
She ran to him and caught him before he fell to the floor.

They were both on their knees, and her father was weeping, his body shaking violently. The words would not form
in his throat, but Cara Lynn knew that nothing could reduce
her father to this state short of a catastrophe. Something
must have happened to her mother.

She held on to him. "Daddy—it's not Mom, is it?"

Her father could only nod. Cara Lynn screamed. Her
mind seemed to go blank, and blackness enveloped her. It
felt like she was falling into a bottomless pit. The next thing
she knew, her father was pressing a cool cloth to her forehead and murmuring to her in a soothing voice. Her col-
lapse had served to bring his grief under control long
enough for him to console her.

"Our Lilli's gone, honey, but she would want you to be
brave. Be strong for her, baby."

Be strong for her. Cara Lynn had taken those words to
heart. So much so that wanting to excel in order to honor
her mother's memory was the impetus that propelled her to
succeed in her chosen career. Whenever she felt like giving
up, her mother's image would come to the front of her mind,
and she would miraculously receive the added strength to
carry on.

Wiping her tears away with the back of her hand, Cara
Lynn returned the photo album and the quilt to the hope
chest. She reverently closed the lid and stood. "I still miss
you, Mama. I always will."

* * *

Cara Lynn was pulling on a pair of jeans when the phone rang. It's Mavis for Dad, she thought.

She picked up the extension in her bedroom. "Hello?"

"Cara—I suddenly had an overpowering urge to hear your voice," Jordan said.

Her heartbeat accelerated crazily as she sat down on the bed.

"Jordan. I was just thinking of you, too. How are you?"

"You tell me," he said, his voice sensuous. "I can't stop thinking about you, girl. And I'll never make it all the way to Friday without seeing you, so I'm coming home tonight. Will you have dinner with me?"

"I'll do better than that," Cara Lynn fairly purred. "I'll make dinner for you. What time will you be home?"

"I'll be there around eight."

"I'll be waiting."

"I'll pick you up, that way I can see you home again," came his sexy baritone. "What have you been up to today?"

Cara Lynn told him about her morning at Baymoor. He laughed when she mentioned that Evan was hosting a fund-raiser.

"I wonder what's in it for him," he commented dryly.

"What do you mean?"

"Fitzgerald is a tough businessman. He strikes me as someone who doesn't do anything unless he gets a percentage. He was willing to break the law in order to bring his building in under budget so that he could pocket the difference. I don't trust people like that."

"Maybe he's doing this because he's trying to change his image. Dad tells me he's been a boon to the black community."

"Just so he doesn't try to make you a part of his image makeover," Jordan said lightly. "I saw you first."

"Actually," Cara Lynn said, her voice playful, "I met Evan years ago. But you don't have anything to worry about," she quickly added. "He's not the one who leaves me breathless."

"I leave you breathless, huh?" Jordan said, his voice husky.

"Can't you hear me panting?"

"I was wondering what that was," Jordan said. "In a minute." He was talking to someone else. "I've got to go, Doc. See you tonight. I will *not* be late."

Cara Lynn was beaming when she hung up the phone. She was going to see Jordan in less than seven hours. Someone up there liked her.

With her father overseeing her efforts every step of the way, Cara Lynn prepared a delectable feast of roasted chicken marinated in various savory spices, a fresh garden salad, green beans, homemade dinner rolls, and a sweet potato pie for dessert.

At the outset, after they'd settled on the menu, Cara Lynn thought she'd be in the kitchen all day, but it only took three hours, and she had plenty of time to pamper herself.

A soak in the tub relaxed her, then she put her hair up. She was sitting at the vanity giving herself a manicure when the phone rang.

She let her father get it. It was seven o'clock, she had no time to waste.

"Cara, Evan's on the line," her father called from downstairs.

He didn't sound too pleased that Evan was calling her. She hoped he'd remembered to place his hand over the receiver.

Cara Lynn picked up her extension. "Hi, Evan. What can I do for you?"

"Marry me and bear my children."

"Besides that," Cara Lynn said without missing a beat.

"Go riding with me tomorrow morning," he offered as a concession.

"I couldn't do that, Evan."

"Why not? I'll keep my hands on the reins and my eyes in my head, scout's honor."

It was tempting. Evan possessed the finest stables in the area. She'd long wanted to get her seat on one of his mounts. Being with him, however, would only make him go after her more aggressively. There would be no compromises.

"Were you ever a boy scout?"

"No, but I wanted to be," he replied, his voice laced with humor.

Cara Lynn laughed. "I'm not going to make excuses, Evan. I truly care for Jordan, and it isn't fair to him or to you if I see you on the side. I'm not that kind of woman."

"I didn't think you were," Evan said seriously. "Okay. But how can we build a friendship when you won't even see me?"

"We meet at social functions. We don't run in the same circles, so that may prove difficult."

"I'm good at difficult," Evan said, sounding up to the challenge. "I know—I'll hire you to be my new veterinarian."

"Harry Bailey is a dear friend—I'd never steal one of his clients. Besides, in case of an emergency, you need someone who's close by."

Evan sighed. "I'll get back to you on this, pretty lady. I'll think of something, I always do."

"Accept it, Evan. There is no solution to this problem. Be a good boy and phone one of those myriad women who'd do just about anything to be with you. I'm sure your little black book is brimming with numbers."

"I would if any of them were half as interesting as you are," Evan said sullenly.

"I've got to go now, Evan."

"Don't tell me you're seeing him tonight."

"I've really got to go, Evan," Cara Lynn warned, losing patience.

"My heart is breaking," Evan moaned.

"Your heart doesn't break. You break hearts," Cara Lynn said, laughing at his melodramatics.

"Normally, yes. Now I know how it feels."

"Now you're breaking *my* heart," Cara Lynn said. "Good-bye, Evan."

Cara Lynn replaced the receiver and went to the closet to get the simple little black dress she was wearing tonight. It was one hundred percent cotton, had a scoop neck, was sleeveless, fell just above her knees, and hugged her every curve. She would have to wear a jacket over it to get it past her father.

She stood in front of the full-length mirror after donning the dress.

Over the years she'd gone from a skinny adolescent to a fit, voluptuous woman. Hard work kept her body trim and taut. And horseback riding was great for the thighs. She wasn't self-conscious about her body any longer and didn't feel as though her physical image directly connected with her self-esteem. She'd like herself no matter how she looked.

She was in the kitchen packing the picnic basket when the doorbell rang.

The smell of roses assailed her nostrils. A tall man stood behind a bouquet of yellow roses.

"By way of apology," said the unmistakable voice. Evan.

Cara Lynn stepped backward so he could enter. Evan placed the roses in her arms, and while her hands were occupied, he leaned over and kissed her full on the mouth.

Cara Lynn angrily broke off the kiss and shoved the roses back at him. "This isn't going to work, Evan. I want you out of here right now."

Evan looked at her as though she were speaking a foreign language. "You look beautiful. Going someplace special?"

Cara Lynn was distracted by the sound of a car door shutting. She looked through the open front door and saw Jordan walking into the yard.

In the meanwhile Evan was making himself at home. He went into the living room and sat down on the couch. "Lovely home you have here. Really charming."

Cara Lynn ran over to him and yanked him up off the couch. "Thanks, too bad you can't stay longer."

Judging from his expression, Evan found the situation amusing. Her ire rising with each passing second, Cara Lynn felt like knocking that smug look off his face.

"Cara!" Jordan called from the doorway.

"Sounds like you have company," Evan commented.

Cara Lynn let go of his arm. "Stay right there."

She met Jordan at the door. More roses. These were red. She smiled at him. "They're gorgeous. Thank you."

Jordan pulled her into his arms. Their mouths met, and Cara Lynn didn't want to end this embrace.

"Mmm, that was better than the roses," she said, slightly flushed.

"Am I interrupting something?" Evan again.

Jordan's smile vanished. "Fitzgerald. What the hell are you doing here?"

"Evan brought me flowers to thank me for helping him out today," Cara Lynn spoke up.

She stood between them. Jordan was the more muscular of the two, and he appeared to outweigh Evan by a good thirty pounds.

They exchanged belligerent looks. Cara Lynn could almost smell the testosterone in the air.

"He was just leaving," Cara Lynn said with conviction.

She took Evan by the arm and escorted him to the door.

"Thanks for the flowers. Good-bye, Evan," she said for Jordan's benefit.

"I don't get what you see in him," Evan said for her ears only. "Those construction types are all pumped up but lacking in the brain department."

"Like my father would say, Evan, you've torn your drawers with me, buddy. After this little stunt, I don't want anything else to do with you."

She closed the door in his face.

Jordan was right behind her. "What did he want?"

He was standing close to her and, as always, her body reacted to his nearness. All she wanted to do was touch him.

"Jordan," she said, looking into his eyes. "Evan asked me out. I realize you and I have just started going out, but I told him I was seeing you and I wasn't interested in him. Apparently he thinks he can change my mind."

She searched his face for any sign of distrust or disbelief. There was none.

He reached out and gently touched her face with one of his big hands. His other arm went around her waist, drawing her into his strong embrace. He smelled of soap, and his breath was cool and clean against her skin. His soft, natural black hair was still damp from his shower, and there was a slight nick on his chin from a hasty shave. Cara Lynn kissed it.

Jordan turned his head so that her mouth found his, and when Cara Lynn gasped for air, he gave her part of his. Cara Lynn felt like she was floating. It was a whole new sensation for her.

The kiss ended, and Cara Lynn thoughtfully wiped her lipstick from his mouth. "How was your drive down?"

"I broke all land speed records," Jordan said, his eyes boring into hers. "Are you ready to go?"

"I am," Cara Lynn answered, but she didn't seem in any hurry to move out of his arms.

Her father cleared his throat loudly as he descended the stairs. His entrance gave them the incentive to separate.

"Hiya, Jordan," Frank said as he stepped into the room. "I thought Cara Lynn was going over to your place."

"Hello, Frank," Jordan said, smiling. The two men shook hands. "She is but I thought I'd pick her up—that way I don't have to worry about her getting home safely."

"Yeah, it is quite a distance," Frank said jokingly. "Well, kids, have a nice time."

Cara Lynn helped her father on with his jacket, then kissed his cheek. "Good night, Daddy. Don't let Mavis keep you up too late."

"You're wearing that?" her father said disapprovingly. "Where's the rest of it?"

Thanks to Evan's untimely visit, she'd missed her chance to camouflage the dress.

"It's a perfectly decent dress, Daddy," Cara Lynn said in a low voice.

"Wear a jacket or something," her father strongly suggested.

"Oh, okay. Get out of here. Tell Mavis hello for me."

When he'd gone, Cara Lynn ran upstairs to get her jacket, then back down to the kitchen to retrieve the picnic basket she was packing when Evan interrupted her.

Just as she was packing the sweet potato pie, Jordan appeared in the kitchen doorway. "Is there anything I can do to help?"

She closed and secured the lid on the basket, then handed it to him.

"All set?" Jordan asked.

"I'm all yours."

He smiled at the prospect.

Seven

Mavis applied a bit of lipstick to her mouth and rubbed her lips together. She didn't look bad, if she had to say so herself. Her brown skin seemed to have an inner glow, and her eyes were clear and bright. It must be love, she thought as she walked out of the bathroom into her bedroom. Forty-nine and I've finally found love. Better late than never.

Her eyes moistened with tears. Happiness had always eluded her. Twenty years of marriage hadn't provided it. Carl Edwards reserved all his affection for the other women in his life—and there had been a long list of them.

The only thing Mavis had was the diner. Carl hadn't been able to give her a child. She'd tried to conceive for years with no results. Mavis begged Carl to go to a specialist, but he'd refused. Unbeknownst to him, she had been examined by a gynecologist who told her she was perfectly healthy.

Adoption was out of the question. Carl wanted a child with his own blood coursing through his veins. They grew further apart. Mavis spent her every waking hour working at the diner, and Carl was away from home more than he was there. A car crash ended his misery and added to Mavis's. She felt like she was in a daze for years following his death. She'd lived with him for half her life, and what did she have to show for it?

Then one day, two years ago, Frank Garrett walked into

her life; actually he walked into the diner, but the moment she saw him, she felt renewed.

He was dressed like every other rancher in their small town, his jeans and khaki shirt seemed to fit him better though.

She beat the waitresses, Bonnie and Chloe, to his booth. She didn't know what she was going to say to him until the words fell out of her mouth. "Hi, I'm your order . . . I mean, hi, I'm Mavis, may I take your order?"

Frank had looked up at her and smiled. "Hello there, pretty lady. I'd like a cup of coffee, that is, unless you really *are* on the menu."

Mavis sat down across from him and offered him her hand. "I'm sorry, I guess I'm a little rusty. I don't usually take orders. I'm Mavis Edwards, I own the place."

"Franklyn Garrett, Frank. I train horses for a living. I have a ranch on the outskirts of town."

"Been in Shelbyville long?" Mavis asked.

"All my life. This is my hometown," Frank replied.

"I've never seen you before," Mavis said easily. "You must not eat out much."

"As a matter of fact, I don't. But I'm familiar with your name, if not your face. I remember when you and your husband opened this place. It was in '83, wasn't it?"

"Yes, it was," Mavis said, smiling at him. "You have a good memory." She liked his friendly, open face.

She automatically looked at his ring finger. He was wearing a wedding band.

Still smiling, she rose. "Nice to meet you, Frank. I'll get your coffee."

Disheartened, Mavis returned with his coffee a couple of minutes later. She placed it before him and turned to leave.

"Wait a minute," Frank said. "Where's the rest of my order?"

"As it turns out, I'm not on the menu after all," Mavis said, looking pointedly at the offending wedding ring.

"I'm a widower," Frank explained. "I just haven't been able to part with the ring yet."

Now Mavis really felt embarrassed. She slid onto the seat across from him. "I'm so sorry. I had no idea. When did you lose her?"

"Seven years ago."

"It's been three years for me."

That's how they met. They were comfortable pals for months. Frank would come into the diner, and they would talk about their respective lives. Mavis told him about her troubled marriage. He told her what a good marriage was like. She listened and a strong craving grew in her for that kind of union.

Things were beginning to get too chummy between them. Mavis knew what she wanted from the relationship, but she wasn't at all sure Frank did.

So one afternoon, near closing time, Frank sauntered into the diner like he did every day. Mavis waited until all the other customers were gone, then she told Bonnie, Chloe, and Nell, the cook, they could all go home early.

She locked the door and asked Frank to sit down. She sat down, too, and for the first few minutes, she simply looked at him.

"What's up?" Frank asked, breaking the silence.

Looking into his eyes, Mavis said, "Your time is, Frank. The last thing a woman likes to admit is that she's getting old, time is running out."

"You're not getting old," Frank said. He had a way of smiling that made her insides quiver.

"I'm going to lay it out for you so that there will be no misunderstandings, Frank Garrett. I'm in love with you. Now you can get up and leave and never darken my door again, and I wouldn't blame you."

"Mavis—"

"No, really," Mavis had insisted. "I would understand. But I can't bear to be around you day after day feeling the way I do, and you acting as though we're poker buddies or something. I told you about Carl. I loved him when I married him, but over the years, after everything he put me through, that love withered up and died. But I never loved Carl as much as I love you."

"I love you, too," Frank confessed, his voice low.

He'd spoken quickly. Mavis didn't think she'd heard him correctly.

"Say what?"

"I said I love you, Mavis. Why do you suppose I'm in here every day? Your food's good, but—" His eyes told her he wasn't coming there for the cuisine.

Mavis grabbed him around the neck and held on to him as though he were life itself.

"You never even gave me a peck on the cheek, Frank."

Frank laughed. "After seven years, a person has to work up to that sort of thing, Mavis."

Mavis kissed his cheek. "You're doing pretty good so far."

The sound of the doorbell brought her back to the present. She smoothed her skirt and went to answer it.

Frank stood on her porch with his hat in his right hand and a bunch of daisies, her favorite flowers, in his left.

He gave her the flowers. "Hello, darlin'."

"Hello, yourself," Mavis said, taking him by the hand and pulling him inside.

"Dinner was delicious, thank you," Jordan said, looking into Cara Lynn's eyes.

"You're welcome. I enjoyed preparing it for you," Cara Lynn said, smiling. "I amazed even myself."

Jordan grasped her hand. "Next time, I'll cook for you."

Cara Lynn looked down at his strong hands, admiring the long fingers, liking how protected she felt whenever he touched her.

She met his gaze. "Wash or dry?"

"Dry," Jordan said. He stood and began clearing the table. Cara Lynn helped him and they made short work of the dishes.

As she was standing at the sink, Cara Lynn peered out the window into the backyard. "You didn't bring Peabo?"

Jordan finished drying a plate and laid it aside. He smiled at her. "No. He's staying at Vince's house tonight. His kids love him. You know, I'm getting a little jealous of all the attention you give that dog."

"He's a hero," Cara Lynn said, turning to look at him. "He'll always have a place in my heart because of what he did for me."

"What did he do for you?" Jordan asked, one eyebrow raised. He'd managed to place both his hands on the sink with Cara Lynn imprisoned between them.

"He kept you from harm," she said, her voice husky.

"You smell so good," Jordan said, bending his head and burying his face in her hair.

"We were talking about Peabo," Cara Lynn murmured, touching the back of his neck. Even that made her senses reel.

"And you feel good," Jordan said, continuing his exploration of her. "I could get used to having you in my arms."

Cara Lynn met his eyes. "I'm going to have to go jump in your pool if you keep this up."

"I can't help it. I missed you, doe-eyes."

Cara Lynn grew warmer at the mention of the endearment. Now she knew why lovers had special names for each other.

Jordan kissed the side of her neck. Cara Lynn was wildly aroused. She moved away from him, feeling intoxicated. Things were moving too fast for her. She needed time to decipher the reason behind the way she was reacting to this man. She was almost thirty, for God's sake, shouldn't she have more control over her libido? Jordan didn't have to actually touch her, all he had to do was be in the same room.

"I'm confused," she cried, putting more distance between them.

"What are you confused about?" Jordan asked, walking toward her.

Cara Lynn ran a hand through her tangled hair. As the evening had progressed, it had come loose and now hung free. She'd taken off her shoes earlier and stood in her stockinged feet. She smoothed down her dress, which had a tendency to inch upwards.

"About you," she finally said.

Jordan covered the distance between them in a couple of steps. When he tried to pull her into his arms, Cara Lynn backed farther away from him.

"That's what I mean, Jordan. I'm having a hard time resisting you."

Jordan smiled. "Honey, you're not supposed to resist."

"Of course I'm supposed to resist. If I did what I want to do, you wouldn't respect me, and I wouldn't respect myself," Cara Lynn said, walking about the kitchen.

"Is that just a woman thing, or do men share in the degradation?" Jordan looked amused.

"I would say that things being the way they are today, we're in it together." Cara Lynn's brown eyes met his across the room.

"Will you be still for one minute?" Jordan requested.

"If you promise not to touch me just yet."

"Fine," Jordan agreed, palms out. "You know, this isn't easy for me, either. I wanted you the first day I met you. Okay, that's out in the open. But I'm a man, Cara, not a boy—and I can wait until we're both ready. Until we're both sure. That doesn't mean I'm going to give up holding you or kissing you or trying to push us both to the limit of our resistance. I want you to understand that."

"I do," she assured him.

Jordan looked at her feet. "What is that?"

"What?"

"That thing you're doing with your toes."

Cara Lynn knew what he was referring to. She wiggled her toes when she got nervous, which was why she enjoyed going barefoot.

But she wasn't ready to share one of her more embarrassing habits with him at this point. "My feet are cold on this tile floor. I'm going into the den. What kind of music do you have? I'll put something on."

Jordan followed her to the den, stopping to observe her from the doorway. She riffled through his CD collection, chose a Terrence Trent D'Arby CD, and slipped it into the player. She began swaying to the music, and her dress began its ascent up her firm brown thighs.

She glanced at him, smiled, and said, "Dance with me."

"It's okay to touch you now?" he couldn't help saying as he walked toward her.

"If you can take it, I can take it," Cara Lynn said sultrily.

"Brave words," he said as he encircled her waist with his strong arms, pulling her close.

Cara Lynn shut her eyes and lay her head on his chest. The denim shirt he wore was soft on her skin. She could hear his heartbeat, and the sound was soothing.

"I'm glad you called. I had planned to bring you lunch tomorrow."

"The guys would've loved that," Jordan said, laughing.

"You mean they would've ribbed you because your sweetie brought you some fried chicken?"

"They've been trying to fix me up with someone for years, with sisters, cousins, their wives' friends. They'd love you. Please come, you'd do wonders for my reputation."

"I doubt if your reputation needs my help," Cara Lynn laughed. "Tell me something—how does a man who builds things get involved with painting?"

"The art came first," Jordan said softly. "I've always had

a talent for drawing. I think at one point my dad thought I might turn out too sensitive, you know what I mean? He started encouraging me to work with him, hoping to ensure my masculinity. I don't know why he associated painting with femininity. The subjects of my earliest paintings were always female."

"Some fathers think that way," Cara Lynn said, looking into his eyes. "It scares them when they see anything remotely feminine in their sons. I think it's wonderful to be born with a talent like yours. The only thing I'm good at is caring for animals—that's why I became a vet."

"I've witnessed the special touch you have with animals, doe-eyes. That's your talent," Jordan said. He bent his head so that their cheeks touched. "Are you my sweetie?"

Cara Lynn fixed him with a questioning stare.

"Earlier, you referred to yourself as my sweetie."

"That was purely hypothetical," Cara Lynn avowed.

"You can't back down now," Jordan said. "You're my sweetie."

"Before I accept the position, exactly what are the requirements?"

"Let's see," Jordan began, pretending he had to actually consider his answer. "You have to be brilliant, beautiful, and sexy."

"Three strikes, I'm outta there," Cara Lynn laughed.

"You're all that and more, Cara. What is it with you and this self-deprecating attitude? It's only a ploy to distract me, right? What's your answer, are you or are you not?"

He kissed her gently on the mouth before she could reply. When they parted, Cara Lynn smiled at him. "Is that something like going steady? Because it's much too soon for that—we've known one another only six days."

Jordan sighed. "Still avoiding the question. Okay, let's talk about something safer, shall we? What was Fitzgerald up to earlier? And a straightforward answer would be appreciated."

"What he was doing was digging himself a hole," Cara Lynn said frankly. "He was trying to cause trouble between us."

The muscles worked in Jordan's jaw. "So he can have you for himself."

"Having me isn't that easy. I'm not attracted to Evan," Cara Lynn said, holding his gaze. "I don't know what it is, but there's something about him I don't trust."

"You're not saying that just for my benefit?"

"No. He doesn't have anything I want." Cara Lynn locked her fingers behind his neck.

"Good, that saves me from having to break him in half," Jordan joked.

"You're cute when you're jealous," Cara Lynn told him, kissing his square chin.

"Then you don't want to see me when I'm angry—I'm downright irresistible," Jordan said, his eyes filled with unexpressed laughter.

"Mr. Hashimoto from Tokyo on line two for you, Mr. Fitzgerald."

Evan's attention was brought back to the present by the insistent voice of his secretary, Joanie.

Frowning, he picked up the receiver. "Mr. Hashimoto, good day to you, sir. Yes, the property you're interested in can be ready for occupancy by the twenty-sixth. An eighteen-hole golf course is no problem. I'll get my people on it immediately. Then we have an agreement? Very good, Mr. Hashimoto. It's been a pleasure to be of service to you."

He replaced the receiver. He should be jumping for joy. His company had just finalized a thirty million dollar deal.

Of course that meant more money in his pockets, but he was finding out that money was a poor substitute for love and was even harder to snuggle up to on a cold winter night.

He buzzed Joanie over the intercom.

"Joanie, I'd like a dozen yellow roses sent to Dr. Cara Lynn Garrett, make that a dozen per hour for the next eight hours. Only the best, do you understand?"

"Yes, Mr. Fitzgerald. Any particular message?"

"Just ask the florist to sign the card: Evan."

He sat back on his soft leather chair and put his feet up. His father would say he was using the old Irish tenacity. Cara Lynn would forgive him by day's end.

She had every right to be angry with him. He knew he'd taken a risk by showing up on her doorstep at an inopportune moment, but it was a risk he'd been willing to take.

He had no personal gripe with Davidson. He was a reputable businessman who knew his field inside and out. A bit of a boy scout though. Three years ago they'd nearly come to blows over the construction of this very building. He'd wanted Davidson to use cheaper materials, not inferior materials. Davidson wouldn't allow his people to work with anything but the best—being chintzy about building materials could cause mishaps, and using them invariably wound up costing more in the long run.

Davidson had won that battle—but Evan hadn't hired him for any more of his projects even though he'd done a superior job on this building. He'd learned that Davidson's business had not suffered due to his personal boycott. His construction company had a sterling reputation.

Besides, Evan mused, no matter what people thought of him, he wouldn't stoop to destroying Davidson in order to win a beautiful woman. Cara Lynn would choose him over Davidson. Everything would be fair and aboveboard, or as fair as love and rivalry could be.

He reached for the phone again and dialed Cara Lynn's number from memory.

He got the answering machine.

"I was a total jerk, please forgive me," was all he said.

* * *

Cara Lynn was sitting at the kitchen table listening to Evan as he spoke. So was her father.

"I told you—you were getting in over your head when you started up with Fitzgerald," Frank said, reaching for the coffee pot to give himself half a cup.

"How was I supposed to know he would develop an attachment to me, Daddy? It was my bad luck to be in Greenwalds' drugstore that day. I don't have any experience with interracial relationships. I thought he was flirting, we all flirt. And when it dawned on me that he was serious, I did everything to discourage him." She exhaled. "I'll ignore him. He'll get the message."

Frank smirked. "Evan is not giving up, Cara. You've got to handle this aggressively. An in-your-face kind of aggressiveness. He isn't going to allow himself to be ignored."

"What can he do about it, Daddy?" Cara Lynn said confidently. She rose and began clearing the table.

"We'll soon find out," her father predicted. He finished his coffee, got up, and put the mug in the sink. "I've got to go into town first thing this morning. Do you need anything?"

"No. After I finish here, I think I'll go for a long walk."

"How did things go with you and Jordan last night?"

"He loved your recipes," Cara Lynn told him, smiling as though she had a secret. "We talked. It was nice."

"In some ways you two remind me of your mother and me when we first met. We had an instant rapport. It was like we were two halves that made a whole, you know?"

"It's so easy to be with him, it's scary," Cara Lynn said, looking up into her father's smiling face. "It feels like I've known him all my life. Does that sound strange to you?"

"No, it sounds like you're learning to let yourself love again, and that's a good thing."

"Are you saying I may be falling in love with Jordan?"

"You're the only one who can answer that," her father

said happily. He kissed her cheek. "Gotta run, tadpole. You have a nice walk."

The phone rang. "That's probably Evan again," Cara Lynn heard him say just before the back door closed behind him.

She answered the phone. "Hello, Garrett residence."

"I know I was a complete ass, but couldn't you chalk it up to stupidity and give me another chance?" Evan pleaded.

"Another chance to do what?" Cara Lynn said, exasperated. "You're not the type of person I thought you were, Evan. You're not a man of your word—"

"Cara, let me explain—"

"I'm not finished," Cara Lynn firmly said. "I don't know what happened between you and Jordan, but you two appear to have very little regard for each other."

"It's true, Davidson and I will never see things the same way, and I wouldn't ask him to be best man at our wedding, but that's neither here nor there. I don't want a friendship with him. I'm only trying to make amends for what I did last night. I caused you to distrust me. I blew it, and I hate that because I think you're a fantastic lady. You don't want a romantic involvement. So be it." He paused. "It isn't because I'm white, is it?"

"No, Evan," Cara Lynn quickly replied. "I told you why."

"Very well, you won't get any more overtures from yours truly. I only want your forgiveness for an unfortunate blunder," Evan ended sincerely.

"I'll think about it," Cara Lynn promised, her voice soft. "I have to go now, Evan."

"Fine. That's all I ask. Good-bye, Cara."

"Good-bye, Evan."

Ten minutes later the doorbell rang, and a delivery man handed her a bouquet of yellow roses.

Cara Lynn offered him a tip, but he refused it. "It's already been taken care of, Dr. Garrett, for all the deliveries."

Cara Lynn closed the door and went to put the roses in

water. She didn't need to read the card. She had a dozen reminders on the dining room table as to who'd sent them.

The delivery man's parting comment puzzled her. What had he meant by "all the deliveries?" Did Evan send all his female acquaintances yellow roses from the same florist?

By noon she knew to what the delivery man had been alluding. Her father contacted her by cellular phone to ask her to tell Evan enough was enough. The sound of the trucks coming and going was making the horses skittish.

Evan was out when she phoned, but Joanie promised to give him the message as soon as he returned to the office.

Two deliveries later Evan returned her call.

"I forgive you," Cara Lynn told him. "Please call off your botanical terrorists, they're scaring the horses."

"I knew you'd forgive me," Evan exulted. "All right, no more roses. How do you feel about orchids?"

"Evan!" Cara Lynn shouted into the receiver.

"You don't hate me anymore?" he asked, sounding contrite.

She sighed. "I never said I hated you, Evan."

"Hold on a minute, I'll have Joanie phone the florist." He was away a few seconds. "Listen, Cara. I realize that I handled things badly. From now on I'll respect your wishes. We'll be pals."

"I'm glad to hear that, Evan. It's settled then."

"I'll see you around," Evan said lightly.

"Yeah, you take care."

"I *will* see you at the ball though?"

"I'll be there."

"Even if Davidson doesn't come?"

"You're doing it again," Cara Lynn warned.

"Sorry, some habits are hard to break," he said, sighing.

* * *

"Boss, come quick. Taylor fell from the fourth floor. I think he's hurt bad."

"I'm leaving now, Vince," Jordan said into the two-way radio. "Lisa, call emergency services. Tell them a man fell four stories and needs immediate medical help."

Lisa Caldfield quickly dialed the emergency number as she anxiously watched Jordan's retreating back. She knew Sandy Taylor well. He'd been with the company five years. He was a practical joker, a family man, an all-around nice guy that everyone liked.

When Jordan arrived on the scene, half the crew, about thirty men, was gathered around Taylor, who, though conscious, was flat on his back with his leg twisted at such an angle that it was evident it was broken.

"Let him get some air, you guys," Jordan ordered, taking command of the situation.

He knelt beside Sandy. "Just lie still."

He looked into Sandy's hazel eyes. Sandy wasn't focusing. Jordan assumed he was in shock. "Vince, get one of those tarps over there and cover him."

He glanced up to where Sandy had fallen from. He didn't notice anything out of place. The scaffolding had held. The building, which would be the new children's hospital when it was finished, was of a skeleton construction made up of steel girders, beams, and columns. Sandy had been welding a beam into place when the accident occurred.

Vince gently placed the clean tarp across Sandy's torso and legs. "Did anyone see what happened?" Jordan asked, looking at his men.

Vince spoke up: "Billy said his torch malfunctioned, and Sandy jerked around, trying to prevent getting burned—and that's when he fell."

Jordan looked over at Billy Chase, another welder. A young, slight man with mousy brown hair and pale blue eyes. "Why wasn't he wearing his harness?"

Billy looked ashen from witnessing the accident. He

shook his head in bewilderment. "Don't know, boss. He usually wears it."

Sandy was trying to say something. Jordan leaned toward him. "You're not to exert yourself, Sandy."

Jordan was grateful to hear the sound of sirens in the distance. "Be still—we're going to get you to the hospital. You're going to be all right."

After the paramedics had left with Sandy, Jordan went up to the fourth floor to try and figure out what had gone wrong. He found Sandy's safety harness hooked on a railing. The belt was broken. Sandy hadn't taken the time to go downstairs to retrieve a working harness. He was an experienced welder, no doubt he figured he'd been doing his job for years without a mishap, he could afford to be a little neglectful. Ignoring safety rules could have cost him his life this time. Jordan saw red.

Many of the workers were still talking among themselves when he got back down to ground level.

"You see what happens when safety precautions are ignored?" he bellowed at them angrily. "The next time I see anyone not following the rules around here, he's out on his butt. Do you understand?"

"Yeah, boss. We got ya," Vince said. Turning to his crew, he said, "Right?"

There was a mutual agreement that Jordan's threat hadn't fallen on deaf ears. Some expressed surprise at his vehemence. Jordan was usually so easygoing. But other more seasoned workers were aware of where his anger came from because they'd seen the results of accidents caused by carelessness on the job.

Turning to Vince, Jordan said, "It's almost quitting time—send everyone home. I'm going to the hospital to check on Sandy, then I'll phone his wife."

Sandy was lucky to have sustained only a broken leg, a broker finger, and two cracked ribs. His condition was soon stabilized, and after being given a strong painkiller, he felt up to talking to Jordan and Shelly, his wife.

Shelly stood next to his bed, holding his good hand, her mascara running down her cheeks from a crying jag.

"I'm sorry, Shel," Sandy said. "I screwed up royally. I got overconfident up there. It's all my fault." Looking at Jordan, he said, "It was all my fault, boss."

"Shh . . ." Shelly said. "I'm just relieved you're alive. I'll kick your butt some other time."

"Same here," Jordan said, heading for the door. "I'll leave you two alone. I'll check up on you tomorrow, Sandy."

In Jordan's absence, Shelly bent over and kissed her husband's forehead.

"This is probably the only thing on you that isn't hurting, isn't it?" she joked. "You had me scared there for a moment."

Sandy had tears in his eyes as he brought his wife's hand to his lips and kissed her fingers. "I love you, Shel. It's funny, when I was falling, the only person I could think about was you."

Shelly started crying all over again. "Thank God, you're going to be all right. I'd hate to have to raise our child alone."

"You mean you're pregnant?" Sandy exclaimed.

"Yeah, you dummy—you're going to be a father."

Sandy cried like a baby.

Eight

A quarter moon hung suspended in the night sky. Cara Lynn stood on the balcony outside her bedroom, looking up at it. It was 3 A.M., but she couldn't sleep. Every now and then she could hear her father softly snoring down the hall. But for the most part the night was silent.

She loved the sounds of the ranch—they'd always been able to lull her to sleep. Tonight was a different matter. She was too keyed up to sleep. Tomorrow morning she would be going back to Louisville. She'd drop by her office to make sure everything was as it should be, then she'd go home and prepare for the first day back to work. All mundane details she'd done so often they'd become routine.

Tonight, though, she felt as if something magical had touched her, something miraculous—and it was all thanks to her father. He had made her realize she shouldn't take her feelings for Jordan for granted. She should accept them and act on them, not be afraid of them.

Consequently, earlier tonight, when Jordan came to pick her up for their date—dinner at a French restaurant and listening to jazz afterward—she was ready for him.

He was dressed semicasually in basic black. The man looked good in anything, but in black he was devastating. He wore a custom-tailored blazer over a crew neck shirt and chinos with a pair of Italian loafers. But it didn't matter what he had on because Cara Lynn liked everything about his square-chinned, clean-shaven face from his rather long, well-shaped nose to his wide, expressive mouth and large brown eyes. Eyes that, to her, were the color of an autumn sunset and were a very interesting contrast to the dark, burnished copper of his skin. What she liked even more than his eyes, though, was the lovely soul behind them.

Jordan reached for her, and Cara Lynn placed her hand in his.

"You look like an angel," he said admiringly.

Cara Lynn wore an off-white macramé over linen sheath that was tapered at the waist, had a halter top, was cut low in the back, and fell three inches above her knees. Her hair fell in soft waves down her back. She'd kept her makeup at a minimum, going with natural shades that complemented her golden brown skin. Her only jewelry was a pair of simple gold stud earrings.

When they arrived at the restaurant, Jordan went around to get her door for her.

"I've been here only once," he said, his hand under her elbow. "But the food's good, and they have excellent service. I hope you like it."

Cara Lynn didn't have the heart to tell him this particular French restaurant was Bill's favorite spot. They'd frequented it perhaps twice a month for over a year, probably because of its close proximity to the hospital.

"I'm sure I'll love it," she said truthfully, smiling up at him.

He clasped her hand in his, and they walked inside. The maitre d' recognized her, but seeing she was with a different companion, chose to treat her anonymously.

"Good evening, sir, madam. Your name, please?"

"Davidson," Jordan supplied.

"Yes, of course, Mr. Davidson. Your table is right this way."

The restaurant was subtly lit and attractively decorated in early French provincial. Cara Lynn had always liked its romantic atmosphere. Sometimes, when she and Bill came here, the atmosphere of the restaurant was the closest she got to romance.

She realized, as she was seated across from Jordan, the setting was no longer important.

"How is Sandy?" she asked when they were alone.

"He's doing a lot better. His doctor says he's lucky. He could have broken his neck or injured his spine. As it is, his leg should mend in a few months. But it really shook him up. Sandy was never afraid of heights before, but I'll wager he'll think twice before going up again."

"What about his family?"

"We have excellent medical coverage. His family will be provided for until he can go back to work. We take care of our own," Jordan said proudly.

"I'm glad he's going to be all right. I hate to see you worried."

They held hands across the white-clothed table.

"You could tell I was worried?" Jordan said, his smile enigmatic.

"Last night you were quiet and introspective. You're usually outgoing. I figured you must have been thinking about the accident," Cara Lynn said. "Jordan, there's something I should tell you."

Their drinks arrived and the waiter, a young man who'd served Cara Lynn on numerous occasions, gave her a cheerful hello.

"Dr. Garrett, I haven't seen you in a while. How've you been?"

"Good, Derrick, thank you, and you?" Cara Lynn said, returning his smile.

"Great. Business has been good. I can't complain. Enjoy your evening," Derrick said with a quick smile in Jordan's direction.

"I take it you've been here before," Jordan said with a faint smile.

"A few times," Cara Lynn admitted. "It's Bill's favorite place."

"And that's what you were about to tell me when Derrick showed up with our drinks," Jordan surmised.

Cara Lynn nodded. "Uh huh."

Jordan laughed. "I suppose we were bound to go someplace you'd already been to with Bill. But next time, speak up, okay? We should be able to tell each other anything."

Out of the corner of her eye, Cara Lynn noticed a familiar figure. "Oh, no, it can't be," she whispered.

She turned her head and saw it most certainly could be. Following her lead, Jordan sighed. "You've got to be kidding me . . . that's Bill?"

"In the flesh," Cara Lynn answered resignedly.

Dr. William Dunlevy was elegantly attired in a blue Brooks Brothers suit. His companion wore an elegant white ensemble.

"The woman with him is Dr. Regina Miles. She's a general practitioner on staff at the hospital."

The maitre d' apparently tried to seat the physicians so that their table wouldn't be facing Jordan and Cara Lynn. Cara Lynn was grateful for his discretion.

"We should go over and say hello," Jordan said to her utter amazement.

Frowning and shaking her head, Cara Lynn said, "Believe me, Bill wouldn't appreciate the gesture. We didn't part on the best of terms."

"We're not going to enjoy our evening if we don't get this out of the way," Jordan reasoned. He squeezed her hand. "I'm not going to have you furtively glancing over there, wondering if he's going to make a scene. Let's go."

"You're probably right," Cara Lynn reluctantly agreed.

Because it was the proper thing to do, Bill rose and shook Jordan's hand when Cara Lynn introduced them. At five-eleven, Jordan towered over him, but what Bill lacked in height, he made up in social graces. Cara Lynn was pleasantly surprised.

"It's good to meet you," he greeted Jordan.

"Same here," Jordan returned. "Cara Lynn told me about the important work you do."

"It's a job," Bill said modestly, but his smile appeared genuine. "I'd like you to meet Dr. Regina Miles. Regina, Jordan Davidson."

Regina Miles, an attractive woman in her midthirties, was originally from England. She was a petite brunette with brown eyes. She grasped Jordan's hand, pulling him toward her.

"Oh, how marvelous," she said, flashing large white teeth. "They do grow them big here in the States."

Bill took the opportunity to pull Cara Lynn aside. "You're looking lovely, Cara. I always liked you in that dress."

"Thank you," Cara Lynn said. It isn't one of those prissy things you bought for me, she thought derisively.

"You're very handsome tonight," she said, returning the compliment.

"He seems a nice sort," Bill said of Jordan.

"Regina looks good on your arm," Cara Lynn quipped. "You make an attractive couple."

"And she doesn't mind the hours," Bill said. His first dig.

Jordan returned to claim her to her great relief. She offered Bill a parting smile. "Take care."

"Yes. You, too," Bill said, turning to look at Regina, whose eyes were on Jordan.

On the way back to their table, Jordan took Cara Lynn's hand and slipped a business card into it. "Regina gave me her card."

Cara Lynn dropped it into a waste receptacle as they passed it. "You won't be needing it."

Back at their table Jordan reclaimed her hand. "That wasn't so bad, was it?"

Cara Lynn laughed. "No, let's do it again."

"You're gorgeous when you're nervous as hell."

"I never want to come here again," Cara Lynn said seriously.

"No?" Jordan feigned surprise. "I thought we'd make this our place."

On the drive back home Cara Lynn couldn't resist stealing glances at Jordan as he drove.

Sensing her eyes on him, he turned and briefly smiled at her. "You know, for someone who was a wallflower in high school, you are very popular."

Cara Lynn sighed. "That's the way it is. Once you meet someone you care for, every mistake you ever made starts coming out of the woodwork."

"There is no one else I should know about?"

"There's the knife thrower with the circus, but he only comes to town once a year."

"A knife thrower, huh? Is he any good?"

"He keeps putting his assistants in the hospital. I think he needs glasses."

Laughing softly, Jordan said, "What are you doing over there? Come here."

Cara Lynn moved closer to him on the leather seat. She laid her head on his shoulder.

"I had a wonderful time tonight."

"So did I," Jordan said.

"Even though Bill showed up?"

"I'm glad I met him. I'm no longer jealous of him."

"You, jealous?" she said with a note of incredulity.

"I was feeling a little inadequate. He's a brilliant surgeon," Jordan said reasonably.

"And you're a brilliant builder. He doesn't have a thing on you. Besides, you're the one with the to-die-for eyes."

Her right hand was on his chest, massaging it, her movements deliberate, sensual.

They were almost home. Jordan turned into a park that

was deserted except for the ducks sleeping on the bank of the pond.

"Why are we stopping?"

"Because I can't do this while I'm driving," Jordan replied, turning off the ignition.

He pulled her into his arms and kissed her proffered mouth. Cara Lynn wrapped her arms around his neck, and Jordan pulled her onto his lap. They were insistent, as though they'd been waiting to do this all evening and had finally gotten the chance.

Cara Lynn straddled him, her dress up around her hips.

"You are the only man I've ever steamed-up car windows with," she said, her breathing uneven.

"I'm honored," Jordan said, kissing her throat, behind her ear, working his way lower.

Cara Lynn moaned. "Jordan, I'm ready. I want you now."

Jordan kissed her mouth again, his tongue parting her lips and entering her soft sweetness. His hands molded her pliant flesh to him. Cara Lynn arched her back in ecstasy, her body burning with the need for fulfillment.

The kiss ended abruptly. "I'm sorry, sweetheart, but I didn't come prepared for this, did you?" Jordan said, his voice drunk with passion.

"No," Cara Lynn answered, regrettably, breathlessly.

"Besides," Jordan told her, cupping her face. "When we make love, I want you in my bed, not in a car alongside a dark road. Our first time will be unforgettable."

They held each other, reveling in the feel of their bodies, the smell of their skin, and the heat being generated between them.

"I'd better get you home, darlin'. It's getting late."

"Just a minute longer," Cara Lynn said, her voice in his ear. "I love it when you call me darlin'."

"I love everything about you," Jordan said, his voice husky with pent-up desire. "And I want you so much, I can think of nothing else. But I want much more from you and for you than sex. You're special to me."

Cara Lynn laid her head on his chest a while longer, thinking about what he'd just said. Special. How special?

She got back in her seat. "Being this hot and bothered is new to me, but I'll get a handle on it."

"I don't want you to get a handle on it. I want you to save it for the right time. God knows, I don't ever want you to change—you're perfect just the way you are."

Cara Lynn smoothed her skirt and adjusted her bodice. She reached into her purse for her comb and ran it through her hair while Jordan watched.

"Your father is going to think you've been necking in the backseat," he said, a smile curving his lips.

"Which is why I'm freshening up," Cara Lynn told him.

Jordan started the car, and they fastened their seat belts. He pulled onto the blacktop, and they were soon back up to the speed limit.

"You seem to have a good relationship with your dad," Jordan said in his easygoing way. "You two seem to be able to discuss anything."

Discerning the meaning behind his words, Cara Lynn laughed. "You want to know what he thinks of you, right?"

Grinning, Jordan shook his head. "Girl, you must be psychic. Okay, yes, I'd like to know how Frank feels about me dating his daughter."

"You can relax. He approves. To quote him, 'That fellow has his head on straight.' That means he not only likes you, he respects you."

Jordan breathed a sigh of relief.

"So," Cara Lynn said, changing the subject. "It's back to work for me, too. Think we'll still find time for each other?"

Jordan reached over and stroked her cheek. "Lady, I'd go without food and sleep before I'd ever give you up."

Cara Lynn smiled at him. He was either the smoothest

talker she'd ever met or the sweetest man alive. She believed he was the latter.

So now, here she was looking up at the moon, thinking of the sweetest man alive and trying to convince herself she was not falling in love. Women like her didn't fall so fast, they took their time. Women who had been hurt before guarded their hearts in fortresses of denial. Women like her lived with the certainty that once you began to trust again, your hopes would be dashed. She knew nothing would come of this thing between her and Jordan. Still, she couldn't resist hoping that for a change, she'd found true love. Hope—the last bastion of the incurable romantic.

On Sunday morning Cara Lynn stood on the front lawn of St. Paul AME Church after the service had concluded. Everyone was gathered in groups, catching up on each other's lives.

Cara Lynn was searching the grounds for her father. They'd come together, and she wanted to leave, but she couldn't unless she knew he had a lift home. He'd sometimes come with her and catch a ride back with Reverend Brown, an old friend.

A little to her left, she could not miss Deborah Sanford in the middle of a lively monologue. Whatever she was talking about must have been riveting because the women gathered around her hung on her every word.

As Cara Lynn walked past Deborah and the other women, she smiled at them and said, "Good afternoon, ladies."

She was stunned when they simply stared at her and started giggling behind their hands.

She kept walking. The last thing she needed on a Sunday morning was a confrontation with Deborah on church grounds. It didn't take the deductive reasoning of a Sherlock Holmes to guess what they'd been discussing: her. What she found unbelievable was the fact that Deborah was behaving the way she had in school with gossiping and snickering behind her back. Why she should be the target of the woman's malicious games was equally unfathomable. Didn't she have anything more constructive to do with her time?

"Hello there, Lillianne Junior."

Cara Lynn's spirits lifted at the sound of that beloved voice.

She turned and walked into Reverend Brown's open arms.

"It's good to see you. How has this old world been treating you?" asked Aaron Brown, pastor of their church for the last twenty years. He was tall, perhaps four inches taller than Cara Lynn, and broad like an oak tree. That's how she thought of him, strong and solid.

"Up until a few minutes ago, I thought everything was going rather well," Cara Lynn said, sighing.

"Let's walk," Reverend Brown suggested, his hand under her elbow.

They made their way across the expanse of the lawn to the century-old cemetery that sat several hundred feet behind the church.

"I saw what happened," Reverend Brown began in his calm voice. "It looks like our Deborah is back up to her old tricks. Lord knows, I've tried to counsel that girl over the years—but it doesn't do any good. Nothing works if the heart condition isn't right. She's an incurable gossip and from what I hear, you're her latest victim."

They stopped at the ornate iron gate which led into the cemetery. On either side of it stood eight-feet-tall marble statues of angels with their wings spread.

"Reverend Brown, Deborah has had it in for me since we were in grade school. I don't know if I want to ignore it any longer."

"Some of us have enemies all our lives, Cara Lynn, whether we deserve them or not. The Lord says we should love them. I know it isn't easy to follow His admonition, but it's better for our souls if we do. I'm not talking about damnation or anything so dramatic. I mean for the sake of your own inner peace, it's best to forgive and go on with your life."

Frowning, Cara Lynn said, "If only I had an inkling as to what her problem is, I believe I could cope with her better."

Reverend Brown had a contemplative expression on his broad, dark face. "Well, let's see. For one thing, Deborah never knew her father. Her mother died when she was a child, and she was reared by a grandmother who told her she was worthless every day of her life. Maybe she picks on you because she believes you possess everything she never had. A stable home in which you were dearly loved. A father who was there for you every step of the way. Face it, Cara Lynn, you're blessed."

"There are lots of people in the world who don't have perfect lives, and they manage to be decent to others," Cara Lynn said, unconvinced.

"Then look at it from this point of view," Reverend Brown suggested, a smile making him look ten years younger than his seventy years. "She's behaving like a child. Don't you be small, too."

"I'm not going to be around to hear her latest lies anyway. My vacation's up, and I'm heading back to Louisville today."

She stood on tiptoe and kissed his cheek. "Thanks. I always feel better after a little chat with you."

"You know whom you must never forget to talk to," Reverend Brown said, his dark eyes shining.

"I always remember Him," Cara Lynn assured the elderly minister.

They began walking back toward the church grounds.

"Is Dad getting a ride home with you today?"

"Yeah, you go on. Frank's dropping by my house to see the fish I caught yesterday."

"Got some big ones, huh?"

"They were so big, I had to strap them on the hood of my car like hunters do deer in order to get them home," Reverend Brown joked.

"That big," Cara Lynn said, laughing. "Almost as big as the last ones you told me about."

She stopped in her tracks and stared intently at his nose.

"What's the matter?" Reverend Brown asked innocently.

"Just checking to see if your nose is growing right before my eyes," Cara Lynn said.

The air was chilly when Cara Lynn walked into the clinic later that afternoon. She'd come in through the back door, and the first room she came to was examination room number three. It was the largest since it housed the X-ray machine. Everything looked in order in there from the stainless steel sinks to the spotless tile floor.

The next room on the left was her office, a small, unremarkable room she didn't spend much time in. It had a desk, a chair behind it, two chairs in front of the desk, a file cabinet, and a water cooler.

She walked into examination room number two and went to the locked closet where she kept most of the drugs and supplies she used in her practice. Nothing was amiss there. She was fortunate never to have had her clinic broken into by thieves looking for drugs. She knew vets whose clinics had been burglarized, usually by thrill-seeking teens. The *Courier Journal* had featured one boy who'd regrettably tried one of the drugs he'd stolen and nearly died from the experience.

The only rooms remaining were examination room number one and the nurse's station, where Carly greeted the patients, did the bookkeeping, and logged in daily records on the computer. It consisted of large counters, cabinets, and drawers. There were several workstations in this area:

the computer station, the billing station, and what Carly called her "I need a break" station. Under the counter in this station, she had an office-sized refrigerator and a microwave. She kept the fridge stocked with colas and fresh fruit for the times they worked through lunch.

The last room was the waiting room. This area was large and comfortably furnished with leather sofas and chairs. On the coffee table were the requisite magazines found in every doctor's office, except here there was also *Ebony, Jet* and *Essence.*

Satisfied that the clinic was as she'd left it, Cara Lynn departed, locking the door behind her.

Stopping by the small market she frequented that was on her way home, she was greeted by the Vietnamese couple who owned it.

"Dr. Garrett! Good afternoon. Beautiful day we have, isn't it?" Mrs. Nguyen was a tiny woman in her late forties.

"One of the best, Mrs. Nguyen. I thought I'd pick up some fresh vegetables."

"Good, good. If we ain't got it, it don't exist," Mr. Nguyen piped in. He was the salesman of the family. He led her back to the fresh vegetable section of their immaculate market of which they were very proud.

Fifteen minutes later Cara Lynn was driving home with a bag full of lettuce, tomatoes, cucumbers, onions, carrots, bell peppers, and sweet corn. She was having a salad for dinner tonight.

It took her several trips to the Jeep to bring in her suitcases, the groceries, and various other things like the watermelon her father had insisted on giving her, plus the ten pounds of beef he'd taken out of his freezer and made her promise to take with her. Her father believed she starved herself when she wasn't under his roof.

When that was all done, Cara Lynn kicked off her shoes at the front door, walked back to the kitchen, opened the refrigerator, got a bottle of mineral water, drank it, then sat down at the kitchen table to listen to her messages. It felt good to be back in her old routine.

"Just wanted to let you know I enjoyed your visit, baby girl. Don't forget to eat those steaks. Maybe Jordan will show you how to cook them. I didn't want to say this to your face, but you're looking a little puny. Eat that beef—it'll put some iron in your blood. I love you!" Her father, of course.

"Cara, aren't you back yet?" Carly's voice said excitedly. "We're home. Got in around midday. Girl, we had a great time. I'll tell you all about it tomorrow, I guess. Eddie and the girls say hey."

Cara Lynn smiled at the enthusiasm in her best friend's voice. She had an impulse to phone her, but she didn't. They were resting up after a hectic week in Florida. She'd see her in the morning.

"Dr. Garrett, Clarence Everett here. I'm sorry to bother you at home, but I'm very concerned about Crackers. He's losing more feathers every day. I'd like to bring him in tomorrow if it's at all possible. Please have your assistant call me at home. Thank you."

Cara Lynn picked up her appointment book and made a note to have Carly phone Mr. Everett in the morning. She would probably work him in around lunchtime.

"Cara, I can see you wasted no time getting over me. For two years I thought I knew what kind of person you were, what you liked in a man. I had no idea you went for the physical type. And all this time I thought you were attracted to intellect. If I'd known you wanted bulk, I would've gone to the gym more often. Call me." Bill.

She thought about it. Did she want to talk to Bill? It had been over three months since she told him she wanted out of the relationship. In the beginning, he had stimulated her, made her feel special. They could talk about their respective jobs for hours, and she felt good about being with him. Then, about six months into the relationship, Bill, who was ten years her senior, began giving her unsolicited advice. He didn't like the way she dressed, so he took her to his favorite shop and picked out her wardrobe.

To this day Cara Lynn still didn't know what had possessed her to allow such an affront to her ego. Perhaps it was because she was still at the stage where she was willing to make concessions.

Bill was a star in his field, and he didn't miss the opportunity to tell her how fortunate she was to be his chosen mate.

Toward the end, he found fault with her business acumen, her choice in friends. When he suggested she cut Carly loose, saying she was a hindrance to her social status, Cara Lynn called him a snob and walked out on him in the middle of dinner at Maison Blanche, his favorite French restaurant. That was the night she decided she could no longer stomach him or his views.

Thinking about it raised her ire. On second thought, she *would* like to speak with him. He needed to know once and for all that she was never going back to him.

She tried his home number first and got the answering machine. She didn't leave a message. She tried his beeper number instead. A couple of minutes later he phoned her.

"Cara, I have to see you." With Bill it was never a question but a command. "That old saying about one not missing the water until the well runs dry is true. I took you for granted. I tried to change you, not realizing it was your unique personality that drew me to you initially."

"Bill, I never thought you had it in you," Cara Lynn said.

"What?" His voice was indolent, relaxed.

"That territorial streak that exists in the male sex. Do you really want me back, or does the notion that a man you consider your inferior may win over you bother you?"

"That's preposterous, Cara." The doctor was perturbed now.

"Is it?" Cara Lynn asked calmly. "And what of the lovely Dr. Miles?"

"She's boring. All she wanted to talk about was her work."

Cara Lynn remembered his work was a popular topic of conversation when they were together.

What he probably found intolerable about Regina Miles was the fact that she could carry and hold the ball when they were discussing work. It occurred to Cara Lynn that Bill quite possibly considered her his inferior as well. And having her as his rapt audience fed his monumental ego. She wasn't in the mood to feed egos any longer.

"She outtalked you?" Cara Lynn said incredulously.

"It's obvious you don't want to be reasonable about a reconciliation, Cara. Look, I invested two years in this relationship. The least you can do is be civil."

"What relationship?" She wondered where his mind had been the two years they were together.

"As I was saying, two years, Cara," Bill countered in an attempt to regain control. "I offered you marriage, the home of your dreams, children—and you could continue to work. What more does a woman want or need?"

"You are aware we're living in the nineties?" Cara Lynn said, laughing. "Come on, Billy—"

"Bill, I hate it when you call me Billy."

"Whatever. You know material possessions mean very little to me. What I wanted, and still want, is a man who loves and respects me."

"I love you. I haven't been able to sleep in my bed since you left. I've been sleeping in the den."

"That should tell you something," Cara Lynn said seriously. "Where else do you miss me?"

"Well I—"

"You can't think of anyplace else, can you?"

"I miss you everywhere," Bill said, annoyed. "What are you getting at, Cara?"

"I've spent too many years working to become my own person, Bill. I don't want to be some man's trophy. I want to be loved for who I am. Maybe it wasn't apparent to you that you treated me like an object, but it was to me. I was never your equal, and that's why I couldn't stay with you. Am I making myself clear?"

"I hear you, but I can't believe you're saying this, Cara. I treated you like an object? No way! I put you on a pedestal. I can't accept what you're saying. I don't consider what we had to be dispensable. Whether you believe it or not, I invested a good deal of myself in this relationship."

"I don't believe it," Cara Lynn said vehemently. "A personal relationship has been secondary, maybe even a poor third, on your priority list. You are first and foremost what you do."

"I don't deny that. I love my work."

"And I love *my* work, but you expected me to be ready to attend any social function with you at the drop of a hat. Solely because I'm a woman, I might add."

"That isn't true, Cara. I wanted you at my side."

"It was good for your image," she accused him.

"It wasn't good for yours?" Bill said, his voice rising.

"This conversation isn't getting us anywhere. Give yourself time, Bill. You'll find yourself someone more suited to your needs."

"Like you've found in Davidson? Has he seen that cute little birthmark you have on the inside of your thigh yet?" he asked vindictively.

"Good-bye, Bill."

"Wait, Cara. I'm sorry—"

Cara Lynn angrily slammed the receiver down.

She listened to the rest of her messages, then got up to put away her things.

The phone rang as she was putting the groceries in the refrigerator. She waited for the answering machine to screen the call. As she suspected, it was Bill.

"Pick up, Cara. I know you're there. I'm so damned jealous. I can't bear the thought of another man touching you. All right, I'm going. Call me when you decide you want to talk."

Cara Lynn sighed tiredly. She had no intention of ever phoning Bill Dunlevy again. Walking out of his life was an inspired decision. She could breathe again.

Nine

"Welcome back. We've got a half hour before Mrs. Switzer brings Tom in. Such an original name for a tomcat, don't you think? Tell me about your visit home. How's Mr. Frank? Mama told me he's dating Mavis Edwards. Girl, I couldn't believe my ears. Mr. Frank, dating. It's a miracle. But it's good for him, don't you think? I mean, he shouldn't have to be alone the rest of his life, a big, vibrant man like him," Carly blurted out the moment Cara Lynn walked into the office the next morning.

Carly usually arrived earlier to open up, set the thermostat, make sure everything was ready for the arrival of their first client.

"Eddie and the girls and I really had a ball at Disney World. Those two kids wore us out. There's so much to see, you can't get to it all in one week." Her pretty, medium brown face seemed to be lit from within. "The hotel was fabulous and so luxurious. Soap carved in the shape of a swan. Eddie's company paid for everything, did I tell you? Oh, I brought you back a stuffed killer whale, we went to Sea World, too. We're thinking of going to Daytona Beach in September, the week before Sharlee and Sharalynn have to go back to school. They'd get a kick out of that."

Cara Lynn felt like telling her best friend and veterinary assistant to breathe between sentences.

Since second grade, Carly had been the talker and Cara Lynn the calming force in their friendship.

They were direct opposites in appearance as well. Cara Lynn was a good eight inches taller than Carly, who stood five feet two inches.

Cara Lynn believed the biggest difference between them was in their personal lives. Carly had married Edward James Needham when she was eighteen. Eddie was a certified public accountant. They had seven-year-old identical twins, Sharlee and Sharalynn, named for their mother and godmother, respectively. To Cara Lynn, Carly went after life with gusto, grabbing it with both hands, whereas she was reticent, cautious.

"I'm seeing someone new," Cara Lynn said hurriedly. The only thing capable of shutting Carly up when she got going was a dose of good news.

"Who? When? Where?" Carly asked, mouth agape with surprise. "Details, girl, details."

"At home this past week. He phoned the house wanting to talk to Dad, and I answered the phone. You've probably already heard about him. He bought the old Collins place."

"Jordan Davidson?" Carly guessed. "Mama told me she saw him in the grocery store. He helped her put her bags in the car. Over six feet of pure heaven," she said. She was so excited, her short, curly hair seemed to be standing on end.

"Miss Rose said that?" Cara Lynn laughed. "What did Aunt Jean have to say about him?"

Carly's aunt Jean was the consummate gossip and kept Carly, who lived in Louisville with her husband and family, up to date about the goings-on in her hometown of Shelbyville.

Cara Lynn and Carly had a running joke about Aunt Jean. If you want news to spread fast, telephone, telegraph, and tell Aunt Jean.

"Well, okay," Carly said, grinning. "There are rumors

that he's the bastard son of Josiah Collins the fourth, and that's why he bought the place. You know, the ancestral home and all that. I think that's pure bunk. Some people think he's into something illegal, but I suspect that's because they don't know about his business here in Louisville. Oh, you've got some competition. Deborah Sanford is reportedly quite taken with Mr. Davidson. She's trying everything short of turning up stark naked on his front porch to get his attention. And don't think she won't try that if all else fails."

"So that's it," Cara Lynn exclaimed. "She wants Jordan."

Seeing the puzzled expression on her friend's face, Cara Lynn explained.

"Deborah tried to intimidate me last Monday night, supposedly because she's never gotten over her adolescent dislike of me. And now she's spreading rumors about me. What kind, I'm not certain of because I haven't heard them."

"Not again," Carly said, scowling. "Forget her. I'm more interested in what's going on between you and Mr. Davidson."

Smiling, Cara Lynn said, "There's a fire, girl. The man drives me totally insane."

"Oooh, Cara Lynn, this is the best news I've heard from you since you broke up with Mr. Freeze."

"Bill wasn't that bad," Cara Lynn said, pulling a face which made her look like she was gagging.

Giggling, Carly said, "Penguins could live on his butt, he was so cold. Back to Jordan, though. How long did it take? I mean, was it an instant flame or a slow burn?"

"Instant nine-one-one. It's like I've just discovered the opposite sex. It's scaring the hell out of me."

"Sounds wonderful to this onlooker," Carly said, her eyes sparkling.

"I embarrassed myself, Carly. I threw myself at him and practically begged him to seduce me."

"That must have pumped up his ego," Carly said, laughing uproariously. "Among other things."

Laughing along with her, Cara Lynn wiped away tears. "Don't make me laugh. This is serious. I don't want to fall in lust again. What if after several months of terrific passion, we find out it isn't going to work? Another one bites the dust? Things were fine with Bill for a while, too, you know."

"You had terrific passion with Mr. Freeze?"

"No, but—"

"I didn't think so. You know what's wrong with you?"

"I'm sure you're going to tell me."

"You don't know what a good man is, aside from your dad and my Eddie, that is. You compare every man you meet to that loser, Keith. If you sabotage a relationship with Jordan before he has a chance to prove himself to you, I recommend intense therapy for you, girlfriend."

"Don't worry—I'm a little panicky, but I'm not entirely stupid," Cara Lynn laughed.

"I knew you'd see reason," Carly told her. "If I didn't have Eddie, I might've shown up naked on his doorstep myself."

Cara Lynn didn't have time to brood about Jordan during working hours. She treated eight dogs, five cats, and Crackers, the cockatoo that was mysteriously losing its feathers.

The owner of the parrot, Mr. Clarence Everett, a designer of computer software, was distraught. He'd had the bird several years and was convinced his friend was dying.

"Birds have been known to lose their feathers due to stress or an allergic reaction to certain irritants. Is there anything in its environment that has been altered recently?" Cara Lynn inquired, a concerned look on her face.

She was holding Crackers, examining him for mites, any

sort of disease that could cause him to shed faster than usual.

Sitting across from her, Mr. Everett looked confused. He smoothed his too-long, limp brown hair away from his face and adjusted his horn-rimmed glasses. Cara Lynn noticed bright yellow specks of paint on his hands.

"Been doing some painting?" she asked.

"Yes, I'm redecorating my office," Mr. Everett explained. "Oh, the walls aren't this bright. They're a pale yellow, trimmed in this shade. My work is tedious, I needed something to keep me alert."

"Does Crackers keep you company while you work?"

"Yes, he always has. He's a great joy to me. Do you think he could be allergic to the paint fumes?"

"That's a possibility. When did you start painting?"

"Two weeks ago. I finished the trim yesterday. I'm afraid I'm a klutz where home maintenance is concerned. I kept procrastinating until my wife lit a fire under me, and I finally completed the job. Come to think of it, it was about a week after I started painting that I noticed more feathers than usual in Crackers's cage. You may have hit on something."

Cara Lynn smiled at him. "I suggest you remove Crackers from your office until the paint has had sufficient time to dry. Try it for two weeks. Let me know if the feathers continue to fall out. If so, we'll have to look into other possible causes."

Mr. Everett stood, taking Crackers from Cara Lynn. The white cockatoo squawked as its owner placed him back into the small travel cage. "Thank you, doctor. You've allayed some of my fears."

Her hand on his shoulder, Cara Lynn walked him to the door. "Try to make Crackers comfortable in a well-ventilated area of your home. Give him a chance to get the pollutant out of his system. He's a perfectly healthy bird aside from this. He'll be all right."

Cara Lynn had never personally seen a case like this before, but she'd read an interesting article in a veterinary science journal about a similar incident. She hoped her instincts were serving her well. She'd hate to lose the good-natured bird.

She glanced up at the wall clock. The day had sped by. It was already five thirty. They would have finished seeing patients earlier, but Mr. Everett had phoned saying he was having car trouble. He finally showed up at five.

A couple minutes after Mr. Everett left, there was a tap on the door. Carly stuck her head in. "I wanted to let you know I disinfected the sink in room three. Everything okay in here?"

"I cleaned up just before Mr. Everett's appointment. I'm going to feed Effi a little information, and then I'm out of here," Cara Lynn told her.

Effi was what they called the office computer. "Have a nice evening. Give Ed and the girls my love."

"Remember to take it slowly with Jordan. No obsessing, Miss Worrywart."

"Okay, already," Cara Lynn said with a long-suffering grin. "Advice taken. Go home to your family."

It required only an hour to add the new patient information to the permanent files. She'd had five new patients today, a record. It was further evidence that her practice was on a good footing. This year they would be firmly in the black.

As she sat down on the swivel chair, she began to feel some of the tensions of the day melt away. She enjoyed working with the computer.

It was actually Carly's job to do the computer work, but Cara Lynn had a natural affinity for it. Carly had a fear of one day destroying all the files with just one press of a button. Cara Lynn tried to explain to her that it was not that easy to erase the files. The computer had an excellent retrieval system, and besides, she kept more than one copy

Get 3 *FREE* Arabesque
Contemporary Romances
Delivered to Your
Doorstep and Join the
Only New Book Club
That Delivers These
Bestselling African American
Romances Directly to You
Each Month!

No Obligation!

LOOK INSIDE FOR DETAILS ON
HOW TO GET YOUR FREE GIFT.....
(worth almost $15.00!)

WE HAVE 3 FREE BOOKS FOR YOU!

FREE BOOK CERTIFICATE

Yes! Please send me 3 *Arabesque* Contemporary Romances without cost or obligation, billing me just $1 to help cover postage and handling. I understand that each month, I will be able to preview 3 brand-new *Arabesque* Contemporary Romances FREE for 10 days. Then, if I decide to keep them, I will pay the money-saving preferred subscriber's price of just $12.00 for all 3...that's a savings of almost $3 off the publisher's price with no additional charge for shipping and handling. I may return any shipment within 10 days and owe nothing, and I may cancel this subscription at any time. My 3 FREE books will be mine to keep in any case.

Name _____

Address _____ Apt. _____

City _____ State _____ Zip _____

Telephone (___) _____

Signature _____
(If under 18, parent or guardian must sign.)

AR0896

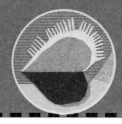
AFFIX
STAMP
HERE

ZEBRA HOME SUBSCRIPTION SERVICE, INC.

120 BRIGHTON ROAD

P.O. BOX 5214

CLIFTON, NEW JERSEY 07015-5214

of the files on discs. Carly persisted in her fears though, and she used Effi as infrequently as she could get away with.

Cara Lynn locked the back door of the office building. The sun was going down, and the temperature was warm and humid. Monday night. When she was seeing Bill, Monday night meant dinner at his home unless he was paged. Then it was a leisurely bath, a tuna sandwich and a thick book. There were many nights she spent alone wondering why, at twenty-eight, she wasn't leading a more glamorous life.

As she climbed into the driver's seat of the Cherokee, she thought of Jordan and smiled contentedly. They had a date for tomorrow night. His voice had sounded so melancholy over the phone last night when he'd told her he had to cancel their dinner plans due to a late meeting. She was disappointed but, as a working woman, had understood.

Driving through the city's streets, she was reminded of when she'd moved here three years ago. Like most newcomers, she'd done the tourist bit. Every weekend was devoted to seeing the sights. It wasn't as if she was unfamiliar with the city. She had often gone shopping with Lillianne in Louisville and walked along Fourth Avenue. They visited the American Saddle Horse Museum on several occasions. She'd been to concerts with Carly and on countless shopping excursions. And then there was the time she and Carly staked out Muhammad Ali's old house when they were juniors in high school. Cara Lynn had just gotten her driver's license and had taken her father's truck. They went joy-riding and wound up celebrity hunting. They sat outside the house for hours before it dawned on them that he didn't live there anymore. It was one of their more embarrassing adventures.

She turned onto Bardstown Road. Her office was near Cherokee Park so she took Bardstown Road to Douglass Boulevard and made her way to the St. Matthews section of town, where she rented a home in Norbourne Estates. The neighborhood was quiet and low key, exactly what she needed after a hectic day at work. The location was ideal for her because it was only a few minutes from Highway Sixty, otherwise known as Shelbyville Road, which led to home. No matter how much she grew to love Louisville, her heart would always belong to Shelbyville.

At home she kicked off her shoes in the foyer and walked barefoot through the living room to the kitchen, where she opened the refrigerator to get a bottle of mineral water before listening to her messages. She sat at the kitchen table, her feet propped up on one of the chairs.

The first message was from her father. "Hi, hon. I had a strange conversation with Harry Bailey today. I don't know what's wrong, but something's up with him and Sara. Maybe you can find out and let me know. I've got a feeling it's serious. Call me later."

Harry and Sara having marital problems? No, it couldn't be. They were the happiest married couple she knew.

The second message was from Bill. Persistent devil. "How long are you going to ignore this, Cara? Be an adult and return my call. You know where to find me."

She pressed the play button on the answering machine, hoping the next message would take her mind off Bill Dunlevy.

Harry Bailey's deep voice said, "Cara Lynn, Harry here. There is something I'd like to discuss with you, and I don't want to do it over the phone. I'll be in town tomorrow, and I'm going to drop by your office—say, at around one? See you then."

Something important. Cara Lynn wondered what it could be. Harry's voice had sounded so serious. It was unusual for Harry Bailey to lack a note of laughter in his booming voice.

"Oh, my God, he's ill," Cara Lynn said out loud.

No, that couldn't be it. Harry had danced every dance

the night of the Founder's Day celebration. Then it must be Sara. They had lied to her about Sara's condition. Now Harry was coming to see her to reveal the truth.

Cara Lynn got to her feet. She had to call them right now. No, Harry wanted to tell her face-to-face. That alone told her what he had to say was likely to be bad news. People could give you good news via any medium: over the phone, in a letter, skywriting. It didn't make any difference. But when bad news was delivered, most people wanted to do it personally so there would be a shoulder to cry on, arms to put around you. Shared misery.

She sat back down and forced herself to finish listening to her messages.

The last message on the machine was from Jordan. "Do me a favor. The next time we're together, don't look so beautiful, don't be so charming, and wear something that's sure to turn me off because the times I'm away from you are hell, lady. I miss you so much, I can hardly concentrate at work and, as you know, that can be dangerous. Call me after eleven. I want to hear your voice before I go to sleep tonight."

Cara Lynn reached over and removed the tape from the machine. In this modern age the answering machine had replaced the love letter. This was definitely a keeper.

Cara Lynn found that even after a long soak in the tub, she still couldn't relax. Her mind was on Harry's message and all the implications behind it. Realistically she knew worrying about something before she even knew what she was worrying about bordered on the insane, but she couldn't shake the feeling that bad news was only a day away.

She lay on the couch in the den with the lights dimmed, trying to concentrate on the evening news, but that was more depressing than her own thoughts so she switched off the television and turned on the radio.

"Reflections" by the Supremes was playing. After it ended, the disc jockey came on. "This is Barry Golden stacking the wax and bringing back the sounds of yesteryear. I bet you don't remember this one, children. It's Sam Cooke telling us 'A Change Is Gonna Come.' "

Cara Lynn let the satiny sound of Sam Cooke's voice wash over her. The disc jockey was wrong, she knew the song. It was one of her favorites. At the moment it expressed exactly how she felt, sad but hopeful that a positive change was coming.

She closed her eyes, and because she was physically and mentally worn out, she drifted off to sleep.

A few minutes later the doorbell rang. She thought she'd dreamed the sound, so she turned over and went back to sleep. The doorbell rang again, and this time it startled her. She quickly sat up, wiping the sleep from her eyes.

Pulling her bathrobe closed, she went to answer the door.

Bill stood on her doorstep, looking haggard and unkempt. She could not recall ever seeing him in need of a shave. He held a cardboard box in his arms. He shoved it at her.

"Here, these are the last of your personal possessions that you left at my home."

Still a bit groggy, Cara Lynn accepted the box. "Thank you, but I could have picked them up some other time. There was no rush."

"I wanted them out of my house as well as everything else that reminds me of you." His voice was cold as ice.

Gathering her wits about her, Cara Lynn looked him in the eyes. "This should do it," she said. "Good night."

She absently kicked the door shut with her right foot, but Bill's shoulder got in the way of its closing.

He stepped into the house and shut the door behind him. He was still wearing his surgical greens, something he never did when he was off duty.

"I did not invite you in," Cara Lynn said angrily.

"No, you didn't—but I wouldn't expect good manners from a low-born person like yourself."

Cara Lynn placed the box on the floor and gave him her full attention. "Get it out, Bill. Say everything you came here to say, then leave because I'm tired of this. I left you months ago. I wanted things to remain civil between us, but if that's not possible then go ahead, I can take it. Get it off your chest, doctor."

Bill's breathing was erratic, and sweat had broken out across his brow. His hands were clenched into fists at his side.

"I don't need this aggravation, Cara. I came here tonight to give you one last chance. When I cross your threshold again, it's over. Are you going to see reason or not?"

"Do I look like an utter fool to you, Bill? Why would I want to be with a man who thinks I'm beneath him?"

"That was anger talking," Bill said, wiping his forehead with the back of his hand.

Cara Lynn scowled. "You were being honest. It's how you feel. At least admit that."

Sighing, Bill stepped toward her, hand outstretched. "Cara, I've never failed at anything."

Backing away from him, Cara Lynn said, "That's what's bothering you, isn't it? Your experiment went awry. Two years invested in the bride of Bill, and everything went bust. Let me give you some advice. Failing isn't so bad sometimes. We learn from our mistakes. Maybe the next woman you get involved with will benefit from this failure. Maybe she won't have to run away from you in order to regain her own sense of identity and purpose. I hope so, Bill. I really do."

Bill grabbed her by the shoulders and forced her to face him. "Is that your final word on the matter?"

"Yes, it is," Cara Lynn said, gaze unwavering.

All the fight seemed to go out of him. He released her and walked to the door. Grasping the doorknob, he turned back to look at her. "I'm done with you. You could have had the world, instead you moan about equal treatment and a little constructive criticism. I guess a zebra can't change its stripes, after all," he said regrettably. "You could have been somebody."

"I *am* somebody, Bill. That's what you never could fathom."

He left without another word. Cara Lynn ran to the door and locked it. She leaned against it, her legs weak. To think that proper, anal-retentive, William Dunlevy could frighten her.

She knew he was controlling and obsessive—but she'd never suspected how he would react when she denied him something.

Still, it was worth it if it was finally over.

Ten

Cara Lynn was on pins and needles all morning as she waited for Harry to show up. When he did arrive, there were dark circles under his eyes.

Carly brought them steaming cups of strong coffee, then closed the door behind her as she left Cara Lynn's office.

Forgoing her desk chair, Cara Lynn pulled up a chair next to Harry's. She placed her coffee cup on the desk, then reached for his hand.

"Harry, what's wrong?" she said, looking into his red-rimmed eyes.

Harry looked down at their clasped hands. "I'm going to retire, Cara. I wanted you to be the first to know."

Inwardly Cara Lynn breathed a sigh of relief. Retirement? She could handle that.

"You're in your prime, Harry. You've got many years ahead of you. Why would you retire so soon?"

Harry's eyes were tearing as he squeezed Cara Lynn's hand. "I told myself I was going to be strong about this. If it were me, I would have no regrets. I've had everything a man could want: a wonderful wife, fine children, good friends. But it's Sara, and it's eating me up inside."

Cara Lynn's stomach muscles constricted painfully. She had to remind herself to breathe.

"Sara's not well?" she asked, her voice trembling.

This time it was Harry who calmed *her*. He took both

her hands in his and held on to them. "Sara has lung cancer, Cara."

Cara Lynn felt faint. The room spun crazily. Harry had to put his arms around her to prevent her from falling off her chair.

The tears came in a deluge. At that moment she realized that when her mother died, she'd transferred some of the love she'd reserved for her to Sara.

The vertigo passed quickly, and she sat up straight, trying to appear composed for Harry's sake.

"Sara never smoked a day in her life, Harry. How did she get lung cancer?"

"The doctors believe it comes from being exposed to asbestos. You remember, the entire school had to be remodeled after that asbestos scare a few years back. It's ironic that the thing she loved most, teaching, should take her life away. It isn't fair," Harry said in a tormented voice.

"Her doctor doesn't think it will respond to treatment? Surely something can be done," Cara Lynn said, grasping at straws. She knew that lung cancer was one of the most difficult forms of the disease to cure.

"We've seen all the specialists. We've gotten second, third, and fourth opinions. They all agree it's only a matter of time now."

"Why did I press her about her appearance? Did I upset her, Harry?" Cara Lynn cried. "I'd give anything to have been wrong."

"It was hard for Sara to lie to you, Cara, but she hadn't made up her mind to tell anyone just yet. She wanted to keep things quiet for a while. She didn't even tell Amy or H.J. You know how strong willed she can be," Harry explained, his voice breaking.

"I can't believe it, Harry. I don't want to believe it," Cara Lynn said, tears rolling down her cheeks. She rose, going to her desk for tissues. She got a few for herself and handed the box to Harry.

"If there's anything I can do for you, all you have to do is ask," she said, her eyes meeting his.

"There is one thing you can do for us, Cara."

"Name it, Harry," Cara Lynn said sincerely.

"You can take over my practice. I don't want anyone else taking over where I leave off. I've built up a solid business. I have the utmost confidence in you. I wouldn't trust anyone else to do the job."

Cara Lynn sat down on the edge of the desk. "You don't know how much it means to me to know you have that kind of faith in me, Harry."

"Do I detect a 'but' in the sound of your voice?" Harry asked, smiling gently. "I know you have some misgivings. You're wondering if some of the old boys are going to object to an African American woman doctoring their thoroughbreds. I intend to set them straight on that score from the get-go. They'll know you are my choice. And if you get any flak or attitude from anyone after that, tell them to take a hike. They'll find out soon enough that they've made a big mistake."

"What about Ted Walsh?"

"Ted's a good vet when he's sober," Harry stated matter-of-factly. "But he lost a couple of valuable foals last year due to negligence, and he's in the middle of litigation. If he doesn't straighten up, his license is going to be yanked. I'm not asking you to take over temporarily. This would be a permanent arrangement. Sara and I are moving back to Arizona. Her parents want her in Phoenix so they can spend time with her. Besides, the dry air is supposed to be good for her condition."

Cara Lynn managed a weak smile. "Give me a day or so to think it over, Harry. This has all been a big shock to me."

"I understand," Harry said, getting to his feet. "You have lots of things to consider. You want to make certain Carly is taken care of. You know, you could have it written into the contract that she comes with the practice. Carly's a very good assistant. She'd be an asset to any vet."

"It's not only the job. Carly's my best friend, Harry."

"You'll have to handle it with kid gloves. But you'd be passing up a great opportunity if you said no. Carly would understand that."

Cara Lynn hugged him. "My heart goes out to you. You know I love you and Sara. I don't want you to have to worry about your practice on top of everything else. I'll do it. I'll find a way to work it out. Tell Sara I'll be home this weekend. I'll drop by and see her Saturday afternoon."

"She'll be happy to see you. But, remember—"

"No hysterics," Cara Lynn provided, smiling. "I promise I'll be cheerful. I'll get my crying over with before I arrive."

"There you go," Harry said, sounding almost like his old self. He gave her a squeeze and then kissed her cheek. "We're okay. Sara and I are handling this better than I ever imagined we would."

"You've always gotten strength from one another."

For an instant Cara Lynn saw the panic in Harry's eyes. He was losing his source of strength. Then they were hugging again, and she walked him to the door, afraid to say anything else.

He forced a smile as he turned to walk to his car.

Carly came into the office as soon as she saw Harry leaving.

She was shocked when she learned Sara was so ill. "Miss Sara has lung cancer? I knew Dr. Bailey was upset when I saw him, but I would never have guessed it was over something this awful. How are they coping?"

"Under the circumstances, Harry seems pretty together. It can't be easy losing someone you've spent most of your life with."

She sank down on her chair, her eyes inexpressibly weary. "Harry wants me to take over his practice."

"You'd be perfect," Carly said immediately. "You love

horses. Dr. Bailey services some of the biggest outfits in the area. You'd be foolish to turn him down."

"What about you? I don't want to leave you, Carly. We're a team. You helped me build my practice, you've been my right-hand woman."

Carly smiled at her. "Yes, I have, haven't I? But listen, Cara, horses and cattle are not my cup of tea, and you know it. You're the one who has a way with horses. You can't have forgotten the time you tried to teach me to ride? I was mortified. Those big, smelly beasts. Flaring nostrils, disgusting noises. No. It would suit me fine to stay here with the cats and dogs and the occasional reptile. What about Brent Bachman over in Frankfort? He's been having a hard time getting established. I bet he'd jump at the opportunity to buy you out."

Cara Lynn had gone to veterinary school with Brent.

"Would it be possible for you to move back to Shelbyville with me?" Cara Lynn posed.

Carly laughed. "With Eddie's job? No way. We've been friends since we were seven years old. I know you as well as I know myself. Working with horses has been your dream for a long time. Do it. Don't pass up this opportunity because of some exaggerated sense of loyalty to me."

Sitting up, Cara Lynn grinned at her. "I'd really miss seeing you every day, hearing your corny jokes and juicy gossip."

"You know where I live, come see me. The girls will have someplace to go on weekends. They love visiting the ranch. Unlike their mother, they aren't afraid of horses."

Cara Lynn hugged her friend. "I don't know what I'd do without you."

"And you aren't going to find out," Carly promised. "Feel better?"

Buttoning her coat and straightening her shoulders, Cara Lynn nodded. "Yes, I'm fine now."

"Good, because you've got a big job ahead of you. I believe Butch is constipated again."

"What is Mr. Peterson feeding that Doberman?" Cara Lynn said, sighing.

"Well it's not bran," Carly joked. "Room three."

"Horses are beginning to look better and better," Cara Lynn complained as she left the office.

Cara Lynn took Carly's advice and placed a call to Brent Bachman when she got home that night. She and Brent were at Tuskegee together. He was the type of man a woman felt comfortable around. He and his longtime sweetheart, Jenny, whom he later married, were good friends to Cara Lynn when she was away from home. So it felt good now to be able to do him a favor.

They talked briefly about their personal lives. Brent told her the latest havoc Casey, their two-year-old, had wrought. He complained about his inability to draw clientele.

"That's why I'm calling, Brent. Harry Bailey is retiring, and he asked me if I'd be interested in taking over for him. I've built up a good business here, and like Harry, I want to leave it in capable hands. Would you be interested?"

"Of course I'm interested," Brent said right away. "The market isn't great here—too many practitioners. I'm looking for a better location. What's your asking price?"

"I haven't worked up any figures yet, Brent. But I'd like to ask you if you'd be willing to hire Carly as your assistant. She wants to continue working here."

"I'd be glad to have her. The man I have now is not working out. He's late for work every other day and gives me attitude whenever I tell him to do something."

"What's his problem?"

"I don't think he likes working for a black man," Brent said, laughing. "Anyway, put me at the top of your list, Cara. Jenny and I would love to be back in Louisville. Both sets of our parents live there. It'd be good being closer to them."

"I'll give you a call as soon as I speak with my lawyer," Cara Lynn promised. "Good talking to you, Brent. Give Jenny and Casey my love."

"Will do," Brent said brightly.

After they hung up, depression got a stranglehold on her. Harry had been so adamant that everything that could be done for Sara had been done. The thought of Sara's imminent death made Cara Lynn cringe. In some ways Sara was an earthly connection to her mother.

Many times she'd visit Sara, and Sara would launch into one of her myriad stories about Lillianne. Cara Lynn especially liked the one about her mother and Sara's luncheon date at an upscale restaurant in Bowling Green. The luncheon was Lillianne's birthday treat to Sara. However, when the waiter came to take their orders, he addressed all his questions to Sara.

The waiter returned with their orders. Lillianne looked him in the eye and said, "Young man?"

When she had his attention, she continued. "My friend and I are here to celebrate her birthday. This is my gift to her. If you would like to be duly compensated for your services, I suggest you at least acknowledge my existence."

The waiter's faced turned beet red, but he soon recovered and was solicitous the remainder of their stay. Lillianne left him a generous tip along with the benefit of a little more wisdom.

Cara Lynn felt like running through the house screaming at the top of her lungs. Simply yelling until there was no breath left in her. Why Sara?

What she wanted was the solace of a pair of strong arms around her. A masculine shoulder to cry on. But she didn't have that luxury. She would've liked to turn to Jordan for comfort, but she felt it was too soon in their relationship for that kind of intimacy. She didn't want to scare him off.

Therefore she had no one, save herself, to get her through the night.

She looked up at the clock on the kitchen wall. Seven thirty. She'd been sitting at the table, her feet propped up on a chair, for over an hour. Feeling sorry for herself.

The phone rang. She reached over and answered it.

"Hello?" she said, sounding wretched.

"I knew you'd go home and wallow in your misery. Eddie and I want you to come over and spend the evening with us. Bring a change of clothing—you can spend the night in the guest room."

"I'm okay, Carly. As a matter of fact, I'm seeing Jordan in just a few minutes." A little prevarication, but it would get Carly off her case.

"Good," Carly said cheerily. "What are you going to do?"

"Supper and whatever," Cara Lynn said offhandedly.

"I want to hear all about the 'whatever' tomorrow. Take notes if you have to. I'll let you go, then. See you in the morning."

"Oh, I spoke to Brent tonight. He says he'd be happy to have you work with him."

"He seems really nice," Carly said, pleased. "I hope things work out for him. Well, I'll let you go get dolled up for Mr. Davidson."

"Thanks for checking up on me."

"Girl, you're closer to me than my own sister. Of course I worry about you."

After she got off the phone with Carly, she got up and grabbed her car keys. What she needed was sustenance, and not just your plain everyday fare. She needed chocolate. Lots of chocolate. Chocolate ice cream, specifically with chocolate cookies on the side, chocolate cookies on top, chocolate cookies coming out of her ears.

She quickly changed into a pair of Levis, the ones with the extra room in the waist, a white T-shirt, her Reeboks, and was heading out the door when she collided with a hard male body.

Jordan barely avoided being knocked over by the whirlwind flying through her front door.

He managed to hold on to the bags of Chinese food he was carrying.

"Hey, what's the rush?"

Cara Lynn looked up at him. She grinned.

"You should never get in the path of a woman in desperate need of chocolate."

"I've got you covered," he said, holding up the bag in his left hand. "Chocolate almond ice cream and Oreos."

"Mmm," Cara Lynn said, relieving him of the burden of the aforementioned bag. "Welcome to my home, big guy. Come right in."

She led him straight back to the kitchen, where they placed the bags on the counter then regarded each other with questioning expressions on their faces.

"I thought you had to work late," Cara Lynn said, still smiling happily.

"I got out earlier than I anticipated. I thought I'd surprise you," Jordan told her, his eyes on her face. "What's wrong?"

"What do you mean? Nothing's wrong," Cara Lynn denied self-consciously.

Jordan touched her cheek with the back of his hand as he moved closer to her.

Cara Lynn's body instantly reacted to his nearness. She could feel herself being drawn into him like a drop of water melding with another.

His hand cupped her chin, tilting it upward. "You've been crying. Tell me why."

His golden brown eyes mesmerized her.

"If I do, I'll start crying all over again."

Jordan put his arms around her. "You don't have to talk

about it if you don't want to, but I want you to know you can. I'm a good listener."

"Your being here is good enough for now," Cara Lynn told him. She kissed his chin, one of her favorite parts of his anatomy. "Thanks for bringing dinner. I'm famished."

They enjoyed the shrimp fried rice, dumplings, and egg rolls in front of the television in the den. There was an old Woody Strode Western on, and they were both fans of the genre.

At the beginning of the film, they were sitting together on the couch, Jordan's arms draped around Cara Lynn's shoulders. By the middle, Cara Lynn was lying with her head in Jordan's lap. This didn't work because Jordan couldn't resist kissing her mouth—and after one heated episode during which Cara Lynn had to leave the room in order to cool off, they decided that she should sit on the floor and he should remain on the couch. That is, if they wanted to watch the movie. By the end of the film, they were both on the floor, and neither of them could recall how the Western ended if his or her life depended on it.

"You smell good, you taste good. Damn, girl—I believe you're edible," Jordan said in her ear.

"I totally missed the movie," Cara Lynn said, shifting to a more comfortable position in his arms. "What happened to the Woody Strode character?"

"He got killed. You know they don't allow brothers to live long in a John Wayne movie."

"You missed it, too, didn't you?" Cara Lynn said, her eyes looking into his.

"I'll rent it for you sometime."

"Thank you," Cara Lynn said sincerely.

"It's just a movie."

"I don't mean for the movie," Cara Lynn laughed. "For the way you came here tonight and cheered me up. You took my mind off my troubles. That was sweet of you."

Jordan's eyes were tender as he regarded her. "It's begin·

ning to dawn on me that there is very little I wouldn't do for you, doe-eyes."

"Oh, yeah?" Cara Lynn said sultrily.

"Oh, yeah," Jordan answered, his baritone voice equally seductive.

"That brings to mind quite a few possibilities," Cara Lynn said as she wrapped her arms around his neck and pulled him down to meet her mouth in a passionate kiss.

The doorbell rang just as Jordan's hand found its way under her T-shirt.

"They'll go away," Jordan murmured.

The person at the door leaned on the bell.

"It could be Mrs. Lerner, an elderly neighbor. She has a heart condition. I'd better get it," Cara Lynn groaned.

It wasn't Mrs. Lerner. The caller was Evan, looking cool and collected in an off-white summer suit of Italian linen. He offered her a bouquet of snowy white orchids. Cara Lynn had a sudden flash of déjà vu.

"Evan, what are you doing here?" Cara Lynn said, trying to keep the annoyance out of her voice.

"Don't ask me to stay—" Evan said, stepping across the threshold.

"I wasn't going to," Cara Lynn said impatiently.

"I told my driver to keep the motor running. I was in town for a late meeting and thought I'd bring you some flowers. A beautiful woman should have flowers given to her every day."

He looked her up and down. "What have you been doing with yourself?"

Jordan appeared in the foyer.

"Oh, is that your car in the driveway, Davidson?" Evan said. "Nice, but I always buy American."

"Did you come here to discuss cars?" Jordan said, his lips set in a thin line.

"No. I came to ask Cara to attend the ballet with me

Friday night," Evan replied, smiling at Cara Lynn. "The Dance Theater of Harlem is performing 'Firebird.' "

Jordan leaned against the wall, his powerful arms crossed at his chest. He was rapidly losing patience with this pompous, self-serving jackass.

"Thank you, Evan, but I have other plans for Friday," Cara Lynn said politely.

"I understand," Evan said magnanimously. "Perhaps another time. It was only a friendly overture. No strings attached. Far be it for me to cross the bounds of friendship." He ended with a glance in Jordan's direction.

Jordan pushed away from the wall. Cara Lynn quickly moved between them, her back to Jordan.

"Your driver's waiting," she said to Evan, then in a lower voice, "How did you get my address?"

"You're a doctor with a heart, Cara. Of course you'd have your address listed along with your home number."

"What happened to our agreement?" she whispered, exasperated.

"I couldn't live with the terms," Evan said.

As she walked toward him to show him to the door, Evan reached out and pushed a tendril of her hair behind her ear. His eyes intimately raked over her face. "Enjoy your evening.

Cara Lynn closed and locked the door behind him.

She sighed. "I don't think he's getting the message."

"Why did you let him touch you?" Jordan said, frowning.

"I didn't let him touch me, he just did," Cara Lynn said, walking toward him. "What was I supposed to do, smack him for putting an errant hair back in place?"

Looking down into her face, Jordan said, "Maybe you like having two men salivating over you."

Frowning, Cara Lynn huffed, "I have never done anything to encourage Evan Fitzgerald."

Moving close to him, she poked him in the chest with her index finger. "And another thing—I'm not interested in having two arrogant males after me like dogs in heat. I'd rather be alone."

Jordan caught her hand by the wrist and pulled her into his arms.

"Next time let me rip his head off. He'll get the message."

"Can we go back to what we were doing before that unpleasant interruption?" Cara Lynn said, her mouth perhaps an inch from his.

"Only if—" Jordan kissed her lower lip "—you promise—" he kissed her upper lip "—not to answer the door again." A full kiss on the mouth.

"I promise," Cara Lynn mumbled.

Eleven

"Harry has always been fond of you, and he *is* your mentor," Frank said of Harry's request that Cara Lynn take over his practice.

They were discussing the matter over breakfast Saturday morning. Cara Lynn had driven to Shelbyville Friday night since she had no plans to see Jordan. He was tied up in negotiations with the company that supplied his company with steel girders.

Due to a mix-up at the factory, they had sent an inferior shipment and until they made good on the order, Jordan refused to do further business with them. The company promised to have the girders there by Friday night, so Jordan stayed on the site to personally inspect the new shipment.

"I'm sorry that Sara's so ill," her father was saying sadly. "She's a fine lady."

Cara Lynn slammed her fist down on the tabletop. "I'm just so mad. Look at her life: a teacher, a mother, a person who is concerned for others. She was right in there fighting when so-called concerned citizens wanted to move the homeless shelter off Main Street."

"And won," her father added, smiling.

"And won," Cara Lynn repeated, her anger subsiding. She looked into her father's face. "Daddy, can you explain to me why awful things like this happen?"

Frank sighed and took her hands into his. "I wish I could. All I know is: life is unbiased. Bad things happen to everybody. Good fortune befalls the evil. Look at the rich robber barons who prospered off the poor. Most of them lived to be doddering old men."

"And people like Mama and Sara are gone too soon," Cara Lynn said sadly.

"You've been given a gift this time, though," her father said.

"How so?" Cara Lynn asked softly.

"You didn't get the chance to say good-bye to your mother," Frank reminded her.

Homes reflect the spirits of those who occupy them. This could be said of the Bailey home, which was a rambling two-story ranch house with a wraparound porch.

Cara Lynn could not enter Sara's home without reliving her childhood. Images of her, Amy, and H.J. running in and out of the kitchen for lemonade and cookies in the summertime or sipping hot chocolate by the fire in winter while their mothers talked. Amy was a year older than Cara Lynn, and H.J. was two years younger. H.J. would follow the girls around like a lost puppy, eager for any affection thrown his way.

Sara, looking more rested than the last time, met Cara Lynn at the door.

The two women hugged without a spoken greeting, and Sara pulled Cara Lynn inside. The air was redolent with spices, cinnamon being the principal one.

"Is that your carrot cake I smell?" Cara Lynn asked hopefully.

Sara released her and looked up at her. "Made especially for you," she said, smiling.

"Sara, you shouldn't be cooking for me. I . . ." Cara

Lynn paused in midsentence, seeing the warning look on Sara's face.

"It smells delicious," she said instead.

Sara smiled approvingly. "Come on, it's such a beautiful day, we'll talk on the patio."

They walked through the living room, past the kitchen, out the Dutch door that led to the patio.

"Where's Harry?" Cara Lynn asked, looking around them.

"I sent him on an errand, I wanted to speak with you alone," Sara told her. "Sit."

The round patio table was topped by a festive floral tablecloth on which sat the carrot cake, a pot of coffee along with Sara's best china, silverware, and cloth napkins.

"Everything looks lovely, Sara," Cara Lynn complimented her.

A lump formed in her throat, and she sat there smiling foolishly, at a loss for words.

"Thank you," Sara said, her green eyes never leaving Cara Lynn's face. "Would you serve us, please?"

Cara Lynn did so gladly, relieved to have something to do.

Finished, she sat down and tasted the cake. It was perfection as always.

"You've done it again," she said. "You've got to give me this recipe. One day I may be brave enough to tackle it."

Sara reached over and grasped Cara's hand, squeezing it.

"You're already that, my dear," she said with admiration.

"I'm going to say this, and then we aren't going to bring the subject up anymore," she continued. "I'm not afraid of what lies ahead, Cara. At first I railed against it. Did everything short of cursing God. Then, to my amazement, a sort of peace came over me," she laughed. "Remember that poem you quoted so beautifully in my eleventh grade English class? 'Invictus' by—"

"William Ernest Henley," Cara Lynn said, delighted she'd recalled the name.

"Yes, do you remember how it goes?"

" 'Out of the night that covers me'," she started. " 'I am the master of my fate; I am the captain of my soul.' "

"Well that's how I feel now," Sara said, smiling. "I'm blessed to have had people like you in my life—and now that this disease threatens to rob me of that life and I am at its mercy, I've accepted what must be. But I don't believe this is the end. You know I have faith that God has a plan for us. I don't believe He'll keep us separate from our loved ones for all of eternity. So don't be sad, dear. Celebrate our time together."

Picking up a small jewelry box covered with brown velvet, Sara placed it in the palm of Cara Lynn's hand.

"I was going to give you this on your wedding day," she said. "But I'm giving it to you now for obvious reasons."

Cara Lynn raised the lid of the box. Inside were a pair of pierced gold earrings, approximately an inch in length, in the shape of leaves. They were exquisitely crafted in eighteen-carat gold.

"They're beautiful, Sara. So unusual."

Smiling, Sara told her the story of the earrings. "They were a fortieth birthday present from your mother. Lilli told me I was turning over a new leaf, and these would remind me that I was finally an adult." Tears sprang to her eyes. "I'm sorry, it's just that I miss her so much." She picked up a napkin and wiped her tears away. "I want you to have them so that you'll have something from the both of us. And if you wear them on your wedding day, some little part of Lilli and me will be with you."

Cara Lynn hugged her impulsively, tears streaming down her face as well. "I'll always treasure them. And if I ever get married, I promise to wear them."

Sara smiled through her tears. "Oh, you will get married, young lady. Perhaps to that fine Jordan Davidson."

Their sadness forgotten momentarily, they held a lively conversation on the pros and cons of marriage.

Harry showed up in the middle of a fit of laughter. Looking at both of them as though they'd taken leave of their senses, he said, "You've been in the mulberry wine, haven't you?"

To which Cara Lynn and Sara laughed even harder.

Cara Lynn was late arriving for her date with Jordan. He met her at the door wearing an apron over his clothes and a ready smile.

Cara Lynn fingered the apron. "You look very sexy in that."

Jordan pulled her into his arms, kicking the door shut. "You, gorgeous one, are forty minutes late."

"I have a good reason."

Her emotions were at the surface, threatening to break through at any instigation. She breathed in deeply, exhaled.

"So what's your excuse?" Jordan asked as he smoothed a lock of her hair away from her face, his fingers lingering on her silken skin.

Cara Lynn told him all about Sara.

"I danced with her at the barbecue," he recalled.

Smiling, Cara Lynn nodded. "She makes an impression."

Holding her tightly, Jordan soothingly rubbed her back. "No wonder you're tense. I'm so sorry about Sara." He laughed shortly. "She wanted to know, in no uncertain terms, what my intentions are toward you. I told her they were most definitely honorable. She looked at me and said, 'They'd better be.' I couldn't do anything but laugh."

"That's Sara," Cara Lynn said wistfully. "She and my mother were best friends, and after Mom died, she sort of became my surrogate mother."

Jordan shook his head sadly. "Is there anything I can do to make things easier for them?"

"Harry and Sara are pretty grounded as a couple. I think

they will be okay. I'm worried about their children, Amy and Harry Junior. It's going to be tough letting her go."

"I can't bear to see you so depressed," Jordan said. "I've got to do something to lift your spirits."

Before Cara Lynn could protest, he swept her up into his arms. Holding on to him, Cara Lynn experienced a rush of longing. Her emotions, being so close to the surface, erupted in the form of passion.

She wrapped her arms around his neck, thinking that this was it. He was taking her upstairs to his bedroom. She was delighted with the turn of events and kissed his cheek repeatedly to show her approval of the idea.

He wasn't walking in the direction of the bedroom, however—he was heading toward the kitchen.

"Jordan, where are you taking me?" Cara Lynn asked suspiciously.

"Stop squirming," he said, a mischievous grin on his lips.

"You wouldn't," Cara Lynn said aghast.

Jordan opened the sliding glass door which led to the pool and deck area.

"I just washed my hair," Cara Lynn protested vigorously.

"Poor baby," Jordan commiserated.

He stopped at the edge of the deep end, holding her aloft. Cara Lynn held him tightly around the neck. "Jordan, don't. I'll do anything."

"Anything?"

"Within reason," Cara Lynn amended, realizing what a broad statement her comment had been.

Jordan threw her into the pool and dove in after her. Cara Lynn was a strong swimmer, so by the time he came up for air, she was waiting to push him back under.

Jordan broke the surface of the water, gasping for air. Cara Lynn grinned at him triumphantly. "That'll teach you not to mess with a woman who just had her hair done."

He swam toward her, but she was already out of reach,

swimming for the pool's steps. He caught up with her as she placed a foot on the first step.

"You don't get away that easily," he said, grabbing her about the waist and allowing their combined weight to propel them back into the water.

"Okay, I give up," Cara Lynn sputtered as they came up for air. "I'm happy, I'm happy."

She clung to him, kissing his face. "You're nuts, you know that?"

"Nuts," Jordan said, his eyes boring into hers. "Yeah, that about describes it. I've known you fourteen days, and I can't think of anything else. I find myself daydreaming about you at the most inopportune moments."

"Is that good or bad?" Cara Lynn said, smiling at him.

"It has to be good because I'm damned content," Jordan answered, cupping her face in his big hands.

"Me, too," Cara Lynn confessed. "When you look at me, I feel so alive."

"And when we touch?" Jordan said, gazing into her upturned face.

Cara Lynn took his hand and placed it over her heart. "Feel that?" she said. "That's what you do to me."

Jordan sought her mouth. Cara Lynn gave herself to him, succumbing to her true feelings. She was whole with Jordan. Unafraid and safe. And yet there was a cauldron of emotions simmering at the edge of her mind. It would take very little for her to fall in love with him. She was already halfway there.

After such an emotionally draining day, she felt like letting go and simply allowing her instincts to carry her along. As long as they led her into Jordan's arms.

Jordan smiled at her. "Come on, I don't want you catching a cold. We'd better get out of these wet clothes."

They climbed out of the pool and began stripping out of their wet clothing down to their underwear.

Cara Lynn watched, her heart pounding, as Jordan peeled

off the soaked apron, denim shirt, and jeans. He was beautiful. His dark brown skin glistened with water droplets. He was like some mythical African god, rising from the depths of the sea. His trim, sinewy body was perfectly proportioned, no doubt from hard work, and there wasn't an ounce of extra weight on him from his broad, hairy chest to his long, decidedly muscular legs.

Jordan was observing her just as closely as she stood shivering in her red bikini panties and lacy bra. Her even-toned, honey brown skin was unmarred. And, he hadn't noticed it before, but she was slightly bowlegged, which gave her shapely frame extra oomph.

He marveled at the definition of her leg and thigh muscles when she moved. With or without clothing, she was the sexiest woman he'd ever known.

He had to consciously fight down his rising libido because at that moment it would've been quite evident how much he wanted her. It was a losing battle, however. He wound up placing his wet clothes strategically in front of him and ushering her into the house.

"I'll put our clothes in the wash," he hastily suggested.

"Can't they wait?" Cara Lynn said sultrily, turning to touch his bare chest. "We've got all night."

Jordan felt his resolve melting away with the implications her words brought to mind.

"You're not spending the night," he laughed, rallying. "I'm not going to have Frank after me with a double-barreled shotgun."

"Is that it?" Cara Lynn murmured, kissing his chin. "My father? I'm not a child, Davidson. I don't need my father's permission to be with you, and I sincerely doubt I'd get it if I asked for it."

"I know how old you are, and it really doesn't matter. It's a no-go on staying over. We're not giving the good citizens of this town anything to gossip about."

Cara Lynn could have told him they were already being gossiped about whether they deserved it or not.

"So I won't spend the night," she said, exasperated. "But the clothes can wait, I can't."

She kissed his chest then and raised her eyes, sending him an unmistakably sensuous message.

"Cara, you're in a vulnerable state. Please don't tempt me. I don't want to take advantage of you."

Cara Lynn politely stepped aside. Jordan went into the laundry room adjacent the kitchen.

Miffed, Cara Lynn turned and went in the opposite direction.

Five minutes later, though, she strode back in wearing his bathrobe. She opened the lid on the top-loading washing machine and placed her wet underwear inside.

Jordan stood to the side, wearing a clean T-shirt and buttoning a pair of dry Levis. She preceded him out of the room.

"You aren't angry with me, are you?" he asked, touching her right shoulder.

Turning to look at him sideways, Cara Lynn smiled. "You throw me in the pool and then ask if I'm angry with you? If you don't mind my looking like a drowned rat all evening, then it's all right with me."

"No more surprises," Jordan said, laughing at her drowned rat comment. If she knew how beautiful she looked to him at that moment, she'd probably get out of there as fast as she could. "And to make up for throwing you in the pool, I'm going to give you a shampoo, and then I'm going to braid those lovely locks of yours."

"Really?" Cara Lynn said, unable to conceal her amusement.

"You don't think I can?" Jordan said, taking her disbelief as a personal affront. "I'll be right back, don't move."

"Don't worry, I wouldn't miss this for the world," Cara Lynn told him.

He went upstairs and returned a couple of minutes later carrying a tray on which were two fresh white towels, a bottle of shampoo, conditioner, a jar of hair dressing, a large-toothed comb, and a natural bristle brush.

"Well, you look like you know what you're doing," Cara Lynn said, still sounding doubtful.

Jordan set the tray on the countertop, reached over and turned on the water, tested it for warmth. "That's good. Now if you'll bend over the sink, we'll get down to business."

Cara Lynn complied, if somewhat halfheartedly. She had yet to meet a man who was comfortable doing a woman's hair, except professional stylists of course. When she was a little girl, her own father had gratefully left the task to her mother.

Jordan's hands felt wonderful to her scalp as he massaged the herbal shampoo into her hair. It was obvious he'd done this before—the question was, to whom? She was jealous of that unknown female who'd previously enjoyed this experience.

"You have beautiful hair," Jordan told her. "Very soft."

"Where did you learn to do this?" Cara Lynn asked, curiosity eating her up. "It isn't something you're born knowing how to do."

"I have three younger sisters," Jordan said, sighing. "And even though I hated it at the time, my mother made me learn to wash and braid their hair. That's the extent of my expertise. She said the knowledge would come in handy one day. What if I had a daughter, and I wasn't able to do her hair? Was I going to allow my child to go around with uncombed hair? Believe me, boys don't care one way or the other. But Mom could make up the most impossible scenarios to get her point across."

"Your mother was right," Cara Lynn said. "All men should know how to do this. It feels great."

"If I had known this would give you such pleasure, I

would have suggested it the first day we met," Jordan laughed.

"No, the timing's right," Cara Lynn told him. "If you had tried this then, I would've thought, 'What is he, nuts?' "

After washing and conditioning her hair, Jordan wrapped one of the towels around her head, turban style.

"Let's go into the den. There's an old movie I think you'll like coming on in a few minutes."

In the den Jordan sat on the couch while Cara Lynn sat on a huge floor pillow in front of him. He towel dried her hair, then gently combed through it.

"Is this hair dressing all right?" he asked, showing her the jar.

"Yes, but only a little, please," Cara Lynn replied. She was so relaxed, she was sure she'd fall asleep if this continued for much longer.

"Wake up," Jordan said into her ear. "The movie's about to begin. I hope you like horror films."

"I love 'em."

"This one's the *Bride of Frankenstein.*"

"Horror? It's too campy to be described as horror," Cara Lynn laughed. "I even wound up feeling sorry for the monster."

"You would," Jordan said, grimacing. "What about the terrified townspeople?"

Cara Lynn humphed. "If they had left him alone, he never would have turned violent. They made him a monster. And that Dr. Frankenstein was a wimp. He created the poor thing and then abandoned him. Didn't try to educate him. A few speech lessons wouldn't have hurt. If you ask me, Dr. Frankenstein was the monster, not the creature."

"I see you've given this some thought," Jordan said, amused by her assessment of the story. He applied some of the hair dressing, massaged it into her hair, and began to comb it back away from her face. "Let's just watch the movie, shall we? Then we'll decide who the monster is."

The film, circa 1935, starred Boris Karloff as the creature and Elsa Lanchester as his bride. Cara Lynn cracked up at the antics of Dr. Frankenstein's maid, who provided most of the comic relief throughout the film, and at the end, when the creature tried to hug his bride and she screamed and hissed at him like a frightened alley cat, Jordan couldn't help laughing. "Now that's gratitude. If it weren't for him, she'd still be so many rotting corpses."

"It definitely wasn't love at first sight," Cara Lynn said offhandedly. "Not like the moment I—I first saw *Old Yeller,*" she said quickly. "I cried my eyes out over that dog. I must have been around five years old."

It wasn't exactly a good save, but it would have to do.

Their eyes met, and Cara Lynn hastily looked away. Her heart hammered in her chest. She'd almost admitted she loved him. Where had that come from? Where was her brain? But then it had hit her suddenly. Wham!—right between the eyes. Without warning. No notice whatsoever. She had tried to convince herself what she was feeling was physical attraction because Jordan was all things physical. He was big and powerful, exuding strength, agility. His movements were those of a sleek panther. His touch made her weak. Made her entertain thoughts that had heretofore never entered her mind with other men.

But love? Love wasn't on her agenda. Love was to be avoided at all costs. Love meant commitment, love required trust. Love was scary. The thought of it made her want to take flight.

She reached up and touched the soft, expertly braided plait that fell down her back. "Thanks, you're a man of many talents."

"It was my pleasure," Jordan said, his voice a caress.

Cara Lynn got to her feet, intending to put some distance between them, but Jordan playfully pulled her down onto his lap.

"Not like the first time you what?" he said in his deep, sexy baritone.

He kissed the side of her neck, his lips lingering on her fragrant skin. Cara Lynn tingled all over. She had difficulty thinking about anything except making love to him.

"I told you, not like the first time I saw *Old Yeller.*"

"And I don't believe you," he murmured in her ear. "There's one thing I've learned about you, doe-eyes. Your lovely lips might hedge, but your eyes don't lie. There was something of a more personal nature you were thinking of just then."

"Not like the first time I saw Keith," she lied. "But I didn't want to bring him up. It was stupid of me, so I tried to cover it."

"You don't need to hide anything from me, Cara. I know Keith was your first love. Do you want to know who my first love was?" Jordan said, still playful.

"Yes, who was she? Some beauty queen from Bangor?"

"Betty Jo Kelly. I was sixteen. She was fifteen. I'd already picked out my tux for the wedding when along came Tabby Ericson, and I realized one shouldn't make a lifelong commitment based on the fact that a girl smiled at me."

"I bet you were fine at sixteen," Cara Lynn said, looking him in the eye.

"I thought I was God's gift to pubescent girls," Jordan said, laughing at the memory.

"I wish I'd known you then."

"You would have been what, nine years old? No, I like you much better now," Jordan told her, tracing her jawline with a finger.

Say it, Cara Lynn thought. Say you love me so I'll know I'm not in this alone.

Instead he kissed her forehead and said, "Are you hungry?"

The moment had passed.

"Extremely," she said. "What have you got?"

"I made you my special pasta primavera."

Cara Lynn followed him into the kitchen, and as he was rummaging through the refrigerator, she set the table.

"Where do you want to be five years from now, Cara?" Jordan asked when they sat down at the table in the formal dining room.

The oak table was large enough to accommodate twenty diners. The polished wood floor was covered with a hand-loomed Persian rug. It was done in earth tones, and there were pictures of exotic birds woven into it.

"I guess I just want to be happy," Cara Lynn said lightly. "I'd like my career to be on a good track. I know this doesn't sound like the independent woman I am, but I'd like to be the mother of two children by then. By the time I'm thirty-five, I'd like to have three, perhaps four."

"Tell me, does a husband figure in anywhere?" Jordan asked, his eyes lit with humor.

"A husband?" Cara Lynn said as though she'd never heard the term before. "Did I leave him out? An oversight, I assure you. Of course I'd like to be married. I don't simply want to be married though—I want to be desperately in love with my husband, and I want him to be equally enamored of me."

Putting down his fork and lacing her fingers with his, Jordan said, "That shouldn't be too difficult to achieve. What man hasn't fallen in love with you after being in your presence more than a minute?"

"I'm looking at one right now," Cara Lynn replied with a hint of a smile.

"How do you know I'm not in love with you?" Jordan said.

Placing her elbow on the table and her chin in her hand, Cara Lynn regarded him. "I know because you haven't told me. It's as simple as that."

"Maybe I don't want to appear foolish," Jordan said, then

quickly added, "Do you really believe it's possible to fall in love after knowing one another two weeks?"

He was scrutinizing her so closely that Cara Lynn was suddenly nervous.

"Is there a time limit on love? It was love at first sight for my folks, and they had a rock-solid marriage. It happened to me once. It was the only time I ever truly loved someone," she said anxiously.

"Keith again?" Jordan said, curious.

"That turned out to be a bad case of infatuation. I was too young and naive to recognize it at the time."

"Bill, the heart man?" he ventured.

"Common interests. No, it wasn't Bill."

"Then whom?" His confusion was written all over his face.

"I don't want to talk about him, it's too painful," Cara Lynn said, looking away.

"Why?" Jordan inquired, his voice rising. "Did he die in a tragic accident or something?"

She met his gaze. "He's very much alive. He just doesn't love *me,* Jordan."

"You're still in love with this person?" he asked, willing her to respond.

"Can we drop the subject? I don't want to talk about it," Cara Lynn said, sounding more morose than she intended to.

Taking a deep breath, Jordan gave her hand a reassuring squeeze. "No—I don't want to drop the subject, Cara. You told me there was no one in your life. Now tell me, who is he? Is he married? Is that it?"

"I'd never get involved with a married man, Jordan," Cara Lynn replied, slightly annoyed.

"Not all married men behave like married men. Maybe you fell in love with him before you found out he had a wife," Jordan proposed.

"I know for a fact he isn't married," Cara Lynn adamantly maintained.

"Chronologically," Jordan said. "He came along after Keith and before Bill, am I right? Why is it you never mentioned him? Does he live around here? Do you see him often? Is he someone I might know?"

Cara Lynn sighed. How could she answer his questions without confessing the truth?

"He lives in Louisville—and yes, I see him occasionally," she said evasively.

"When you say 'see,' do you mean in a romantic sense, or do you just happen to run into him every now and then?"

"We aren't dating, if that's what you mean. I'm not seeing anyone but you."

"But you're still in love with him," Jordan persisted, his eyes boring into hers.

She swallowed hard. "Yes, I love him."

Jordan released her hand. Placing his elbow on the table, he rested his forehead in his hand. He sighed. "Then what are you doing here with me?"

"I'm having dinner with you."

"Don't be cute, Cara. If you love this man, why waste your time with me?" he said bluntly.

Once again, he searched her eyes.

"I told you—he doesn't love me. Can I make it any clearer than that? And the reason I'm with you is because I want to be. I'm very attracted to you, Jordan. You—"

"Turn you on?" he said angrily.

"I like being with you. We can talk to each other," Cara Lynn said, trying to remain calm. "At least most of the time. This particular conversation seems to be deteriorating before my eyes."

Eyes narrowing, Jordan blew air between his lips. "The fact is, I'm just a passing fancy for you. You're still hoping he'll come around, aren't you?"

"No, I—"

She had taken the game too far. Jordan was visibly upset. She watched him with a compelling fascination.

Pushing his plate away, he stood and walked around to her side of the table and pulled her to her feet.

"Jordan, I'm not using you, if that's what you're thinking. I genuinely care for you," Cara Lynn said softly.

He bent his head and kissed her roughly. His eyes were ablaze with a mixture of pent-up passion and anger when he looked down at her. "If this is all you want from me, Cara, you've got it."

His hands were inside the robe she wore, caressing her satiny body.

Cara Lynn placed both hands on his chest in an effort to resist, but her resolve was swept away in an instant as he kissed her again, his tongue forcing her lips apart. She moaned with pleasure.

She found the strength to tear herself away momentarily. "Jordan, this isn't all I want from you, believe me."

"That isn't what your body's saying," Jordan replied, pulling the robe down off her shoulders. Gravity did the rest.

"You're beautiful, Cara," he said, his voice hoarse with longing.

Suddenly shy, Cara Lynn tried to pull the robe back up. Jordan took it and flung it across the room. It landed on a rubber plant in the corner of the dining room.

"Don't be modest now, Cara. A minute ago you were eager to share yourself with me. What is it? Can't get him out of your mind?"

"Why are you so upset?" Cara Lynn cried, pushing out of his embrace.

Jordan let her go, his eyes devouring her as she walked over to the rubber plant, picked up the robe, and wrapped it around her.

"I'm not upset," he denied. "I'm most definitely not upset."

"Then stop this," Cara Lynn said, turning to look at him. "Every time I've come on to you in the past, you've put me off. It wasn't the right time. Now all of a sudden you're forcing the issue. What gives?"

"I realized that you don't want to gradually build a relationship. You want instant gratification, something to tide you over while you pine away for the man you're in love with. I wanted more, but if you want a stand-in, I'm your man. Take me."

"You don't understand," Cara Lynn tried to explain. "I was playing a game with you. A harmless, if ill thought out, game."

Seeing the thunderous expression on Jordan's face, Cara Lynn knew she couldn't have chosen more inappropriate words.

"Let me reword that. I don't mean a game as in I was leading you on. I was just trying to make you jealous, okay?" she blurted.

Coming to stand in front of her, Jordan seductively rubbed her arm with a finger. "You do many things well, Cara. Lying isn't one of them. You led me on. Admit it."

"I did not lead you on," Cara Lynn denied, grasping the hand that was busily inciting her nerve endings. "What was I supposed to do, tell you I'm in love with a man who doesn't love me, a man whom I probably don't have a chance with? He isn't in my life. What more do you want from me?"

She couldn't believe the words spilling from her mouth. Instead of admitting there was no other man, no unrequited love, she was digging herself in further. The next thing she knew, she'd be giving the mystery man a name.

Jordan took her hand and gently pulled her toward him.

"I want everything from you, Cara. I'm drawn to you like a moth to a flame—and the sad thing is, you're probably as bad for me as the flame is for the moth. But I've got to have you anyway."

Cara Lynn reached up to touch his cheek. "Jordan, I want you, too. I just don't—"

"No, don't say anything else," Jordan said and silenced her with a kiss that left her weak in the knees.

When they parted, he swept her up into his arms and carried her upstairs to his bedroom.

He laid her atop the comforter on the big, four-poster bed and removed his shirt. As he lay down beside her, their bodies curled around each other. Cara Lynn's face was buried in his chest as she inhaled his male scent between fluttery kisses.

Jordan tilted her head up so that their eyes were level.

"There's nothing to stop us this time, doe-eyes. Are you sure?"

"Yes," Cara Lynn breathed. "I'm sure."

Jordan rolled over onto his back, pulling her on top of him. He slowly loosened the robe's sash around her waist, and Cara Lynn allowed the robe to slide off her shoulders.

She felt his sharp intake of breath at the sight of her full breasts and his arousal not long after. She boldly unbuttoned his jeans, taking her time.

Jordan stayed her hand on the final button and pulled her down to meet his mouth in a lingering kiss. He felt all his anger leave him. There was no room left for any emotion except love when he was holding her. He didn't know how he'd fallen so fast, so hard. But he had, and she was everything he wanted. Everything he needed. And although it was gut-wrenchingly painful knowing she loved someone else, at least he would have this night, this moment to cherish.

"Hold on, my love," Jordan told her, getting off the bed. He left the room and returned.

Cara Lynn had gotten beneath the covers, and she held them up for him to join her.

Their eyes met, and they both smiled as Jordan climbed into bed beside her.

"I missed you," she said.

"Not as much as I missed you," he said, bending his head to kiss her smooth stomach.

Cara Lynn giggled. "I'm ticklish there."

Jordan kissed her breast, his tongue lingering on the nipple.

"There?"

Cara Lynn could have sworn her toes were curling. "No, not there," she said breathlessly.

All her reactions to his caresses were an expression of her love for him. She gave herself to him in an undiluted frenzy of passion. Her exquisite body answered his every need, surpassing all his expectations.

He was in no rush to end this coupling of souls. He kissed her thighs, her legs, her flat, smooth belly. He savored every inch of her, enjoying the sound of her soft gasps of pleasure from deep in her throat.

Then their loving became more intense, urgent. Cara Lynn held on to him, her body aching with the desire for release. Sweet perspiration covered their writhing bodies.

She grasped him tighter, ever tighter. There was only a matter of seconds before the culmination of their melding of minds and bodies. Sensing this, Jordan kissed her deeply, heightening the sensation for both of them.

He watched her beautiful face as she came down from the peak. She was precious to him.

He lay beside her, spent himself. Momentarily he rolled onto his back, his breath coming in short intervals.

"How can you make love to me like that and be in love with another man?" he asked as he laid his head on her belly.

Cara Lynn tenderly stroked his cheek. "There is no other man."

"You mean at this moment—here and now—no one else exists except the two of us?"

Cara Lynn sat up in bed, forcing him to sit up as well.

"I don't think you're listening to me, Jordan." She thought she'd try a different angle. "How do you feel about me?"

Jordan ran his index finger along her thigh. "I think you're the sexiest woman alive. But I hate the way you change the subject whenever you don't want to answer a question. You can't possibly be in love with the guy in Louisville and be here with me."

Cara Lynn was preoccupied with what he had said. Sexy? Who cares about sexy? She wanted to hear him say he loved her.

"Cara?" Jordan impatiently called her name.

"There is no other man, Jordan," she said resignedly.

She looked for the robe. She couldn't find it. No wonder, the way they had carelessly tossed their clothes aside an hour ago.

An hour ago—when she still harbored the hope that he could be in love with her.

"I know you told me he didn't love you, but you obviously continue to care for him," Jordan said. "Otherwise you wouldn't have brought him up. Perhaps you feel guilty for having such a good time with me. Like you're cheating on him."

He simply would not let go of the notion that there was another man. She stared at him. "Jordan, what happened here tonight?"

"You opted for a real man instead of a fanciful dream. And I'm grateful you did because I'm not ready to give you up, Cara."

Cara Lynn took this as a positive sign. He didn't love her yet, but he was falling in love with her.

He pulled her down next to him, and their bodies automatically sought each other underneath the comforter.

They lay there for a few minutes, relishing the feel of their bodies touching. Then Jordan broke the peace of the moment with "Tell me about him."

His voice was so low, seductive, that Cara Lynn didn't grasp his meaning at once.

She languidly turned to him. "Whom?"

"The man you can't forget."

Her temper flared. She sat up in bed. "I told you—"

"Yeah," Jordan said lightly, tossing her explanation aside. "There is no other guy. Come on, Cara. If this is going to go anywhere, we've got to be honest with one another."

"I am being honest," Cara Lynn said huffily. "He doesn't exist, Jordan. I made him up to cover up something else I didn't want to reveal to you at the time. He's a figment of my imagination, you read me?"

"Well," Jordan returned, looking pleased. "That, at least, is a step in the right direction. Soon you'll be over him. Maybe you aren't as in love with him as you think you are."

Cara Lynn angrily pulled the top sheet off the bed and wrapped it around herself as she got to her feet. "I can't believe you're jealous of someone who doesn't exist."

Jordan got out of bed, too. "I can't believe you're protecting him."

"Protecting him? Protecting him from whom? He isn't real!" Her voice was shrill.

Pulling on his jeans, Jordan said, "Calm down, Cara. Okay, if you don't want to talk about him tonight, we won't. Let's drop the subject for the time being."

Angry beyond reason, Cara Lynn glared at him. "You're impossible, Jordan Davidson. You're also about the most stubborn human being I've ever met. I shouldn't have come here tonight. It was a mistake." Then she bolted from the room, the sheet trailing behind her.

Jordan ran after her. "Cara, what the hell am I missing here?"

"Where are my clothes? What did I do with my sandals?" she cried, ignoring him.

Once downstairs she looked for her missing shoes, first

in the den then outside on the deck. Peabo was happily chewing on one of her leather sandals.

"Oh, let him have them," she said, on the verge of tears.

She turned to go into the laundry room and ran into Jordan.

"Would you please get out of my way?"

"As soon as you tell me why you're so upset."

She faked a left, he went in that direction, and she quickly went right, getting past him.

"You won't pull that one on me anymore," he said, still dogging her steps.

"What counts is that I got away with it that time," she said over her shoulder.

In the laundry room she took her clothes out of the dryer and began putting them on.

Jordan stood in the doorway as she quickly dressed.

"What did I say? I thought I was being pretty understanding. I mean—it's not every man who'll try to overlook the fact that the woman in his arms is in love with someone else."

Fully clothed, except for her sandals, Cara Lynn stood with her hands on her hips. "In your desire to be so understanding, you entirely missed the point. But," she paused, "I can't blame you. This whole fiasco is my doing. I brought up the mystery man, who remains a bone of contention between us, even though I've tried to convince you he isn't real. You don't believe me. I can't force you to believe me. I'm losing patience with it all. I think we should forget tonight ever happened."

Looking into her eyes, Jordan touched her arm, and Cara Lynn drew away from him, afraid she'd give into him without a fight. He had to listen to her, otherwise they'd be building a relationship on half-truths. Why was he being so obstinate? She'd admitted to her deception. Why couldn't he accept her apology and let them go on from there?

"You were right when you suggested we take things slowly," she said, the fight gone out of her.

"Don't do this to us, Cara. You made love to me. There's nothing wrong with that. We—"

"We what? We like each other? We're friends? We're drawn to each other? What, Jordan?"

"We just need to take time to work through this," Jordan said quietly. "You're feeling guilty because you think you're in love with someone else. Give yourself time, you'll get over him."

Throwing her arms up in disgust and resignation, Cara Lynn spun around, preparing to leave.

"All right!" Jordan called after her. "He never existed."

Cara Lynn cautiously faced him. "You truly believe me?"

One look into his eyes told her he did not.

Sighing, Cara Lynn continued walking. "Good-bye, Jordan."

Exasperated, Jordan pulled her into his arms, holding her tightly. "So I'm not completely convinced," he breathed. "You should have seen the look on your face when you mentioned him. The emotions you expressed were very real. All I'm asking for is the chance to help you get over him."

He bent his head to kiss her, and Cara Lynn met his mouth with all the fervor of a woman about to lose something precious. Couldn't he sense her need for him?

If she told him she loved him now, what would his reaction be? He'd probably laugh and say, "Once you get over *him*, we'll talk about *us*." Or he'd play psychiatrist and tell her she only thought she was in love with him. Yes, she'd certainly dug a hole for herself this time.

Jordan kissed the fragrant hollow between her breasts, his hands busy unzipping her skirt. Cara Lynn felt dizzy with the heat of sexual hunger.

"Tell me you want me, Cara."

"I do. I want you so much it hurts."

"Good, then his hold is weakening."

His words were like a cold shower to her senses. She froze. The spell was broken. She pushed out of his arms. "You're a man with a mission, aren't you? Make Cara forget him. If I'm so in love with him, what makes you think you can cure me? Maybe I don't want to be cured."

"Then you were using me, Cara," Jordan said, releasing her. "I suppose it would be best if you left. I'd be willing to do anything for you except be your fool. That isn't my style."

"I'm a big enough fool for the both of us," Cara Lynn said sadly.

Jordan blocked her path, not yet ready to give up. "You lied to me from the beginning. Saying you were not involved with anyone. What kind of woman are you? You seemed so sincere. I thought I had found the perfect woman."

"Perfect?" Cara Lynn said, rounding on him. "Why is it every man on the face of Mother Earth wants a perfect woman? You're not perfect, Jordan Davidson."

"I never said I was!" he said angrily. "But I thought we were pretty damn close to being perfect together. If I didn't know better, I'd believe you were making this other man up just to blow me off. You got what you wanted, so you're done with me."

Cara Lynn was so shocked, all she could do was laugh.

This infuriated Jordan. "Why don't you go all out, Cara? You've got all the right equipment to ensnare a man. God knows you did a good job on me. Go get him."

Cara Lynn stood there wondering how she could be in love with such an arrogant, bullheaded man.

"Maybe I will." She ran out into the night.

Jordan slammed the door with a thud. For the life of him, he couldn't figure out why she wouldn't admit she'd lied. She was the most infuriating, stubborn piece of work he'd ever had the displeasure of meeting. It was too bad he was too in love with her to ever give up on her. She might think it was over, but she hadn't seen the last of him. A dream lover, indeed. He was the real McCoy and before long, Miss Cara Lynn Garrett would know it.

He went outside and rescued her sandals from Peabo, who whined pitifully when he took them away.

"You think *you* feel bad?" Jordan said. "I just sent the only woman I ever loved running out into the night without her shoes. I'm the one in the doghouse."

Twelve

"I don't understand you, Cara Lynn. The minute you feel yourself falling for a guy, you do something to ruin it," Carly said, taking the opportunity to chastise Cara Lynn in the twins' absence. It was Saturday afternoon, they were having lunch downtown at Mavis's diner. Carly had sent the girls over to the jukebox to choose a few songs more to their liking. At the moment "You Send Me" by Sam Cooke was playing. "It's nice, Mom," Sharalynn had informed her mother. "But it isn't jammin', you know what I mean?"

What she meant was, it wasn't rap music. The twins were addicted to TLC and Salt N' Pepa. They got up in the morning listening to Queen Latifah and went to bed boppin' to Arrested Development.

"I didn't exactly screw things up all by my lonesome," Cara Lynn said in her defense. "I tried to tell that thick-headed boob that there is no other man—but he refused to listen."

Taking a sip from her cola, she sat back. "You know, you hear about the differences between the sexes and everything. How we don't think alike. But it's amazing to witness it up close. Carly, I was talking but the man just couldn't hear me."

"Why did you bring it up in the first place?" Carly asked, glancing over at the twins. Sharlee was about to give the jukebox a good, swift kick.

"If you do that, young lady, you won't be able to sit for the rest of the day," her mother said sharply.

Sharlee placed her foot back on the floor. "I wasn't really going to do it," she said, giving her mother a sheepish grin.

"Yeah, right," Carly said, unconvinced. "You see that empty booth over there? Go sit down, and I don't want you to move until I tell you to."

Sharlee hastily obeyed, knowing her mother didn't brook any back talk.

"We were discussing the possibility of love at first sight. I told him that's what happened with my folks—"

"I never knew that," Carly interrupted. "That's so romantic."

Nodding, Cara Lynn continued. "Uh huh, Dad told me he took one look at Mom and he was gone. She told me the same thing. Anyway, I mentioned to Jordan that it had also happened to me like that."

"With whom?" Carly said, frowning. "I don't recall anyone in your past that you fell for so quickly."

Cara Lynn gave her a knowing look. After twenty-one years of being best friends, that's all Carly needed.

"Are you positive it isn't lust?"

"Unfortunately, yes."

"So you almost admitted it to him, caught yourself, and invented the other man to cover your blunder."

Cara Lynn nodded. "And I would've gotten away with it if he hadn't been so insistent about knowing who the man is."

"That only means one thing, girlfriend," Carly concluded.

"What?"

"He's in love with you, too."

"He may be in love with my body but not with me."

"How long did it take for him to come on strong? The first date? Second?" Carly asked expectantly.

"Actually I was the one who put on the pressure," Cara Lynn confessed. "He was a perfect gentleman."

"Then he could be under the impression that you wanted him only for his body," Carly said, lips pursed.

"He told me as much," Cara Lynn said, sighing. "He said I was amusing myself with him until my mystery man came around."

"Girl, you two really made a mess of things," Carly told her. "But since you love each other, I think we can save the relationship."

"How?" Cara Lynn plaintively asked. "I don't see how."

Looking at Cara Lynn as though she were annoyed with her, Carly said, "You've got to convince him that there is no other man."

"I tried. He wouldn't listen."

"Try again," Carly said fiercely. "And this time don't leave until you've made him understand."

The bells over the door jangled, announcing new customers. Out of habit, Cara Lynn turned her attention to the newcomers. Her jaw dropped.

Jordan walked into the diner with Deborah Sanford hanging on his arm.

A week, Cara Lynn thought. One week and he's with someone else.

"Cara Lynn, stop staring," Carly ordered under her breath.

Cara Lynn lowered her eyes to her hands. "Still think he's in love with me?"

"He's doing the typical male thing, trying to get over a good woman with a bimbo. It's so obvious. Don't let it get to you," Carly informed her. Then, "Oh, Lord, she's coming over here to gloat. Be cool."

Deborah Sanford was five feet, six inches tall and had the type of body men desired and women envied. Curves in all the right places. She had big brown eyes, skin the color of Georgia pecans, and lips that were made to look fuller than they were with the aid of artifice. She never went out in public without being "turned-out," which meant her hair, makeup, clothing all had to be perfect.

Today she looked like a beautiful pixie with her raven hair cut short and layered, framing her heart-shaped face. She was wearing a hot pink miniskirt with a silk blouse in a darker shade, and heels that made her legs even more becoming than they already were.

Cara Lynn felt underdressed in her customary Levis and denim shirt. But then she'd dressed this way because after lunch, she was going riding.

"Carly, Cara Lynn, still together I see. I haven't seen you two in ages," Deborah gushed. "When Jordan and I came in and I saw you, I told him, 'You've got to meet these gals.' I swear, seeing you two makes me feel like I'm back in high school."

"Hello, Deborah, how've you been?" Carly said, smiling politely.

"Oh, I've been keeping busy. I'd like you to meet Jordan Davidson, he's new to Shelbyville. Jordan, this is Carly Needham."

Jordan reached over and shook hands with Carly. "It's a pleasure to meet you, Carly."

"The pleasure's mine," Carly said. "I finally get to meet the man I've heard so many good things about."

"Oh?" Jordan said, his eyes briefly meeting Cara Lynn's.

"Yes," Carly replied, smiling. "Cara Lynn told me you gave her a tour of your newly renovated home. She says you're a master carpenter. And then there are the jobs you've given to several local men. News like that travels fast. The employment situation being what it is, I'd say you're somewhat of a hero in this town."

"That's far from accurate," Jordan said. He instantly liked the petite woman. She seemed to complement Cara Lynn, being more open—whereas Cara Lynn was self-contained. "I needed the extra men, and they were skilled at their jobs."

"He's so modest," Deborah said, possessively taking his arm. "I think he's a fine asset to our little town."

"I couldn't agree more," Carly said.

"I didn't know you and Cara Lynn knew each other," Deborah lied. Her eyes sent daggers in Cara Lynn's direction. Her smile, however, never wavered.

"We met when Cara Lynn was kind enough to examine a stray that followed me home," Jordan said, his eyes on Cara Lynn. "How are you, doc?"

"Doing good, and you?" Cara Lynn said much too brightly.

"Feeling better every day," Jordan replied, matching her tone.

Rightfully assuming the subject needed changing, Carly glanced up at Deborah and said, "I've been thinking of dropping by your shop. Got in anything interesting?"

"We've gotten in some new things that would look darling on your petite figure," Deborah began. To Jordan, she said, "Carly was head cheerleader three years in a row when we were in high school. You'd never think, looking at her, that a tiny thing like her could bellow out cheers. But she was the best. And Cara Lynn. Cara Lynn was a bookworm. She was so smart, most of the boys were too intimidated by her to ask her out. Did you have one boyfriend in high school, Cara Lynn?"

"I'm sure none of this is of interest to Jordan," Cara Lynn said, forcing a smile.

"But she had her horses," Deborah continued sympathetically. "She won so many prizes for her riding that her picture must have been in the paper every week."

Jordan knew then that Deborah was envious of Cara Lynn and probably had been for years.

"I hate to break up this reunion," he said, bestowing a charismatic grin on the ladies. "But if we're going to have lunch, we should order soon. I have a meeting in Louisville this afternoon. It was nice meeting you, Carly. Cara Lynn."

"Same here," Carly said. "And welcome to Shelbyville."

"Thank you."

With one more quick glance in Cara Lynn's direction, he escorted Deborah to a booth.

"I like him," Carly announced once they were alone. "He's definitely the man for you."

Cara Lynn angrily cut her eyes in Deborah's direction. "That girl is always itching for a fight," she said. "It's a good thing he stopped her. I was about to go off."

"But he did stop her, didn't he? And you know why?" Carly inquired, looking especially satisfied with her deductive reasoning.

"Because he was embarrassed," Cara Lynn answered.

"No, because he couldn't bear having you ridiculed. Deborah succeeded only in cutting her own throat. I'd be willing to bet that today is the first and last time those two will go anywhere together. He loves you, Cara. I could see it in the way he was looking at you. And don't look now, but he's staring at you."

Cara Lynn kept her eyes lowered, fearing she might do something stupid like running over to him and flinging herself at him. She reached across the table and grasped Carly's hand, squeezing it. "I hope you're right."

"Those two have been together forever," Deborah said, vying for Jordan's attention. "It makes one wonder."

"Wonder about what?" Jordan said, picking up a menu.

"If it's more than friendship," Deborah replied.

She moistened her lips and smiled at him.

Jordan laughed shortly. Deborah would go to any lengths to poison his mind against Cara Lynn. Did she think he was so damned gullible? Cara Lynn was all woman, and he had concrete proof of that.

"I think it's a waste of time and brain cells speculating

about what other people are doing in their private lives," he said, not looking at her. The menu was more interesting.

"Oh, me, too," Deborah quickly changed her tone. She reached over and lowered his menu. "I didn't mean that maliciously. We're old friends."

"I see," Jordan said.

"We go all the way back to grade school. But enough about that. The Horsemen's Ball is coming up, and I was wondering if you've thought about going?"

"I don't think so. I'm not big on dances."

"But it's the social event of the year," Deborah said excitedly. "Everyone dresses to the hilt. This year, donations are being made to the Boys' Home. Quite a few of our black youths benefit from the ball. In the past proceeds have provided scholarships for kids who wouldn't have gone to college otherwise. So it's not just for show."

"I'm sure it's a worthwhile endeavor," Jordan said. "Whom do I see about making a donation?"

"You can do that at the bank across the street," Deborah said offhandedly. "Do you have plans for next weekend?"

Jordan smiled at her. Underneath her caustic exterior, she was just someone who wanted to be liked. He'd known people like her. They were insecure about themselves, and that insecurity made them hurt others before they could get hurt.

"I'm thinking of flying home to see my parents," he said, letting her down easy.

"Too bad you have to miss it," Deborah said, disappointed. "Evan Fitzgerald is hosting this year. Just being at Baymoor will be worth the money. You do know Mr. Fitzgerald, don't you?"

"I'm acquainted with him," Jordan said.

"Of course. You know Cara Lynn, so you've probably heard of Evan Fitzgerald. They're good friends."

"Are you implying they're more than friends?" Jordan asked, knowing she was baiting him.

"No, I'm not. I just know she's been seen at Baymoor.

I also hear he allows her to ride his prize horses. You figure it out."

"We should order," Jordan said abruptly. "I have to be in Louisville in two hours."

Her words had affected him though, and he couldn't resist wondering if Fitzgerald was the man Cara Lynn couldn't get over. The race issue could be the cause of the unrequited love. No, he was letting his imagination run wild. If Fitzgerald was the man Cara Lynn wanted, all she had to do was whistle and he'd come running.

He watched as Cara Lynn and Carly, along with two small girls, left the diner. This was what pain was, this aching in his gut. It took all his inner strength not to get up and run after her, apologizing profusely.

He returned his attention to the beautiful woman sitting across from him, and he realized that for all her physical assets—her exquisite face, expertly madeup, her hair, cut in the latest, most flattering style, her perfect body—she was missing something basic and vital to the human being. She had no heart.

He felt sorry for her, so sympathetic that he did not tell her what he really thought of her. She was miserable enough.

"Harry wasn't exaggerating when he said you were good at what you do," Evan said, grinning at the newborn foal as it struggled to get to its feet. "Look at him, he's a winner if I've ever seen one."

Cara Lynn got to her feet, brushing hay off her jeans. "He's a beauty all right."

It had been a fairly easy delivery. The mother was young and strong, and the foal had been positioned correctly in the birth canal. No problems.

She was sure Evan's flattering words were sincere, but in her opinion, they weren't warranted. The mare had done all the work. She'd merely assisted.

She turned to look at Joey Gardner, Evan's stable boy. A young man of twenty, Joey was already a fine horse handler. He had assisted Cara Lynn during the birth by keeping the mare calm. It took a unique personality to be able to do that. It was clear to her that he loved animals. She had been interviewing veterinary assistants all week. No one had been to her liking thus far. After watching Joey for the last few hours though, she thought he would be a good candidate.

"You did an excellent job, Joey. Thank you."

Joey's good-looking dark brown face brightened. "Gosh, thanks, Dr. Garrett."

Evan was at Cara Lynn's side, ushering her out the stable door. "Come into the house. I've some champagne I've been saving for the occasion."

Smiling at him, Cara Lynn seriously thought of saying no. Evan had kept his word about not pursuing a romantic relationship with her, but he still sent flowers at least once a week to remind her he was still interested should she change her mind.

"That sounds good," she said at last. "I can stay only a few minutes though, I've an early call in the morning."

As they walked out into the coolness of the night, Cara Lynn looked heavenward. The stars shone brightly in an ebony sky. While she was admiring the stars, Evan was marveling at a more earthly beauty.

"It's a gorgeous night to be born on, isn't it?" he said, placing his hand under her elbow.

"Beautiful," Cara Lynn agreed, but her thoughts seemed to be even farther away than the stars.

Evan, at thirty-seven, was a fifth-generation Kentuckian. He had inherited Baymoor, his ten-thousand-acre estate, from his parents. An only child, he was cherished from birth and even more so because he was male and would carry on the Fitzgerald name. In all his life he had never desired anything he didn't eventually possess.

By the time he was seventeen, he knew his attractiveness to women was primarily due to his bankroll. It wasn't that he lacked sex appeal. At six feet tall with dark brown, wavy hair and warm brown eyes, he knew he turned heads. He was honest enough with himself, however, to acknowledge that his looks took a backseat to his wealth in many people's eyes.

Cara Lynn Garrett was unfathomable to him. She continued to rebuff his romantic overtures, even though he had it on good authority that her love affair—it hadn't lasted long enough to be referred to as a relationship—with Davidson was kaput. What's more, he had nothing to do with their breakup. So why wouldn't she give him a chance?

When they were alone, as they were now, she was careful not to hold his gaze too long. She was so professional with him, he felt like screaming.

In the sunroom, which was his favorite room in the house because of its coziness, he handed her a glass of chilled champagne. It was the finest bottle from his personal stock. He'd hoped to drink it with her their first night together, but it appeared as though that might never happen, so he'd decided to enjoy it with her while he could.

Their fingers touched and he smiled at her. "To Kid Galahad."

"May he have a long, healthy life," Cara Lynn offered, returning his smile.

They drained their glasses. Evan was about to refill her glass, but Cara Lynn asked him not to.

"I'm driving and I'm already tired."

"Perhaps I should have suggested coffee instead. It would be no trouble to brew a pot." It would give him the opportunity to spend more time with her.

"It's kind of you to offer, Evan, but as I said, I should be going," Cara Lynn said, stifling a yawn.

Evan moved closer to her on the sofa. "Let me drive you home, Cara. After everything you've done tonight, I feel it's the least I can do. One of my men will return your car to you in the morning."

It was a kind and generous offer but Cara Lynn declined. "It isn't necessary. I'm fine, really. It's only a few miles."

Resigned, Evan walked her to the door.

"Have you decided whether or not you're going to allow me to escort you to the ball? You remember our agreement?"

"I remember," Cara Lynn said, laughing. "How can I forget when you sign the card that comes with your flowers, 'two weeks till the ball,' or something similar?"

Evan smiled. "I don't suppose you'd consider having dinner with me some night? I know this wonderful Italian restaurant in Lexington I think you'd love."

"I'm sorry, Evan, but I don't think it's a good idea to date clients. It makes for an awkward situation if something goes wrong."

"Then I suppose I'll have to fire you," Evan joked.

Stepping outside, Cara Lynn turned to look up into his face, "It's easy to find a dinner companion but difficult to find a good vet," she said, confidently calling his bluff. "Thanks for the champagne, Evan. Good night."

Evan sighed. "Isn't there anything I can do to convince you to snap out of this funk you're in over Davidson and let me see you, Cara?"

They stood looking into one another's eyes.

Then Cara Lynn propositioned him. "I'll gladly go to the ball with you. No, not only will I attend, but I'll act as the hostess right by your side, if you'll fire Joey."

"What?" Evan cried. He hadn't seen that one coming. "Fire Joey Gardner? What did he do to you?"

"I want to hire him. He's a great kid. My workload is becoming too much for me to handle alone. I've interviewed a handful of applicants, but no one suited me until I saw Joey in action tonight. I'd treat him well. A good salary, dental and medical insurance. He'd have a future with me."

"He has a future with me," Evan said. "He isn't always going to be a stable boy, you know. I see the makings of a first-rate trainer in him."

"Working for a veterinarian will only help him then, don't you think?" Cara Lynn countered. "The more he knows about horses, the better."

Evan sighed. "If Joey wants to go to work for you, I won't stand in his way. But whatever he decides to do, you still have to be at my side the night of the ball, agreed?"

"Fair enough," Cara Lynn said, offering her hand so they could shake on it.

Evan grinned. "I obviously took the wrong tack with you. I had to give you my stable boy for a date. What will you take in exchange for a kiss?"

Cara Lynn stood on tiptoe and planted a kiss on his cheek. "Kisses are free. Good night, Evan."

Cara Lynn pumped up the volume on the cassette player in the Jeep as she drove. The funky beat of TLC surrounded her. She let down the windows, needing the fresh air on her face and blowing through her hair to help keep her alert.

In the four weeks since Harry handed over the reins to her, she'd been so busy she barely had time to eat or sleep, which was ruining her health but served to take her mind off Jordan.

Perhaps Carly was right and his bringing Deborah to the diner that momentous Saturday was his desperate attempt to forget her—but that didn't make her feel any better. He could have thrown himself into his work or taken up a hobby if work wasn't sufficient. He didn't have to date the sexiest woman in the tristate area and her sworn enemy. And if he was truly in love with her, as Carly suspected, why didn't he pursue her? Wasn't that what normally happened in a love affair? Love affair. Was it really an affair of the heart or a one-night stand? Her heart was involved, but was his?

Suddenly as she took the curve in the road, the Jeep started making a strange gurgling noise. She glanced down at the dashboard. The fuel indicator flashed red. The car began to lose speed. She was fortunate to be able to coast to the soft shoulder of the dark country road before the engine came to a complete halt.

Out of gas. She'd laugh if she didn't feel like crying. She was becoming absentminded about the small things like filling the gas tank of her car. If it were physically possible, she'd kick herself.

After getting the flashlight and her wallet from the glove compartment, she locked the doors and set out for home on foot. She should have listened to her father when he'd advised her to have a cellular phone put in her car. It wasn't that she hadn't heard him, she simply hadn't had the time to comply.

She estimated that she was about four miles from home. Four miles was no great distance for her when she was well rested. However, in her present state, she was dreading the long trek.

This was a first for her. Ordinarily she was diligent about car maintenance. What was she turning into, a workaholic whose mind was solely on her career and oblivious to everything else? This was a wake-up call, an occurrence in her life telling her to slow down and pay attention to the details.

"The trouble with you, Cara Lynn, is you're scared of life," she said, berating herself. "You could be having a nice romantic rendezvous with Evan if you hadn't chickened out. He would've probably rolled out the red carpet if you'd shown some interest. But no, because you're in love with a man who has already forgotten you, you run away from one who is clearly taken with you. You need your head examined. Make an appointment Monday morning."

She wondered where Jordan was at this moment. Plying

Deborah Sanford with wine, not that she needed any encouragement. Or Deborah feeding him strawberries dipped in chocolate. Her imagination was constantly torturing her.

Lightning zigzagged across the night sky, and faint rumblings could be heard in the distance, then tentative raindrops fell to the earth. Cara Lynn pulled her jacket close around her and picked up her pace. The sprinkle turned into a downpour, and Cara Lynn hoped she wouldn't catch pneumonia.

She was already approximately a mile from the Jeep. Should she turn around and head for the relative safety and dryness of her car? That question was answered for her when the rain let up just as abruptly as it had begun. She smoothed back her hair and wrung the water out of it. She was thoroughly soaked.

She hadn't seen a car for quite some time. This road was not well traveled during the day, what did she expect at night? Her watch told her it was after midnight. In this day and age she would've been wary about accepting a ride with a stranger anyway. A little rain never hurt anyone.

About a half hour later, she spotted a pair of headlights coming toward her. She moved off the paved road to wait for the car to pass. Instead of speeding by, the car slowed down, and the driver parked it on the grassy shoulder.

When the lights were extinguished, she could see the vehicle more clearly. Jordan's Range Rover.

Jordan got out of the car and began walking toward her. "Cara, is that you?"

"Yes, your eyesight isn't failing you," Cara Lynn said. Why couldn't her rescuer have been someone else, anyone other than Jordan?

"I didn't think it was," he said dryly. "I passed your car about a mile back. Come on, I'll take you home."

Cara Lynn didn't have to be asked twice. She slipped onto the leather seat and closed the door. Thankfully, Jordan was alone. She would've died of embarrassment if Deborah had been sitting next to him, looking immaculate and smelling of expensive cologne.

Jordan reached behind him and retrieved his coat from the backseat. He handed it to her. "Here, put this on—you look chilled to the bone."

"I'm freezing," Cara Lynn said, grateful to him. "Thank you."

Jordan put the car in drive and turned onto the blacktop. They rode in silence for the first couple of minutes, then Jordan asked her what had happened to her car.

"I ran out of gas," Cara Lynn said, chagrined. "I've been so preoccupied with work, I forgot to fill up."

"So you felt like taking a stroll in the rain?" he said incredulously.

"It was better than spending the night in my car and having my father worry about me all night. Besides, it wasn't raining when I started walking," Cara Lynn said defensively.

"Knowing you, you were too obstinate to go back to the car when it did start up. Look at you—you look like a drowned rat."

The instant the words were out, he regretted them. Using that analogy made him recall the night she'd referred to herself as a drowned rat and how the evening had ended.

Trembling Cara Lynn turned to him. "You don't say? And I thought I was a raving beauty, what with drenched hair and soaked clothing. If I had known you were coming, I would've fixed myself up."

Jordan switched on the heater. "And on top of that, you're going to be sick."

"Thanks," Cara Lynn retorted, referring to the heater. Then, "What do you care, Davidson? Just drop me off at my father's gate, and you'll have done your good deed for the day. You won't have to suffer my presence for much longer."

"That will suit me fine," Jordan said angrily, his eyes on the road.

"Good. Now, can we ride the rest of the way in silence?"

"Oh, no, my dear. You don't get off that easily. What were you doing at this time of night anyway, leaving your lover's arms?" he said accusingly.

"No! Were you leaving yours?"

"No, I had to work late. I've been doing a lot of that lately."

"Just so you'll know," Cara Lynn said, still irritated. "I don't have, nor do I want a lover."

"Sure you do. He just doesn't want you."

"Stop the car," Cara Lynn ordered, angrily pounding on the door. "Stop the car. I'd rather die of pneumonia than take another minute of this."

Jordan slowed the car and pulled off the road. He cut the engine.

Cara Lynn reached for the door's handle, and Jordan's hand covered hers. "Don't go out there, Cara. I won't badger you anymore."

Cara Lynn withdrew her hand. Jordan's face was a couple of inches from her own. She held her breath, but it was too late—she'd inhaled his aftershave lotion.

He looked into her eyes. "Deal?"

She nodded her assent. Jordan started the car, and she retreated to her corner.

"I'm sorry," Jordan said. "I guess I still have some angry feelings left over from the last time we were alone together. We never did talk things over. You left me hanging."

"I didn't mean to hurt you, Jordan," she said, her voice low, remorseful.

"I know you didn't," Jordan said calmly. "You can't help it if you're in love with someone else. I suppose it was a good thing you left so early in the relationship. Otherwise I may have been in love with you."

That hurt more than anything he'd previously said. She knew now, without a doubt, he didn't love her. She was right to get out when she did. She had spared herself further humiliation.

She pulled the coat closer around her, feeling colder than ever.

Five minutes later, she was happy to see the lights of the house and barn up ahead. A few more minutes. She could last that long, couldn't she?

"Since we weren't in love, being civil to each other should be a breeze," she said. Perhaps she couldn't wait. "I'll be sure to invite you to my next barbecue."

"Don't mention a barbecue—that's what got us in this mess," Jordan said, looking at her as he slowed down to turn onto the unpaved road that led to her father's ranch.

"Are you saying we can't be friends?" Cara Lynn innocently asked.

Jordan stopped the car in the driveway. The porch light gave off enough illumination for them to see each other clearly.

"Friends?" he said, a pensive expression on his face. "I don't think I can be your friend, Cara. I can't even be near you without wanting you. Maybe in a hundred years we can be friends."

He held her gaze like a magnet. Cara Lynn's heart accelerated at his admission of longing.

"But you said you weren't in love with me," she said. Hope—a thing with wings—prepared to take flight at the first sign of acquiescence.

"You didn't give us time for that, Cara. What I feel for you is like an addiction. I want to hold you, feel your heart beat against mine. Run my fingers through your hair. I remember every detail about that night, Cara. Images of you play over and over in my mind. I miss you."

Suddenly she didn't feel cold any longer.

"I've missed you," she said, her voice husky.

She reached up to touch his cheek and Jordan bent his head to kiss her. Her arms went around his neck and they kissed hungrily. His big hands were on her back, sending a river of fire along her spine.

He kissed her neck, her face, the tip of her nose. Cara Lynn was drowning in a sea of conflicting emotions. The intense loneliness she'd previously suffered from was instantly gone when he touched her.

"I need you, Cara. I don't give a damn about the other man. He was a fool for letting you go. I keep reliving that night, wondering what it was I did that upset you so much. Whatever I did, I'm sorry, my love. Say you'll come back to me."

"When? Where?" Cara Lynn breathed.

"Tomorrow night. My place. I'll make dinner for you, and this time you'll stay long enough to eat it," he said, his hand at the small of her back, pressing her closer to him.

"And then?" Cara Lynn said.

"And then it's up to you, doe-eyes," Jordan answered, gently kissing her generous mouth.

"You wouldn't think I'm using you until I win the man I'm supposedly in love with?"

Sighing, Jordan said, "Don't make this harder than it has to be, Cara. I miss you. You miss me. Do we have to make it something cheap and sordid?"

"That's what it would be, Jordan. You still don't believe me—therefore I'd be using you and you'd be using me. We're drawn to one another. There's no denying that. But until you can truthfully say you believe me when I say there is no one else in my life, we can't have anything between us. You want to give me part of you. I don't want part of you. I'm sorry I forced the issue. Something happens when a couple makes love. I suppose that's why it's called *making* love. It's a mistake to become intimate when feelings haven't reached that stage yet."

"It wasn't a mistake, Cara. Badly timed, yes. But we both wanted it. The problem was, you were already in love with someone else so there was no room left for you and me."

"You won't give up your obsession with my alleged lover, will you?" Cara Lynn said, voice rising.

"Please, Cara," Jordan implored. "Stop denying it. Until you can face reality, you're right, we can't have anything between us."

"I'm not the one avoiding reality," Cara Lynn said accusingly.

"If you're in love with him, you're involved with him. It's as simple as that."

"The man I'm in love with is a stubborn, opinionated, chauvinist who wouldn't recognize love if it fell on his thick head," Cara Lynn said angrily.

"You can't possibly be in love with someone like that," Jordan ridiculed.

"God help me, I am."

"You can really pick 'em," Jordan said, his eyes narrowed.

"I sure can," Cara Lynn snapped, throwing his coat at him.

She went to open the door and Jordan prevented her, forcefully pulling her into his arms and kissing her roughly. He wasn't able to hold on to his angry frame of mind—the feel of her body, the softness of her mouth, the taste of her skin all worked to arouse him. He wanted her, and there was nothing he could do about it.

He released her, and Cara Lynn hurriedly opened the car door and jumped down out of the cab, slamming the door.

"Thanks for the lift, you're a godsend," she spat out.

"Don't mention it," he called after her. "See you tomorrow night. I'll help you expend some of that pent-up aggression."

"In your dreams!"

"You always are, sweetheart."

She ran up the steps of the house, not looking back at him. Jordan sped out of the driveway, the car's tires throwing gravel in every direction.

Thirteen

Evan was relishing the sight of Cara Lynn astride Moon Dancer, the palomino he'd recently bought for her at an auction in Lexington. She rode a few feet ahead of him. It was a lovely Friday afternoon, and neither of them could think of a better way of spending it than riding.

He coaxed the stallion he was riding alongside the palomino. "You're smiling," he said.

Cara Lynn's smile broadened. "He's wonderful. I wish I could take him home with me."

She patted the palomino's muscular neck with her gloved hand. "He's so intelligent. It's like he knows what I want him to do before I give him a direction."

Grinning, Evan said, "He's yours."

"Did you say he's mine?" Cara Lynn asked, sure she'd heard him wrong.

"He's a belated birthday present," Evan replied.

"My birthday isn't until August," Cara Lynn told him, laughing.

"Then he's an early gift," Evan said, refusing to be outdone.

He tapped the stallion's right flank, and the magnificent black beast took off at a gallop. Flustered, Cara Lynn followed on the palomino.

After a few minutes Evan slowed the pace of the stallion

and halted him underneath a copse of young oak trees. He dismounted and waited for Cara Lynn to catch up.

When she joined him, he went to her and helped her down off the palomino. His arms lingered about her waist as their eyes met.

Cara Lynn took a moment to catch her breath. "He's a gorgeous animal, Evan, but I can't accept him."

Evan's eyes reflected his disappointment. "Why not?"

"Because if I did, I'd be giving you an erroneous message. I like you, Evan, but I'm not attracted to you the way a woman should be attracted to a man who gives her extravagant gifts."

Evan gently stroked her cheek. "Cara, I'm falling in love with you. Don't you feel anything for me?"

Her eyes searched his face. Yes, she felt something for him. She was empathetic toward him. She knew how frustrating it was to love someone who didn't love you in return.

"It's Davidson," Evan said angrily. Turning away from her, he said, "I'll be happy when he's gone—lock, stock, and barrel—back to Louisville—no, Maine. Maine would be even better."

Facing her again, his eyes flashed with amusement. "He's put his property on the market. Did you know that? My realtor told me about it. She thought I might be interested in buying it. And I might do it, just to get the satisfaction of tearing it down brick by brick."

Cara Lynn felt like her heart was in a vise. Jordan, gone forever? "When did she tell you this?"

"Yesterday," Evan said dismissively. "What difference does it make?"

It made all the difference in the world to her. She had no time to waste, she had to go to Jordan.

Evan must have sensed her thoughts. Grabbing her by the shoulders and making her face him, he said, "The man has caused you nothing but pain. Give me a chance, Cara, and I'll make you happy. I promise you. And I never break my promises."

Cara Lynn stared at him. "Why, Evan? Why do you want me? Aside from our love for horses, what do we have in common?"

"We have more in common than you think, Cara. My mother was one-quarter African. Her mother was half Nigerian. She met her husband, an American Jew, while attending university in New York City."

"No one around here knew?" Cara Lynn felt compelled to ask.

Evan laughed. "Only my parents' closest friends and relatives. You know the history of slavery in America. Practically all of us have a person of a different race in our family tree. Even before my father, who was Irish, married Mother, he had some African blood. He would have married her even if he didn't. He adored her."

Cara Lynn wasn't exactly stunned by his revelation. It would explain his swarthy good looks. And she, like plenty of African Americans, also had people of a different race in her family.

On her mother's side her great-great-grandfather was a Frenchman. On her father's side of the family, her grandmother was half Cherokee. So she certainly identified with him.

"My grandmother is a smart, lovely woman—she's still living. I visit her several times a year," Evan continued. "So does my attraction to you seem so out of place?"

Smiling at him, Cara Lynn sighed. "It wasn't your race that prevented me from being drawn to you, Evan. By the time we met, I was already involved with Jordan. I've been honest with you. I can't get Jordan off my mind. I feel like I'm going through withdrawal. And knowing how you feel about me makes me feel even worse. I should go. I'm only hurting you by being with you."

Shaking his head, Evan said, "Let's not go through this

again. I don't care if my heart breaks in two each time I see you, I'd rather be with you than without you. Don't even think about not attending the ball with me, Cara. You gave me your word."

"I'll be there," Cara Lynn said. "I don't intend to go back on my word."

Evan held her in his arms, breathing in her heady essence, "Good. As for Davidson, give it time. His image will fade. We could have everything together, Cara. Love, a real home, a house full of children, a legacy to leave behind. I want it all—and that includes you."

Jordan frowned as he applied paint to canvas. Yes, that was right, it was the sensuous curve her mouth took when she gave him just a hint of a smile. Her come-hither challenge, as if he needed to be coaxed to kiss her.

He finished and stepped back to examine his work. He'd painted her from memory as he'd done the other three, no, four canvases, since their split twenty-eight days ago. In this painting she was standing with the sun behind her, framed in its golden light, just as she had been the first moment he'd seen her.

He sighed. Damned if he was going to spend the rest of his life painting her from memory as some form of therapy. He had to do something to get her back. But the only thing he could think of to do was to lie to her and tell her he believed her when she said the mystery man was a figment of her imagination. He'd already tried that, and she'd seen right through him.

The only thing left was to go to her and tell her he didn't care if she was in love with another man—he could live with it. That wasn't true, either. He could not share her loyalties. He could not bear to be of secondary importance in her heart. There was the matter of pride to consider. What kind of man would he be if he took a backseat to a "might-have-been"?

The doorbell rang. He ran downstairs to answer the door, hoping the caller was Cara Lynn.

Evan Fitzgerald stood on the other side of the door, wearing a pair of dark glasses and a grim expression.

"What the hell do you want?"

"I have a proposition for you," Evan said, removing his glasses.

Preparing to close the door, Jordan said, "I don't discuss business on my day off, and especially not with someone I have no regard for."

Evan quickly stepped into the foyer. "I'd like to buy this house and the surrounding property. Name your price."

Jordan laughed shortly. "You don't have enough money, Fitzgerald. What do you want it for, a trinket for Cara? Believe me, you don't want to give her this house, not if you want her to forget me."

Evan got his meaning. "So you've made a few memories here. All Cara needs is a little time—she'll be fine without you. I'll see to that."

Looking around him, he smiled. "You've got good taste, Davidson. I'll give you that much. In houses and in women."

"Neither of which you'll ever possess," Jordan said, teeth clenched.

"The house, perhaps not. The woman . . . well, that's debatable. It's true, she's having trouble getting you out of her system—but like a bad case of the flu. Her immune system will kick in and flush you out, leaving her a bit weak, disoriented, but very much alive and well."

"And that's where you come in," Jordan said. "While she's still weak and in need of consolation. It'll never happen. Cara will come back to me."

"Don't hold your breath."

"If you leave now, you stand the chance of getting out

without any broken bones," Jordan warned him. "Cara isn't here to save you this time."

"Come now," Evan said, looking smug. "Let's handle this like gentlemen, shall we? You didn't like my first offer. Perhaps you'll be more receptive to my second. I want you to come to the ball tomorrow night. I'd like Cara to see the both of us in the same setting, under the same circumstances. You get her alone, plead your case. It will be a romantic evening. Perfect for a proposal. If she accepts, I'll step aside—but if she does not, you step aside. You sell this place and ride off into the sunset. A perfect solution, *n'est-ce pas?*"

Jordan glared at him. "Everything is a business deal with you, Fitzgerald. When I propose to Cara, I will choose the time and the place and they will not be per your instructions. Get the hell out of my house."

Jordan turned to go back upstairs. "You know where the door is. Use it."

Evan dogged his steps. "You dumb jackass."

Jordan faced him, and Evan threw a right cross, connecting with Jordan's jaw. "That's for hurting Cara, you son of b—"

He didn't finish the sentence because Jordan silenced him with a fist to his solar plexus, rendering him breathless.

Jordan got great satisfaction seeing him doubled over in pain. He gingerly touched his jaw. He tasted blood, but nothing seemed broken.

Evan stood up straight, groaning. "I suppose I asked for that, but I still think we should settle this, Davidson. Why do you object to my idea so strenuously? Afraid you can't compete in my arena? Physically you could beat me to a pulp, but are you man enough to win the woman you love?"

"I'm not the one who threw the first punch," Jordan reminded him. "So don't call me a violent man. And in answer to your question, I will win Cara back. I'll see you tomorrow night. But I'll be on the lookout for any traps you've set for me, Fitzgerald."

Attempting a smile and failing due to the pain in his midsection, Evan said, "Would I come here if I had anything up my sleeve?"

"Yeah, you would," Jordan replied.

"You're far too suspicious," Evan insisted, running a hand through his hair. He was feeling more himself. "I simply want whatever is between you and Cara to be over and done with. I know I can make her happy once you're out of the picture."

"Good-bye, Fitzgerald, I've got things to do," Jordan said, brushing him off. "And sit-ups will strengthen those stomach muscles."

"I'll have my secretary phone you with the name of my dentist," Evan shot back.

Evan saw himself out, and Jordan returned to his painting.

Not ten minutes later the doorbell rang again. Irritated by the interruption and half expecting the caller to be Evan, Jordan yanked the door open, his face a mass of frowns.

Cara Lynn completely lost her nerve when she saw his expression. "I . . . I um—"

Jordan laughed. "I thought you were someone else."

She visibly relaxed. "Thank goodness, I was about to tuck my tail in and run."

Noticing the paint stains on his overalls, she apologized for taking him away from his work. "I can come back another time," she said timidly.

Jordan's pulse was thundering in his ears. It took all his willpower not to pull her into his arms.

Smiling at her, he said, "It's all right, Cara. I was going to take a break anyway. I'm pleased to see you. I wanted to apologize for the way I acted the night of the rainstorm."

"You don't need to apologize. I was as much at fault as you were. I was already in a rotten mood when you came along. And on top of that, I was embarrassed to have to be rescued. I felt foolish running out of gas."

"I haven't been myself lately either," Jordan told her. "Are you going to stand out there all day?"

Cara Lynn stepped inside. She got a good look at his face as she moved closer to him. "My God, what happened to your face?"

Jordan was warmed by her concern. "Don't look like that, it's only slightly swollen."

Cara Lynn gently touched his cheek. "You should put ice on that. I'll get some."

She began walking toward the kitchen.

"Cara, that isn't necessary," Jordan said right behind her.

"Why? Have you done it already?"

"No, but—"

"I didn't think so."

She got a dish towel out of one of the drawers, put ice from the freezer in the center of it, and wrapped the towel around the ice.

"Sit down," she said, pointing to a chair.

Jordan sat.

She held the ice-filled towel on the swollen area. "How have you been since the last time we spoke?"

"Keeping busy," Jordan said, his words unclear because of the compress on his jaw. "I wanted to know what you've heard from the Baileys since they moved back to Arizona. How's she doing?"

"I spoke to her this morning. She's enjoying her family. Her parents are happy to have her back. She sounds strong. Maybe the change will be good for her."

Jordan reached up and grasped the hand she was holding the towel with. "How've you been?"

Her voice sounded as though she was fighting back tears when she, spoke. "I um—" clearing her throat "—I've been staying busy so that I don't have to think about everything that's going on in my life."

Then it occurred to her how Jordan had sustained his injury.

"This doesn't have anything to do with Evan, does it? We went riding this afternoon. He told me his realtor informed him you were thinking of selling this place. By the time we got back to the house, he was in a weird mood, said he had to go somewhere, then he tore out of there like a crazy man. He came over here, didn't he?"

"Don't worry, I haven't killed him and stashed his body," Jordan said dryly.

"I'm not worried about that," Cara Lynn said, putting the towel down on the tabletop. "Is it true?"

"About my putting the house up for sale? Yes, I'm done with the remodeling and it's much too big for me, alone."

Going around to look him in the face, Cara Lynn said, "I thought you loved this house."

"I like the house, Cara. You're the one who's in love with this place. Why don't you take it?"

Upset, Cara Lynn shook her head. "I couldn't live here."

"It would be perfect for you," Jordan said, painting a picture for her. "You could turn the barn into a stable for horses. And there's plenty of room for your clinic."

"Where will you go?" Cara Lynn asked, not listening to him.

"Louisville for the time being, but I'm seriously thinking of selling my business and moving out of state."

Cara Lynn scrutinized him to see if he was serious. He appeared so. "Why would you do that? I thought your business was doing great in Louisville."

"It is. My pockets are fat, but I need a change."

"What you mean is, you need to get away from me."

Jordan got to his feet. Arms crossed at his chest, he looked into her face. "Am I supposed to stick around here waiting for you to make up your mind about us?"

"I'm not the reason we're apart. You don't trust me. You

think I used you for sex. If sex was all I wanted from you, I'd still be with you, playing the game."

"You have a point there, Cara. But tell me one thing. If the other man doesn't exist, why did you bring him up?"

"I told you. It was to cover something else I wasn't prepared to tell you then."

"Are you prepared to tell me now?" His eyes were relentless.

"I don't believe you're ready to hear it."

"Try me." Jordan placed his hand on her shoulder reassuringly.

She couldn't do it. Her stomach muscles constricted painfully. Her mouth was dry.

"Tell me, Cara," Jordan pleaded with her, his voice rising.

"I can't," Cara Lynn cried. "You'll just have to trust me, Jordan. I don't want anyone else. There is no one else. Why can't you simply trust that I'm telling you the truth?"

Jordan angrily turned away. "How can I trust you when you can't confide in me, Cara?"

"I have confided in you. I'm telling you now, I don't want you to go. That's why I came to see you. Don't go away." She was the one pleading now.

"Maybe I should get out while I can," Jordan said, his eyes cold. "For a woman who didn't even date in high school, you have a devastating effect on men. Fitzgerald wants you so badly that he'd give me anything for this property in order to get me out of the way. Men fall for you, Cara—but what do you do for them? Do you love them in return? Keith hurt you. Was there ever a chance for Bill? Maybe you've turned off your emotions to guard against being hurt again. You say I don't trust you. The fact is, you don't trust me. You don't trust any man. If you did, you'd let down your guard and let me in."

Cara Lynn's eyes welled with unshed tears. She wanted to tell him he was wrong about her. She certainly was not devoid of emotion. If she were, his words would not feel like razor-sharp knives piercing her gut.

She opened her mouth to say the words, but clamped it shut. There was only one thing left to do. She fled.

Seeing the hurt in Cara Lynn's eyes, Jordan knew he'd gone too far, but there was no turning back. Either Cara Lynn was going to face up to her fears and come to him free of them, or he really was going to have to sell the house and move away.

"What do you think of this?" Carly asked, holding up a frothy white creation that fell to her ankles.

"Too busy," Cara Lynn said. "And you should wear something short, show off your legs."

They were in an exclusive dress shop in downtown Lexington. They'd been in the store about ten minutes, and the saleswoman hadn't taken her eyes off them once.

"Do you suppose she actually thinks we're going to stuff dresses down our jeans?" Carly said. "This really ticks me off. Here we are patronizing her shop, and she's watching us like we're criminals."

"We'll go someplace else," Cara Lynn suggested.

"I don't want to go someplace else," Carly said. "I like the clothes in this shop."

"Then ignore her."

"Fine," Carly said, cutting her eyes in the woman's direction. "Are you still going to wear that cream-colored satin gown with the train?"

"That's right," Cara Lynn confirmed.

"What do you want to do, give Evan a heart attack?"

"I feel like cutting loose. I'm tired of worrying about whether Jordan and I are going to be together or not. Now that I know how he really feels about me, that I'm some kind of femme fatale, a woman who delights in breaking the hearts of unsuspecting males, I can get on with the program."

"Bitterness doesn't suit you," Carly said with a laugh. "Do you really believe that's what he meant?"

"What do you think he meant?"

Pulling her attention away from the dresses and on to Cara Lynn, Carly said, "I think your heart is too involved for you to see your situation clearly. Jordan recognizes your fear of commitment for what it is: a reflex action you've developed over the years to protect yourself. He wants you to stop being afraid and let him love you."

"No. What he wants is to dictate how I should behave. It's all a power struggle. If it isn't his way, it's no way."

"You're wrong. Jordan loves you," Carly said, annoyed by her friend's pessimism.

"If he does, he has a peculiar way of showing it," Cara Lynn said, remembering his last words to her.

"Can I help you, ladies?" The saleswoman had appeared silently, seemingly out of nowhere.

"Yes," Carly said. "I'd like to see this in a size six."

She handed the woman a truly gauche red dress. The woman smiled as all good saleswomen do when the customer's choice leaves a lot to be desired. "Of course, I'll only be a moment."

"You hate red," Cara Lynn said when the woman was out of earshot.

"It'll keep her out of our hair for a while. I just thought of a solution to your problem. All you have to do is go to Jordan and tell him you love him. You think you can do that?"

"That's the easiest way to make him head for the hills."

"Your logic escapes me," Carly said, looking heavenward for divine help. "I know what you're thinking. You're remembering that when you confessed to Keith that you loved him, the next thing you knew, he'd married Diana. But Jordan isn't Keith. He's a good man, and if you keep putting up roadblocks, you're going to lose possibly the best thing that ever happened to you."

"Don't you think I know that?" Cara Lynn said sadly.

Carly stood right in front of Cara Lynn, looking up into her face. She sighed. "No, I don't think you know it. Not really. You don't realize that life is a risk—and if you're not willing to risk anything, you're not likely to gain anything worthwhile, either. Jordan is yours for the taking, but first you've got to sacrifice a little of yourself. Tell him you love him. I truly believe that's all he wants from you. Say the words, Cara Lynn."

"I'm sorry, but we don't have this particular style in your size," the saleswoman said upon her return.

"Great, honey, because I've decided I hate that dress," Carly said, holding up her final selection. "This one is in my size. Show me your dressing room."

Carly left with the saleswoman, and Cara Lynn sat down on one of the upholstered chairs provided for customers.

An attractive African American woman in her early thirties walked past her, saying a polite hello.

Cara Lynn smiled at her, "Hi, how are you?"

"Fine, thank you," the woman replied.

Cara Lynn knew she'd seen the young woman before. She was of average height, trim, with shoulder-length auburn hair which she wore in a pageboy cut. She had high cheekbones, a well-shaped nose, and dark, almond-shaped eyes.

"Don't I know you?" Cara Lynn said, smiling.

"You might if you watch Channel Four News. I'm Susan Waters. I'm an anchor with the station."

"That's where I've seen you before," Cara Lynn said, delighted to meet her. She stood and offered Susan her hand.

"I'm Cara Lynn Garrett. I'm a veterinarian."

"You don't say," Susan said easily. "That's fascinating. I don't know many black women vets. Actually you're the only one I've ever met."

"Well, you're the only anchorperson I've ever met, so we're even," Cara Lynn replied. They shook hands.

Carly came out of the dressing room wearing a royal blue gown that fit her petite body perfectly. It was short and sleeveless with a low-cut bodice.

She turned around excitedly. "Would Eddie die, or what?" Then she noticed Susan. "Cara Lynn. Do you know who this is?"

"Susan Waters," Cara Lynn said, zipping the dress for her.

"You're Susan Waters," Carly gushed. "What are you doing here—picking out a dress for a hot date?"

Susan laughed. "I wish. I'm here to find a dress to wear on an assignment. Since I'm the new kid on the block, they've got me covering some dorky country dance in a small town near here. It's called—now get this—the Horsemen's Ball."

Cara Lynn and Carly looked at each other and burst out laughing.

"It isn't that funny," Susan said, confused.

"We're attending that dorky country dance tonight," Cara Lynn explained.

"Horses, veterinarian." Susan looked embarrassed as she made the connection. "I really put my foot in it, didn't I?"

"Forget it," Carly said. "We've called it worse things than that."

Her tone became conspiratorial as she walked over to Susan and took her by the arm. "Tell me, Susan—I'm Carly Needham, by the way—does Douglas Grant wear a toupee? I mean the man's hair never moves. It's either a rug or he's singlehandedly destroying the ozone layer."

Susan laughed delightedly. "I've been asking myself the same question. If I ever get up the nerve to ask, I'll let you know."

* * *

On the drive back to Shelbyville, Carly wanted to know Cara Lynn's impression of Susan.

"She seems nice. Why do you ask?"

"I felt sorry for her," Carly said. "Three thousand miles from home. No friends, no family. I can't imagine that kind of life."

"That's because you've never been without friends or family," Cara Lynn said, watching her speed. "You're related to half the population of Shelbyville, and you've been married since you were a child."

Carly laughed. "I was pretty mature for eighteen. And unlike some people who bemoan their lot in life, I enjoy every minute of mine."

"Is that a sneaky crack at me?" Cara Lynn said, smiling.

"If the crack fits."

"I do not complain about my life," Cara Lynn emphatically stated.

"I'm your best friend, so I can be brutally honest with you. It's rule number two thirty-five in the best friend code book. You have a wonderful, almost charmed, life. A little screwed up at the moment but basically a wonderful life. I wish you could relax and enjoy it more."

"Having a man in one's life is not a prerequisite to happiness," Cara Lynn said stiffly, sensing what her friend was getting at.

"I would like to see you happy with a man. Eddie is my friend, my helpmate, my lover—I feel like I'm involved in an eleven-year love affair. All the intrigue and forbidden passion, it's still there. Don't let anyone tell you that romance dies once that wedding ring gets on your finger. It only dies if you forget to fan the embers."

Briefly glancing at Carly, Cara Lynn grinned. "I don't think I've ever heard you expound on the advantages of marriage so eloquently. I know marriage can be wonderful, and I want all that someday."

"Your someday could be next week, tonight even—"

"I don't want to talk about Jordan," Cara Lynn said bluntly.

"He hurt you because he told you the truth. The truth isn't easy to face. We lie to each other so much that we get used to it, and that's a shame. The mere fact that he had the courage to tell you what was on his mind proves he loves you. I swear, Cara Lynn, if you can't see that, you're not as smart as I thought you were."

"I know I have a problem, Carly. I'm afraid I've allowed it to go on for so long that it's become a part of me," Cara Lynn cried, asking for her friend's help.

"The first step in solving any problem is recognizing you have one. You're halfway there. Now, what are you going to do about it?"

"Try again. This time I'll make him listen."

"And you won't run away?"

"I'll give it my all."

"Good enough," Carly said with a sigh of relief. "Hey, if he comes to the ball tonight and sees you in that dress, you might not have to say a word."

"What are you trying to say, Peter? Out with it. Are you going to be my escort tonight or not?"

"Sorry, Deborah—but Jackie's back from her trip. You know the rules. I can't be anywhere near you when she's in town."

"It's four hours before the ball begins. What am I supposed to do?"

"Consult your little black book, sweetheart. I'm sure you can come up with someone."

"You creep. You could've given me more notice," Deborah said, very upset.

"Hey, baby, I didn't have to call."

"Don't bother calling in the future."

Deborah slammed down the receiver and lay back on her

bed. She should have known she couldn't depend on Peter Tanner. A man who would cheat on his fiancee was not innately reliable. But then she always entered a relationship with her eyes open. The only reason she'd asked him was because he was prominent in the community. He owned the hardware store downtown. By Shelbyville standards, he was the most eligible bachelor in town next to Jordan Davidson and Evan Fitzgerald.

It didn't matter to her that he'd been engaged to Jacqueline Bradley for the last two years. After all, she wasn't twisting his arm. She was doing Jackie a favor. Served Peter right if Jackie heard about his extracurricular activities. Jackie could save herself the hassle of a nasty divorce five years down the line.

She wished Bobby wasn't in Anchorage. Bobby had never let her down. Which made her feel guilty for dating other men in his absence. But was she fool enough to believe Bobby wasn't seeing some Alaskan woman? Get real. He *was* a man. And from all indications, Bobby wouldn't be coming home anytime soon. Was she supposed to embrace celibacy?

She laughed aloud. That was something Miss Cara Lynn Garrett would do in her man's absence. If she ever got a man. The girl was pitiful. She'd heard her relationship with Jordan was over before it had begun properly. Even with everything Cara Lynn had going for her, she could not hang on to a man. She wasn't all that!

"Deborah! Do you have to play that stereo so loudly?"

Deborah grudgingly got up and turned the volume down. "Sorry, Grandma."

She caught her reflection in the mirror as she passed the bureau. She looked at herself critically, as always. Her eyes, though nice, were spaced too wide apart. Her nose was too long. Her mouth, too thin. She needed more fullness in order to maintain a sexy pout.

She pursed her lips. Not bad altogether. Her body, though,

she knew to be drop-dead gorgeous. Her face was something she couldn't change. She was afraid of cosmetic surgery. With her luck, she'd end up looking worse. However, her body she could pummel and mold into shape. She didn't put anything into her body that might put on pounds, and she exercised religiously. Step exercises three times a week at the gym and jogging the remaining days of the week. Five miles each way. Her legs were legendary.

Her grandmother, Essie Sanford, appeared in the doorway. At sixty-five, Essie was in excellent shape. She was about the same height as her granddaughter, trim from staying busy in her garden and various church activities. She wore her silver hair in a short, natural style.

"If you'd play that music a bit lower, you'd be able to hear the doorbell, and I wouldn't have to come all the way back here to tell you you have a visitor."

Getting to her feet, Deborah wondered why her grandmother could never give her a message without editorializing.

She quickly pulled on a pair of shorts and a T-shirt. "I'm coming, Grandma. Who is it?"

"That Johnson boy," Essie said, sniffing disapprovingly. "I don't know what you see in him. He can't keep a job. Here he is back from Alaska months ahead of the time he said he'd be back. Probably got fired."

Deborah had sprinted from the room before her grandmother finished complaining about Bobby.

"You're a fine pair," Essie said, getting her second wind. "He can't care anything about you. If he did, he wouldn't have run off up north. And going up north wasn't enough for him, he had to go clear to Alaska. If you put that boy's brain in a bird's head, it would fly backward."

Deborah didn't stop running until she was in Bobby's arms.

"Bobby, Bobby!"

"Oh, baby, you are a sight for sore eyes," Bobby said, enfolding her in his two strong arms.

They kissed.

Essie came into the room, clearing her throat loudly.

Deborah and Bobby parted.

"Grandma, could we have a little privacy, please? It's been a long time since we were together."

"That's what marriage is for," Essie said, sitting down on the couch and propping her feet up on the coffee table. "You get to live in your own home and enjoy your fill of privacy."

"She's right," Bobby said, grinning down into Deborah's frowning face. "Marry me, baby."

Deborah looked startled. "You want to marry me?"

Pulling her back into his arms, Bobby hugged her tightly.

"I love you, Deb. I've loved you for years. And while I was up in Alaska, I came to the conclusion that I was going to ask you to be my wife."

Bobby's boyish, open face gave Deborah such a feeling of hopefulness, her spirits soared.

Her vision was blurred by tears. She took a deep breath. She *did* love him. It took an eight-month separation for her to come to that realization. Bobby, who had been her standby for more years than they cared to remember. Since their senior year in high school. All the years she was trying to self-destruct, he was like a guardian angel on her shoulder, telling her she was special and a worthwhile person.

When no one else believed in her, Bobby did. When she didn't even believe in herself, Bobby did.

"I'm not good enough for you, Bobby. You deserve someone much better than I am," Deborah said regrettably.

Bobby caught her by the shoulders and made her face him. "Listen, Deb, I don't want to hear that kind of talk from you anymore. I love you and I don't care about the past—"

"You should care," Essie interjected, sitting up on the couch.

"I mean this with all due respect, Mrs. Sanford," Bobby said, his dark eyes determined. "But please stay out of this."

Essie's mouth dropped open with shock. She sat quietly, however.

"I have watched you become what your grandmother intended for you to become: an embittered, unhappy woman," Bobby said with conviction. "That's all she knows, so that was all she had to give you. But, Deb, that isn't all you are. You're also smart and loving and giving. Look at the way you run your dress shop. That takes ingenuity and flair, baby, two things you have plenty of. And the last three years you've been a Big Sister to Karen. That means a lot, Deb. Because of you, Karen will be going to college this year."

Tears were streaming down Deborah's face. "Bobby, I've been unfaithful to you."

His gaze steady, Bobby said, "I know that, Deb."

"Then why? Why would you want to take a chance on me?"

"Because I believe you're ready to start believing in yourself, Deborah Sanford."

Deborah threw her arms around Bobby's neck. Her tears wet his collar. She couldn't speak for her sobbing. Each teardrop was like an individual pound of pain being purged from her.

Essie stood. She wasn't about to let a man who'd probably never amount to anything tell her how to behave in her own house.

"Nobody talks to me like that under my roof, Bobby Johnson. Get out of my house. Get out before I call the police."

Sighing and shaking her head in regret, Deborah pushed out of Bobby's arms and turned to her grandmother. "Oh, Grandma. You hate to see anyone happy, don't you? Bobby's right. You have never had a kind word for me. You resented me from the start, didn't you? Your teenaged daughter got pregnant by a traveling musician, had me, and left me in your care. Don't you think I've wanted to know if she's living or dead all these years—"

"I thought your mother was dead," Bobby said, confused.

"No, that's just a story Grandma made up to hide her shame. For someone who loves to gossip, she hates to be gossiped about, so when my mother ran away after having me, Grandma told everyone she'd died in a car accident in Louisiana where she'd gone to be with her musician husband, which was another lie. My parents were never married."

"How can you stand there and talk about family business in front of him?" Essie said angrily, waving her arms.

"Family business—I'm so sick and tired of family business. Now, here's something *you* aren't even aware of yet, Grandma. Grandpa left this house to *me* in his will. He made me promise to take care of you until your death. I made that promise out of respect for him because, frankly, I was going to leave Shelbyville after he died six years ago. But since he was the only person, besides Bobby, who ever loved me, I stayed."

"Liar!" Essie screamed. "You're no better than that two-bit horn player who fathered you."

"You're too stubborn to learn to read, I figured you'd never find out," Deborah explained, her fury abated.

She turned her back on her grandmother, and the most peaceful expression came over her face as she smiled at Bobby.

"Yes, Robert Wilson Johnson, I'll marry you."

Bobby hugged her. "I've never loved you more than I do right now, Deb. Go on, pack a few things. We're leaving."

Deborah didn't hesitate any longer. She went to her bedroom and hastily packed her suitcase, being sure to add her evening wear. She was going to that ball tonight, she didn't care what it took. She had an old score to settle with Cara Lynn Garrett.

When she got back to the living room, her grandmother was sitting on the couch, angrily mumbling to herself. Bobby stood like a sentinel, next to the door, waiting for her.

She approached her grandmother. "I do care what happens to you, Grandma. I don't want to leave here with bad feelings between us. I don't hold any hatred for you in my heart. I know you thought you were doing what was best for me. Maybe your mother, somebody, treated you the same way when you were growing up. But it's got to stop somewhere, and I figure now's as good a time as any. This house is yours as long as you want to stay here. And when Bobby and I set a date, I'll let you know. I hope you'll come to our wedding."

Essie kept her eyes on the television screen.

"Go on and leave," she said, her voice trembling. "Leave your poor grandma who worked her fingers to the bone to make sure you were fed and clothed, got a decent education. If I said cruel, hurtful things to you, it was because I wanted you to be better than your mother and amount to something in this world."

"What you failed to see, Grandma, is I turned out all right. I graduated from college with a 4.0 average, and I run a successful business, and still—for the longest time—I thought of myself as dirt. I thought I didn't deserve to be happy. For the life of me, I couldn't figure out why. Well, now I know, and I'm going to change my life. I know it isn't going to be easy, but nothing in my life has ever been easy. Good-bye, Grandma. I'll check up on you in a few days."

Deborah turned to Bobby. Bobby opened the front door for her. He took her suitcase and placed an arm about her shoulders.

"Everything's going to be all right," he said reassuringly.

Essie refused to watch her go. "Don't bother checking up on me, you Judas. I'll be fine without you. I never needed you, you're the one who needs me. You'll be back. That boy can't take care of you. He can't take care of himself."

"Good night, Mrs. Sanford," Bobby said cheerfully as he shut the door behind them.

They stood on the porch for a few moments, gazing at one another.

"You won't regret it, Deb," Bobby solemnly promised.

"I know that, Bobby," Deborah told him, unable to stop smiling. "You've been the best thing in my life for a long time."

He firmly grasped her by the hand. "Come on, girl. We've got a lot of catching up to do."

They ran down the steps of the porch like two small children, happy, content, ignorant of what the future held but not caring. They had each other.

"How would you like to go to a dance tonight, Bobby?"

"We'll go wherever you want to, babe. My time is yours."

Fourteen

Mavis grimaced at her reflection in the full-length mirror. Basic black covered a multitude of flaws. The sequined dress had a ballet neckline and quarter sleeves, fell to her ankles, and was split up the sides to her knees. Stylish, sophisticated, classy. All words she would never have attributed to herself two years ago. Pre-Frank. Pre-love. Prehistoric in her estimation.

Everything was new to her. She felt like something wonderful was going to happen every day of her life. For years she thought she was desensitized to deep emotions. Being the wife of a blatant adulterer had made her develop a thick hide. Little did she know, she possessed a hidden waterfall of feelings. She was passionate about her work, passionately interested in her friends and family. Passionate about Frank.

Recently she had more to be passionate about. She'd decided to adopt a fourteen-year-old girl.

She was called Beany. Her actual name was Benina, but she hated it—so when a friend dubbed her Beany, the name had stuck. Beany came into Mavis's cafe one afternoon with a group of ninth graders, a rowdy bunch. When the noise spilling from their booth began to drown out the jukebox, Mavis had gone over and told them to quiet down or hit the sidewalk.

As she was walking away, she overheard Beany say, "Who's that mean ole witch?"

One of the boys, Terrell Jacobson, told her in no uncertain terms. "Girl, you'd better watch your mouth. Miss Mavis don't play."

"I ain't afraid of her," Beany had replied confidently.

"That's 'cause you ain't got sense enough to be. Miss Mavis has been running this place a long time, and everybody loves her."

That made Mavis tear up. She left them to their burgers and fries and didn't bother them when they started getting loud all over again.

The next week Beany was back and as pugnacious as before. Mavis watched her as she got into a shouting match with another girl. Before it could turn into a physical fight, Mavis went over to their booth and pointing at Beany said, "You, up. I'd like a word with you."

A chorus of uh ohs arose from her chums. Beany obeyed, which surprised Mavis. She could have sworn Beany was a hard case to the core.

Mavis took her into the kitchen, where they faced each other.

"What's your name, little miss?"

"Beany," she said, lips pursed.

"Beany? What kind of name is that? Your given name, child."

Beany huffed. "Benina Russell."

Shaking her head, Mavis said, "You related to Polly and Burton Russell?"

"No. I live with the Morrisons."

"You live with them, but you aren't related to them?"

Beany stared at Mavis. "How many questions are you going to ask, lady?"

"As many as I need to," Mavis said sharply. "Well?"

"The state pays them to allow me to live with them," Beany said, frowning.

"Then you're a foster child."

"I ain't no foster child," Beany promptly denied. "I have parents. I'm going back to live with them real soon."

"Where are they?" Mavis asked, determined to get to the bottom of the mystery surrounding this child's situation.

"My dad's an international businessman, and my mom's a rock star. What's it to you, lady?"

Translation: her father was a drug dealer and her mother, a crack cocaine addict.

Mavis had been mortified, but she would never have let Beany see pity in her eyes. No one likes to be pitied.

Mavis laughed. "Think you're tough? I've seen tougher. I was on my own by the time I was sixteen. My mother died of pneumonia. I never knew my father. He could walk right through that door, and I would not know him from Adam."

Beany stared at her as though she were a crazy woman, but Mavis's revelation made her open up. "I saw my dad once," the girl said. "I was around eight. He came to the apartment. My mom wasn't there, I don't know where she was. She used to do that, disappear for days. There was no food in the house. I'd only had a slice of bread since the day before. Anyhow, this man shows up at the door. I recognized him from pictures Mom kept in a drawer in her bedroom. I'm like happy to see him, 'cuz I'm thinking maybe he'll take me away from there so I can live like a normal kid, you know? He looks at me real funny like, he can't decide what to do. Then he digs in his pockets and comes out with a five dollar bill. 'Here,' he says. 'Go get you somethin' to eat.' He makes like he's gonna be there when I get back. I run down to the corner store and get a sandwich and some milk. By the time I got back, he was gone. I never saw him again." She ended with a shrug of her shoulders.

"How did you wind up a ward of the state?" Mavis said, moved by Beany's story.

"I think he must have called somebody, because the next day a lady came and took me to a temporary foster home."

"You mean you've been in the system since you were eight years old? How old are you now?"

"Thirteen," Beany said with a faint smile. "Five more years and I'm outta prison."

"Is it that bad?"

Beany laughed. "Nobody mistreats me, if that's what you want to know."

"You could still find a permanent home," Mavis said, hoping what she said was true.

"Nobody wants a teenager," Beany had said as though Mavis was about the most gullible adult she'd ever met.

Mavis had hugged her impulsively. "You're wrong, there are plenty of people out there who'd love to be able to give you a home."

Today Mavis had received a phone call from a Mrs. Epstein from the office of Health and Rehabilitative Services. Mrs. Epstein told her Felicia Russell had finally signed the legal papers making it possible for Beany to go to a permanent home.

"I know it's unusual receiving a phone call from a government servant on Saturday, but I got bogged down yesterday and didn't get the chance to phone. You've been waiting a long time to hear about Benina's fate. Her mother has no intention of ever getting her back. So if you'd like to give Benina a home, I'm willing to work with you on this. I've known Benina since she came under our care. She's a bright kid. Lots of potential there. I'd personally like to see her placed in a good home, and I have a feeling that you'd provide that for her."

"I'd like to do that more than anything," Mavis told Mrs. Epstein. "Just tell me what I need to do."

"Come down to the office Monday morning at nine, and I'll get the ball rolling for you," Mrs. Epstein said.

So here she was, soon to be a mother at forty-nine. The Lord definitely works in mysterious ways.

The doorbell rang. Frank. She couldn't wait to give him the good news.

The orchestra was warming up as Cara Lynn walked into the ballroom. She had worn the dress she'd told Carly about earlier. It was champagne satin with a scoop neckline that accentuated her bosom with soft folds. The dress itself was straight and hugged her curves, the hem falling three inches above her knees. However, the train, which was attached at the cinched waist, fell to the floor. She wore satin pumps of the same shade with it. Her hair was a soft halo of curls, framing her face and cascading down her back.

She was a half hour early. Evan had wanted to pick her up in his limousine, but she'd declined. She didn't want him assigning too much meaning to her being at his side tonight. She was fulfilling a promise, nothing more. She was to serve as a stand-in hostess, which entailed greeting the guests along with Evan and dancing the first dance of the night with him.

The ballroom was beautifully decorated. The tables along the wall had white linen tablecloths on them with center-pieces made of white gardenias floating in crystal bowls. The chandelier lent its sparkling light to the already enchanting atmosphere. The hardwood floor gleamed.

The orchestra, a twelve-man band specializing in tunes from the Big Band Era, was now playing "When I Fall In Love." They were very talented, and when they finished, Cara Lynn applauded enthusiastically.

They smiled their appreciation, and setting down their instruments, filed out of the room to take a break before beginning the first set promptly at nine.

"She walks in beauty, like the night . . ." Evan quoted as he crossed the room, his eyes riveted on her.

"Lord Byron," Cara Lynn said, smiling at him.

"You are breathtaking," he said, his hand over his heart.

They met in the center of the room. "Thank you. You look rather splendid yourself."

He was attired in a black tuxedo with a white silk shirt and a white bow tie.

"I admit to being nervous. I wish I could call the whole thing off."

Laughing, Cara Lynn said, "Nonsense. It's going to be an evening we'll never forget. Everything looks fabulous. The buffet, the bandstand. You've got servants bustling all over the place. I just heard the orchestra, they're remarkable. Everything is perfection. Except—"

"Except?" Evan said, his voice cracking.

"Where is the chanteuse?"

Evan breathed a sigh of relief. "She's changing into her costume."

"Have you heard her sing?"

"On tape, yes. She sounds like a cross between Miss Ella Fitzgerald and Whitney Houston."

"That good?"

"I just hope she sounds that good live."

"What's her name?"

"Billie Goodnight. And she says she was born with that name."

Hearing the click of heels on the wooden floor, Cara Lynn turned to look in the direction of the ballroom entrance. A petite, plump black woman made her way across the room to them. She wore a glittering white gown and in her short, curly black hair, she wore a single gardenia over her right ear. She reminded Cara Lynn of Billie Holiday.

"Ah, here is our songstress," Evan said, beaming at Miss Goodnight. "I'd like you to meet the hostess of tonight's affair, Dr. Cara Lynn Garrett."

"How do you do, Dr. Garrett?" Miss Goodnight said pleasantly in her deep, lilting voice.

"It's a pleasure to meet you, Miss Goodnight. Mr. Fitzgerald tells me you have a lovely voice."

Miss Goodnight blushed. "I try."

"What are some of the songs you're going to do for us?" Cara Lynn asked.

"I'm starting off with 'When I Fall In Love,' then we'll go into 'Someone To Watch Over Me' and 'You Made Me Love You.' After that, the band will play something upbeat while I take a short break."

"I'm looking forward to it," Cara Lynn said.

Miss Goodnight went up on the bandstand to go over her sheet music while Cara Lynn and Evan walked through the house to the foyer to await the guests. They sat down on the antique bench near the door and regarded one another.

"I want to thank you for being here, Cara. Until I started getting dressed tonight, I didn't realize how much I needed your support."

"You, who can stare down the most cutthroat business-men?" Cara Lynn ribbed him.

"Yeah, but have you ever tried to maintain eye contact with C.C. Cuthbertson? That's one scary woman."

Catherine Creel Cuthbertson was a blue blood to be reck-oned with. She owned more land than God. It was rumored that she'd once been involved with Him in a land deal. It had come down to a draw. He'd taken heaven and C.C. had taken earth. It was one of the many tall tales folks in Jefferson county made up about a woman who was larger than life.

"She RSVP'd?" Cara Lynn asked.

"She wrote a note on the card: 'Make sure you serve good Kentucky bourbon.' "

Cara Lynn laughed. "No wonder she's so well preserved."

"I can put up with C.C. for an evening," Evan said. "Af-ter all, she donated ten grand to the Boys' Home. Altogether, we raised one hundred twenty thousand. That should cover the cost of the additions they need to make to the dormi-tory."

He took Cara Lynn's hand in his. "I have to tell you something before the guests arrive. I did something rather impulsive. After I had time to think about it, I regretted having done it. But it was too late. I went over to Davidson's and we traded blows—"

Cara Lynn sighed. "I know, he told me."

"Then you're okay with his being here tonight?" Evan asked, searching her face.

She sat up straight. "He didn't mention anything about coming tonight," she said, trying to keep the excitement out of her voice.

"Maybe he changed his mind," Evan said offhandedly. "At any rate, I thought I'd better warn you, so you'll be on your guard."

Cara Lynn's temperature had risen at the thought of seeing Jordan. She fanned her face with her hand.

"Does the prospect of seeing him make you uneasy?" Evan said, not missing her reaction.

"A little, but I'll be okay," she admitted.

"Of course you will be," Evan said. "Just ignore him and everything will be fine. Even he wouldn't dare make a scene."

Cara Lynn stood, looking down into Evan's face. "Jordan isn't the type of person who'd publicly humiliate anyone, Evan."

She walked over to the door, peering out into the night. Evan went to her.

"If you say so, Cara. It wasn't my intention to besmirch Davidson's sterling reputation. For someone who's supposedly on the outs with him, you were certainly quick to jump to his defense," he said indignantly.

"I never lied to you, Evan," Cara Lynn said, turning to face him. "You know how I feel about Jordan."

"Then it was to my disadvantage to have invited him to join us tonight," Evan said, laughing at his own expense.

"You invited him?" she said, her voice rising in disbelief.

"I thought you knew—"

"I knew nothing of the sort," Cara Lynn said sharply. She sighed. "I assumed he'd decided to come on his own. You threatened him, didn't you? Or the two of you made a wager. May the best man win?"

Evan colored slightly. "There were no threats made," he adamantly denied.

"Don't lie to me, Evan," Cara Lynn warned harshly.

"I may have told him to stay away from you," he wavered.

"And what was the wager?"

Evan looked pained. "Either make a commitment or move aside for someone who's ready to."

Cara Lynn laughed. "So I'm supposed to decide between the two of you tonight?"

"In a word, yes."

Angrily turning away from him, Cara Lynn sat back down, crossing her legs. "If I hadn't promised I'd be here, and if the Boys' Home wasn't benefiting from this affair, I'd leave." She looked up at Evan. "I hate the way men assume they have to take control of a situation. What made you think Jordan's presence would force my hand? Did you have some plan to make him look so absurd in my eyesight that I'd go running into your arms?"

Sighing, Evan attempted a smile. "Bad move, huh?"

"Extremely bad," Cara Lynn acknowledged. "I can't imagine what you could have said to Jordan to get him to come here tonight. It isn't like him."

"I've told you everything," Evan insisted.

"I believe you have." Then that could mean only one thing: *Jordan does care for me.*

Her smile was brilliant.

Relieved by her brightened demeanor, Evan sat down next to her. "You're taking this better than I thought you would."

Cara Lynn fixed him with a stony stare. "Keep your distance. If you and Jordan can scheme behind my back, then I can certainly cook up something to match your sorry efforts."

Actually she wasn't that upset with him. The prospect of seeing Jordan cancelled out any acrimony on her part. But in payment for his chicanery, she would let him squirm for a while.

"Come on, Cara. I've apologized. I confessed everything," Evan whined.

"Don't beg, it's pathetic."

The doorbell sounded.

Cara Lynn stood, cool and poised. "Shall we go greet your guests?"

To Evan's relief, Cara Lynn behaved as though they hadn't argued minutes before the ball commenced. She was charming and gracious. She was the epitome of good taste and decorum. It didn't even faze her when C.C. patted her on the behind and told her what a pretty filly she was.

C.C.'s actions surprised Evan. He'd expected her to be standoffish as she usually was.

When she arrived, the other guests gave her a wide berth. People did this in C.C.'s presence for two reasons. First, because they didn't want to be too near when she let loose that caustic tongue of hers. A person could be cut to pieces by that sharp member. Second, she never went anywhere without her entourage, consisting of her husband, whomever he might be at the moment, her personal secretary, and her bodyguards. A person carrying that much baggage needed the extra space.

C.C. arrived alone tonight, however. A tall, thin woman in her fifties or sixties—few people knew for sure—she was striking with her fine-boned features, blond hair swept off her high cheekboned face. Wide-spaced blue eyes that didn't miss anything. She was wearing a red beaded gown that was long sleeved, low cut, and fell to her ankles in sparkling waves.

She glided past the butler, who was announcing the arrival of each guest.

"Don't waste your breath, sugar. Everybody knows me."

She walked straight over to Evan and Cara Lynn. "Evan. Your parents would be so proud of you. Carrying on the family tradition of hosting the most fabulous parties. How I miss your dear parents."

"Thank you, Mrs. Cuthbertson," Evan said, smiling down at her.

"Call me C.C.," she told him, her eyes raking over him. "Who is this adorable child at your side?"

"C.C., I'd like you to meet Dr. Cara Lynn Garrett. Cara Lynn is my companion for the evening."

C.C. looked Cara Lynn in the eyes. "Not just for the evening, I should hope."

The two women clasped hands. C.C. smiled. "You're the vet who took over for Harry Bailey."

"Yes, I am," Cara Lynn answered, liking the woman's directness.

"It's no wonder we haven't met. I must be the only person in Jefferson county who detests horses. I was thrown when I was a child, and after I blew the dumb beast's brains out, I decided that riding wasn't for me," C.C. said, not cracking a smile.

Seeing Cara Lynn's horrified expression, she laughed heartily. "I'm only kidding, child. I don't believe in abusing animals, just men."

"Aren't they animals?" Cara Lynn returned.

C.C. laughed her deep, throaty laugh. "I like this one, Evan. She's got more spirit than the others you've been linked with. And she's a pretty filly, too."

That was when C.C. gave Cara Lynn the rap on the rear, after which she disappeared into the burgeoning crowd.

"You've made quite an impression on C.C.," Evan commented, laughing.

"Her hand made quite an impression on me," Cara Lynn said, briefly touching her backside.

Evan wasn't listening. He was staring at the newest arrival. Cara Lynn followed his gaze. Jordan. Solo. Thank God.

"Mr. Jordan Davidson," the butler announced.

Cara Lynn thought she heard a collective sigh from the females in the room. She didn't like it a bit.

Jordan didn't make it across the room to them because he was waylaid by a buxom redhead of the bottle variety.

Cara Lynn knew the huntress. Paula Kingston. When they attended Shelbyville High together, Paula had been a brunette and wore a training bra. It was amazing what a few years could do.

"Go ahead, Cara," Evan goaded her. "If you hurry, you can wrestle that little redhead for him. I think you can take her."

Cara Lynn eyed him through narrowed slits. "Oh, shut up, Fitzgerald."

"Miss Deborah Sanford and Mr. Robert Johnson," announced the butler.

"You can have this one by your lonesome," Cara Lynn said, turning away. "I'm going to the powder room."

From across the room, Jordan watched Cara Lynn beat a hasty retreat.

"Excuse me," he said to Paula. "I think I've spotted the person I came here to see."

"Save a dance for me," Paula cooed, her hand trailing down one of his arms.

"I'm sure your dance card is already full," Jordan told her.

He'd gotten only about five feet before someone grabbed him by the arm.

"Jordan! I see you made it after all. Whom did you come

with, Cara Lynn?" Deborah said. "Let me introduce you to my fiance, Bobby."

Jordan paused to shake hands with Bobby. The two men were approximately the same height, but Bobby was slimmer with less muscle definition. They instantly recognized in each other a working man, someone who wasn't afraid to dig in and get his hands dirty. This put them on an equal plane of respect.

"How ya doin', man?" Bobby said.

"Good to meet you, Bobby. Congratulations on your upcoming marriage."

"Jordan, Bobby just returned from Alaska," Deborah cut in. "He's a top-notch construction worker. He's a carpenter, a brick layer, welder—you name it, he can do it."

"Deb—" Bobby protested. "Now isn't the time to ask for a job."

"It's no problem," Jordan said, reaching into his tuxedo's coat pocket and producing a business card. "Give me a call on Monday, Bobby, and I'll see what we can do."

"Okay, I will," Bobby said, his momentary embarrassment evaporating. "Thanks, man."

"Don't mention it. You two enjoy yourselves," Jordan said, looking anxiously into the crowd.

"She went that way," Deborah said, pointing in the direction she'd last seen Cara Lynn.

"Thanks," Jordan said, smiling.

He left them, and Bobby pulled Deborah into his arms. "What was that all about?"

"Oh, Jordan and Cara Lynn were dating, and something happened to break them up. I hope they can work things out," Deborah explained.

"I believe you mean that," Bobby said as he kissed the tip of her nose.

Deborah grinned up at him. "I do, babe. I need to make amends. That's why I wanted to come tonight. Maybe if I apologize to some of the people I've wronged over the years, I'll heal faster."

Bobby hugged her tightly. "That's all it takes, Deb. One step at a time."

"Where are you going in such a hurry?" Carly asked Cara Lynn, stepping into her path.

Cara Lynn paused in her headlong rush. "Carly. Hi, Eddie. You two look great, did I tell you that already?"

She pecked both her friends on their cheeks. Carly was wearing the royal blue dress she'd purchased in Lexington that morning. Eddie was attired in a black tuxedo. He was an inch taller than Cara Lynn, which made him look like a giant next to his wife. He was very fair skinned, had green eyes with brown specks in them, and wore his light brown natural hair in a conservative style.

"Yeah, all the niceties have been said," Carly said impatiently. "Who're you running from, Jordan or Deborah?"

Blowing air through her lips, Cara Lynn said, "Take your pick. Oh, and add Fitzgerald to the list. He invited Jordan so that they could have an old-fashioned, may-the-best-man-win battle over yours truly."

"Girl, your life," Carly laughed, shaking her head. "We'll be back in a few minutes. We're going to the little girl's room."

"All right, sweetheart," Eddie said, pushing his glasses back up on his nose. He felt a bit out of place here. He'd only agreed to come to please Carly and to spend some time alone with her, away from the kids. Between her job and his, they didn't get many nights out together.

He didn't mind the interruption. Cara Lynn was a good friend to the both of them. They'd all grown up together. Like Carly, he was concerned about Cara Lynn's apparent fear of commitment. If the girl kept running, she'd never get caught.

He looked up and saw Jordan heading in his direction. They'd never met, but he'd noticed him when he'd arrived earlier and Carly had whispered in his ear, "That's him. That's the one Cara Lynn told to go jump in a lake. That girl gets on my nerves sometimes."

So when Jordan walked past Eddie, he was detained once again.

"Jordan Davidson, isn't it?"

"Yeah," Jordan replied, a look of curiosity on his face.

"Edward Needham," Eddie told him, offering his hand. "Carly's husband."

"Oh, yeah." Jordan smiled, shaking hands with him. "Cara's friend. How's it going?"

"Good. Listen, I know it isn't any of my business, but if you're looking for Cara Lynn, she just went to the ladies room with Carly."

Jordan looked down into the shorter man's face. "I get the feeling everyone knows why I'm here tonight."

"I take it you want to patch things up with Cara Lynn," Eddie ventured.

"I'd like to at least talk to her. She won't stick around long enough for us to have a decent conversation."

"Don't you know why she keeps running away from you?" Eddie asked. He reminded Jordan of a college professor with his ultraconservative dress and wire-rimmed glasses.

"I think she cares more for me than she's letting on. She seems to think caring for a man automatically makes him leave her. She's a complex woman," Jordan said. "You've known her a long time. Why do you think she's avoiding me?"

"I agree that she does care for you," Eddie said in his measured way. "I'll tell you what Carly told me because I'd like to see Cara Lynn happy, and you obviously make her happy." He briefly scratched his head. "The misunderstanding about the other man was a total screw-up. She tried to tell you, but you weren't ready to listen. Cara Lynn has a big problem with rejection. She claims she can sense it before it happens. She sensed it in you, and that's why she's avoiding you now. She doesn't want it to be over between you."

"My ego got in the way," Jordan admitted. "It's not easy being with a woman who has men standing in line to date her. Look at how Fitzgerald has been behaving the last few weeks."

"Should a woman be penalized because she's attractive?" Eddie asked sagely. He laughed. "As for being attractive, Cara Lynn would be the last person to believe that of herself. She was a late bloomer. Very shy and studious as a girl. The important thing is, Cara Lynn considers Fitzgerald a friend, nothing more. She has no control over how he feels about her."

"So you're saying we've both been too stubborn to listen to each other," Jordan gathered.

"That's the way it looks to someone on the outside looking in," Eddie said. "Only you and Cara Lynn can rectify the situation."

"And in order to do that, we need to talk."

"Don't let her run away from you this time," Eddie admonished. They shook on it.

"Welcome to small town life," Eddie joked. "Where everybody gets into your business."

"Nice," Jordan said, smiling.

He spied Mavis heading purposefully in their direction. Sensing he was in for a prolonged lecture, he quickly said farewell to Eddie and was swallowed up by the crowd.

Eddie was lying in wait for Mavis when she arrived. "Why, Miss Mavis, don't you look lovely tonight."

"Eddie, I haven't seen you in a month of Sundays. Where's Carly?" she said, looking around them.

"She went to the powder room," Eddie said pleasantly. "I hear good things about you and Mr. Frank."

At the mention of Frank's name, Mavis's eyes sparkled. "I suppose you could say we're a couple. And speaking of a couple, where are those twins of yours?"

"They're with their Grandma Rose. We're all staying with Carly's parents tonight."

"Oh? Tell Rose and James I said hello, will you? Did you see which way Jordan went? I have something I need to tell him."

"It looks like Mr. Frank is beckoning you," Eddie said, avoiding Mavis's question.

Mavis pretended not to see Frank across the room, enthusiastically gesturing for her to join him. Eddie assumed Frank didn't want Mavis getting involved in Cara Lynn's and Jordan's problems. She seemed to have chosen to ignore his wishes.

Frank was smiling as he approached them. "Hiya, Eddie." They shook hands.

"Good evening, Mr. Frank. You're looking well."

"So are you. How are Carly and the girls?"

"They're all doing well."

"Good," Frank said. "I know you're a hard-working man, but when Carly comes to the ranch with the girls, you ought to tag along. We'd be glad to see you."

Nodding, Eddie said, "I get your meaning. Carly has been after me to lighten my workload."

"She's a smart woman, your Carly," Frank said, grinning. Turning his attention to Mavis, he said, "I thought we'd get some fresh air. Will you excuse us, Eddie?"

"Of course," Eddie said, amused by the look of disappointment on Mavis's face.

She went reluctantly, stealing glances over her shoulder.

"You didn't tell me you were the hostess of this event," Susan said, her brown eyes alight with interest. "And Evan Fitzgerald is your significant other."

"You're mistaken on both counts." Cara Lynn laughed.

When she and Carly had entered the tastefully decorated powder room, Susan was already there, freshening up her makeup.

Cara Lynn reapplied her lipstick, pressing her lips together. "Evan is a friend, and I'm only a stand-in. I'm here because he isn't involved with anyone at the moment."

"But he's gorgeous," Susan said, unable to hide her ebullience.

A meaningful look passed between Cara Lynn and Carly.

"You're okay with the interracial thing?" Carly asked, not one to beat around the bush.

"I've dated an Italian in Chicago and a Jewish man in New York. What can I say? A man is a man."

"Then what are you doing wasting your time with us?" Cara Lynn asked. "Go introduce yourself, and ask him to dance."

"I'd feel awkward," the attractive newswoman said. "Couldn't you introduce us?"

"No. If I did, he'd know something was up," Cara Lynn began.

"Evan thinks he's in love with Cara Lynn," Carly put in.

"But he isn't," Cara Lynn was quick to add. "And the thing is, I've been trying to get him interested in someone else. If I introduced you, he'd immediately put two and two together and we'd be busted. But if you were to walk up to him and begin to gently flirt with him, he might be more open to you."

"I get you," Susan said, smiling appreciatively. "All right, I'll do it. If I can appear on television every night, I can walk up to a man and ask him to dance."

An introduction wouldn't have been needed if, when Susan arrived with her cameraman, Larry Powell, earlier in the evening, Evan was not being monopolized by Colonel Edmund Stewart and his wife, Elizabeth "Bitty" Stewart. Bitty was short for "little bit." She was very petite, no more than five feet tall—and the colonel had thought it romantic to give her the appellation some years before they were wed. Unfortunately for Elizabeth, it had caught on.

"Go, girl!" Carly urged Susan on.

"Wish me luck," Susan said, heading for the exit.

"You don't need it," Cara Lynn assured her. "You've got it going on."

Susan left, and Carly playfully punched Cara Lynn on the arm.

"You are so bad."

"What?"

"Encouraging Susan to make a play for Evan because you want him out of your hair."

"It's a solution to a problem," Cara Lynn said reasonably. "I like Evan, even with his infuriating behavior. But I'm in love with Jordan. I hope Evan and Susan fall in love at first sight."

"Me, too," Carly giggled. "Girl, I'd be in the front row at the wedding. Now that would be an event Shelbyville would never forget."

The door swung open and Deborah strode in, resplendent in a sleeveless slinky black gown with a white princess collar. She wore her short black hair slicked back in a sophisticated style. She was followed by three other women who needed to use the facilities.

There were friendly hellos all around, then Deborah smiled at Cara Lynn and said, "Could I have a word with you in private?"

Instantly suspicious, Cara Lynn stepped close to Deborah and said in a low voice, "Not on your life. I am not in the mood to get into it with you."

Expecting that reaction, Deborah smiled at her. "I'm not up to my old tricks tonight, Cara Lynn. I came here to apologize for behaving the way I have toward you. I'm sorry for the lies, the intimidation, generally making your life miserable."

Looking down at her, Cara Lynn laughed. "You won't be surprised if I don't believe you."

"I realize I have to prove my sincerity by my actions," Deborah said serenely. "But I'm trying to change. I've known I have a problem with insecurity and jealousy for some time now. But tonight I had a sort of spiritual awakening. For the first time in my life, I know I can change if I want to, and I don't have to continue being a spiteful person. I can abandon her and recreate myself. I'm starting by apologizing to you."

"Damn—I think she's on the level," Carly exclaimed, backing away from Deborah as though she was witnessing a miracle.

"I am," Deborah said, her voice low. "I was so immature. I ridiculed you out of envy, Cara Lynn. You seemed to have everything I didn't: parents who loved you. I know that isn't an excuse for my behavior. I just want to try to explain."

The other women in the room hastily left after attending to their needs, guessing they were intruding on a private moment.

"I'd better get back to Eddie," Carly said, excusing herself.

Cara Lynn and Deborah were alone. She sat down at the vanity. Deborah stood, leaning against the sink.

"I wouldn't do that if I were you," Cara Lynn said. "It could be wet."

Deborah pushed away from the sink. Then she laughed.

"What?" Cara Lynn asked, watching her.

"You're innately nice, Cara Lynn. It comes as easily to you as breathing. You even wanted to save your oldest enemy the embarrassment of a wet evening gown."

"It wasn't that much," Cara Lynn told her. "And I'm not so nice. There were many times I felt like punching you out."

"But you didn't," Deborah said, smiling at her. "And about Jordan. Nothing happened, believe me. He couldn't wait to get rid of me after we left the diner that day. The only reason he took me to lunch in the first place was because I cornered him on the sidewalk in front of my shop, and I made a perfect ass of myself trying to make him interested enough in me to actually notice me. He took pity on me."

Cara Lynn was still suspicious. "Why are you telling me all this?"

Deborah sighed. "Because if I'm the reason you and Jordan aren't together, then I've eliminated the reason. Bobby asked me to marry him tonight, and I said yes. I feel like I've been given a new lease on life—and believe it or not, I didn't want to cause you any more heartache."

"You're not the reason," Cara Lynn informed her. But she didn't go so far as to confide in her.

"I'm glad to hear that," Deborah said, coming around to stand in front of her. "Well, I've had my say. Is there anything you'd like to say to me, some gem you've been saving up and would like to get off your chest?"

Cara Lynn got to her feet. "This is definitely an anticlimax. I expected us to have a knock-down drag-out slugfest before it was over, and here you are with your 'I've seen the light' routine. I'm a little disappointed."

"You want to smack me around a little?" Deborah joked.

Cara Lynn laughed. "The little girl in me does. But the adult would like to wish you and Bobby the best. Bobby's a decent fellow. I often wondered why he stuck by you all these years. I guess he was looking a bit deeper than the surface. I accept your apology, Deborah. I'm tired of the petty childishness and besides, Reverend Brown would tell me I'd have no inner peace if I didn't."

To Cara Lynn's surprise, Deborah's eyes were misty.

"Thanks," Deborah said.

They regarded each other with solemn expressions on their faces, then Cara Lynn broke the mood with a genuine smile.

Deborah smiled back. "I'd better go," she said and swiftly left the room.

Cara Lynn sat down for a minute or so before leaving. She felt emotionally drained. Her bitter enemy asking for her forgiveness. There was something terribly wrong with this picture. But if Deborah could change, she certainly could. She was right when she'd told Evan tonight would be an evening to remember. She wondered what else fate had in store for her before the night was over.

Evan knew his brain was turning to mush. A minute longer having to listen to Colonel Stewart's war stories and he'd go berserk. Where was Cara Lynn? If she were here, he'd have the excuse of asking her to dance. Miss Goodnight was singing her rendition of "Embraceable You," and it was liltingly beautiful.

"Excuse me, Mr. Fitzgerald. May I interrupt? I'd like to ask you for this dance."

She had a lovely voice and an even more captivating face.

"Why, Miss Waters, you can interrupt me anytime," Colonel Stewart said, grinning broadly. "Evan, you didn't tell me we'd have a celebrity here tonight."

Evan didn't watch much television. He didn't know to what the colonel was referring.

"This is Susan Waters of Channel Four News. Evan, you really should get out more," Colonel Stewart said with a jolly laugh.

Evan graciously kissed Susan's hand. "Please excuse my ignorance, Miss Waters. I'd be honored to dance with you. Excuse us, Colonel."

Colonel Stewart watched them glide effortlessly onto the dance floor, then he went in search of Bitty.

"You have a lovely home," Susan said, her voice warm.

"Thank you. It's been in the family for nearly a century," Evan told her.

She smelled of jasmine, and her skin was silky to his touch. The nearness of her triggered his libido the moment he took her into his arms. He fleetingly thought such feelings made his love for Cara Lynn a mockery. Surely this was a fluke. He pulled back just a bit.

Susan smiled up into his eyes. "Please stop me if I'm being too forward, but was that Mrs. Fitzgerald I saw you with earlier?"

The deception grew.

"No, I haven't had that pleasure," Evan said. "And you?"

"I was engaged once, but I got transferred and the relationship didn't survive the separation," she replied in a soft voice.

"It must be difficult to meet someone when you're so busy."

"And I'm new to the area. I don't know anyone," Susan revealed, sounding a mite depressed by her situation.

"Allow me to show you around," Evan found himself offering.

Cara Lynn was angry with him anyway, and she wasn't over Davidson. Her behavior tonight made that more than clear. Maybe a little harmless competition would make her sit up and take notice.

"That would be nice," Susan said. "It's a date."

She laid her head on his shoulder. He was practically undone by her sweetness.

Cara Lynn felt a strong hand on her arm. She looked up into Jordan's face. She smiled. He smiled back.

"Hello."

"Hello."

She fingered the leather lapel of his black tuxedo. His cummerbund and bow tie were both made of Kente cloth.

"Nice. You look very handsome."

He caught her hand in his and leaned toward her. "You

in that dress . . . I have no words that would adequately describe you."

Cara Lynn's skin tingled.

"We need to talk, Cara," Jordan said quietly.

Their eyes met and held.

"We can go outside," she suggested, taking him by the hand.

They made their way through the jubilant revelers, past the kitchen staff, out the back door.

Once outside, they were alone on the patio. The silence was a welcome treat after the bedlam of the partygoers. Cara Lynn looked up at the velvet black sky. It was sprinkled with diamondlike stars. As she returned her gaze to Jordan, she said, "I didn't expect you to come. Evan told me how he challenged you to either patch things up with me or move aside. That was very presumptuous of him. He knows how I feel about you."

"How *do* you feel about me?" Jordan said, gently touching her cheek.

Tears moistened his fingers. "I'm so lonely without you."

Jordan's arms went around her in a warm embrace. "I've been lonely without you, sweetheart."

Her body trembled. He kissed her wet face, tasting her tears. "The last time we spoke, I hurt you. Unintentionally—nonetheless, I hurt you. I never want to cause you pain, Cara. I'd just had an argument with Fitzgerald, and then you came along to kiss my bruises, and I was like the snake who bit the woman who'd nursed him back to health. I turned on you," he said, kissing her forehead. "I know you aren't some kind of femme fatale. Maybe you do have a problem with rejection, but so do I."

"A femme fatale?" Cara Lynn said, smiling. "I'm about as naive about men as they come. That's why I can't get it right with you. And I truly want to."

Cupping her face between his two strong hands, Jordan laughed. "Why don't we start over. Forget about all the misunderstandings. I don't care about anyone else except us. Can we agree on that?"

"Yes," Cara Lynn said, looking into his eyes.

They kissed. Gently, yet urgently. Their bodies pressed close. Cara Lynn's arms went around his neck, and Jordan's arms encircled her waist. Her hands found their way to his hair, which was soft to her touch, the curls playing between her fingers. His moved downward to her hips, molding her to his male hardness.

All her senses were heightened when he touched her. She breathed in his scent, remembering how good it had been between them.

Their mouths parted and they held one another, regaining their composure.

"I don't know if I can take many more of these separation-reconciliation scenarios," Jordan told her. "They take too much out of me."

"Come dance with me," Cara Lynn said, wanting to extend these sensations.

"No—I came here to talk to you. I know you have an obligation to Fitzgerald tonight. I'm not going to behave like a jealous fool. You go back in. I'm going home."

"I'd rather go with you—"

Jordan silenced her with a kiss. "We're starting over. I trust you, Cara. I believe you when you say Fitzgerald is only a friend. I'm not going to start picking your friends for you."

"I'll leave early," Cara Lynn promised.

Jordan was right, it was Evan's night. It would be unkind to take the spotlight from him.

"I'll wait for you," Jordan said with another gentle kiss to her mouth.

He turned to leave, walking around the well-lit mansion to the front lawn, where the parking attendant had left his car.

Cara Lynn wasn't back in the ballroom five minutes before Evan sought her out.

"Where have you been?" he asked reproachfully.

"I went outside for some air," Cara Lynn said lightly, still feeling the effects from being with Jordan.

"With Davidson?" he asked, looking around for Jordan. "Well, are you going to tell me what happened?"

"Thanks to your kind invitation, we had the chance to talk and we've decided we'd rather be together than apart."

"What the hell," Evan said with a shrug. "I gave it my best shot."

He took her hand. "May I have this dance? We haven't danced all night."

Miss Goodnight was crooning "Unforgettable."

"I see they managed to work in a Nat King Cole number," Evan commented as he pulled Cara Lynn into his arms.

Cara Lynn relaxed and went with the flow of the music. Evan was an accomplished dancer. They moved well together. She closed her eyes and imagined it was Jordan who held her so possessively. That it was Jordan's hand tenderly massaging her back.

She allowed the fantasy to go unchecked for too long however, for when Miss Goodnight stopped singing and the band stopped playing, all eyes were on her and Evan. Evan, being an opportunist, saw his chance and took it. He passionately kissed her, much to the delight of their audience, who applauded enthusiastically.

Cara Lynn pushed out of his embrace. Stepping backward, she glared at him. Turning on her heel, she looked straight into Jordan's face. He was standing near the entrance, a dozen red roses clutched in his right hand.

Their eyes met across the room. His held disappointment, hers were pleading. He turned around and walked away.

Evan grasped Cara Lynn's arm. "Let him go, Cara."

Cara Lynn wrenched her arm free. "Drop dead."

By the time she got outside, Jordan was in his car, about

to pull out of the parking area. She crushed the discarded roses under her heels as she ran toward him.

"Jordan, please listen. That wasn't what it appeared to be."

She fell against the door of the Range Rover. "He kissed *me*. He took me by surprise. Can't you see it's just another one of his stunts?"

"Move away from the car, Cara. Please," Jordan said resolutely.

"You said you trusted me," she cried.

"I spoke too soon. I spoke from my heart, not my head. I can't keep going through these changes with you, Cara. You say one thing and do another. To me, that isn't truthfulness. I'm beginning to think you'll eventually go to the highest bidder—and I'm not in Fitzgerald's league."

Cara Lynn angrily hit the car door. "I don't know who's the worst, Evan for being underhanded and willing to go to any lengths to achieve his goal—or you for being so eager to believe any blessed thing about me."

She stepped away from the car. "Not fifteen minutes ago you held me and told me we were starting fresh, that you trusted me."

"I've already been burned once, Cara. I trusted her, too," Jordan said stonily.

"I'm not Gail," she said heatedly.

"It's obvious we still have problems we need to work out about past relationships. I talk a good game, but I guess I'm still wary of beautiful women who tell me they care for me and then fall into another man's arms."

Cara Lynn simply stared at him. She was numb. "Leave," she said. "I don't feel like fighting anymore."

Jordan hit the accelerator and pulled off. Cara Lynn turned her back, refusing to watch him go.

She walked slowly back to the house. She was going to get her purse and go home. No use prolonging an absolutely miserable evening.

A tall man walked toward her in the darkness.

"There is nothing you can do or say to make up for what you've done. So don't try," she warned Evan before they were within striking distance. "You have done everything in your power to wreck my relationship with Jordan since the day we met. And I have been foolish enough to allow it. Well, this is it, Fitzgerald. We're through."

"Don't believe for one moment that if I'd seen Davidson kissing the woman I loved, I'd have reacted the way he did," Evan began smoothly. "He's not worthy of you, Cara. He won't fight for you. What does that tell you?"

Cara Lynn kept walking. "You have connived and made it appear I'm not trustworthy. To anyone looking on, it seems I'm incapable of choosing between two men. You're good, Evan. It's too bad I realized too late what a snake you really are."

Evan reached out to her and Cara Lynn spurned his touch. "I'm going home now," she said and left him standing there.

"To do what?" Evan called after her. "To cry over that spineless SOB who left you standing out in the cold?"

He caught up with her and grabbed her by the shoulders, pulling her around to face him. "I played to win, Cara. It's the only way I know how to."

He dropped his hands, releasing her. "But I also know when to cash in my chips. You haven't said it, but I think you're in love with Davidson, not just strongly attracted to him. If you are, you should tell him. Men can be pretty dense about these things," he smiled. "It's been some night, huh?"

Cara Lynn shook her head, wondering what kind of upbringing produced men like Evan. Men who thought they could be forgiven anything as long as they were charming.

She sighed. It was a waste of energy being angry with him.

"Not exactly my dream night," she said, agreeing with him. "More like a nightmare."

"Mine either. But we got to the truth. You're no longer confused, are you?"

"No, things are crystal clear."

"And I lose. But I'm a big boy. I can take a little heartache. Would you like me to talk to Davidson? Confess my sins?"

"Please don't," Cara Lynn was quick to reply. "You've done quite enough already."

"Then let me take you home."

"I have my car, I'll drive myself."

They began walking back to Baymoor. He draped his arm about her shoulders, and she promptly shrugged it off.

He laughed. "You know, Cara, these past months with you have been the best I've had in a long time. You kept me on my toes. I could say you've been a worthy fencing partner. Exceedingly stimulating."

"The next time you get bored, I suggest you try scaling Mount Everest or scuba diving in shark-infested waters."

"That's cold."

"There's more where that came from."

"I deserve it."

"Yes, you do."

"Let me make it up to you," he said, sounding despondent.

"Okay, I want you to fall in love and get married. But don't invite me to the wedding."

"It would serve Davidson right if you'd marry me. That would teach him a lesson," Evan quipped.

"I'll choose my own form of punishment for Jordan."

"It was only a suggestion."

Cara Lynn laughed shortly. He was incorrigible. "Yeah, right."

Fifteen

At six thirty on Monday morning, Cara Lynn felt as though she needed a pair of clothespins to keep her eyes open. She'd been up all night, tossing and turning. Three cups of strong black coffee hadn't done the trick.

"Mavis and I are going to get hitched," Frank announced. That statement woke her up.

"What happened to all those jokes about your being too set in your ways to ever consider marriage?"

Frank smiled contentedly as he buttered his fourth piece of toast. "I figure there's still some life left in the old boy yet. And don't look so thrilled for me."

"I'm surprised, that's all. I didn't think things had progressed this far with you two," Cara Lynn said, wrinkling her nose at how much butter he was using.

"I love her," her father said simply. "She's gotten under my skin. After ten years of being alone, I'm as shocked as you are that I've found someone I want to share my life with. I expected to be alone the rest of my days. I loved your mother with all my heart, but I don't think she'd want me to be lonely."

Cara Lynn yawned and grasped her father's hand, squeezing it. "Daddy, I'm happy for you. In fact, I'm proud of you. God knows somebody in this family deserves some happiness. I'm going to welcome Mavis into the fold with open arms and as a wedding gift, why don't you let me give you a nice reception? We could have it right here on the front lawn, it would be nice."

"Mavis and I were just thinking of having a civil ceremony at City Hall, nothing big or drawn out."

Sighing, Cara Lynn said, "Marriage isn't something you do every day, Daddy. Let me give you a good send-off."

"No," her father objected. "That's my role. I'm supposed to marry you off, not vice versa. Although you don't seem to be cooperating."

Cara Lynn took another sip of her coffee. "I'll marry you off in style, and when my turn comes—sometime in this century, hopefully—you'll return the favor," she said, grinning at him. "Come on, Daddy, say yes."

"Okay. It's about time I got back some of that college tuition," Frank acquiesced.

Cara Lynn got up to rinse out her coffee mug. "I might be late getting home tonight, Dad. I have to go to Lexington to pick up a few medical supplies. I can't believe I let my stock get so low before reordering. I'm usually much more organized."

"That comes from burning the candle at both ends," her father said. "You've got to slow down before you fall down."

"I am. This weekend, I'm going to go shopping and generally spoil myself," Cara Lynn told him.

"Good girl, you deserve it." Her father joined her at the sink. "There's something else I need to tell you before you run out the door. I know you remember Beany . . ."

"Sure," Cara Lynn said, smiling. "I liked her, she's got spunk to spare. Wait a minute, did everything go through? Mavis can adopt her now?"

"That's right. We're going to adopt her after we get married," her father confirmed.

Cara Lynn laughed. "I'm going to have a kid sister. I always wanted a sister. When did Mavis find out?"

"Saturday afternoon. She told me that night."

"Has she told Beany yet?"

"Yesterday, after church. She was very happy. Mavis said she threw her arms around her and hugged her and then asked if she could borrow the car."

Laughing, Cara Lynn said, "She's a teenager. Have you and Mavis given any thought to what you're going to go through being the parents of a teenager?"

"I'm going to do exactly what I did with you, tadpole," her father said. "I'm gonna wing it."

"You are nuttier than those fruitcakes you make every Christmas," Cara Lynn said, shaking her head. "But you're also the most giving human being I know."

"I'm glad you're taking it so well. Now there's one more thing I'd like to touch bases with you on."

"I'm going to be late, Daddy."

"This won't take a minute. After Saturday night's goings-on I want to know what you're going to do about Jordan."

Pursing her lips, Cara Lynn said, "It's over this time. We said some things that are not going to be easy to forget or forgive. He told me he thought I would choose Evan over him because Evan is wealthier."

"People always say things they don't mean in the heat of the moment, Cara. If only you two could have had tunnel vision, capable of seeing each other but blocking out all other obstacles that sidetracked you. Obstacles like Evan Fitzgerald. I knew that man was nothing but trouble. But I also know that if you and Jordan are meant to be, you'll find some way to be together. That's the way life is," he rhapsodized.

Cara Lynn smiled at her father, with her love for him glowing in her eyes. "It's much too early in the morning to wax philosophical, Daddy. Let's face it—Jordan is out of my life now. I need to concentrate on my work. It's the only thing that hasn't let me down. I can get satisfaction out of a job well done. There are no egos to tiptoe around, and I can wear jeans every day if I want to. What more could I ask for?"

Her father wasn't deceived by her performance. He kissed her forehead like he used to do when she was a little girl. "Go on to work, but don't give up on Jordan. Things have a way of working themselves out."

Cara Lynn smiled at him. "Thanks, Daddy. You always make me see things in a better light."

"It's in the job description."

He watched her as she walked out of the back door. His heart went out to her. He couldn't bear to see her this way. Denying her feelings in hope of salvaging her dignity. It was then that he decided to have a talk with Jordan. Unbeknownst to Cara Lynn, of course. A father has the right to interfere in his child's love life. That's what he planned to say to Cara Lynn if she ever found out about his snooping.

Jordan answered the door attired in worn overalls. There were paint stains on the bib, and his hands were caked with black soil.

His eyes registered surprise when he saw Frank. "Frank, how are you? Then his eyes were panicked. "It isn't Cara is it? Nothing's happened to Cara?"

"No, it's nothing like that," Frank said quickly. This boy's got it bad, he thought. "I just came by for a neighborly visit."

Jordan breathed easier. "Come in—I was in the backyard digging out weeds in the garden. The tomatoes are doing great, but worms are trying to eat up all the sweet corn before it ripens."

Frank removed his Stetson as he stepped into the room. "I can see you've been busy. The last time I was here, the place was falling down. Still living in two places? Ever thought about bringing your business here, actually living in this house full-time?"

"Come on back to the kitchen, I'll get us a couple of beers from the refrigerator."

They went to the kitchen, and Jordan pointed him to the kitchen table while he got the beers.

"It was my plan to live here. My business is doing well in Louisville, so I wouldn't want to change anything there. But I do love this house, and I think it would be a great family home, just not my family's home. I'm thinking of selling."

Handing Frank a bottle of beer, he sat down across from him.

"How is Cara?"

"That's what I came to find out from you," Frank said, eyeing him over his bottle. "What went on between you two?"

Jordan smiled and shook his head in dismay. "Frank, what happened between Cara and me is private. She wouldn't want me discussing it with her father, that much I'm sure of."

"You're not seeing each other any longer. Why do you care what she thinks?" Frank asked, his keen eyes not missing the dark circles under Jordan's eyes.

Jordan hesitated for a second, then he was talking as though he'd been dying to confide in someone. "To tell the truth, I don't know what happened. We were getting along fine until Fitzgerald came along and muddied the waters. And there was this mystery man she's never come clean about." He sighed. "Maybe you can give me some insight into the workings of your daughter's mind. She told me she was in love with someone else, and then she turned it around and said she wasn't. I accused her of lying to me. She explained she hadn't lied because the man she's in love with doesn't love her."

"Are you convinced there's another man?" Frank asked, leaning forward.

"Yes and no," Jordan replied. "Yes because when she

told me about him, she was very sincere, Frank. Her heart was breaking right before my eyes. I wanted to rip the guy's lungs out for treating her so badly. And no, I don't believe there is another man in the picture because I'd like to think there's a chance for us."

"Does this man have a name?" Frank said, amusement in his dark eyes.

Frowning, Jordan said, "She told me he lives in Louisville and she sees him occasionally."

Frank laughed. "She does, does she?"

Seeing he'd finished his beer, Jordan offered him another one.

"No thanks, one's my limit. They put me to sleep," Frank said. "She wouldn't tell you his name? Well I'll tell you. There is no unrequited love in her life, Jordan. She made him up. And I'll tell you something else, son. Cara is in love with you."

"You're mistaken, Frank," Jordan said with certainty. "She doesn't even want to see me—and I don't blame her after what I said to her Saturday night."

"You're both a pair of wounded souls," Frank told him. "Cara told me how you were jilted. You know she was treated badly by a man she fancied herself in love with. Her problem goes deeper than that though. I believe it started with her mother. She was killed when Cara was seventeen. She's never really gotten over it. So now she has it in her mind that everyone she loves leaves her. You came into her life at a stressful time anyway. You know about Sara?"

Jordan nodded. "I met her a few months back. Nice lady."

"Uh huh. So don't give up just yet. Cara must really care for you, otherwise she wouldn't be behaving so irrationally."

"She sabotaged the relationship before I could hurt her," Jordan deduced.

Frank grinned. "She eliminated the threat."

"She was falling in love with me?" Jordan said in disbelief.

"Bingo," Frank said with a slap to Jordan's back. "There may be hope for you yet."

"You have a clever daughter, Frank. Making up another man was smart, but then denying it and making me distrustful—well, that took genius."

"And you fell for it."

"I didn't say I was a genius."

Frank got to his feet, replacing his Stetson as he did so. "I have to be going."

They shook hands, then Jordan briefly hugged Frank.

"Thank you, Frank. You've made my day."

"If you ever tell Cara Lynn I told you any of this, I'll deny it to my dying breath," Frank said at the door. "I was never here."

"I don't know what you're talking about," Jordan said, straight-faced. "Who are you, anyway?"

"It pays to have a touch of amnesia when you're dealing with a woman," Frank advised him. "Remember the good and forget about the bad."

Then he was jogging down the steps, looking like a man half his age.

Jordan closed the door behind him. "She loves me," he said.

He went back outside to his garden and attacked the weeds with renewed vigor.

While he worked, he was mentally going over his stratagem for winning Cara Lynn. She'd massacred him in the first two battles, but the war wasn't over yet. If she thought she would go through life running away from love, feeling safe in her cocoon of loneliness, he would prove her wrong before they called a cease-fire to the fighting. He would help her to embrace love, revel in it—because what was life without love . . . and what was love without her?

* * *

George Braddock scrutinized Cara Lynn as she stood holding the reins and smoothing the mane of the four-year-old mare while it was being mounted by Sir Lewiston, an eight-year-old stud he hoped would sire a winner. Joey held the reins of Sir Lewiston while Braddock's groom, Tom Peterson, patted the muscular neck of the stallion.

The process completed, Sir Lewiston was led outside to the paddock. Cara Lynn continued to calm the mare. "Easy girl, if everything goes well, you're going to be a mother in a few months."

"If you've done your job right, she should be," George Braddock said caustically, stepping out of the shadows.

Cara Lynn looked down into his flushed face. "Nature does the work, I'm here to assist."

"You're the expert, and I'm paying a hell of a lot for your so-called knowledge," Braddock said the word "knowledge" with such venom, Cara Lynn thought he was about to spit on her.

Turning to Joey, she said, "Would you please take Marabelle back to her stall, Joey?"

"Sure, boss," Joey said, tossing a defensive look at George Braddock as he left to do the task.

Cara Lynn placed her hands on her hips, her legs slightly apart. Her fighting stance. She didn't back down as she met Braddock's mean brown eyes.

"My fee is standard for this kind of procedure, Mr. Braddock. Do you have a complaint about my qualifications that you'd like to lodge?"

George Braddock shoved his hands into his jeans pockets. "I'm sure Harry wouldn't have recommended you if you weren't qualified," he allowed, looking uncomfortable admitting that she had a license to practice veterinary medicine.

Cara Lynn held her tongue, choosing her words carefully.

She had known she would face opposition when she agreed to take over for Harry. "If you'd rather have another vet taking care of your animals, by all means, hire someone else. But I'm more than qualified to do this work. I was at the top of my class—and what's more, I'm dedicated to giving my patients the very best of care." She paused. "It's apparent to me that you are barely tolerating me. Whether the reason is that I'm a woman or because of my skin color makes no difference to me—I'm not about to change either one of them to suit you. All I ask is that you be straight with me."

George colored profusely and nervously ran a hand through his thin, gray hair. "I don't give a damn what color you are, young woman. You people are always bringing up race. My concern is whether or not a woman is up to a job of this magnitude. You're not built for heavy lifting."

Cara Lynn had trouble concealing her amusement. He wasn't a racist, he was a sexist.

"I'm not going to be carrying your horses on my back, Mr. Braddock. Veterinary Science is a field equally accessible to both sexes. There is very little muscle required. What should matter to you is if I have it up here or not," Cara Lynn concluded, touching her temple.

"Well, you seem to be fine so far," George Braddock conceded. "But I'll be watching you."

"I'm sure you will be," Cara Lynn said, which elicited a smile from the taciturn George Braddock.

By five on Saturday afternoon, Cara Lynn's feet felt as though she'd been running in the Boston Marathon. She had some difficulty carrying all the packages onto the elevator at the downtown hotel she was spending the night in. A bellboy had to place most of her purchases on a luggage cart and wheel them into the elevator.

Cara Lynn leaned against the wall and closed her eyes.

"You must have bought out the stores," the bellboy, a good-looking black youth of perhaps seventeen, said jokingly.

"Almost," Cara Lynn said, opening her eyes and smiling at him. She hadn't been entirely narcissistic—some of the packages held gifts for her father, Mavis, Beany, Carly, Eddie and the twins, Joey and Sharon. But she had purchased a certain little emerald green number that fit her like a glove. And when she had tried the dress on in the exclusive shop in downtown Lexington, she had fleetingly wondered what Jordan's reaction would be if he could see her in it.

"I bet you would look good in a flour sack," the bellboy said, giving her the benefit of his most brilliant smile.

"Do you flirt with all the female guests, or am I just lucky?" Cara Lynn inquired lightly.

"I'm not flirting. I'm dead serious. On the money. I'd drink champagne out of your shoe, babe."

Cara Lynn laughed. She'd put him in his place if the situation wasn't so comical. Here she was stuck in an elevator with a Denzel Washington wannabe.

Five minutes later he was seeing her to the door of the suite. He went in and deposited the packages on the sofa in the sitting room.

"Here," Cara Lynn said, handing him a generous tip. "You're cute. Slow down and enjoy your youth."

The young man appeared upset by her comment, then he glanced the single bill in his hand and his expression brightened, his moment of discomfiture forgotten. "Gosh—thanks, miss. Have a nice stay."

"Thank you, I will," Cara Lynn said, closing the door.

Alone, she threw herself onto the bed and stared up at the stark white ceiling. Her body was tired, but she still couldn't shut off her mind. She had hoped that after her last encounter with Jordan, she would have begun to get him out of her system. But no, she thought about him all day—and at night as she slept, he invaded her dreams.

She kicked off her flats and turned over onto her stomach, preparing to take a nap. When she awakened, she planned to dress up in one of her new outfits and go downstairs to dinner. After dinner she'd stroll over to the hotel's nightclub and listen to the blues singer who was scheduled to appear tonight.

She'd been sleeping a little over an hour when the phone rang. Thinking the caller might be her father, she answered. "Hello?" The caller hung up.

"Nuisance," Cara Lynn muttered and tried to fall back under Morpheus's spell. When she didn't succumb immediately, she knew it was useless, so she climbed out of bed and went to run a bath.

While the tub was filling up, she examined herself in the full-length mirror. Her body had gained more muscle in the past few months. Her calves were more defined as were her biceps.

She let her long, curly hair fall over her shoulders. "Maybe I ought to get a haircut," she said.

She piled it up on her head, imagining herself with short hair. "Maybe not."

Minutes later she was sitting at the vanity, putting her hair in a French braid. Finished, she stood up, removing the hotel bath towel she'd wrapped around her, and slipped into a pair of satiny emerald panties and matching lacy bra.

She chose the simply cut, straight emerald green dress with spaghetti straps and a low-cut neckline. A short-waisted, long-sleeved jacket went over the revealing bodice, and the hem fell a couple of inches above her knees, exposing a tantalizing view of her legs. Black suede pumps and a matching clutch completed the outfit.

Her reservation was for seven thirty. She made it with only a minute to spare.

The maitre d' gave her an appreciative once-over as he escorted her to her table. "Right this way, Dr. Garrett. Your dinner companion arrived early. He's waiting for you."

Cara Lynn glanced in the direction the maitre d' was indicating and stopped in her tracks. Jordan smiled at her from across the room and even had the nerve to give her a little wave.

"Is there anything wrong, Dr. Garrett?" the maitre d' asked nervously.

"No," Cara Lynn said quickly, willing her legs to function normally. "Everything's lovely, thank you."

Jordan rose and pulled out her chair for her. The maitre d' wished them a pleasant evening, assuring them their waiter would be along momentarily, then returned to his post.

"Surprised?" Jordan asked sweetly.

Cara Lynn had to restrain herself from kicking him in the shin underneath the table.

"What are you doing here," she hissed. "And more specifically, what are you doing at my table?"

"I had some business to transact here in town," Jordan said.

He could not tell her that her father had phoned him with the news that she was in Lexington for the weekend and that he'd dropped everything in order to get here.

No, he would tell her years from now, after their firstborn was in college. By then, she'd probably think nothing of it.

"I often stay here when I'm in town," he said instead. "I may have mentioned that to you in our happier days. Anyway, as I was checking in this morning, I saw you leaving the hotel. I had a hunch you might be staying over, so I phoned the restaurant to see if you were expected for dinner. I arrived early, bribed the maitre d', and here I am." Well, most of his story was true.

"You went to a lot of trouble to be here. Why?"

Jordan leaned forward. "You aren't still angry with me? I was hoping you'd be over our little spat by now."

"Spat?" Cara Lynn said angrily, keeping her voice low.

"Is that what you call it? You accused me of being a mercenary bimbo. Yeah, I'm still angry."

"I apologize for my rather bad choice of words the night of the ball. Please forgive me," Jordan said sincerely, his hand over his heart.

"Are you also going to apologize for being bullheaded. Oh, and narrow minded? And don't forget your tendency to jump to conclusions," Cara Lynn said, her eyes on his hands. She'd always loved his hands.

"I'd apologize for anything if it meant you'd be back in my arms. I miss you, Cara. What do you suppose that means?"

"I don't know what it means," she said, meeting his eyes. "I thought you detested me."

"Hate has nothing to do with the way I feel about you. Give me five minutes alone with you, and the word 'hate' would never enter your mind."

Cara Lynn had butterflies in her stomach and her heartbeat had quickened. Calm down, she chided herself. You're melting right before his eyes.

"I can do without meaningless sex, thank you," she said, lowering her eyes.

"Can you? You look like you could use a little right now," Jordan returned, his golden brown eyes alight with humor.

Cara Lynn inhaled deeply, exhaled. "You enjoy watching me squirm, don't you?"

"I enjoy watching you, period," Jordan said with a crooked smile.

He reached across the table and touched her cheek with the back of his hand. "Haven't you missed me, doe-eyes?"

Cara Lynn watched his mouth as he spoke. Those beautifully shaped lips. Those soft, pliable lips that she ached for, dreamed of, had vivid recollections of the way they felt on her mouth, her throat, the backs of her knees.

"You really have some nerve," she cried, getting to her feet. "Stop torturing me, Jordan. Leave me alone."

She turned on her heels and walked swiftly from the dining room.

Jordan smiled triumphantly as he rose to follow her. The maitre d' walked up to him. "You're not dining with us this evening, sir?"

"We've decided to dine upstairs," Jordan said, discreetly handing him a gratuity. "Thank you very much for your help."

The maitre d', a distinguished-looking black gentlemen in his late fifties, smiled. "It was my pleasure, sir. Come again."

Jordan caught up with Cara Lynn at the elevator. She ignored him as they waited for the doors to open.

A minute later they stepped aside as several diners exited the conveyance, then they walked into the empty car.

"Where do you think you're going?" Cara Lynn asked.

"You didn't bother to turn around. How did you know I'd followed you?"

"I could—"

"Feel my presence?" he ventured, grinning.

"Don't get metaphysical on me. I was going to say I could smell your aftershave," Cara Lynn flatly stated.

"Too much?"

"No, it's fine."

"Then you like it?"

The doors slid shut with the two of them as the sole passengers. Cara Lynn pressed the fifth floor button and looked up at Jordan.

"Yes, I like it, okay? What floor are you on?"

"Fifth," he replied happily. "Lucky you. We get to ride all the way up together."

Sighing, Cara Lynn moved to the other side of the elevator. "You ruined my evening."

"You ruined more than my night, lady," Jordan countered, loosening the tie of his tuxedo. The silk bow tie unraveled in his hands, and he shoved it into his pants pocket. A man more accustomed to jeans, he abhorred being confined in this monkey suit.

"Hot under the collar?" Cara Lynn said, seeing her chance to get the upper hand in their war of words. She wanted to see *him* sweat for a change.

She removed her jacket, her movements calculated and deliberately sensual. "Are you warm, or is it just me?"

"You couldn't possibly be warm in that dress. It's indecent," Jordan said, but his eyes were riveted on her.

"You sound like my father," Cara Lynn said, standing within two feet of him. "I'll tell you a secret, Davidson—when I was trying this on in the shop where I bought it, I was hoping you'd see me in it. How do you like it?"

A trickle of sweat rolled down the side of his face. He undid the top button of his shirt.

Cara Lynn didn't wait for his answer. "You want me to open up to you? Well, here goes: you cut me to the quick when you accused me of being a gold-digger who would willingly give herself to whoever has the fattest wallet."

"I was angry, damn it," Jordan said in his defense. He looked into her eyes. "I got to my car that night and realized I'd forgotten to give you the flowers I'd brought for you. I went back in to give them to you and found you in a lip lock with Fitzgerald. What would you have done?"

"I would have believed you," Cara Lynn said loftily.

Jordan placed a hand against the wall of the elevator, leaning in toward her. Their faces were inches apart. He moved closer.

"Are you sure about that?" he breathed.

Cara Lynn tried to turn off her emotions. But her wall of resistance was rapidly crumbling.

"I would have been jealous—and no, I probably wouldn't have listened to you. But I would have come to you the next day and attempted to get things straightened out."

"I'm here now."

"You're too late," she said sadly.

"Don't say that, doe-eyes."

Jordan felt as though he was drowning in her liquid brown eyes. He wanted to kiss her doubts away. But she would have to be the one to make the next move. She would have to find it in herself to come to him. He'd done all he could.

He pushed away from the wall and backed away from her. She stood there, looking at him as though she were trying to say something but could not find the words.

Then she was in his arms, kissing him. She had taken him completely by surprise. All he knew, or cared to know, was she was kissing him like he'd never been kissed before.

Their bodies, having a natural affinity for each other, molded her soft curves to his male hardness. Lord, but she felt good to him.

They would have gone on like that for an indeterminate length of time if the elevator hadn't stopped and the doors opened to admit an elderly couple on the fourth floor.

They parted for the sake of decorum, but their hands were entwined, their eyes locked. The petite, white-haired woman playfully nudged her husband. "Young love," she said loud enough to be overheard. Then to Cara Lynn, she said, "Newlyweds?"

"Reconciliation," Cara Lynn provided, smiling at her.

"Even better. Making up is worth the fighting." She smiled at them. "You make a handsome couple."

The elevator arrived on the fifth floor. Cara Lynn and Jordan allowed the elderly couple to precede them off the car.

"Good luck, kids," the man said with a wave of his hand.

"Thanks," Jordan said, holding Cara Lynn close to him as they made their way down the hall to his suite.

When they were out of earshot of the older couple, they laughed uncontrollably.

"I feel like a teenager caught necking on the couch by my parents," Jordan laughed.

"Well, I don't feel anything like a teenager," Cara Lynn said, her hand on the small of his back. "When I was a teenager, I never imagined anyone like you."

Jordan couldn't unlock the door fast enough. The minute they stepped into the room, they were undressing each other between light, teasing kisses.

"Cara Lynn, we need to talk."

"Jordan," Cara Lynn said, sighing deep in her throat. "I have been going crazy remembering how you feel and not being able to touch you. Now do you really want to talk before, or can it wait a little longer?"

"I don't need words to tell you what I want you to know," he said, his baritone husky with longing.

He kissed her, leaving her weak in the knees. Cara Lynn felt bereft of her lifeline when their lips parted, but that thought lasted only a second for Jordan had charted new territories to explore. Her knees buckled when he kissed her shoulder and worked his way slowly down to her cleavage.

Jordan unzipped her dress and pushed the straps down off her shoulders. Cara Lynn undid the snaps on her bra and tossed it aside. Jordan was having some difficulty with the small buttons on his silk shirt, so Cara Lynn quickly unbuttoned it for him and that, too, fell to the floor.

Flesh touched flesh, and Jordan felt like a dying man who had been given the cure for his malady. This was all he needed—Cara in his arms, her body welcoming his, her exquisitely lovely eyes looking into his with explicit desire and sweet expectation.

Neither of them spoke as they fell onto the bed wrapped in one another's arms. It was as though their minds were joined in a mutual, sensual synchronization. He gave, she accepted. She knew precisely where to touch him for maximum effect, for every inch of him was attuned to her.

Jordan reined in his passion as he brought Cara Lynn to her peak. There was no rush. He wanted to revel in his victory. She loved him. Even if she hadn't said it. He felt it, and that was enough for now.

Cara Lynn was nearly weeping with the want of release, but Jordan withheld her ascension knowing how intense the descent would be for her when it was kept at bay for as long as possible.

He was looking into her face, loving each curve, each angle of it. She held his gaze, and there was a small smile playing at the corners of her generous mouth. Her tongue slowly licked her lips, and it was that minute act that turned the tide for him. He could hold on no longer. He lifted her so that she lay on top of him, and they rode the wave of fulfillment together.

Spent but happy, Cara Lynn lay on top of him. "I believe you did miss me."

Jordan pulled her into his arms. "Can we talk now?"

"Can we order something to eat from room service first? I'm starving," Cara Lynn said, rolling over to pick up the phone, placing it on her lap.

Jordan sat up in bed. "Have them send up a good bottle of wine while you're at it."

Cara Lynn placed the order, then got out of bed.

"Where are you going?" Jordan asked, watching her.

"To freshen up. I'm not going to be lying in bed when room service brings up the food."

Jordan took his cues from Cara Lynn. They showered together, dressed, and ate on the balcony.

They dined on grilled trout and a fresh garden salad. Cara Lynn drank two glasses of the delicious white wine and was about to pour a third when she began to feel the effects of the alcohol and placed the bottle back on the tabletop.

"I'm glad I'm not driving tonight."

Jordan had been enjoying the view. Cara, sitting across from him, dressed in that killer number with her hair in wild disarray. Her neat French braid had come loose while they were making love, and he'd asked her to leave her hair down—he liked it that way. She looked more relaxed than she had in a long time. It was satisfying knowing he'd put that grin on her lips.

"I don't want you more than a few feet away from me all night," Jordan said, reaching for her hand.

She grasped his hand, covering it with her other one. "You really mean that?"

"I do, Cara. We've been apart long enough for no good reason," Jordan said.

"The reason was I'm no good at relationships. I told you I was trouble the day we met," Cara Lynn said, eyes downcast.

"Look at me, Cara," Jordan said. "Have you ever considered the possibility that the other men you've been involved with were incompatible? Don't blame yourself for everything. Sometimes it's best if things don't work out the way you expect them to. In our case though, I think we have the chance to build something special and lasting. All we need is the patience to let it grow."

"I'm not normally so impatient. I'm usually very much in control. With you, it was different from the beginning."

"It's nice to know I can make you lose control," Jordan said, smiling into her eyes.

"It's scary to me because if I'm out of control, it means someone else is in control," Cara Lynn explained.

"You're afraid to feel too deeply because you equate loving a man with giving up your personal power?" Jordan asked, trying to understand her.

"When someone has too much power over you, he also has the capability of hurting you," Cara Lynn reasoned.

"But if he loves you, Cara, he will not want to see you harmed. Sometimes you just have to have faith in him, let him prove his love."

Cara Lynn rose, going over to the railing to look up at the stars.

"That's what's so hard for me to do," she said morosely.

Jordan came up behind her and wrapped his arms around her.

"I don't expect you to trust in me all at once, my love. I'm willing to wait."

Still in his embrace, Cara Lynn turned to face him. "I'm still hungry."

"I'll go order you some chocolate ice cream."

"Not for food."

Jordan smiled down at her. "What do you think I am, a machine?"

Cara Lynn kissed him. He lifted her in his arms and carried her back inside.

Sixteen

The next day, when Cara Lynn returned home, she found a disturbing message on the answering machine. Sara had taken a turn for the worse. Harry had left her the name and telephone number of the hospital in Phoenix where they could be reached.

She hastily dialed the number. A nurse answered, and Cara Lynn asked for Harry.

Harry came on the line in a matter of seconds. "Cara, honey, things don't look well. Her lungs collapsed last night. She's not breathing on her own any longer. I—" His voice broke. "I don't think she's going to last another night."

"Harry, hang in there," Cara Lynn told him. "I'm on my way. I'll get the next available flight."

She phoned Joey and told him he would have to contact all the clients they were scheduled to see tomorrow and explain that she'd been called out of town on an emergency.

Then she phoned Brent to ask if he could cover any emergencies her clients might have in her absence. He readily agreed.

The airline she phoned said their next flight to Phoenix departed in four hours, and yes they could accommodate her.

Next she scribbled a note to her father telling him she was on her way to Phoenix and why. She'd give him a call when she arrived.

Finally she tried Jordan's number and was relieved when he answered.

"Jordan, I'm glad I got you. I've got to go to Phoenix as soon as possible. Sara's failing fast—" she spoke hurriedly. "I'm leaving for Frankfort now."

"I'll drive you," were the first words out of his mouth.

"Are you sure?"

"Sweetheart, I can tell how upset you are by the sound of your voice. I don't want you to have to worry about driving all that way alone, then parking and racing through the airport. No. I'll leave right now."

In Phoenix Cara Lynn was met at the airport by Amy Bailey Serrano, her husband, Alec, and their two-month-old daughter, Sara Jean.

Cara Lynn hugged the petite, blond, green-eyed woman as Alec stood in the background cuddling Sara Jean.

"I'm so glad you came. Mom would've been pleased."

Cara Lynn's heart skipped a beat. "You mean she's—"

"Yes," Amy said, putting her arms around Cara Lynn. "We were all with her. She fell asleep and didn't wake up. Dr. Carter says she wasn't in any pain."

Tears sprang to Cara Lynn's eyes. "I was out of town and didn't get the message in time. I should have been here for her."

Amy hugged her tightly. "Now stop that, Cara. You know Mom wouldn't put up with self-recrimination. Come on, you haven't met our new addition yet."

Alec was a quiet bookish man in his early thirties. He was dark haired and dark eyed. Around five ten, he was trim and wore horn-rimmed glasses.

He smiled shyly at Cara Lynn as he shook her hand. "Good to see you again, Cara Lynn."

"Yes, it's good to see you, too, Alec," Cara Lynn said, smiling at him.

It was an effort to be congenial at a time like this. She felt like she was in a fog. Sara was gone. It hadn't quite registered.

"This—" Amy said, holding the infant in the crook of her arm "—is Sara Jean."

Cara Lynn took the baby into her arms, looking down into her sweet cherubic olive-skinned face. "She's beautiful, Amy. You know, I think she has—"

"Mom's eyes?"

"Yes, Sara's eyes," Cara Lynn said softly. Tears welled up again. "I'm really going to miss her."

The Baileys refused to be maudlin about Sara's passing, aware of how Sara felt about such things. They chose instead to concentrate on all the positive influence Sara had effected while she was with them. They remembered her wit and charm. The sound of her laughter and her passion for teaching. They talked about the way she had with an apple pie and her off-key singing in church on Sunday morning. Or the way she used to fall asleep at the drop of a hat: "I think I'll take a nap before I go to bed," she used to say.

Cara Lynn sat between her father and Harry Junior in church two days later as family and friends gathered to say good-bye. H.J. was taking it particularly hard—because of a heavy workload at Tulane, he hadn't been able to be with Sara as often as he would have liked. Sara wouldn't hear of it when he'd suggested taking a semester off from his studies.

Cara Lynn thought Sara had been too stubborn in that instance. School could have waited. Being with his mother was a limited-time offer, so to speak. That time could never be made up.

Afterward many of them met at the home of Sara's parents, Isaac and Madeleine Swensen, both in their sixties and extremely healthy robust people.

Madeleine pulled Cara Lynn aside, leading her into the

kitchen for a private chat. They hadn't seen one another in years, yet Madeleine knew Cara Lynn the moment their eyes met across the room.

"Cara Lynn Garrett, right?"

Cara Lynn was surprised because she had assumed Madeleine wouldn't know her after nineteen years. She had been ten years old the last time she'd seen Isaac and Madeleine Swensen. They'd visited Sara for the summer, and at that time Cara Lynn was a frequent addition to the Bailey family.

Madeleine smiled at her and took her by the hand. "Sit down. I'll get us some coffee."

Cara Lynn took a seat at the kitchen table. Madeleine poured two cups of coffee from the coffee maker on the counter, then joined Cara Lynn at the table.

"When I saw you walk into my home this afternoon, I momentarily thought I was seeing a ghost. I thought to myself, Lillianne has come to pay her respects. You're very much like your mother. And you have her smile."

"I do? No one has ever told me that before."

"Well, it's true. I never forget a face. My mother was full-blooded Navajo, and she used to tell me the dead live on through their children. Of course we know that, but I believe she meant spiritually as well as physically. It's peculiar how some people can behave like their parents without being aware of it. When I was a teenaged girl, I used to hate being compared to my mother because I saw her as old-fashioned and totally unaware of how the world worked. But today I'm pleased I inherited her wisdom. Old people are supposed to be wise, you see."

Cara Lynn said, "You don't have to worry about getting old, Mrs. Swensen, you'll always be young at heart. Now I can understand why Sara was the way she was."

"We are all better off for having known her," Madeleine said, sighing. "She made her father and me very happy."

* * *

Cara Lynn dozed on the flight home, her head on her father's shoulder. She hadn't slept well the night before. She and Harry had sat up late talking. He was trying to pretend he wasn't broken up by Sara's death. Cara Lynn found herself wishing he'd let it out. But then it occurred to her that each individual has his own way of coping with grief. He'd have to figure it out on his own. But still it tore her up to see him in such pain. "I'll see her again. Time is relative," he kept saying.

"You will, Harry," Cara Lynn had assured him. "In the meanwhile, though, you have to go on with your life, take care of yourself. I feel certain Sara would want you to do that."

He'd nodded his agreement, but his eyes were sad and dejected. He was consumed with loss. She understood that.

When he'd seen her off at the airport this morning, they'd clung to each other as though neither of them wanted to let go. In some ways Harry represented a part of Sara to Cara Lynn and, conversely, Harry saw Sara in Cara Lynn. They were all linked.

She looked back at him as she and her father boarded the plane. His face was wet with tears. Touching her face, she realized hers was, too.

"Stay," Jordan said, pulling Cara Lynn back down onto the bed.

"I've stayed too long already," Cara Lynn said. It was true. Since Jordan had picked her and her father up at the airport in Frankfort at two this afternoon, after a brief detour to drop her father off at the ranch, she had been with him.

She kissed his chin and snuggled closer. "It's nearly midnight. I have to get up early in the morning."

"I want to wake up with you in my arms. I always feel like we're rushing," he complained.

"I need a place of my own, then it would be possible for us to spend the night together."

"Move in here with me."

Cara Lynn laughed and felt his forehead. "You feverish?"

"Marry me, Cara. What do you think about a December wedding?"

"I think we'd better have it inside."

Jordan didn't get the joke. "What? Don't you want to marry me?"

"Yeah, I want to marry you, but for the right reasons. I don't want to marry you because we're slightly inconvenienced."

"Why would you marry me?" Jordan said, looking amused.

Cara Lynn got up and slipped into the bathrobe Jordan had left at the foot of the bed.

"Do you recall our first fight?"

"Like it was yesterday. It was over the mystery man, whose identity you've never revealed, I might add."

"Well, I'm ready to now," Cara Lynn said, meeting his eyes.

Jordan sat up in bed, his attention wholeheartedly hers. "I'm listening."

"Prior to my bringing up the subject of the unrequited love, we'd been discussing love at first sight. I told you I'd fallen in love with someone that quickly, and you wanted to know with whom." She smiled. "It was you, Jordan. I fell in love with you in an instant, it seemed. Of course I didn't want to face it. The more I saw you, though, the less I could deny it. I loved you—but I couldn't tell you because you didn't return my feelings."

"I'm the mystery man? How dense can I be?" Jordan said, hitting his forehead with the palm of his hand.

"Hold on," Cara Lynn said. "I'll let you know in a second. After we made love, I asked you how you felt about me, and you told me, in essence, I was the best you'd ever had. A woman in love doesn't want to hear that. She wants to hear: I love you. You didn't say that. So . . . in an effort to save myself further embarrassment, I left. Do you know how it feels to love someone who doesn't love you?"

"Yes, I do," Jordan said, climbing out of bed, the top sheet wrapped precariously around his lower half. "Because for the first few months we were together, I was certain I was in this alone. You put me through emotional hell. First, I thought you were using me for sexual release while you'd given your heart to Mr. X. Then there was Fitzgerald. Believe me, it wasn't easy to love you, through all that. But I did."

Cara Lynn grinned. "You were in love with me then?"

"I was so in love with you, I couldn't think straight. Hell, I must have painted you a dozen times."

She looked awestruck. "You painted me?"

"Will you stop asking questions and listen to me?" Jordan insisted. He stepped forward, taking her face between his hands. "There have been a lot of misunderstandings between us. I don't want you to misunderstand this. I love you, Cara—and we're going to be husband and wife."

Cara Lynn wrapped her arms around his neck, kissing his face all over. "You put me on canvas?"

Jordan smiled at her enthusiasm. "I know every curve and angle of your face, my love."

"Why haven't you shown them to me?"

"The same reason you didn't tell me you loved me until a minute ago. I was afraid of looking foolish. Let's get back to the subject at hand. When are you going to marry me? This weekend? I could have my folks here by then."

"Everyone will wonder why we have to get married so soon," Cara Lynn said.

Jordan grinned. "The end of the month?"

"I need more time to plan. I want a church wedding."

"January first, no later," Jordan said firmly.

"January first. Fine. We'll be Mr. and Mrs. by January first."

Her eyelashes tickled his cheek. He felt her tears before he saw them.

"Why are you crying?"

"You fill me up. I love you so much."

"You're nuts—you know that, don't you?"

"And you want to marry me. What does that make you?"

"Crazy in love," Jordan answered, kissing her full, red lips. She tasted salty.

"I've got to go," Cara Lynn murmured as they fell back onto the bed.

Jordan kissed her neck. "Hold on to me, doe-eyes, we'll go together."

Dear Reader,

I hope you've enjoyed reading *Affair of the Heart*. I had a good time writing it. If you're like me, I'm sure some of the characters in the novel reminded you of yourself or someone you know. If so, then I've done my job because I'm writing for you, the reader.

I invite you to drop me a line and tell me what you liked, or didn't like, about *Affair of the Heart*. All comments are appreciated. Don't be shy.

Until our next adventure together.

Sincerely,

Janice Sims

Janice Sims

P.O. Box 811
Mascotte, FL 34753-0811

About the Author

After working as a journalist, a loan officer, and an Elementary school tutor, Janice Sims decided to dedicate her life to writing poems, short stories, and full-length novels. She lives in Central Florida with her husband and daughter.

Look for these upcoming Arabesque titles:

August 1996
WHITE DIAMONDS by Shirley Hailstock
SEDUCTION by Felicia Mason
AT FIRST SIGHT by Cheryl Faye

September 1996
WHISPERED PROMISES by Brenda Jackson
AGAINST ALL ODDS by Gwynne Forster
ALL FOR LOVE by Raynetta Manees

October 1996
THE GRASS AIN'T GREENER by Monique Gilmore
IF ONLY YOU KNEW by Carla Fredd
SUNDANCE by Leslie Esdaile

SENSUAL AND HEARTWARMING
ARABESQUE ROMANCES FEATURE
AFRICAN-AMERICAN CHARACTERS!

BEGUILED   (0046, $4.99)
by Eboni Snoe
After Raquel agrees to impersonate a missing heiress for just one night, a daring abduction makes her the captive of seductive Nate Bowman. Across the exotic Caribbean seas to the perilous wilds of Central America . . . and into the savage heart of desire, Nate and Raquel play a dangerous game. But soon the masquerade will be over. And will they then lose the one thing that matters most . . . their love?

WHISPERS OF LOVE   (0055, $4.99)
by Shirley Hailstock
Robyn Richards had to fake her own death, change her identity, and forever forsake her husband, Grant, after testifying against a crime syndicate. But, five years later, the daughter born after her disappearance is in need of help only Grant can give. Can Robyn maintain her disguise from the ever present threat of the syndicate—and can she keep herself from falling in love all over again?

HAPPILY EVER AFTER   (0064, $4.99)
by Rochelle Alers
In a week's time, Lauren Taylor fell madly in love with famed author Cal Samuels and impulsively agreed to be his wife. But when she abruptly left him, it was for reasons she dared not express. Five years later, Cal is back, and the flames of desire are as hot as ever, but, can they start over again and make it work this time?

Available wherever paperbacks are sold, or order direct from the Publisher. Send cover price plus 50¢ per copy for mailing and handling to Penguin USA, P.O. Box 999, c/o Dept. 17109, Bergenfield, NJ 07621. Residents of New York and Tennessee must include sales tax. DO NOT SEND CASH.

DANGEROUS GAMES   (0-7860-0270-0, $4.99)
by Amanda Scott

When Nicholas Barrington, eldest son of the Earl of Ul-
combe, first met Melissa Seacort, the desperation he
sensed beneath her well-bred beauty haunted him. He
didn't realize how desperate Melissa really was . . . until
he found her again at a Newmarket gambling club—being auctioned off by her father to the highest bidder. So,
Nick bought himself a wife. With a villain hot on their
heels, and a fortune and their lives at stake, they would
gamble everything on the most dangerous game of all:
love.

A TOUCH OF PARADISE   (0-7860-0271-9, $4.99)
by Alexa Smart

As a confidence man and scam runner in 1880s America,
Malcolm Northrup has amassed a fortune. Now, posing
as the eminent Sir John Abbot—scholar, and possible
discoverer of the lost continent of Atlantis—he's taking
his act on the road with a lecture tour, seeking funds for
a scientific experiment he has no intention of making.
But scholar Halia Davenport is determined to accompany
Malcolm on his "expedition" . . . even if she must kidnap
him!

TIMELESS LOVE

Look for these historical romances in the Arabesque line:

BLACK PEARL by Francine Craft (0236-0, $4.99)

CLARA'S PROMISE by Shirley Hailstock (0147-X, $4.99)

MIDNIGHT MOON by Mildred Riley (0200-X; $4.99)

SUNSHINE AND SHADOWS by Roberta Gayle (0136-4, $4.99)

Available wherever paperbacks are sold, or order direct from the Publisher. Send cover price plus 50¢ per copy for mailing and handling to Penguin USA, P.O. Box 999, c/o Dept. 17109, Bergenfield, NJ 07621. Residents of New York and Tennessee must include sales tax. DO NOT SEND CASH.